FORTUNE'S BLIGHT

Also by Evie Manieri

Blood's Pride

FORTUNE'S BLIGHT

Shattered Kingdoms Book II

Evie Manieri

TOR®

A Tom Doherty Associates Book

New York

This is a work of fiction. All of the characters, organizations, and events portrayed in this novel are either products of the author's imagination or are used fictitiously.

FORTUNE'S BLIGHT

A Tor Book
Published by Tom Doherty Associates, LLC
175 Fifth Avenue
New York, NY 10010

www.tor-forge.com

The Library of Congress Cataloging-in-Publication Data is available upon request.

ISBN 978-0-7653-3235-6 (hardcover)
ISBN 978-1-4299-6006-9 (e-book)

First published in Great Britain by Jo Fletcher Books, an imprint of Quercus

First U.S. Edition: February 2015

Printed in the United States of America

0 9 8 7 6 5 4 3 2 1

For Lou and Prudence

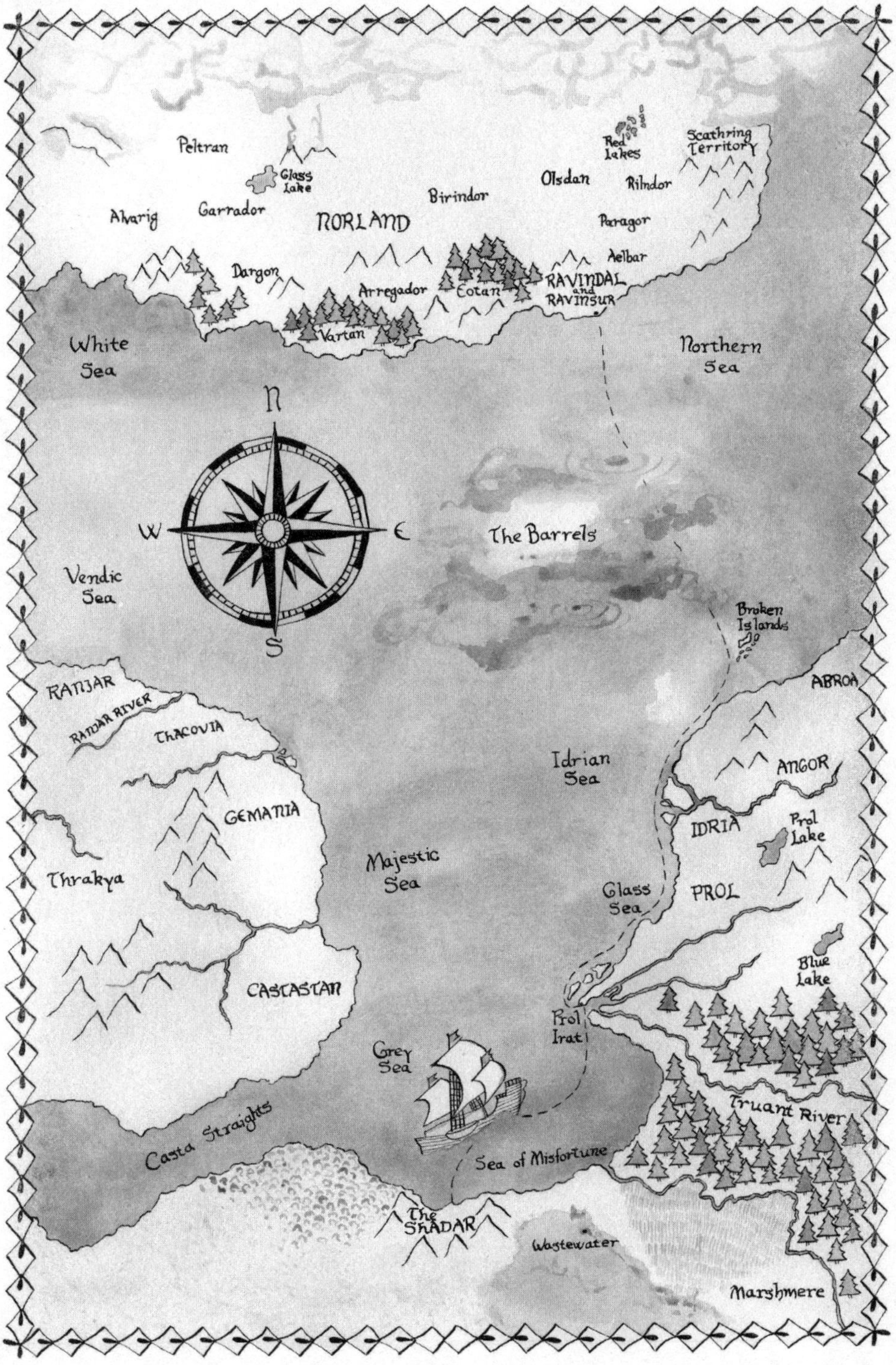

Peltran
Glass Lake
Red Lakes
Scathring Territory
Olsdan
Rilndor
Birindor
Alvarig
Garrador
NORLAND
Paragor
Aelbar
Dargon
Arregador
Eotan
RAVINDAL and RAVINSUR
Vartan
White Sea
Northern Sea
N
W
E
S
The Barrels
Vendic Sea
Broken Islands
RANJAR
RANJAR RIVER
ABROA
THACOVIA
Idrian Sea
ANGOR
GEMANIA
IDRIA
Prol Lake
Majestic Sea
Thrakya
Glass Sea
PROL
Blue Lake
CASTASTAN
Prol Irat
Grey Sea
Truant River
Casta Straights
Sea of Misfortune
The SHADAR
Wastewater
Marshmere

Valrigdal
Onfar's Circle
NORLAND

AELBAR
ar's helm
Ravindal
Ravinsur

Dramatis Personae

The Norlanders

Aline—Kira's hand-servant, Berril's sister
Arvald—a soldier in the Shadari garrison
Bekka Eotan—a high clanswoman
Berril—Cyrrin's assistant, Aline's sister
Betran Eotan—presumptive heir to the Norlander throne
Cyrrin—a physic, founder and leader of Valrigdal
Dara—a resident of Valrigdal, a cook
Dell—a soldier, friend of Rho
Denar Eotan—elderly Norlander general
Eofar Eotan—current governor of the Shadar, brother to Frea, Isa and Lahlil, Oshi's father
Falkar—lieutenant of the Shadari garrison
Frea Eotan—deceased, sister of Eofar, Lahlil and Isa
Gannon Eotan—Emperor of Norland
Gothar Peltran—a high clansman
Gyr—a soldier in the Shadari garrison
Herwald—a soldier in the Shadari garrison
Ingeld—a deserter from the Shadari garrison
Isa Eotan—youngest sister of Eofar, Frea and Lahlil
Jaen Arregador—a high clanswoman
Kira Arregador—wife of Trey Arregador
Lahlil Eotan—sister of Eofar, Frea and Isa, also known as the Mongrel, the General and Meiran

Laine—Ani's prison guard
Olnara Eotan—Gannon's daughter, Scion of Norland
Orina Arregador—Exemplar of the Arregador Clan
Peel—a tavern keeper
Remi Arregador—a friend of Trey's
Rho Arregador—a soldier in the Shadari garrison, brother of Trey
Tovar—a soldier in the Shadari garrison
Trey Arregador—lieutenant in the Norlander Army, brother to Rho
Vrinna Eotan—Captain of the Guards at Ravindal

The Shadari

Ani—a Shadari asha also known as Anakthalisa
Binit—leader of a group of dissidents
Daryan—daimon, King of the Shadari
Dramash—a young boy with asha powers
Harotha—deceased, Eofar's wife, mother of Oshi
Falit—Omir's man
Omir—a government official
Tamin—Omir's man
Yash—Omir's man

The Nomas

Arva—bursar on the *Argent*
Behr—wagon-master of Jachad's caravan
Callia—queen-to-be of the Nomas
Grentha—first mate on the *Argent*
Hela—a sailor on the *Argent*
Jachad Nisharan—King of the Nomas, son of the sun god Shof
Leth—cook on the *Argent*
Mairi—healer on the *Dawn Gazer*
Mala—healer on the *Argent*
Nisha—Queen of the Nomas, captain of the *Argent*
Sabina—second mate on the *Argent*
Tobias—King of the Nomas, deceased

Triss—Behr's young daughter
Yara—cabin girl on the *Argent*

Others

Alack—a mercenary in the Mongrel's crew
Bartow—a mercenary in the Mongrel's crew
Dredge—a mercenary in the Mongrel's crew
Fellix—an Abroan, a former strider
Jaspar—Dredge's lover
Josten Drey—a bounty hunter
Nevie—a mercenary from Marshmere
Oshi—infant son of Eofar Eotan and Harotha of the Shadar
Savion—an Abroan strider

The Gods

Amai—the Nomas moon goddess
Onfar—the Norlander god
Onraka—the Norlander goddess
Pengar—a Stowari god
Shof—the Nomas sun god
Valrig—Norlander traitor god, god of the cursed

The Norlander Progenitors/High Clans

Aelbar—color: yellow; sigil: a cudgel
Alvarig—color: red; sigil: an ember-flower
Arregador—color: forest green; sigil: a pine bough
Birindor—color: white; sigil: an icicle
Dargon—color: brown; sigil: a pine tree
Eotan—color: blue; sigil: a wolf's head
Garrador—color: pale blue; sigil: an ursa
Olsdan—color: orange; sigil: a flame
Paragor—color: pale green; sigil: a thorn branch

Peltran—color: purple; sigil: a plum
Rilndor—color: black; sigil: a hawk
Vartan—color: gray; sigil: a mountain peak

The Swords

Blood's Pride—now Isa's sword, formerly her sister Frea's
Fealty's Strength—Falkar's sword
Fortune's Blight—Rho's sword
Honor's Proof—Trey's sword
Strife's Bane—Eofar's sword
Virtue's Grace—Kira's sword
Valor's Storm—Eowara's bronze sword, claimed by Gannon

Prologue

Excerpt from the manuscript, *The History of the Shadar,* by Daryan (Daimon, ninth of that name)

This is now. This is the present.

This is the time to lay aside our past, and the nostalgia that buffs our happy memories until they gleam. We must keep our eyes from straying toward the future, with its hazy aura of wishful thinking. The present is yet the hot ground under my feet, the hunger in my belly, the insect buzzing in my ear. It is the pause after the question I cannot answer.

I spent most of my life living apart from this city. I could look down on the Shadar from the windows in the temple, but I could not remember what it felt like to walk through the streets with the dirt kicking up in clouds around my feet or the heat pulsing from the whitewashed houses in the flaming noonday sun. I could only imagine what it felt like to have running children knock into my legs and then dart away, laughing, while I pretended to scold them. I used to be able to smell the sea when the wind blew from the east, but I only could imagine standing on the beach with that same wind blowing through my clothes, listening to the thin voices of the men on the fishing boats calling out to each other or singing ancient songs.

It was nearly thirty years ago that the Dead Ones came to the Shadar, with their white hair and skin, their blue blood, their silent language and their gleaming swords, to dig the black ore out of our mountains. They housed their flying beasts in our sacred temple, enslaved our people and made weapons—black blades, mixed with their own blood, that obeyed their minds as well as their hands—which they then used to carve the rest of the world into the mighty Norland Empire.

The temple is gone now, destroyed by the mad ambition of the Norland governor's elder daughter, and by the grief felt by one little boy—a Shadari child with the ancient power of our people to move the rocks and sands—for his murdered mother. The entrances to the black ore mines are now blocked up with boulders and the Shadar is free from the rule of the Norland Empire. The city is my home now—but it is not as I once imagined it would be.

Now I walk past houses charred by the fires that swept through three months ago on the night when Frea Eotan, the White Wolf, tried to destroy it all. I see children sitting among the rubble, hungry and crying. I no longer need to imagine the beach, but I have to hold my breath as I pass between smoking funeral pyres to make my way down to the sea. The men on the fishing boats don't sing anymore.

Ours is a victory counted in losses.

We have sent emissaries to the emperor across the sea to bargain for our continued freedom: the Norland governor's son, Eofar; the child Dramash, whose terrible power to move the sands cannot be controlled, and the soldier, Rho, atoning for his crimes.

Our allies are few. King Jachad and the Nomas have come to our aid again and again, but they must roam: their men to the desert, their women to the sea. The Mongrel has disappeared, taking her secrets along with her. A drink in any tavern will buy you an account of her death, but I know this: if the Mongrel is dead, it is only because someone new has walked away in her boots.

And there is Isa, the Norlander governor's youngest daughter, sister to the White Wolf, who stood with us in the uprising against her own people. Victory took her sister, her status, her sword, her left arm, and the love of her gods. It took the hopes she had for a future with the man she loves, who loves her more than his own life. Victory did not take Isa's courage, nor her honor, because nothing ever could.

Our Shadari ancestors decided to protect our future by destroying our past. It was a decision made in fear and exhaustion. Now our history goes no further back than a glance over our shoulder, and yet I can feel that past closing in on us now, edging its way toward a reckoning. Forgetting what went before neither erases it nor absolves its debtors. Just because you don't remember drinking in the morning doesn't mean you don't have to pay for the wine.

And I fear the bill for our victory is about to come due.

Chapter 1

Lahlil sat on the carpet beside her nephew's cradle, waiting and willing something to happen. The light filtering in through the sailcloth tent had faded down to nothing and the hush of twilight had replaced the noises of the Nomas camp outside, but she hadn't yet lit the lamp. Oshi looked up at the ceiling of the tent with his round silver-blue eyes shining faintly in the darkness, indifferent to her presence. She reached into the driftwood cradle to adjust a fold of his swaddling and accidentally set the finely balanced vessel rocking. The clinking noise of the little suns and moons dangling over it drifted through the tent. A dozen versions of herself winked back at her from the twisting medallions, illuminated by the pale gray glow of her skin: the smooth oval eye-patch, the nicks and tiny scars, the jagged line pulling up her lips at one corner.

At least the sleeve of her Nomas sailor's blouse hid the scaly pink scars that ran over her left forearm—scars nearly as old as she was herself.

Let all so afflicted be numbered among the damned.

For three months she had been waiting, holding on to the elixir's promise that somehow Oshi was going to take all of her broken pieces and put them back together, but here she was at the end of another monotonous day, and still nothing—*nothing*—had changed.

A feeling like tiny needles jabbed her behind the eyes as Oshi wriggled in his cradle: he was just about to cry. He owed his Norlander ability to communicate without making any noise to his father, Lahlil's brother Eofar, and got the vocalized crying from his Shadari mother, Harotha. She lifted Oshi up against her shoulder, patting his back to calm him before his upset could turn into shrill, nerve-shredding wails. She felt him trying to lift his head—he could still only just manage it—and his soft hair brushed against her ear as she started off in the well-worn circuit around the tent. On the tidy side were Oshi's little things, the washbasin, the low chair on rockers that Callia had demanded she get, and the cold lamp hanging from its sun-emblazoned stand, while her side of the tent still bore the hallmarks of her seizures: bedlinen in a tangled heap, table knocked onto its side, shards from a broken cup sticking up from the carpet. She paused for a moment by the door and looked down at her over-full pack, weighed down by all of the supplies she and Oshi were going to need for their journey—everything except for the medicine she needed to withstand the attacks that came on her every day at dawn and dusk. Without something to at least keep her alert and breathing, she would be putting Oshi's safety at risk.

She couldn't deny that her fits were getting worse, any more than she could deny the bits of pottery crunching under the soles of her boots or the cuts on her hastily bandaged hand. Sunset had only just passed and she was already dreading tomorrow's dawn. She had come back to the Nomas caravan with the thin hope that her return would somehow placate the two different gods to whom she had accidentally been consecrated. Instead, Shof, the sun god worshipped by the men of the Nomas caravans, and Amai, the moon goddess worshipped by their sea-faring women, had pushed their claims on her further and further. They were quarreling over her like two children wrestling over a rag-doll until it was spoiled past wanting.

She might have appealed to her own Norlander gods for protection, if they had not decided to make her a plaything of their own for having the affront to go on living with the scars that should have mandated her expulsion and death. She had gambled on the constant movement of the caravan to keep those cold gods from catching up with her, even while knowing, like all gamblers, that losing became more certain the longer she played. She was quite sure Onfar and Onraka enjoyed twisting her life into knots too much to stop the game now.

She made her way back to the cradle and set Oshi down, pulling her hands out from underneath him only when she felt him slide down into a deep sleep. Then she knelt down next to the cradle and drew out the parchment from her shirt pocket. The crack along the fold would split soon; the crumbling edge had already nibbled at the fading ink. She didn't need any light to read it. She knew the text by heart.

Let all so afflicted be numbered among the damned.

She traced her finger along the edge of the watery blue stain darkening the corner.

Let them not remain among you, for they will be your destruction; let them be stripped of their garments and set out in the wilderness, for by these marks on their flesh, their twisted limbs, the corruption issuing from them, our brother Valrig has claimed them and will have dominion over them. He will bring them to his hall of Valrigdal in the deep forbidden places, and they shall be his Army of the Cursed. Then be ready against the day they will rise up and strike at the Righteous. On that day let a Hero be prepared with the sword we have given you, to subdue them, lest they corrupt all that is pure in this land.

Her mother had taught her to read from *The Book of the Hall.* Lahlil had drawn chalk maps on the floor of her hidden room and reenacted the battle poems with her toys. She had read the story of Lady Onraka breathing life into the twelve genderless progenitors after Lord Onfar, her brother, had fashioned them out of snow. She had imagined the blood of her own progenitor, Eotan, spilling from his wounds as he battled ice-trolls and sea monsters, and every drop springing to life as the first warriors of the Eotan clan. She had pored over the stories of Lady Onraka outwitting Haggah the she-wolf, and Lord Onfar wrestling the last leviathan out of the black sea.

The sound of clinking bracelets came tinkling through the tent wall.

Yet as Lord Onfar is merciful, and as Lady Onraka is just, if the afflicted be found worthy, so their wounds shall be healed and their steps guided back to the fires of their clan. For by this sign, they are to be embraced without prejudice. Then let the wine be abundant and the rejoicing long and full of praise for the gods and the progenitors. Let the clan make rich sacrifice from the hunted beasts, and all of that fellowship partake in the burned flesh.

The tent wall behind her rustled as someone lifted the flap. She folded up the parchment and put it back in her pocket.

"Why is it so dark in here?" asked Callia, wiping her feet on the rug and shaking out the wet, sandy hem of her pink dress.

"Oshi's sleeping."

"No he isn't."

Lahlil got up and lit the lamp. As the wick caught, Callia's dark eyes swept over the mess. She made her way over to the cradle, her great round belly sailing before her, leaving streamers of scent in her wake.

"He's hungry. If a Nomas like me can feel that from halfway across this marsh, a Norlander like you can certainly feel it sitting right next to him." Oshi began to cry again as he sensed the proximity of his next meal and Callia scooped the baby out of the cradle with a smooth competence that Lahlil could never emulate.

"He was asleep. You woke him up," said Lahlil.

"Crying babies," said Callia as she settled him on her shoulder, "an army of them. That's what I'd send against you in battle, not soldiers. Quickest retreat in history." The impending Queen of the Nomas made some ridiculous clucking noises as she settled down in her rocking chair to nurse. "You didn't give him that goat's milk again, did you? If my milk's good enough for the son of a god, it ought to be good enough for this little sprat."

Lahlil started picking up the pieces of broken pottery and tossing them into the rubbish sack. "Idrian women don't nurse when they're pregnant. They say it makes the baby come early."

"Good thing I'm not from Idria, then," Callia said tartly. "Mairi told you to tell me that—don't bother denying it, I know her meddling ways right enough. I've had just about enough of that potion-pusher and her bad temper and the way she fusses over everything. No one asked her to leave the *Dawn Gazer* to look after me. You'd think I hauled her ashore like she was the catch of the day, the way she complains about being here. But this is Shof's baby in my belly and if a god can't see his own son into this world in one piece then we ought to chuck him overboard and catch ourselves a better one."

The material pulled tight over Callia's belly rippled as her baby rolled over; perhaps the little demi-god was jealous of another child stealing his mother's milk. Lahlil sometimes wondered exactly how Shof went about fathering the Nomas kings, but only the women chosen by the goddess Amai as her proxies had that knowledge and Nomas' tact kept anyone else from inquiring. Jachad had come into this world in the same way, though Callia and *his* mother, Queen Nisha, could not have been less alike.

"Where are you going?" asked the girl.

Lahlil had only just picked up her cloak. "Jachad's, to look at the maps."

"Oh," said Callia, packing a whole trunk-load of insinuations into the syllable. Lahlil knew better than to respond; it only encouraged her. "When was the last time you changed that shirt?"

Lahlil looked down at the soft gray linen, a gift from Nisha herself before she sailed for Norland on the *Argent*. A spot or two she hadn't noticed before stared back up at her. "I don't remember."

Callia sighed and shook her head, her big gold earrings flashing in the lamplight. "You do it on purpose, don't you, just to torment me?"

"No one asked you to leave the *Dawn Gazer* either." Lahlil pulled the cowl up over her head and adjusted it to make sure it concealed her face.

"And live with the smell of fish all night and all day? Not hardly. I could stand it before, but now . . ." She sniffed the air scented with her perfume, then stuck out her pink little tongue. "Anyway, you couldn't cope without me. You've been too used to getting your own way, that's your problem. You need someone to tell you what's what. Admit it."

"Next time I need a vain little chit to talk my ear off, I'll come find you."

"Lahlil Eotan!" Callia cried in mock astonishment. "Do I have water in my ears, or did you just make a joke? Be careful not to hurt yourself, now. Start slow. I have a few limericks I can teach you when you get back."

Lahlil turned back for a last look at the baby. Every time she left him she was afraid she would miss the moment—like a highwayman bending down to take a stone from his shoe while a fat merchant rides right by him. As she ducked out of the tent, she heard Callia serenading the suckling infant with one of the most brazen limericks she had ever heard.

She walked through a stand of squat trees toward the heart of the camp. The lights of the tiny town of Wastewater twinkled in the middle distance and she remembered old King Tobias telling her that Wastewater was the kind of place where retired purse-snatchers and cutthroats came to die of boredom. Inside the tents, the men of Jachad's caravan were sitting down to their evening meal with their children, brothers, fathers and friends, their shapes moving across the canvas like a shadowplay as she passed. Plates and cups rattled; someone plucked the strings of a harp.

A shriek cut through the background hum and a little girl in a striped robe darted out from a patch of tall grass with four or five other children in hot pursuit. She was smaller than they were but faster, moving over the sandy ground as smoothly as a snake. Lahlil tracked their procession until they blundered into one of the shallow pools right in front of her and splashed her with water.

The children froze, and the hectic rise and fall of their little chests reminded her of a family of mice after the box under which they'd been hiding had been whisked away.

"Sorry," squeaked one of the boys.

She went around them and continued on her way.

"Where's your sword?" asked the same boy.

"In my tent."

One of the girls asked, "Why did you leave it there?"

"I don't need it right now."

They were trailing behind her now, taking courage from each other. She picked up her pace.

"Besides, anyone from Wastewater would know she wasn't one of us if they saw her with it," said another boy. "Did you really kill the striders? All of them?"

"Yes."

"But they weren't hurting anybody, were they?"

"The emperor wanted the striders to work for him." She stopped next to a tree blotched with dry yellow moss and turned to the children. They shrank back, shifting closer together. "The striders said no."

"Why didn't they just stride away?" asked the girl in the striped robe.

Before she could come up with an answer, one of the other children grabbed the girl's arm and whispered, "Triss, your dad's coming."

"Triss!" Behr the wagon-master called as he hurried up the path with his robe hitched up and displaying a pair of knobby ankles. "What are you all doing here? Go and wash your feet and get ready for bed. Come on, now, get going."

The little huddle broke apart and Triss trudged off with her head lowered, but Lahlil didn't see much penitence in her expression.

"Sorry if they were bothering you," said Behr. "They're just curious."

"Forget it," said Lahlil. She started off through the trees, then a memory of Behr as a strong, wiry-haired boy with gentle eyes and a shy smile made her turn back around. "She looks like you."

The shy smile returned and he mumbled some awkward acknowledgment before jogging after his daughter and putting his arm around her slender shoulders.

Mairi, the only other grown woman in the caravan besides her and Callia, had wedged her tent on a ridge between two trees. An untended fire smoldered in front of it, and a band of lamplight marked out the tent flap in the deepening gloom. Mairi glanced up as she entered, then immediately returned to the task of scraping the skin from a gnarled purple root into a bowl.

"Why are you here? Isn't it time for your thingummy? Your fit?"

"The sun is down. My seizure is over."

"Move out of my light." The healer waved her into a corner while she measured water into the bowl, counting each drop under her breath.

Lahlil pulled back her cowl and stepped away from the lamp, but she couldn't move any further because of the collection of things from Mairi's cabin aboard the *Dawn Gazer*: clay pots, wooden bowls, gourds made into bottles, dippers and mortars sat on every flat surface. Casks of wood bound with iron bands were pushed almost to the tent walls, and garlands of dried plants hung from the supports or sat heaped in baskets. Lahlil nearly upset a shiny clay vessel in which a thick, oily sludge was reducing over the flame of an unshielded candle. As she watched, a heavy bubble glugged up to the surface and burst with an odor so foul it made her eyes water.

"And don't touch that," Mairi called out sharply, finally looking up. Her eyes were bloodshot and stormy with frustration and fatigue. She reached across to a low wooden chest and tossed a clanking missile to Lahlil—her silver flask—not some base metal polished up or covered in a thin sheet of silver but real, solid silver. She felt the weight resting in her hand, heavier than she remembered.

"That's what I've got: nothing," said Mairi. "I can't lay hold of half the ingredients, and I can't find substitutes for more than a third. I told you it was hopeless from the start. If you need more of it so badly, then go back to where you got it in the first place."

"I can't," she said. "I need you to keep trying. I have to have it before the caravan leaves for Prol Irat."

"You think I'm not trying? Believe me, you don't want to go half as much as I want you to leave." Storm clouds swept across Mairi's face. "We're going to have a new princeling in a few weeks and, Amai help us, a new queen-in-waiting. No one expects Jachi to marry Callia, but he's the baby's near-father, like it or not, and he has responsibilities."

"That's nothing to do with me."

"Glad to hear it," said Mairi. "Then go away and leave him alone."

Lahlil tossed the flask back to her. "Make me something that works and I will." On her way out of the tent the candle caught her eye and she stood for a moment, watching a drip of hot wax slide down and solidify into a white tear. In its depths she saw fields of snow under a slate-gray sky.

She walked along the paths until she came to Jachad's tent, just south of the dead tree.

"Come for supper?" he asked after he bade her enter, half-rising from a meal neatly laid out on a folding table in the corner. Even in the lamplight she could pick out a dozen different shades of red and orange in his hair. He had grown a wiry beard in the months since they'd left the Shadar, but his freckles still made him look barely older than the boy who had shared his tent with her after his near-father, old King Tobias, rescued her from a burning death in the desert. "Pull up a stool. There's too much food here for one person—there's some bread, and stew, though not as good as my mother's, I'm afraid." He trailed off as he read her mood, then dropped his napkin onto the table beside his plate. "The maps, then. Help yourself."

She flipped open the top of the tall map-box by his desk and located the one she wanted. Rolling out the vellum on the desk, she anchored the corners with a plate of fruit and a silver ewer.

"Where's Oshi?" asked Jachad.

"With Callia."

"Better him than me," he sighed. A few sparks played around his fingers: the gift of fire from his sun-god father. "Why couldn't she have stayed on her ship? She's always on about something, and those clothes—she's like a refugee from a Thacovian wedding party. How Shof could choose her after my mother, I can't fathom, any more than I can understand why *you*—of all people—are the only one in my caravan who can tolerate her."

She found the Ranjar River on the map and traced it south: rivers, hills, forests, and then the massive bog. She'd never met anyone who'd been south of Balt; at least, no one who'd ever come back. "She reminds me of someone."

"Callia reminds you of someone you know? Who could that possibly be?"

"No one important. A mercenary." She lifted up the ewer and the map rolled itself up. She put it back in the box and brought out a different one. "Her name was Nevie."

"*Was?* What happened to her?" asked Jachad. He paused. "On second thought, don't tell me."

He got up from his unfinished meal and came to stand beside her. The desert had woven itself into the fabric of his robe and the air felt suddenly warmer for the scent. He took a sprig of berries from the dish by her hand and she caught a hint of their sourness as he bit into the fruit. "I love these. They're the best part about the caravan coming here. Do you remember Wastewater, when we were little?"

She remembered the squat trees, the insects, the pools with sucking sands at the bottom, and the smell of dry grasses, reeds and decay. She remembered the snapping lizards hiding by the edge of the water, and how she had lain on her belly alongside Jachad with the other Nomas children to catch them by their tails. She remembered running with the reeds waving over her head, swatting the blood-sucking insects away from her face; running because Jachi was chasing her and just for the sake of running. She remembered the time they'd blundered into a stand of knife-grass, and how sternly Tobias had scolded them as he'd dabbed some stinging sap on their shallow cuts, and then spoiled them with cake and warm spiced milk for supper. She remembered lying in her cot and listening to the insect chorus as she looked up at the striped silk of the tent above her, and how Jachad had pretended to be asleep in the cot beside her.

"I remember the lizards," she told him.

He made a faint sound in his throat that might have been a stifled sigh. "That's a map of Norland. I thought you wanted to go south."

"I am going south."

"Decisive, as always," said Jachad.

"A bad decision is better than none at all. Hesitation loses battles."

"Are we in a battle? Someone should have told me." He ran his knuckles across his beard. "Do you still think you're taking Oshi with you?"

"He's got to stay with me." The mapmaker's spiky mountain peaks blurred. "Harotha gave him to me for a reason. I'm going to see it through."

"I don't care what the elixir promised you, Lahlil. You can't take a helpless infant with you into Shof knows what. Not even you could be *that* selfish."

"Other people have done it," she said, refusing to flinch; he had called her "selfish" before. "Settlers. Refugees."

"Of which you are neither," Jachad pointed out. "You can't take that child out into the wilderness and make him run from *your* past. If you want to keep him with you, you'll have to stay with us."

"I'm leaving before the caravan goes on to Prol Irat." She automatically noted the quickening of her pulse and the dryness in her throat; a habitual awareness drilled into her by a lifetime of relying on her instincts. She stepped back from the desk. "They'll be looking for me there. There's a price on my head."

"Not on *your* head—on the Mongrel's. That's not who you are any more."

"I've done things I can't take back, Jachi," she said, "and that's not going to change because we want it to. It's not that simple. Anyway, you knew from the beginning I couldn't stay."

"I knew nothing of the sort, and neither did you." He pushed himself away from the desk, rattling the brass hinges on the folding top. The water jug tilted, spun on its edge, and then dropped onto the carpet. Water glugged out from the narrow mouth and turned the rug's blues to black and the reds to scarlet, but neither of them bent down to retrieve it. "You were content enough just to have Oshi, and us, after that mess in the Shadar. You weren't expecting some great change to happen. Maybe the real reason you don't want to leave Oshi behind is because you love him. People *do* love their babies occasionally, you know."

"Don't make this about Oshi," she said. "I've tried staying in one place before. It didn't work. I'd be putting everyone here in danger, including you."

"You don't have faith in anything, do you?" asked Jachad. Little tongues of flame were twisting around his fingers. "Not even me."

"Faith is dangerous."

"Why, for Shof's sake?" he asked.

"Because it makes you drop your guard."

He smiled, but the light didn't reach his eyes. "Well, there it is, isn't it?"

Jachad turned away from her and went back to his cold dinner. She rolled up the map of Norland, retied it, and placed it back in the partitioned box. The hinged lid clicked shut.

Lahlil took a sprig of berries from the dish before she left.

The darkness outside had deepened and clouds of tiny glowing insects swarmed from one patch of tall grass to another. She crushed one of the berries between her fingers, feeling the wet juice as the skin broke open. A stringy, yellow-eyed nightwing shot out of a patch of reeds and alighted on a leafless branch over her head. Some small rodent dangled from its curved beak, dripping blood onto the branches below. The bird eyed her for a moment, then tipped its head back and gulped down its prey in one bite.

Mairi was never going to be able to make her medicine for her. It wasn't the healer's fault; Lahlil had always known that medicine could only be made in Norland.

Norland. She still remembered every detail of that day on the snow-covered plain, sitting down by her fire to skin the dappled hides off the two lagramor she'd bagged that morning. The instant she had taken out her knife, the grachtel that had been following her for more than a week swooped down and dug its talons into the crust of ice on the other side of the fire, tracking the stroke of the blade with its white-rimmed eyes, until Lahlil had tossed it a few scraps of offal. She could almost hear Nevie's voice calling out to her, but Nevie was long dead . . .

"General! Surprised to see me here, eh?" Nevie's mercenary patois sounded even more garbled than usual: she was eating one of the hard green fruits that grew in the hot spring dells, chewing the fibrous flesh with her usual unhurried grace. She had always said that the only advantage of being from Marshmere was that there was nothing she couldn't or wouldn't eat. Her figure had come into view long before she reached Lahlil. The two shortswords at her waist and easy swing of her shoulders made her easy to identify; but, of course, it was always going to be Nevie.

"Knew you were tracking me," Lahlil answered economically, feeling the cold burn her throat. There was a reason Norlanders communicated without opening their mouths.

"The emperor—he found out about the bloody striders, you know," Nevie told her. "Just like you told us. Eoban put a big price on your head. Big price. That why you take this crazy job, eh? Kill him, before he kill you?"

"Close enough." She stuck the spitted meat into the thawed ground by the fire, then walked out across the snowy plain to meet her visitor while the grachtel took wing in a streak of bright blue against the gray sky. "We could kill him together. We've done it before."

"Like King Carder? Nah. Kill one of them assholes, you just get another. You know it." Nevie tossed the pit of her fruit out onto the snow, making a black pockmark in the unbroken whiteness, then wiped her sticky gloves on her thighs. "Better to kill you instead. Nothing personal."

"By yourself?"

"Too much gold, this job," Nevie sighed, as if expecting her to commiserate. "I bring a crew, they turn on me, sure as a swamp witch got tits."

"A full share of nothing is still nothing." The slate-gray Norland sky was beginning to darken to a starless, moonless black and she could feel her seizure beginning. Even here in Norland, where the sun and moon were little more than ideas—things she had seen once in a dream, and then forgotten—there was no escaping the Nomas gods' tug-of-war. Her muscles were already beginning to weaken. She had battled straight through it before, but not against someone as deadly as Nevie. Soon she would be at her most vulnerable, and Nevie knew it.

Lahlil circled around with the snow pulling at her boots, watching Nevie's hips. Her hips would move first. The mercenary's dark eyes took on a gleam without warmth, like the twilight sky reflected in the snow, and she chuckled. Her hips didn't move after all, only her arm. The throwing motion was little more than a clever flick of her wrist, but the sword whirled out with impressive accuracy.

Lahlil twisted out of the way, but the weakness in her legs made her just a fraction too slow, and the tip of the blade caught her thigh as it flashed by. She felt a warm burst of blood and then pain, but Nevie dived at her before she could bother about it. Too late to block, Lahlil dropped her sword and writhed sideways, then grabbed for Nevie's sword-arm, forcing the mercenary's next blow wide of her body. But the edge of it caught Lahlil in the face, opening up a gash at the corner of her mouth. Blood trickled down her throat.

She managed to throw Nevie off and used the respite to fish her sword out of the snow. This time when Nevie rushed her, Lahlil had enough time to bring her blade up to block. She pushed whatever strength she had into her trembling arms and fought off the Marshmere woman, not trying to gain the offensive, not yet, instead getting first to her knees, then to her feet. They launched into a volley of sword strokes.

"You not doing so good, General. Not the same. I see it, after the striders." Nevie's blows came quickly, efficiently; she was testing her exactly the way she would any other opponent even though they had fought side by side a

hundred times. Lahlil knew her reactions were slow and her thrusts weak. "I think you know it. I think maybe you come to Norland to die. I make it easy for you."

"Stop now, and you can go." Blood welled out from the gash in Lahlil's mouth and down her chin, and her wounded leg was as responsive as a chunk of wood. No one had hurt her this badly in a long time. "You're a pawn. The Norlander gods are using you."

"What for?" asked Nevie.

"To punish me."

The light dipped, and snow began falling in fat, heavy flakes. Lahlil strained her good eye as Nevie's shortsword darted through the whiteness with a bright agility she couldn't match. She was too late on one parry and had to fall back one step, then another. On the third step she put her weight on her injured leg and it folded beneath her.

Nevie had been so focused on Lahlil's leg that she had not seen her draw her knife. She charged, fully committed.

Lahlil pivoted out of the way at the last moment and saw Nevie's sword slide past within an inch of her chest, but by then she was punching her dagger straight through Nevie's breastbone. The mercenary's terrible rattling cry flew out over the plain. Lahlil caught her in her arms before she fell and sank down with her into the snow.

"General." Nevie's chest heaved under the knife and blood flecked her gaping mouth.

Lahlil bent her head low to make sure her voice found its way into the dying woman's ear. "The Norlander gods wanted to make me kill you," she said. "To prove how much I disgust them." Her own dark blood ran over her lips and pattered down onto Nevie's face. "You were the closest thing I had to a friend."

Nevie's death came as a restoration of the heavy Norlander silence. Already the snow was working to bury the evidence of their intrusion, covering over the blood and settling in the hollows of Nevie's half-lidded eyes. The snowy plain tilted to one side and wouldn't go straight again. The fight had drawn her thirty paces away from the fire, and with her affliction draining what remained of her strength, it might as well have been fifty leagues. With no way to seal the wound in her leg, she would soon be dead as well. She had gone from freezing to being uncomfortably warm—so warm that she would have taken off her coat if she'd had the strength—and she could no longer feel either the cut on her leg or even the leg itself.

As her sight faded away to nothing, she moved her eye-patch to uncover the silver-green Norlander eye on her left instead of the brown Shadari eye on her right. When she saw the figures walking toward her through the snow, she thought it was Lord Valrig's minions—the cursed—finally coming to claim her. When they were close enough for her to see their scars and missing limbs, she was sure of it.

Chapter 2

Daryan, the King of the Shadari, had fallen asleep.

Isa leaned over him and touched his shoulder with the tips of her fingers just as a gust of wind blew over the ridge and set the prickly grasses brushing against her cold Norlander skin. She shifted her body, trying to get away from a sharp rock gouging into her thigh through her worn trousers. The straggly bushes dotting the slope high above the city clacked their dry branches: an urgent conversation in a percussive language that was only just beyond her understanding. The thickness of the smooth wool robe she had pulled up over Daryan's naked body shielded him from the chill of her touch as he slept. She noticed how the moonlight drained the color from the fabric as she skimmed her fingers over his chest.

They both knew the risks of these trysts, however infrequent, but the urgency of satisfying their passion made everything else, even the constant pain of their touch, irrelevant. She pitied ordinary couples whose embraces cost them nothing, whose lovemaking came so cheaply that they could undertake it on a whim and forget it just as easily. They couldn't know what it was like to have a lover's arms circle around the small of their back like a pair of blacksmith's tongs straight from the fire, or have kisses rain down like a shower of embers.

But now a different kind of pain shot down through the stump of her left shoulder and into her missing arm and she fished out one of the dense little green balls from the pouch around her waist, not allowing herself to remember that she had taken one just after Daryan had fallen asleep, or that she had only a few left and ought to be saving them, or that the Nomas healer who had given them to her might not be back for months. She tasted the medicine's bitter tang the moment it touched her tongue and made herself chew slowly, needing the herbs and roots and whatever else made up the concoction to take the pain away.

"Daryan," she said, gently pressing her hand down on his heart.

She drew her hand back a moment later when she heard the rumbling—it wasn't very loud, but she still heard it, because she listened for it every day, all the time, with the vigilance of someone too accustomed to sudden catastrophe. The ground beneath her shuddered briefly, and then she knew for certain that the unsettled ruins of the old temple had shifted again, like a sleeping giant gnashing his teeth, grinding her happier memories down into gritty red dust.

"Was that the temple again?" asked Daryan, bolting upright. He pulled his robe on over his head then fumbled around in the stiff grass beside him for his gold circlet. His mouth turned down a little as he looked over at her and she was conscious of the way her old trousers had worn thin at the knees and of the unwashed state of her heavy braid. Since she could not do the braid up again with one hand, she rarely let her hair down any more. "You're already dressed."

"We should go down before someone gets hurt." She waded through the tall weeds to where Aeda was waiting, breathing in the pungent sea-air-and-musk scent of the triffon's bristly hide. She took a moment to scratch the ridges and the coarse tuft of fur between Aeda's round little ears before beginning the methodical process of checking the harness for faults, while Aeda poked her blocky head around in the weeds looking for lizards and rodents to eat.

"I didn't mean to fall asleep." Daryan sent small stones skipping away down the slope toward the city below as he strode toward her, tying his belt. "Why didn't you wake me up?"

"You needed the rest," she said, swallowing against the dryness scraping at her throat. No matter how often she spoke Shadari, speaking aloud still burned. "You work until you're ready to drop."

"That doesn't matter. I don't want to waste a moment of the time we get to be alone together." Daryan came up close behind her and circled his arm around her waist. "I need you more than sleep. You give me the strength to keep going."

Her eye caught the glint of gold among his dark curls even as the heat of his body wrapped around her like a blanket through the layers of clothing between them. She closed her eyes and stood still as he rested his cheek against her white hair.

"We should go," she told him, whispering even though there was no one but the goats on the next hilltop over to hear her.

"I know," said Daryan, but he didn't release her. "Tell me what's wrong first. Something's been bothering you all night. And don't say 'nothing.' I've seen you sneaking those pills, and rubbing your arm like you do when it hurts. It always hurts more when you're upset about something."

"Later." Isa jammed her foot in the stirrup, ready to swing herself into the saddle, but Daryan's hand clamped down over her wrist like a cuff of red-hot iron and pulled her back.

"Now," Daryan demanded, his mouth twitching with worry. "Please, Isa. Don't leave me to wonder about it. Just tell me what's happened."

"I overhead something," she confessed. Had Daryan been a Norlander, he would have been able to feel the uncertainty sweeping through her. She reached down and squeezed the little pouch, feeling the shapes of the pills inside. Only four left. "This morning in the palace, I heard Omir say they want to take Aeda away from me and have a Shadari fly her for you instead."

"That? Is that all?" Daryan gave the shaky little laugh that meant he had been caught out. "That was just talk. I didn't agree to it."

"I know," she said. Cool air snaked up underneath the untucked tail of her brother's old shirt, but sweat still itched on the back of her neck. "You told them you'd think about it."

"I had to say that," Daryan insisted, his voice hardening suddenly. "You know how things are right now. Binit will jump on anything to turn them against me. But I'm not going to do it—I would hardly ever get to see you."

"But I *want* you to think about it," said Isa. He drew back like he'd been pricked with a pin. "You can fly Aeda yourself, and I can do something more important—train your soldiers, help with the fortifications, even translate the mural in the ashadom." She and the rest of the Norlanders had taken up residence in the ashadom—the cave Harotha had discovered, where the ancient ashas had painted constellations and writing all over the walls. Daryan claimed to have chosen it for them because it was large and cool; Isa suspected it was because his people's superstitious fears kept most of the Shadari away.

"Isa," he said, drawing out her name in the way he did when he was trying not to be angry. He moved his hand toward the hair curling over the back of his neck, but stopped short. He had decided the old gesture was a childish tic, not in keeping with the dignity of his office. "I don't think that's a good idea, not right now. Binit will just say something about me letting the 'Dead Ones'—sorry, but that's what he'd say—run things again."

"The Shadar is my home. I need to help. I want to be accepted."

"You are," Daryan insisted. "You're a hero."

"Yes, for killing my sister," Isa reminded him. "I don't want to be a hero for that. It's not enough; I'm never really going to be accepted as one of them if I stay shut up in the ashadom."

She hooked her fingers into the front of his robe and pulled him into a kiss. He made a soft sound deep in his throat even as his shoulders stiffened from the shock of her cold lips and seized her round the waist. She wanted to melt into him until nothing was left of her but a pool of water: melt out of existence . . .

"Isa," Daryan said, pulling away from her. She leaned back with her heart thumping as he tilted his head down toward the dark city. "I know it's been hard for you, but we can't let it drive us apart now. Real change takes time and there's not much I can do while I'm bouncing from one crisis to another. I need you to be patient, not do anything that's going to cause more problems. You understand that, right?"

Aeda's side pushed against her back as the creature breathed in and out. She could feel the rhythm somewhere deep within her: steady and relentless, and so much bigger than herself, like the whirl of the stars over their heads.

"We should go," she said. She thrust her foot back into the stirrup and this time swung herself up, grateful that she'd finally found a way to fasten the harness so that she could wriggle in and out without having to manipulate the buckles one-handed. Daryan climbed up behind her and looped the harness over his shoulders. Then she wrapped the reins around her hand and whistled Aeda into the sky. A moment later, they were in the air with the triffon's wings beating their slow rhythm beneath them.

The ascent was still the worst part, when the angled climb slid her backward in the saddle and the harness was the only difference between life and death. She held on to the pommel and pushed her heels down the way her brother Eofar had taught her. For years after watching her mother fall to her death, the thought of even getting on a triffon's back had terrified her to the point of insensibility; now, ironically, she had taken on the job of flying Daryan around to whatever crisis needed his attention most. In the last three months she had done enough flying to make up for the previous seventeen years; she thought she would have a hard time judging whether she or Aeda was the more exhausted. Still, she much preferred that to skulking around in the cave with the other Norlanders, watching them do nothing but wait for her brother Eofar—now their leader—to come back from Norland. They cared for nothing except drowning their boredom in the wine the Shadari provided as a cursory token of gratitude for taking their side against Frea.

The city below looked peaceful under the cover of night, though dawn would reveal the stark truth: the neighborhoods reduced to scorched rubble; the bleached skeletons of fishing boats wedged among the rocks; the crowds of hungry people washing like a muddy tide toward the scaffold-covered palace for their daily rations. Isa doubted that whatever fate the ashas, those ill-fated Shadari priests of yore, had sought to prevent could have been any worse than the future their very machinations had brought about.

She spotted four pyres blazing in a line along the shore and a strange feeling fizzed through her empty stomach. *Resurrectionists.* They fascinated her as much as they repulsed her, with their self-appointed task of digging up the Shadari dead her people had entombed in the Norlander manner so the bodies could instead be burned on ritual pyres, according to Shadari custom. Some of the bodies they'd exhumed were so old there was no one left to remember their names. She suspected Daryan of being a little envious—the resurrectionists had brought the Shadari together with apparently no effort whatsoever, while so many of Daryan's attempts had failed. When he'd asked people to donate food to a common store to help feed the destitute, they'd claimed not to have enough for themselves. When he'd asked them to work the mines so they could make weapons to defend the Shadar, he'd been accused of trying to profit from their labor. And on it went.

Isa remembered the night three months ago, when she had convinced Daryan to stay in the Shadar to lead his people instead of running away together, the way they had planned. She had thought they needed his passion to reclaim the culture they had lost, to grow strong and independent once more, but she hadn't anticipated how much of his secret, hard-earned wisdom would be viewed with skepticism and fear, or how a few ambitious men would exploit the uncomfortable fact that he had allied himself with her brother—a Dead One—to secure their victory.

"I wanted to go down to the beach to talk to them tonight," Daryan shouted just behind her, his frustrated sigh snatched away by the wind. "Omir still thinks they have some kind of secret agenda. You know I rely on Omir—I'd never be able to manage without him—but he's wrong this time. We need the resurrectionists on our side. I really need to speak to their leader, but they keep saying they don't have one."

Isa turned them north toward the ruins of the temple. The wide ring of debris from the original explosion had been picked over long ago, but the bulk of the structure had fallen back in on top of itself, and the rest—the remains of countless rooms and corridors and staircases—teetered in an increasingly unstable pile. In among the rubble was everything from straw mats and broken broom handles to massive carved chests and sacks of coins from her father's imperial treasury. Every time the ruins settled, people who had lost everything in the war went looking to recover some scrap of their former lives, although too often they ended up getting themselves injured or killed in the process. Ever since Daryan had proclaimed the ruins off-limits in the interests of public safety, a few opportunists had seized on the issue as another chance to undermine his authority.

Darkness hid the clouds of red dust and grit kicked up by this latest collapse, but Isa could smell it in the air and taste it on her lips. Somewhere in that rubble was the other half of her burned left arm, still wrapped up in Eofar's old shirt. Maybe it was nestled among the remnants of her mother's tomb, near the carved lid of the sarcophagus a deranged slave had turned into her torture table, or even close to her mother's broken body. Maybe the undiscovered dead watched over it for her. Another rumble signaled that the pile had not yet settled; sometimes that went on for hours.

A triffon rose up from behind the hills and crossed their path, beating back the cold night air with its leathery wings. It had no saddle, which meant it was one of the feral beasts, those which had fled after their berths in the temple had been destroyed.

As they flew on, tiny points of light—torches and lanterns—appeared around the ruins like a new constellation. Isa saw a fairly large group of Shadari winding through the streets in a loose column and she brought the triffon down lower until the crowd sharpened into individual figures. Relatively few of them carried lamps, but she numbered them at about a hundred. Some shouted when they saw the triffon.

"This isn't good," Daryan mused. "I know it's that little prick Binit whipping them up again. Why do they even listen to him? Everyone knows he was Faroth's laziest crony. He knows I'll go down there—he just wants a confrontation so he can show off."

Isa brought them down over a rutted street lined with derelict houses. Daryan was right: Binit was in the lead, his flabby arm sagging under the weight of a torch stinking of fish oil. Aeda's heavy feet came down hard on the dusty street, sending up a cloud of dirt as her claws hit the ground. Her tail swept out and collided with a broken wall, sending more loose bricks into the street. Isa ducked her face into the crook of her arm to keep from breathing in the dirt while the crowd clogging up the narrow street jostled to a reluctant halt.

"Wait here. I'll handle this," Daryan said, as he unbuckled himself and slid down from the triffon's back. "And don't draw your sword," he added.

"I won't." She stopped herself from reminding him that Blood's Pride wasn't *her* sword. Her sword, Truth's Might, lay somewhere on the ocean floor. No matter how often she oiled and honed the plain steel blade or how many times she drilled with it until her shirt was dripping with perspiration, Blood's Pride would always belong to her dead sister, Frea.

"Those ruins aren't safe. No one should be going near them," said Daryan, squaring off against Binit. Isa shifted uneasily in the saddle as tools swung, clanking, from the hands of those in the crowd.

"We're here to do our duty. People were buried alive in there," said Binit. The remainder of Faroth's revolutionaries oozed out of the crowd and congealed around him. "We just want to give them a proper funeral. Don't you, Daimon? Or is that another tradition we're supposed to abandon now?"

"We can look for our dead in the morning, when we can see and the ruins have settled," said Daryan. "Anyone who goes in there now is just being selfish."

"Selfish?" Binit repeated, turning his chin to the side so the people behind him could hear. "Selfish! That's what you said, isn't it, Daimon?"

"Yes, *selfish*," said Daryan, projecting his voice out over the crowd. A chill wrapped around the back of Isa's neck. "It's not just your lives I'm worried about, it's the people I'll have to send in after you when you get yourselves trapped in there."

Daryan walked further into the street and gestured for Binit to come closer. The rabble-rouser hefted his torch a little higher and came out to meet him.

"I know why you really want to get in there," said Daryan. He kept his voice low under the sound of the spitting torch, but Isa could hear him clearly. "Wait until dawn when it's safer, and I'll let you treasure-hunt as much as you want."

"Sure, with Omir and his toy army right behind us, taking anything we find."

"For the treasury," Daryan corrected patiently, "but no, not this time: if you find anything, take it. You can swaddle your babies in the governor's monogrammed napkins if you want. But I need you to do a few things for me."

Binit rubbed his shoulder in a distasteful attempt at coyness and pursed his fleshy lips. "What?"

"First, stop spreading these rumors about a plague. There isn't any plague."

"You're denying it?"

"No one is sick," said Daryan. Isa didn't need to see his face to know he was clenching his teeth to keep from shouting. "I've got to hand it to you: not many men could convince people there's a plague because there *aren't* any bodies. Every time some family moves house, you and your friends are out there the next day parading up and down in front of the palace, claiming I've carried them off in the night. Gods help us, don't you think people are scared enough already?"

"I'll think about it," said Binit.

"And stop discouraging people with the asha powers from coming forward. There's absolutely no guarantee Eofar is going to be able to talk the Norland emperor out of invading again, and what have we got to defend ourselves? Some half-built walls in the mountain passes that wouldn't hold back a herd of goats and fewer than a hundred imperial swords that we barely know how to use. It isn't a sin for people to use their powers. Harotha told us so; she gave her life so we would know the truth."

"Oh yes, Harotha's 'visions,' " said Binit, with an insincere laugh. "We're just supposed to believe what she said, are we? And it just *happened* to be exactly what she wanted? Too bad she didn't leave any elixir so we could see for ourselves. But maybe she thought of that, eh?"

Daryan lunged forward as if to grab Binit's robe and Isa reached for Blood's Pride despite his warning, but he remembered himself in time, instead balling up his fists and shaking his head in frustration. "What's the *point* of all this, Binit?" he demanded. "What exactly are you trying to accomplish?"

"The Shadar needs to go back to the way it was before the Dead Ones came," Binit answered. For once the arrogant smirk dropped away and he reminded Isa of a boy who had just come out into an unfamiliar street and no longer knew his way home. "You want to change everything. You want to change what we've believed for hundreds of years. I say what my father and my grandfather believed in is good enough for me. Who do you think you are?"

"I'm the daimon, whether you or anyone else likes it or not," said Daryan, raising his voice, "and it's my responsibility to protect the Shadar. You say that what your father and grandfather believed is good enough for you: maybe you've forgotten that what they believed was of no help at all when the Dead Ones came. What they believed led to the pointless suicide of every asha in the Shadar. We have to take back the knowledge and the power we've lost if we don't want to be slaves again."

"Well, you won't silence us," said Binit, his eyes bulging in his reddening face.

"You know, I think I understand you now. You're afraid. You're so afraid of looking stupid that you're trying to make ignorance a virtue. Don't do it, Binit. You can be better than that."

Isa heard the sound of rapid footsteps stomping through the alleys and Omir appeared, followed by a dozen red-robed guards, each armed with one of the first black-bladed swords they'd produced after taking control of the mines themselves. Omir was the tallest and most imposing Shadari she had ever seen. His black eyes were set in a face that could have been carved out of stone.

"Of course, here come the Reds," Binit shouted for the benefit of the crowd, recovering his sense of outrage. "Using the weapons we made with our own hands to oppress us, just like the Dead Ones. How come you're not at the palace, counting the tax-money you've bled from these people?"

Omir growled something in response in his deep, slow voice, but Isa did not hear what he said; she had heard something else. Wings. She stood up in the stirrups and searched the night sky until she saw the triffons' silhouettes blotting out the stars. The other Norlanders were coming.

"Daryan!" she called down to him.

She saw him blanch as he followed the lift of her chin.

"They can't be here now," he whispered up to her. "You have to stop them."

With a heaviness in her chest she collected the reins and whistled for Aeda to take off. Omir and the others dashed out of the way as the triffon stretched out her wings; Isa saw Daryan turn to her just before Aeda bunched her legs and thrust her bulky body up into the air. As soon as she was aloft she saw all six triffons—the only ones left who would still tolerate being saddled—turning toward the temple. Every triffon carried two or three riders. Falkar, Frea's erstwhile lieutenant and their leader in Eofar's absence, led the formation.

<You have to go back,> Isa called out to Falkar, their silent Norlander language giving her aching throat some relief at last. She could feel his dark determination like a gray cloud around him. She tried to hide the flash of panic she'd felt seeing those triffons heading straight for her as she flew in front of them to cut them off. <Daryan's not allowing anyone close to the ruins until dawn, when it's safer.>

<Oh, of course,> Gyr called out, pulling his triffon up and over her head. <Dawn, when we'll be stuck hiding in that stinking cave.>

<Falkar, those're our friends buried under there,> said Arvald, appealing to the lieutenant. The other Norlanders almost never spoke to Isa directly, a fact that she had carefully kept hidden from Daryan so far. <We got the right to take back our own.>

<Daryan is trying to break up that crowd,> Isa told them. She turned Aeda back around toward them, but kept her distance. <You're only making it harder for him. Falkar, please, just go back. Just for now.>

<Our people in there deserve a proper burial,> said Falkar as he flew toward her. He was the only one of them still clean-shaven, the only one bothering to wash his clothes on a regular basis. He had followed Eofar instead of Frea because the law made Eofar the rightful head of the colony. Isa envied the simplicity of his world: black and white, right and wrong.

<You can't go against Daryan,> Isa insisted. <You swore to respect his authority until my brother gets back. Daryan has kept his side of the bargain. He's made sure we have what we need to live, even while his own people go hungry. Are you going to break your word now?>

Falkar brought his mount alongside her and both triffons instinctively fell into formation, beating their wings in unison. <What do you think the Shadari see when they look at you, Lady Isa?> he asked. It was the first time any Norlander had spoken directly to her in weeks, and it felt as if someone had crept up behind her and put their hands around her neck. <What do you think they see?>

Falkar gave the order to return to the ashadom and though Isa could feel the others griping, they had just enough discipline left to obey him. He brought his triffon around and flew away back to the cave, following his men.

Isa took in a great breath of the night air as soon as he was gone and tried to focus. Daryan needed her. She wouldn't think about anything else. She wouldn't think about the pain shooting down from her shoulder into her missing arm, or what she would do when the Nomas' pain pills were gone. Above all, she wouldn't think about the fact that she would eventually have to go back to the ashadom, to live among people who considered her an abomination, because she had nowhere else to go.

Flying up over the ashadom with the moon setting over the water behind her, Isa caught sight of her shadow on the cliff-face, elongated by the moonlight into a silent, string-limbed specter atop a gigantic winged beast. The leaning cross of Blood's Pride poked out from her saddle, stark and menacing. Where her face should have been was a blank oval, incapable of seeing anyone's suffering or offering any pity, and yet she knew it was looking right back at her.

Chapter 3

Rho Arregador awoke to the feeling of hot blood scalding his hands and his tabard soaked and dripping with gore. He closed his eyes again as the hammock swung beneath him, hooking his fingers through the netting and listening to the scrape of the iron rings just over his head. *Just a nightmare,* he told his racing heart. His stomach churned with acid and he felt like he was going to be sick, but he couldn't blame that on the dreams: every morning on the *Argent* began with the contents of his stomach trying to abandon ship by way of his throat.

He rolled gracelessly out of the hammock and dropped to the floor, letting his forehead rest against the strut for a moment before checking Dramash's hammock below. Except for a rumpled blanked and a vacant-eyed poppet made by one of the Nomas sailors, it was empty. The pouches of Shadari sand they had brought so Dramash could learn to control his formidable asha powers were underneath, furred with the dust of another wasted day. Rho knew he couldn't keep letting Dramash wriggle out of practicing. He had watched the boy's ability to command the ore within the Shadari rocks and soil; he'd seen him destroy a stone monument the size of a small mountain and suck people down under the sands—but those deeds had been the acts of a terrified child. Dramash needed real control over his powers if he was ever going to live in the Shadar again, or even be around swords forged from Shadari ore.

At least this morning Rho didn't have to jam his arm against his side and wait for the pain to stop. He ran his fingers over the right side of his abdomen and felt only smooth skin. Mala, the ship's healer, had said that the pain could be coming from scar tissue deeper under the surface, invisible but enduring, like the memory of Dramash's father dragging his rusty blade through Rho's flesh.

He grabbed his boots and took the single step over to the nearest stool, which skidded over the floor as it took his weight until he pushed his back up against the table bolted to the floor.

<Where are you going?> asked Eofar Eotan, his shirtless back glowing in the hammock on the opposite side of the cabin. He had been brooding again, but Rho much preferred that to the drunken, violent grieving.

<I'm going to find Dramash,> he said, tugging on his left boot.

<I dreamed about Ravindal,> said Eofar.

<Did you?> Rho would have liked a dream once in a while that wasn't blood-spattered and reeking of failure.

<It shone, like it was made of moonlight.>

<There is no moon in Norland. Or sun either, thank Onfar,> said Rho, as he pulled on the other boot.

<My mother made it sound so wonderful in her stories. I don't know why—she knew our tainted bloodline meant we could never go back.> Eofar shifted in the hammock and set it swinging violently back and forth.

Rho's stomach rocked along with it and he had to look down at the table, fixing his eyes on the model of Ravindal he had put together after a rummage through the galley junk-box: a slanted stone chopping block with a crack in it for the Front; a weather-bleached clothespin with a bit of red fabric stuck on top for the beacon; lidless spice jars and biscuit boxes for the crowding castles of the twelve clans, except for Eotan Castle, which was represented by a long box that his nose told him had once housed a cheese. The model had not helped them come up with any better course of action than walking into Ravindal and stupidly suggesting to the emperor that he proclaim the Shadar's independence, and then disingenuously presenting Dramash as one of any number of temple-destroying maniacs ready to do battle for his people.

<I don't suppose you've come up with a new plan?> Rho asked his commanding officer.

<No. Why?>

<I just don't think Dramash is ready to give any demonstrations. We can't expect him to be able to control all of that power, particularly in a strange place where he's surrounded by Norlanders with swords made from Shadari ore. Anything could happen.>

<We knew how risky this would be from the start,> Eofar reminded him. <The freedom of every person in the Shadar depends on us. It's too late to start second-guessing now.>

<We didn't know Emperor Eoban was going to die when we left the Shadar,> Rho pointed out. <He was a greedy politician who liked power and didn't like getting his hands dirty. His son's a warrior: Gannon hasn't stopped campaigning since his Naming Day. War is the only thing he knows, and the only thing he truly likes. Trust me, I got to know him much better than I wanted to when he took my brother as one of his lieutenants. Gannon's not the kind of person who negotiates; he's the kind of person who burns down your village and then makes your homeless children wipe the ashes off his boots.>

<So? If we have to fight to get what we want, we'll fight,> said Eofar. He climbed out of his hammock and lurched over to the other stool so he could pour himself a cup of wine from the jug on the table. Drowned rage for the wife, son, sister, father, home, and everything else he had lost lapped around him. <If you think we can walk in and out of Norland without getting bloody, then you're just as big a fool as Frea always thought you were.>

Rho didn't mind Eofar lashing out at him, even if throwing his insane relationship with Frea in his face represented a new low. It was still better than picking up shattered crockery or wrestling knives away from him. <You know, I sometimes think you want it all to go sour,> he commented, picking up the oblong red box representing Arregador House from their model and setting it down carefully on its narrow end. <I think you hate Norland so much for ruining your family that you *want* to fight them, even though you'd be dooming yourself and me, and everyone back in the Shadar.>

As Eofar slumped over his cup, Rho wondered if anyone in the Shadar would recognize their new governor now. He'd lost weight, his white hair was lank, and Rho didn't even want to think about the last time his clothes had been laundered.

<You know the rumor that ruined my family?> said Eofar. <Our irrevocably compromised bloodline—the reason Emperor Eoban gave for banishing my father to the Shadar with such touching consideration? Frea never believed it.>

<I know.>

<She said it was just court politics.>

<I know. I remember.> Rho tapped the block; it rocked, but it didn't fall over. He really didn't want to talk about Frea. <But the Norland of your mother's stories doesn't exist either, Eofar. I'm not sure it ever did.>

The ship swayed and creaked around them as it swept forward into something they couldn't see. Rho listened to the hammock rings grinding behind him and wondered what it would feel like to get some real sleep.

<Rho,> said Eofar, leaning back to watch the lamp swinging over his head, <what did you do to get sent to the Shadar?>

<It's not a very interesting story.>

<I want to know.>

<No, really, it's not,> said Rho, tying back his hair so he could wipe the perspiration from the back of his neck.

<Consider it an order from your governor.>

<I bedded my brother's wife while he was out campaigning.> He hoped it came out as glibly as he'd tried to make it. He didn't even know why he was admitting to it after all this time . . . except that it felt perversely satisfying to dredge it up, like poking an old bruise to see if it still hurt. <I decided it would be better for everyone if I wasn't in Norland when he came back from Angor with Scion Gannon.>

<Oh,> said Eofar.

<So I left, and then Trey died a few months later in a hunting accident, only he didn't die right away. He fell from his triffon and the trees tore him up so much that he knew he wouldn't heal without scarring, so he made his wife and Gannon and his other friends leave him alone in the woods to die. He always had a morbid fear of becoming one of the cursed. Too much time spent reading the *Book,* I guess. Not a problem I ever had.>

He needed some air. He retrieved his ancient family sword, Fortune's Blight, from its dubious place of honor in a dark corner, where it leaned above whatever trash had rolled there: a monolith surrounded by cut-rate acolytes. The massive emerald in the crosspiece glimmered faintly in the glow from his hand as he looped the buckled belt over his head, just as his long-dead father had done, and a dozen ancestors before him. Any one of his older half-brothers could have claimed it, but no one nowadays wanted to be seen lugging around an old-fashioned steel blade.

<But how did you end up in the Shadar, a common soldier?> Eofar asked again as Rho fetched his sun-proof cape from the hook by the door. <You're a high-clansman, an Arregador—you could have got a better post.>

<You don't get it, do you? If being high clan was all that mattered, we'd all be born generals. You have to have money, status, ambition or a lot of talent to get anywhere. Trey had two of those, at least. I don't have any.>

<But why the Shadar? You must have done something. I once heard you cheated at cards, and another time that you ran naked through the Arregador exemplar's chambers on a bet.>

<Oh, it was something much worse,> said Rho as he pulled his hood up and swung open the cabin door. <I volunteered.>

Rho stepped out into the shadow of the forecastle and took a moment to adjust his senses to the onslaught. The glare of the morning sun was the worst of it, but the thump of the wind against the sails, the voices of the women and the rush of the salty air all hit him at once. At least the freshness of the wind and the cool northern air purged the stale cabin funk from his lungs.

An unusual number of sailors were gathered over by the starboard rail, watching the sea below. Their loose garb rippled in the steady breeze, and a few wind-tossed locks trailed down beneath their bright scarves and over the backs of their sun-darkened necks. Some of the girls were up in the shrouds—the younger crew-members did most of the climbing—while others busied themselves at tasks he still didn't understand. He had learned virtually nothing about sailing since he'd come aboard: the women had made it very clear that they preferred him lying in his hammock to stumbling around the decks and getting in their way, although a few had pointed out—some jestingly, some not—that he did possess one asset a ship crewed exclusively by women could well put to use. He shouldn't have been surprised, not given the fancifully pornographic cartoons he had found carved all over the ship, particularly that one with the octopus.

Rho searched the crowded deck for Dramash, but didn't see him—he was probably down in one of the holds playing with his little friend Yara, the cabin girl, or scrounging something to eat in the galley. There was no place else for him to go except overboard. Eofar followed him out of the cabin, walking steadily across the deck despite the fact that he was still straddling the space between badly hungover and newly drunk.

"Rho! Come and see." A young woman with a round face and a little upturned nose shoved one of her comrades out of the way and beckoned him to the rail.

"That's cheating, Hela," the other girl protested.

Rho went over to her, resisting the urge to hold on to things as he passed so he wouldn't have to listen to the girls giggling at his expense. He leaned over the gleaming brass rail and looked down at the white-flecked blues and greens as Eofar came up alongside him.

"Is that what I think it is?" asked Hela.

"Yes," said Rho, as Eofar turned his back to the rail and crumpled weakly on the nearest locker. "It's a dead triffon."

The Nomas had snagged the atrocity bouncing along on the waves in their net. One of the wings had been partially torn off and flopped sickeningly over its side. The creature's snout hung open and its huge eyes, shiny and black in life, had clouded over to a milky white.

"I was just about to fetch you," called out Captain Nisha as she crossed the deck. Strands of hair, brown and sun-streaked gold and silver, played around her face and the silver moon medallion she always wore flashed in the sun. She leaned close to Rho and whispered, "Don't you let those girls bother you, especially Hela. That girl would cheat at solitaire. Don't you worry about their bet. You do just as you like."

"Bet?"

"You mean you don't know?" asked Nisha. "I would never have given them credit for being so subtle. Things must have changed since I was young. Or maybe you spend a little too much time watching Dramash, and not enough looking at the . . . scenery."

As Grentha, the *Argent*'s first mate, emerged from the wheelhouse and came to join them, the girls at the rail immediately straightened up and left off their chattering. Nisha was both their captain and their queen, but it was Grentha who kept the discipline.

"Somebody cut that damned thing loose," said Eofar, still looking sick.

<Poor thing,> said Nisha, switching easily from Nomas to Norlander. She spoke it as well or better than most Nomas, but her feelings wove and darted like a school of quick little fish: the moment Rho tried to grab hold of one, it was gone. <Could it have come from the Gemanese ship Frea's men hijacked in the Shadar?>

<I doubt it,> said Rho. The ship pitched, and his stomach rolled anew. <The emperor still sends triffons to the provinces sometimes. This one probably got sick, so they dumped it overboard.>

Grentha made no reply, but she regarded him with the frank skepticism in which she held all land-dwellers, most men, and Rho in particular. She bore a striking resemblance to the *Argent*'s carved figurehead, right down to the cracked skin and leaden eyes, and had slightly less charisma.

<Then you still don't think Ingeld and those others are headed for Norland?> Nisha asked.

<Without Frea? No. The only thing they can do now is desert,> said Rho. <They're heading for the Broken Islands. It's the only place I've ever heard of connected with Norlander deserters, and since Ingeld has never had an original thought in his life, he's bound to go there. Why does it even matter?>

<The Barrels, that's why,> said Grentha.

He had been hearing the sailors whispering about the Barrels for some time—he had seen it on the map, nothing more than a few swirling lines far out away from any land, but no Nomas ship had ever crossed it voluntarily. Those who had been forced in by storms or bad navigation had returned with tall tales of stars that moved in circles, winds that blew from four directions at once, waves as high as mountains, swirling whirlpools with snapping jaws at the bottom and calms that never lifted.

<The Barrels. I can't say I'm looking forward to it,> said Nisha, as the second mate, a willowy woman named Sabina, came over to join them. <I think we'll have enough excitement without having to worry about being boarded by renegade Norlanders.>

Rho suddenly became aware of an unfamiliar sound mingling with the wind in the sails and the hum of the ropes: a rattling sound. Nothing on Nisha's immaculate ship had ever had the temerity to rattle like that before.

Eofar rocked to his feet and twisted around to look behind him, reminding Rho of a dog chasing his tail; he found it amusing until he realized the cause. He jumped up on the locker behind Eofar and grabbed the hilt of Strife's Bane. The sword was shaking so hard he could barely hold on to it.

<What are you doing?> asked Eofar. <Stop that—let go!>

"Where's Dramash?" Rho shouted to the sailors. "He's doing this: it's the ore in the blade, he's controlling it. Somebody find him!"

"Why would he do that?" asked Nisha.

"He must have seen the dead triffon." Rho was hanging on to the black-bladed sword as Eofar tried to unbuckle the belt and free himself from it. "He loves them. That's how Frea lured him away from his mother in the first place."

Nisha's eyebrows shot up. "Oh, I see."

"He's over there," said Sabina, pointing, just as a knot of girls backed away from each other. The boy was sitting hunched over below the rail, with his head buried in his arms.

Sabina, Nisha and half a dozen sailors all made some version of the same soft, pitying noise and started toward him.

"No, don't," Rho warned them. "He doesn't like people looking at him like that—"

His warning came too late: Dramash looked up to see the women coming for him and power exploded out of his small body. Eofar got the buckle of his swordbelt loose at the worst possible moment and the sword and sheath flew sideways out of Rho's hands, knocking him over. Eofar leaped for them, missed, and fell headlong into a coil of rope. Sailors scattered out of the way as the sword shot past them and crashed into the side of the landing boat, punching a hole straight through the wood.

Rho heard the sound of Dramash's bare feet slapping against the boards and got to his feet in time to see him disappear into their cabin and slam the door behind him. From inside the room came a sound like a volley of arrows loosed at a wooden target.

"Rho," said Nisha significantly. The curve of her mouth had straightened to an emphatic line. "We can't have this."

"I know—I'm sorry. I'll calm him down. It will be all right," Rho told her and the dismayed crew as he climbed down from the locker and headed for the cabin. He paused with his hand on the latch, feeling the deck swinging beneath him and obeying an instinct to give Dramash another moment to calm himself.

By the time he opened the door, everything inside was quiet. Rho pulled the door shut behind him, blocking out both the light and the activity on deck. Dramash sat curled up in a little nook behind his hammock with his arms around his knees. Pieces of Rho's model, the wine jug and the cups littered the floor. The bags of sand lay strewn all around the room, no longer dusty.

"I have to go," said the boy, crawling out from under the hammock without looking at Rho. "Yara's waiting for me." He started wading through the junk like there was nothing unusual about it being there.

"Wait, Dramash. You can't go now. You need to practice," Rho told him.

"I have to go. She's going to teach me a new game."

"Dramash," Rho said, kicking one of the sandbags away, "you have to practice. You can't keep putting it off. Do you know you just wrecked one of the boats?"

"I'll do it later."

"Later?" Rho swept his arm at the mess all around them, feeling a tickling of panic in the palms of his hands. "How much later? After someone's been really hurt? Or later, when this ship is at the bottom of the sea?"

Dramash glowered down at the cabin floor. "I don't *want* to practice."

"And I don't want you to kill anybody," said Rho, and then instantly regretted it.

"You can't make me do it." He looked up at Rho, his dark eyes as fixed and cold as a raptor's. The Shadari gods may have given Dramash the power to cause destruction and death, but that look . . . Rho's knife had called that into being, the moment he had pulled it across the throat of the boy's helpless mother.

Rho reached behind him for the stool and sat down. For a long moment, he watched the shadows rock back and forth with the swing of the lantern. "What game?" he asked finally.

The disturbing look on Dramash's face slackened away, but his chest still rose and fell like he'd been running.

"What game is Yara going to teach you?" Rho asked again.

Dramash picked up an old biscuit box at his feet. "I don't know what it's called."

"Oh."

The boy turned the box over in his hand. "Yara says everything in Norland is made of glass."

"Green-glass," said Rho. "It's ice with minerals in it, so it doesn't melt like regular ice. It's mostly for decoration. The buildings are made of stone, just like other places."

"And there are big cracks in the ground," Dramash went on, "and if you fall into one, you have to serve an evil god and be in his army."

Rho's already miserable stomach knotted up even further and he cleared his throat against the burn of the acid. "That's just a story," he said.

Do not go down into the deep places. For there Valrig will curse you, and into his service forever will you be bound.

Dramash opened the door and was just about to step over the raised threshold when he came back and dropped the biscuit box into Rho's hand. "I won't fall in. I'll be careful."

"That's fine," said Rho, closing his hand around the box. "Careful is just fine."

Dramash was out the door and gone before the ship pitched down again into the waves. Rho covered his eyes against the light sliding back and forth across the cabin wall. He was beginning to feel like he'd never be on solid ground again.

Chapter 4

Kira Arregador made one final assessment of her reflection in the mirror. It was real mirrored glass, not just a polished silver plate, but a fault in the casting made the image wavy and distorted. Still, it confirmed what she already knew: the necklace did not become her. The orange stones clashed with her blue-and-white complexion, and the chain still reminded her of a noose about to be pulled tight no matter how she adjusted the heavy gold links over her collarbone.

<What do you think?> she asked Aline.

Her hand-servant paused in the act of coiling and pinning up her braids in the arrangement that best framed Kira's silver-gray eyes and chose a small jar from among the scents, creams and powders crowded onto the dressing table. <Maybe some of this?>

She took the jar and leaned in for a closer look in the mirror. Veins webbed the whites of her eyes, and the delicate skin underneath had begun to sag. A few nights of real sleep would set it all right again.

<"Pleasant sleep is the reward of a pure heart,"> she quoted, dabbing a tiny amount of the pearly cream under each eye. <Isn't that what they say?>

<That's what it says in the *Book,* my Lady.>

<My old tutor once made me copy that out fifty times to punish me for falling asleep during my lessons. He had quite the sense of humor.> Kira replaced the lid on the jar and straightened the collar of her shirt. <There, is that better?>

<Yes, much better,> replied Aline.

<But?>

<I'm afraid you'll be the only one wearing white.>

<Yes, I don't doubt it.>

<Then why do it?> asked Aline. <The emperor wasn't even from your own clan.>

<Because somebody should,> she said as she buckled on Virtue's Grace over her spotless mourning whites. She admired the sheen Aline had buffed into its hilt; it certainly had not been sullied by use for quite some time. Someday she would likely regret not keeping up even her meager skills. <Emperor Eoban's only been dead three months. The man built the whole empire up from nothing. He deserves a little more mourning than that, don't you think?>

<I think you like showing them up, that's all,> said Aline.

<Do you?> asked Kira. She waited while Aline slid the sleeveless fur robe over her arms and settled it on her shoulders. The silver ursa pelts weighed practically nothing at all, but they were warm enough to make her uncomfortable in the heated room. <Well, you may be right. I'm afraid court life is making you too sharp for your own good, my girl. What happened to that innocent creature I found scrubbing floors in the Aelbar kitchens? I blame myself for your degeneracy.>

<Yes, my Lady,> said Aline, preening a little at the compliment, but not feeling the real regret hiding behind Kira's teasing. <We were a lot more moral in the Aelbar kitchens.>

<I don't doubt it. Have you noticed how people's morals tend to decrease in direct proportion to the length of the sword they carry?>

<You could stay home tonight. I know you haven't been sleeping. I can take a note to the emperor and say you're ill.>

<On Eowara's Day?> Kira thought longingly of taking off her coat and sitting back down in front of the fire, listening to the wood pop and snap as the heat lapped around her. <No one's allowed to be ill on Eowara's Day, least of all me. Unless you want to wait and see if Emperor Gannon sends Captain Vrinna to drag me from my bed?>

<No, my Lady,> said Aline, casting a proprietary eye around the

one-room palace Kira had moved into following her husband's death. The chamber, though large, was tucked in an out-of-the-way corner of the Arregador clan's magnificent house in Ravindal. Tapestries were piled in heaps on the floor, waiting for Kira to make up her mind where to hang them. Her bed had so many cushions that she couldn't even see the furs underneath. Crates leaking sawdust and pine needles held ornaments she'd yet to unpack, and bolts of fabric stood propped up in the corners while the tailors awaited her instructions.

<Then we'd better go. I think we're already late.>

They left through the tiny entrance hall and passed through several corridors, then out into the gallery overlooking the great hall. The slanted green-glass panels of Arregador House's elegant atrium gleamed overhead, but the people who usually congregated beneath it had already left for the feast in Eotan Castle. Cold air slashed its way inside the moment the door-warden opened up for them, and Kira pulled her coat closer to her body before striding out into the evening.

<Let's go the back way,> she told Aline as a pair of guards at the end of an afternoon patrol flew by on their triffons, making their way back to the stables. <It's quicker.>

Their boot-nails crunched through the ice as they walked through the alleys and yards between the Arregador and Vartan houses. Snow clung to the sloping roofs of the outbuildings and pushed up against the walls in sweeping drifts, and icicled thawvine branches bobbed and snatched at their clothes as they brushed by. Clusters of tiny purple berries were just beginning to appear: she remembered eating the warm fruit by the handful as a child, trying to keep from breaking the branches so the hot sap wouldn't ruin her clothes.

Work had ceased early for Eowara's Day and a thin layer of ice covered the firepits and cold furnaces. The alleys were deserted except for vermin forging tunnels from the kitchens to the slop-yards. They passed through Saddler's-yard and out into Smith's-yard, where the tang of charcoal and the taste of hot metal sharpened the rest of Kira's senses to a needle-fineness. At the end of the alley, they climbed up the green-glass slope of Knife Bridge, named for the shape of the ravine it spanned in the black rock.

Kira ran her hand along the etched railing and looked down into the depths of the crevasse as they passed. Luminous mist from the hot springs deep in the rock puddled in some spots and twined out in ribbons in others. She still remembered her sister telling her that the mist concealed Lord Valrig's twisted minions, who came up from the Under-realm to snatch away naughty high-clan children and boil them up for soup.

Once across the bridge, they passed into wider streets sheltered from the snow by green-glass canopies and protected against the wind by frequent turnings. They crossed yet another bridge and hurried on, passing no one but street-sweepers clearing away the snow and scattering fresh pine needles. Finally they came out into the Front—the open space in front of the gates of Eotan Castle—where the headland, cracked in too many places to build upon, sloped up gradually to the sharp rise under which lay the sealed tombs of Norland's most ancient monarchs, including the first and mightiest of them all, great Eowara herself. Kira was not fond of the Front. She preferred the narrow streets and little courts; here, she felt like she was being watched from every angle: from the towers and apparently empty slit-windows of Eotan Castle; from the huge green-glass terrace on the western side, supported by two twenty-feet-tall statues of wolf-headed Eotan the Progenitor; from the worn faces on the carvings of the ancient monarchs lining the rise; from the top of the hewn steps between them to the headland's highest point where the beacon burned day and night to guide ships into the harbor; and where the skull of Gargrothal, last of the great sea monsters, gaped down at them.

The gates of the Eotan clan's castle stood open and a wholly unnecessary contingent of extra palace guards with Eotan tabards stood at attention in front of them.

<It's Captain Vrinna,> Aline said, slowing.

<Don't worry. I'll handle her.>

Vrinna Eotan, scion of a particularly stiff branch of Norland's highest clan, stood in the center of her command in her bronze helmet, no doubt kept warm by her zealous devotion to the emperor who had ordered her to stand out in the cold while he feasted. Vrinna watched them approach for a while before coming down the steps and circling around them like a crag-cat climbing down for a closer look at her prey. Kira felt Vrinna in her mind for a moment like a hand darting out for a slap, but then retreating so swiftly one couldn't be sure it had happened at all.

<The feast has already started, Lady Kira,> said Vrinna.

<Oh, no! Has it really?> asked Kira, looking around the empty Front with dismay as if she was only just noticing she was alone. <Now, how did that—? You see, Aline, I told you not to fuss so long over my hair. Now the emperor is in there talking to an empty chair. He's bound to notice eventually.>

<I'm sorry, my Lady,> said Aline, playing along with just the right amount of sullen apology.

<You can go in behind the dais. You should know the back passages well enough for that,> said Vrinna.

Kira let the clumsy innuendo swing right over her head and replied, <Oh, no, I don't want to walk all the way around. If the skits haven't started, I'll just go straight through.> She felt Aline's trepidation: they had of course planned on entering discreetly from behind the high table; now she faced a long walk down the entire length of the hall, but she would not give Vrinna the satisfaction of seeing her bothered. Summoning up her most aggrieved inflection, she said, <What are you waiting for, Aline? Merciful Onraka, do you want me to freeze into a statue out here, like old Progenitor Eotan over there?>

Vrinna moved back just far enough to let her pass. Aline went up the stairs ahead of her, dragging her feet through the slush left by the passage of the six hundred or so high clansmen and their attendants already inside. Kira followed until her coat caught on something and yanked her shoulders backward. She flailed her arms, trying to regain her balance, but could not compensate for the weight of the sword across her back and crashed down, hitting her shin and elbow particularly hard before she stopped herself from sliding any further.

<My Lady!> Aline cried, rushing over to help her up. Kira breathed through her anger, deflating it until it was small enough to fit back in the little box where she kept it. As Aline tried to brush the dirty slush from her beautiful coat, Kira noted the bootprint on the fur just at the spot where Vrinna had been standing beside her.

Virtue's Grace thrummed against Kira's back, coming alive with her loathing. She had never won a tournament or even seen a battlefield. She knew it would be suicide—and a very quick one at that—to draw on the captain, but Vrinna knew it, too, and her smug certainty galled Kira far more than her graceless tumble. Vrinna was the woman who had brought "battlefield justice" to her new position; apparently the captain saw no point in arresting someone and holding a trial when she could just slice off a few of their fingers and set them out to die.

<All right, Aline, you can fix my coat later,> Kira trilled brightly, pausing on her way back up the steps. <You really should know, Captain, there's a very unfair story going around about you. They're saying you sleep with your breastplate still on and that anyone who wants to bed you has to bring along a stout pair of smith's shears. Isn't that preposterous? How could you possibly sleep with all those buckles digging into your back? That's what I told them, anyway.>

<Thank you, Lady Kira.> Vrinna's anger flashed out in a shower of sparks, but they weren't bright enough to conceal the prudish embarrassment squirming below.

<How *do* these things get started; that's what I'd like to know?> Kira nattered on as she started up the steps after an admirably composed Aline.

Aline looked back over her shoulder as they crossed the wide stretch of paving up to the doors. <She's watching you,> she said, switching back to a private pitch.

<I know.>

<She knows you were teasing her.>

<I know. I suppose I should pity her—unrequited love and so forth,> Kira said, with some small twinge of remorse. <If she could just see for herself how much her fawning disgusts the emperor, she might actually get somewhere. And I know it's dangerous to keep provoking her, but she just makes it so much *fun*.>

They passed the thick iron-and-wood doors and into the entrance hall; Aline took Kira's cloak, hood and gloves and went off to join the other servants in the kitchens for their dinner. Wide stairways on either side led up to the second story, while directly in front of her were the carved doors featuring the Eotan clan's snarling wolf's-head sigil. Beyond those doors lay the venerable Great Hall, around which the rest of the castle had been built in ever-increasing layers, like an onion.

Kira adjusted the orange necklace as the doors swung open to admit her.

At first the clattering of dishes and the scraping of benches across the floor swallowed up her footsteps, but as she walked out under the arcade formed by the yellow and brown ribs of the great leviathan, Kira saw first one head turn, then another, and soon everyone was watching her walk toward the dais through the shimmering heat of the braziers. She affected a careless stroll, setting herself up as too oblivious to the awkwardness of her situation to feel embarrassed. She and the other nobles wearing white could have occupied a linen cupboard without crowding. The stone floor and walls, the heavy oak benches and tables, the iron braziers and chandeliers were old and solid, but the stuff of empire covered them like a gaudy mummer's mask. Gilded plates heaped with exotic fruits and sweetmeats dotted the tables. Paned glass lanterns swung overhead and cast colored shadows onto the floor. Bright tapestries looted from the castles of Enderland held back the drafts. Arms and armor, statuary, musical instruments, shelves bowing under the weight of polished brass vessels in the shape of beasts with flattened faces, more shelves holding glistening glass ewers and pottery so fine as to be nearly transparent: all of it crowded the walls. The hall even boasted, on a special plinth of its own, the bearded head of King Castan of West Angor, preserved in a jar.

A space had been marked out in the center of the hall for the skits, but the mummers had not yet been admitted.

Emperor Gannon Eotan sat his place in the middle of the table, halfway through talking over the particulars of one of his military triumphs with yet another Eotan, the old Lord Denar. Gannon continued his conversation as she approached the dais, but she felt him tracking her like a bear raising its snout to sniff the air. His two old war-dogs did the same before lying back down in front of the high table in a rug of unwashed fur and ashes.

<Opportunity. That's what makes legends,> said the emperor, tapping the edge of the platter with the flat of his knife. Kira

could feel the restlessness prowling back and forth through his words. <How many great Eotans lived and died before Eowara with no adversaries except the other clans, before the Scathrings came down from their mountain? If they had come a little sooner, we might be feasting for someone else right now. Opportunity. That's what I pray for, not victory. Victory can't be given by the gods, or anyone else, for that matter: it has to be taken.>

She stopped at the bottom of the steps, ignoring the yellow-eyed stares of the dogs.

<An interesting point, your Majesty,> Lord Denar began. <It's a long time ago now, but in my day we believed that—>

<There you are, Kira,> said the emperor. He leaned out with his hands braced on the table, calling attention to the fluid elasticity of his muscular arms, shoulders and chest. She looked up into a face that had been chiseled by centuries of carefully arranged marriages and then composed around a pair of silver-blue eyes that outshone the jewel-box display of the courtiers arrayed around him. He was in his fifty-third year, as much in his prime as any man or woman in the empire. She remembered when the sight of him had still impressed her, before his brutishness had worn her down. <You took your time.>

<My time? Oh, no, I would never do that,> she said, bending in a courtly little bow before him. <I don't suppose I could. Everything in Norland belongs to your Majesty, isn't that what they say? So then I took *your* time, not mine. Now that I think of it, I suppose I shouldn't have taken something that doesn't belong to me, but after all, you're so generous>—here she stopped her chattering to stroke her necklace with the subtlety of a sledgehammer—<I'm sure you don't mind me taking a little bit. If you can spare it, naturally.>

Gannon's eyes met hers and she felt him probing, as he often did. She let him in as if she had nothing to hide; the trapdoor in her mind was locked, the key long gone, the cracks filled up with dust.

<Take your place, then,> said Gannon, before resuming his seat.

Kira had been seated next to Lord Denar and the pompous Lord Betran Eotan, the latter spearing the food on his plate with resentful little jabs. He had been knocked out of the morning's tournament in only the third round: a disappointing performance by anyone of significant rank, but especially for the man who, by virtue of being the highest-ranking Eotan in Ravindal at the moment, was technically heir to Gannon's throne, thanks to the law that was in place to ensure the throne remained occupied at all times. Betran was of the opinion that Norland had been steadily going downhill in the century since the Stonewood Treaty had ended the Second Clan Wars; he firmly believed that the only high clan belonging in Ravindal was the Eotan. At least she could count on the sullen lord maintaining a frosty silence with a mere Arregador—and only by marriage, at that.

Betran should have been happy that most of the guests at the emperor's table were Eotans, with the exception of a few warriors from other clans who had distinguished themselves under Gannon's command during his three decades of campaigning, and Kira herself. Gannon had not learned much from his recently departed father about politics if he thought this slight to the other eleven high clans would go unnoticed.

<Still in mourning, then, Kira?> Lady Bekka Eotan observed, from slightly further down the table. Her Eotan blue shirt appeared to be drowning under the weight of its silver embroidery, and was competing for attention with a pair of jeweled combs and a gold cuff bracelet heavy enough to bash in someone's skull. <You surprise me, when the emperor himself has put off his grieving for Eowara's Day. Is there some reason the Arregadors mourn Emperor Eoban more than the rest of us? Or is it just you?>

Kira looked around in consternation. <Am I the only one? But I thought—? Isn't the mourning six months? It's only been half that, hasn't it? Did I count it wrong? I'm afraid I've no head for that sort of thing at all. And when I have so many other nice things I could have worn tonight, too. Now my whole evening will be practically spoiled.>

Discomfort rippled down the length of the table. Most of the courtiers had put off mourning for the old emperor and worn their gaudiest clothes in a transparent attempt to curry favor with Gannon; a few had even exchanged traditional Norlander attire for expensive foreign clothes in thin, garish fabrics. Small wonder the mid-clan physics now did a booming business in cold potions and ague powders and had more money than many of their high-clan patients.

Kira wondered what the physics would see if they looked inside her these days: if they would see a gaping chasm at the core of her, veins dangling over the edge, organs sliding toward the blackness. It amused her to think of their discomfort as they dithered over their potions and poultices, afraid to tell her they had no cure—or maybe even that she was dead already.

She picked one of the yellow fruits from a dish on the table and pressed her thumbs into the indentation at the top, ripping it open and spilling its black arils. A wine-bearer came forward to fill her gold-plated goblet and another bearer leaned in to offer a tray of meat congealing beneath some lurid pink sauce before she waved him away. These elaborate meals had lost their appeal for her. She longed for the dull food of her humble childhood by the Aelbar cliffs: goat meat cured with orange-root; crumbly pannisseed cakes steaming inside a cloth; sour pineberry jam. All these feasts were beginning to blur together, with the same people eating the same food, wearing the same clothes, having the same conversations, all stuck in place like a colony of jewel-beetles in a dollop of sap.

The castle warden swept into the playground rattling his chain of keys and called in the mummers. Kira settled back in her chair with her goblet in her hand, anticipating the customary skits that had ceased to amuse her when she was eight years old. The opening playlet always commemorated the first battle with the Scathrings: a pretend Eowara in a ludicrously tall fur hat fought off an ambush by Scathrings wearing dark scraps to represent their scaly skin and masks painted with staring yellow eyes. The crowd immediately began heckling the mummers and their wooden swords, calling out tips and correcting their fighting techniques, or mockingly cheering the Scathrings on to victory. *Clack, clack, clack* went the mummers' swords and the Norlanders fell around Eowara one by one, unfurling blue silk scarves to represent the blood flowing from their wounds. Some of the Scathrings made a show of lapping up the blood, at which point missiles of fruit and bread came out of the crowd to chase the monsters away from the dead.

That skit ended, and others followed, until eventually the caped figure of Lord Valrig appeared to taunt a man with a line of charcoal across his face to represent a scar, kicking at him and darting forward to squeeze his muscles like a stock-warden inspecting an animal for purchase. Apparently satisfied, he came to a halt in front of the man and threw back his hood. Splotches of black and purple paint covered his face and neck in an unconvincing representation of Valrig's terrible sores. The crowd roared in feigned outrage.

Kira's jaw tightened and acid gouted up from her stomach: a ridiculous reaction to a low-clan mummer dressed in an old robe who'd collect his gold piece after the feast and then go back to mucking out the stables or chasing rats out of the storerooms. The crowd soon tired of him and drove him out with another volley of scraps. The traitor god earned a cheer when he caught a large chunk of bread and took a bite as he dragged his new subject away with him. Kira drained the rest of the wine from her cup and held it out to the wine-bearer, who instantly appeared beside her chair.

The mummers played out a few more old favorites. After a well-received jape where a greedy Vartan choked to death on a fish bone, the stage was cleared for the climactic arrival of the Scathring king. First the mummer playing Eowara came out again, this time with Onfar and Onraka tottering on stilts beside her, and the gods made her the first Norland monarch by handing her a painted circlet and a wooden representation of Valor's Storm.

Then out doddered an old man, or the comical likeness of one, stooped with age, blinking, with a slack mouth and trembling hands. His Scathring King costume had strips of blue among the green and black—Eotan blue—and he wore a painted wooden crown. His sword was a flaccid affair made of rope and twigs. When Eowara challenged him, he looked around as if confused, and then scratched his arse with his useless weapon. Eowara danced around him, jabbing the clueless creature over and over again until he fell to his knees with ribbons of blood leaking from half a dozen pockets in his costume.

Not a single person there could have failed to notice the

similarity between the scene being played out and the ritual combat in which Gannon had killed his father three months earlier. Poking fun at recent events was a tradition, but it stunned Kira that anyone could be either so bold or so ignorant as to stage such a reckless jest. She could only imagine what would happen when Vrinna found out about it.

Kira felt the low rumble of Gannon's anger. She knew this change of mood: the shadow passing in front of the candle, the gust of wind through the broken windowpane. Now he laid his hands flat on the table as if he was about to spring up and his sword trembled in its scabbard over the chair behind him. Everyone else at the table fixed their eyes on their plates and tried to disappear. The rustle and clinking in the room fell away and the roar and snap of the fires leaped up to fill the silence.

Gannon's dignity won out over his anger in the end and he sat back down in his chair. The movement signaled the real end of the skits, and the more serious drinking began. The atmosphere grew more raucous as smoke and the intoxicated emotions of six hundred people thickened the air. She wasn't surprised when the emperor bolted up a short time later and bade the rest of them an off-handed farewell. His dogs lurched up on their thin legs and trotted after him, their nails clicking over the stone floor.

People began leaving in small numbers after he'd gone, but the feast would go on all night. Eventually the tables would be pushed back as boasting gave way to challenges, and challenges to blows. Kira tossed back another cup of wine and cast a longing look at the side doors, which were now gently rocking along with the rest of the hall. She could slip out now and go back to Arregador House, to her bath, her bed. Sleep might come if she laid her head down now and let the black roll over her.

<My Lady,> said Aline, stepping up beside her chair.

<I've been summoned, yes?> Kira looked down into the bottom of her cup for alternatives, but this time it remained empty. She rose with the slow elegance perfected over the many occasions on which she'd ended her evening a little worse for wine.

<I heard some gossip in the kitchens,> said Aline, as they left the dais. <A ship came into the harbor. People seemed excited about it.>

<Why?>

<I don't know, but Captain Vrinna was called away because of it.>

<Well, that explains it, then,> said Kira, as they pushed aside a tapestry and went through into a freezing, pinched little corridor. <The personality she ordered must have finally arrived.>

Chapter 5

They came up through the servants' corridors to a low door fitted with a heavy iron ring. It opened noiselessly on well-oiled hinges when Aline pulled. Kira didn't need to give her any further instructions; after so many months, the girl had sorted a place to sleep until morning.

Kira stepped into the room and the door closed behind her.

The fire had only just been lit and the room was still freezing cold, but Gannon wore no shirt under his fur robe: another volley in his personal war of outrage against the cold; she felt like he was daring her to find any flaw in his masculine beauty. She unbuckled her sword and laid it on the table. Her body responded as his heavy arm came around the small of her back and pressed her to him. His mouth tasted of good wine.

<We'll go hunting tomorrow. We'll go to Thornwood,> he said. <The dogs need to get out. Good sport there, this time of year. Red-tails, if the gods favor us.>

Thornwood was a whole morning's ride away, and the run of fine days they'd had lately meant the weather was likely to turn foul. Kira pictured the dripping black trees and the barbed bushes that gave the forest its name, and the blue algae growing along the reedbeds that made the streams look as if they ran with blood.

<I didn't think you'd want to leave Ravindal now,> she said, fishing gently for more information. <Didn't some ship come in tonight?>

<Merchants, ambassadors,> said Gannon, plucking at the knot

holding her shirt ties together. <My father's empire: contracts and agreements, borders on maps of places he'd never been.> He gave up on the knot and flicked the strings away for her to manage. <Who told you to dress up like a hired mourner?>

<How was I supposed to know not to wear white?> Kira pouted. Aline had tied the knot so tightly that she was having trouble with it as well. <No one ever tells me anything. And here I thought I was being so daring, wearing my new necklace.>

<I never know with you.> He ran a few links of the chain through his fingers before sliding his hand down to her breast.

<Me? What's to know?>

<Trey—that day in the forest, dragging you away from him when he was dying. You hated me for it then. Maybe you still do.>

<Why would I be here if I hated you?> Kira asked rhetorically. Neither he nor anyone else had the slightest idea how much she hated *herself* for being there. <Trey got what he wanted.>

<*You* didn't,> he said, lifting her up against him. His desire gnawed at her with sharp little teeth. <Maybe that's why I haven't got tired of you, like the others. I don't want surrender. I'm a general—generals get bored once there's no one left to fight.>

<I have no idea what you're talking about,> she said, pulling the pins from her hair and tossing them down onto the side table. The little pile of books there had not changed position since her first visit to his chambers.

<Vrinna thinks you're hatching some scheme,> said Gannon.

<How droll of her. Anything I'd been hatching this long would be able to lay eggs of its own by now.>

<Just remember, she's watching you.> He leaned in closer until his weight pushed her back against the servants' door she had just come through. Then he pressed one hand up against the stone beside her head, pinning her, before he kissed her again. <Everything gets back to me. No one plays me for a fool.>

The darkness of his threat wound down through his fingers and she arched her back as they dug in to her flesh. His lips grazed her neck and worked their way up to her ear and she tightened her grip on his arms. She could feel the power banked down in him, straining to get out, as he slid the robe from his shoulders and let the fur drip down into a soft puddle on the floor behind him. His muscles moved beneath skin as smooth as the silver plums that had grown near her family's house when she was a girl: beautiful fruit, but bitter-tasting.

Then she blinked, and there were the scars.

They were everywhere, crawling all over him: scars slashed over his eyes, scars turning his perfect mouth into a child's scribble. His chest oozed with sores; his fingers ended in blackened stumps. His ears were torn off, his hair was shorn and his scalp flaked away beneath the scabs. He opened a mouth full of rotting teeth and his silver-blue eyes dripped blood.

She slammed a door on her emotions before he could sense the distress brought on by her morbid hallucinations. She had sworn not to keep tormenting herself this way; there was no point at all to it because as everyone well knew, Trey Arregador was dead.

A loud knocking startled Kira from her sleepless reverie. Gannon stretched beside her and pulled the blanket from her shoulders. With the bed-curtains closed, his naked back glowed like a lantern. The knocking came again and Kira could feel Vrinna's hammering urgency even from the other side of the chamber door.

Gannon bolted upright and swept the curtain aside. He stepped into a pair of fur slippers and looked around for his robe, still lying by the wall where he'd abandoned it. He didn't bother to fasten it before allowing the attendant in the antechamber to open the door. The hem swirled around his ankles as he picked up his dagger, then headed for the floor-mosaic of the Eotan wolf's head in the center of the room; it looked ready to sink its teeth into anyone who walked too near. Kira's unbraided hair fell around her shoulders, wafting the unwelcome smell of stale smoke into her face as she sat up to pull the curtains closed against the draft.

<This had better be worth getting me out of bed,> Gannon told Vrinna as she entered.

Through a small gap between the velvet panels, Kira saw the captain reposition the fur-lined helmet under her arm. Vrinna knew perfectly well that Kira was there, but she had no choice but to pretend otherwise. For a moment, Kira considered walking stark naked across the room to fetch her clothes, just to tweak Vrinna's prudishness, but the thought of the cold floor deterred her almost as much as her desire to hear news important enough to get the emperor out of bed in the middle of the night.

<It's that Gemanese ship,> said Vrinna. <They have deserters on board: filthy traitors from the Shadari garrison, headed for the Broken Islands. They say Governor Eonar's dead and there's been an uprising in the Shadar.>

The Shadari garrison. The trapdoor in Kira's mind rattled, but she pushed it down firmly. A prisoner. A deserter from the Shadari garrison. *It couldn't be.*

<The temple?> asked Gannon.

<Destroyed.>

<You're sure?> The emperor's elation rose up like an icy wave.

<They're not smart enough to lie,> said Vrinna. <Their leader's right outside. I knew you'd want to question him yourself.>

<Bring him in,> Gannon commanded, pacing the room.

The presence of the deserter slid into the room like the fetid air in a ship's hold. The man was manacled hand and foot, and his clothes, clearly intended for warmer climes, were stiff with old sweat. Two of Vrinna's guards marched him to the center of the room and forced him to his knees. Vrinna put her boot between the prisoner's shoulder blades and pushed him down in front of the emperor's feet, the shackles grating against the stone. She bent his neck until his head was right between the wolf's jaws.

Kira relaxed. It wasn't her brother-in-law.

<His name's Ingeld,> said Vrinna. <No clan that matters; no rank. Went to the Shadar from Thrakya. Not sure why.>

Gannon circled around the prisoner. The man's ordeal, whatever it had been, had obviously left him as weak as a baby, but the will to fight still glowed in him like a live coal. He might have ended up as a deserter, but Kira had the feeling he had begun as something else entirely. <So?> the emperor asked, running a fingertip across the flat of the dagger's blade. <Tell me what happened in the Shadar before you deserted.>

<We didn't, your Majesty,> Ingeld said, lifting himself up on shackled hands already purple with cold. <We weren't deserting. We were coming here to tell you what happened. Our ship blew off course and those bastard Gemanese took the boats and left us to die.>

The emperor said nothing for a moment. He held up the dagger and turned it from side to side, examining it in the torchlight. <Tell me what happened,> he repeated.

<The governor died and left Lady Frea in charge,> Ingeld began. <Lord Eofar didn't like being passed over, so he sided with the Shadari against Lady Frea, and us—and you. *He's* the traitor, and a filthy coward, too. We were coming here to warn you.>

He was such a poor liar that Kira could feel his deception sitting in her stomach like a stone. Vrinna grabbed the chain between Ingeld's hands and hauled him to his knees.

<We know you're lying. What really happened?>

<It's true. I swear to Onfar.>

<Then it's not the whole story.> Vrinna yanked the chain, and Kira could feel Ingeld's agony as his joints strained.

<It is—you'll see when—> But pain or plain fatigue overcame him and he slumped down in a heap.

<Forget him now. He's useless like this. Get Ani,> Gannon told Vrinna. <I need to know more. I want every detail this time. The rest of you—get out.>

Kira pressed her palms down on the mattress as Vrinna and the guards dragged their hapless prisoner away, burying the trapdoor in her mind under layers: first dirt, then rock, then ice, then finally a deep blanket of softly concealing snow, until even she wasn't sure where to find it. She concentrated fiercely; whatever happened, she could not let Gannon feel her screaming apprehension at what was about to occur.

As soon as the door creaked shut, Kira slid her hand between the curtains and drew them back so that Gannon could see her. A freezing draft wrapped itself around her naked body, but she refused to let him see her shudder.

<Do I have to go, too?> Kira asked, sliding her fingers down the velvet panel.

<No. You can stay,> said Gannon, finally fastening his robe as he came back over to the bed. He pinched her chin between his fingers, tilting her head up to him. <You can hear it for yourself this time. Just in case you didn't really believe me.>

<If I hadn't believed you, I wouldn't be here,> said Kira, turning her head to the side so she could graze his knuckles with her

teeth. <That's why you told me about the witch and her prophecies, wasn't it? To coax me into your bed with visions of your future glory?>

<You didn't need much coaxing.>

Kira nearly gagged on the steely bite of his conceit, but now was certainly not the time for him to discover the real reason she had agreed to become his mistress—and as long as the witch saw nothing in her visions to touch on Kira's dreadful secret, he never would know. Gannon went back to pacing the room, his fur slippers making a sweeping sound that Kira found more annoying with each turn. Just when she didn't think she could stand it a moment more, Vrinna knocked again and the doors swung open at the emperor's bidding.

Laine, the witch's only guard, entered alone except for his charge. He was still in his outdoor garb, with nothing of him visible but his eyes. His emotions were just as shrouded as his body: not so much evasive as elusive, floating somewhere behind a cloud of smoke. Kira had felt something like it before, a cousin who had lost the better part of his wits after a bad fall. Laine pushed the Shadari witch before him like a sweeper moving a pile of rags.

Kira crawled forward for her first actual look at the woman who had brought the ore to Norland more than thirty years ago and foolishly set in motion the conquest of her own people. This gray-haired, frail little creature in the greasy fur robe, with her wrinkled skin hanging loosely like she had shrunk within it, had altered the course of the entire world.

Gannon stalked toward the old woman. Towering over her like a giant he said, <Tell her the Shadari temple fell. That's the second sign, isn't it?>

The witch's keeper bent toward her and spoke to her in the Shadari's hideous language. The old woman's mouth moved in response and a small sound issued from it while tears pooled in the wrinkles below her eyes.

<Yes,> the guard said.

The burned-wood perfume of Gannon's eagerness flooded the room. <Tell her to take the elixir. Tell her I want to know more.>

Laine unfastened the catch of his cloak and drew out a chain. At the end hung a little glass bottle—that could only be the magical Shadari divining elixir. The old woman waggled her head and started to move away, whimpering like an animal as her keeper stripped away the wax and removed the cork. Gannon snatched up a glove from the table and grabbed the Shadari's wrist until she crumpled. Laine handed her the bottle and without a word she took a sip, then handed it back to him.

Kira had been out hunting once when one of the low-clan bearers had eaten the wrong kind of berries. The way the old woman now tensed and shook by turns reminded her of how that man had suffered before he died. Gannon had left the servant's body in the snow and continued on with the hunt, and she'd wondered if the man's family had ever been told why he never returned.

The witch began to speak like she was choking, spitting out words that hung painfully in the air. A drop of sweat crept down Kira's face, clinging like a spider, but she dared not even reach up to wipe it away. She held her breath while the old woman muttered to the guard.

<The battle with the cursed is coming,> said Laine, lowering himself to one knee to hear her better.

<But when?> Gannon demanded. <I need to know *when*. She said I would be emperor first, then the temple would fall. I am emperor. The temple has fallen. When will the cursed attack? Today? A week? A month?>

The guard and the old woman exchanged another stuttering series of words, then Laine reported, <Soon. She can't see more. But now she sees a woman, leading the army: a living woman, with one eye and gray skin. Scars on her arm and face.>

Kira felt Gannon's emotions liquefy and spill out of him. <That's the Mongrel,> he said, savoring the name. <It must be. Lord Valrig's chosen his champion to set against me.>

<She sees you with a sword,> Laine went on. <Not a black imperial sword. A bronze sword, with writing on the blade.>

<Valor's Storm,> Gannon exclaimed. <Eowara's sword. Of course. Of course, it must be.>

Kira raked her mind for the passage of the gods' words to Eowara: the same scene she had just seen acted out in the skits. *Then be ready against the day they will rise up and strike at the Righteous.*

On that day let a Hero be prepared with the sword we have given you, to subdue them, lest they corrupt all that is pure in this land.

The witch looked up, and Kira saw her eyes for the first time. Warmth like molten gold rolled over her, and in a rush she understood something Gannon didn't seem to realize: that pathetic little body, for all its fragility, was just a piece of something much larger, like the corner of some buried monolith poking out from beneath the snow.

<What else?> Gannon demanded.

The guard stood up. <That's all.>

Kira moved back from the curtains and sagged down against the fur blankets. The witch had said nothing new about the cursed; they were all safe, for a little while longer at least.

Gannon flung open the door and called for Vrinna.

<I want dispatches written,> Gannon told the captain the moment she hurried back in. <I want a third of our troops—no, make that half—recalled from the holdings. Every clan must send their share. I don't want to hear any guff about defending their provinces, either. And get Olnara back from Bilthwile. I want my daughter in Ravindal; I can't have that ass Betran at my back.>

<They need Scion Olnara in Bilthwile—the insurgents in the hills. We could still—>

<And as soon as the Mongrel sets foot in Norland, I want to know about it. Understand?>

<But the Mongrel's dead,> Vrinna said, confused. <Josten Drey killed her a month ago.>

<I don't want to hear those lies from you or anyone else—do you understand me?> Gannon thundered. Vrinna flinched as if he'd cut her; Kira could almost feel the bite of hot steel and the scent of cauterized flesh in the air. The captain might have fought a hundred battles at Gannon's side, but she had never overcome her craven need for his approval. <And bring that prisoner back in here.>

Vrinna ordered the guards to drag Ingeld back in. His head still lolled on his shoulder, but he was conscious.

<Get that stool and put his arm up over it,> Gannon said.

One of the guards dragged the stool over and unhooked the manacle from Ingeld's right wrist. The emperor took his sword from its stand by the door and went to the fire. Kira watched the flames curl around the blade as the black metal sucked in the light.

<No, please—> Ingeld begged, realizing what they intended to do to him. <Kill me—I told you everything. Please kill me, your Majesty, I beg you. Don't— You can't—>

Gannon turned the blade over in the flame. <You're going to do something for me.>

<Anything!> Ingeld screamed. <I'll do anything! Just don't—>

<I want you to deliver a message to the Mongrel.> Gannon took the blade from the flame and crossed over to the stool. <Tell her I'm ready. Tell her I'm waiting.>

Vrinna stepped back just in time for Gannon to slice straight down through Ingeld's wrist. The blade sank deep into the wood, and both Ingeld and the severed hand fell back when Gannon yanked it out again. The stool clattered onto its side as Vrinna grabbed Ingeld's maimed arm and held it up so that Gannon could hold the flat of the heated blade against the stump.

Kira wanted to close her eyes, but she was afraid she would faint if she did. Instead she tried to focus her senses away from the bile rioting in her stomach and her gaze fell on the witch, standing in the corner where she'd been led. The old woman had her eyes fixed on the blood dripping from the cleft stool. Kira couldn't see her face; something made her glad of that.

<Strip him,> Gannon commanded, <and set him out. And send someone in to clean up this mess.>

Chapter 6

Kira summoned Aline the moment Gannon took himself off to be dressed. The danger of discovery might have passed, for now, but there was no question of going back to bed.

<Oh, let's just go through the throne room,> she said as she followed Aline's torch down one of the dark little stairways, increasingly irritated by the whole pretense of secrecy. Everyone in Ravindal knew about her affair with Gannon, and on top of that, the empress had never bothered to make a secret of her dislike for her husband. She had been happy enough in Ravindal while Gannon was stomping his way through one foreign campaign after another, but as emperor, he had to stay in Ravindal: those were the rules. The empress had vacated Eotan Castle for her own lavish estates the day after her husband's coronation with no intention of returning. Kira could have marched past her apartments banging on a shield and it would have made no difference.

Aline opened the door and pushed back the curtain so that Kira could precede her into the empty throne room. At the far end, a pair of wooden doors let in a bitter draft from the terrace. The late Emperor Eoban had stuck the terrace on the front of the castle, apparently in emulation of the grand houses of Thrakya, although his never-ending campaign there had reduced the originals to rubble. Gannon liked to rail against the vulnerabilities it opened up in the castle's defenses, and kept vowing to have it knocked down.

A magnificent map of the world hung behind the throne; it had been recently updated to show the foreign provinces held by each of the twelve high clans. Only the gray-green seas occupied more space than Eotan blue, but the Arregadors' deep green made a good showing, while the Aelbars were little more than an orange smudge here and there. Far south and a bit off to the left was a tiny blue crescent between the sea and a curving mountain chain: the Shadar. It looked small, harmless, and reassuringly distant.

There were smaller maps, framed in wood, and the ceremonial copies of *The Book of the Hall* and the *Genealogies,* each on their separate stands; they cast angular shadows on the walls.

The play of the torchlight as they passed the throne made it look as if the boiled bones of Norland's extinct enemies were straining to free themselves from their unnatural union. It was traditional for the throne to be covered with the pelts of animals killed by the emperor's own hand. Gannon had occupied it for only a few months, and already the pelts looked deep enough to lose a baby in.

They continued past the simple carvings of Onfar forming the twelve progenitors out of snow, and Onraka bringing them to life with her breath. The genderless progenitors all had the same body, but their tokens distinguished them: Aelbar's iron-wood cudgel, the wolf's head Eotan wore like a helmet, the fir wreath in Arregador's hair. A rendering underneath showed the battle with the ice-trolls, when the first Norlanders had sprung to life: the high clans from the progenitors' blood, the middle clans from their sweat, and the low clans from their bile. She no longer believed any of it, of course, but she still liked the picture.

Her steps slowed near the center of the room as memories crystalized around her like ice. Over there, in front of the throne, was where Trey Arregador had been standing the first time she saw him. He had just returned from the Redland campaign with Scion Gannon and no one had talked of anything except how his bold actions had broken the siege. She remembered how impossibly handsome he had looked as he came forward to receive his accolades from the emperor, Gannon's father, with his helmet under his arm, his battle-scarred shield and the warm torchlight kissing the shining hilt of Honor's Proof. The moment their eyes had met across the room—she a wholly insignificant girl from a craggy little Aelbar estate and he the hero of the mighty Arregador clan—she'd known she would have to be better than she was to be worthy of him, and she'd wanted nothing more than to spend the rest of her life trying.

Then her mind locked on another equally fateful night three years ago, when she'd crept down to the stables in secret and flown her triffon back to the spot where they'd left Trey to die. Even numbed with grief and guilt, she'd known she would never believe in his death unless she had viewed his corpse for herself—even if it meant seeing him after the wolves and ursas had been at the body first. But by the time she reached the place, she couldn't find him . . .

She flew through the dark sky until she found Onfar's Circle, the standing stones encircling the sacred place where Ravindal's cursed—the maimed, scarred and deformed—were left to perish. But not Trey. Even that bit of ceremony had been denied him. They'd left him to die in the woods to the west, discarded like an old bait-sack.

She landed near the patch of bloody snow where he had fallen, but there was no drag-trail leading away. A wolf pack would have torn the body to bits, but there were no tracks, no bones or shredded skin or clothes—there was no evidence of him at all. She paced in frantic circles until she finally worked out that all those footprints leading to the plain had not been left by their hunting party. Then she realized that she knew the area of forest beyond the plain by reputation, if not by name. There was no game worth hunting, not with packs of lagramor that could strip a triffon down to the bone in no time at all.

She got back in the saddle and flew in that direction, keeping low so she didn't lose the trail. She landed when it led into the trees. She knew better than to enter the forest alone, but she went anyway, following the trampled undergrowth until she came to a clearing. In the center stood an ancient ice statue, scrubbed of its identity by weather and time, but something about its facelessness gave it a terrible power, very different from the comforting familiarity of Ravindal's green-glass gods. A sacrificial basin at its feet held a rounded mound of snow.

A man darted out into the clearing so suddenly that Kira leaped back, fumbling for her sword, but before she could draw, she saw that the right sleeve of his bedraggled coat had been sewn together at the wrist. She froze. He had no right hand.

<What are you doing here?> he demanded. She stared at the closed sleeve, afraid that if she moved her eyes at all she would faint.

<She's alone, at any rate,> announced a woman who appeared from the shadowy forest. The woman, who wore no hood, had scaly purple blotches covering her face. Kira could almost see the cursed rising out of Valrigdal behind them, just like the picture in her mother's copy of The Book of the Hall. *They both had steel swords; she might have been able to take them with Virtue's Grace, but she still didn't draw. She had the worrying feeling her blade would pass right through them.*

<Trey. My husband,> she said finally, startled to find she still had the power of speech. <He's here, isn't he? Someone must have brought him here. Where is he?>

Their reaction left her no doubt. She spotted the gap in the briars and ran for it as the one-handed man reached out, too late to stop her. She followed a tunnel of sorts through the hedge, tearing her coat and her skin in the process, until it led her into the remains of a courtyard in front of a vine-covered ruin. Trey sat on the ground with his back up against a pile of stones, next to a lamp shining in a circle of melted snow. A woman stood by his side holding a cloth soaked in something so pungent it made Kira's head spin, pressing it against the fist-sized wound in Trey's shoulder. A young girl clung to her side as if their ragged cloaks had been sewn together.

Enough blood had been cleared from Trey's face to show his mangled ear and the deep cut on his head. Kira waited for the shock and revulsion she knew she was supposed to feel, but it didn't come. He was still Trey, and she didn't know what to do about it. She wanted to take him in her arms and cradle him like a broken doll, but the moment he noticed her there, his rejection pushed her back like a bitter wind.

<What are you doing to him?> Kira demanded of them.

<Cleaning this wound so it doesn't sour,> said the woman. Her words were precisely clipped, as if she had few to spare, and even less time.

<But,> Kira stammered, <he wanted to die.>

<We don't always get what we want. Anyway, it's too late now. He's out of danger.> The physic pulled up one shoulder and twisted her neck, and only then did Kira notice the bones of some kind of cage or case bulging

under her wool cloak, holding her upright. The little girl wasn't just standing next to her but providing support. With a twist of mockery, the physic added, <He'd have to do something on purpose to die now, and you know what happens to suicides in the After-realm.>

The man and woman from the clearing came pounding into the yard. <Sorry, Cyrrin,> said the woman with the burned face. <We didn't expect her to run past us.>

Trey turned away as Kira pulled off her hood and walked over to stand beside him. Blood still leaked out from his shoulder, and those swollen cuts on his face and neck not already scabbed over were weeping a yellowish fluid.

<The gods—Onfar and Onraka—they've abandoned me.> Trey's words were feverish and too quick, like the pulse throbbing in his neck. <They were going to let me die like that, in an accident, right in front of Gannon. Leaving me to scrub floors in the After-realm. How could they do that? After everything I did for the glory of Norland?>

<It was just an accident, Trey,> said Kira, grasping for some way to comfort him. <It's all right now. These people saved you.>

<Lord Valrig didn't want me to die,> said Trey. <He's the one who saved me, so I can help him in return. Lord Valrig wants to raise his armies and he needs my help. That must be the reason. It has to be.>

Kira knelt down on the frozen ground and brought up her gloved hand to touch his face, but he flinched, then shut his eyes and drew away from her.

<I don't believe any of that. You're a hero.> She tried to take his hand, but he jerked it away. <You're not cursed. I don't care what the Book *says. You're Trey Arregador, the hero of Redland. You're my husband.>*

<You don't have a husband any longer,> said Trey. <Your husband is dead. Go, Kira. You need to go.>

<I'm not taking orders from a corpse,> Kira snapped back, feeling hysteria creeping up on her. <Look at me, Trey. Just look at me once, and then I'll go, if that's really what you want.>

His arm came around her—she'd been afraid to hurt him, but he held her fiercely—and she felt the coolness of his cheek against her forehead and the flutter of his eyelashes. Then he drew his arm back and pushed her away, and whatever chink had remained open in the wall he had put up against her sealed over, shutting her out completely.

<Trey.>

<Tell my brother I'm dead.>

<Please don't ask me to lie to Rho,> Kira begged him.

<I think you owe me that much, don't you? Or did you think I didn't know?> He turned away again, even before the flush of shame had finished sweeping over her. <Go. Go away.>

Kira stood up as more broken people melted out of the darkness: three at first, then six, then a dozen, wearing patched furs and old woolen cloaks. She saw missing limbs, twisted torsos, scarred faces, bodies damaged in every possible way. They lifted Trey up and helped him toward the ruin and were gone before Kira had even thought to say goodbye to him.

Cyrrin turned to the small child at her side. <It's all right, Berril.>

The girl—she might have been about seven or eight, but she was small and malnourished—took a crude wooden medallion from around her neck and placed it in Kira's gloved hand.

<Berril was four years old when they set her out. She crushed her fingers in a doorjamb,> Cyrrin explained. Kira looked at the girl's hands, but the child's over-sized mittens made it impossible for her to tell which hand had been maimed. <Her sister Aline hid her for days before they were found out. Find Aline and give her that and tell her Berril is all right.>

<You'd let me go back?> Kira asked, astonished. <Just like that?>

<Why not?>

Kira stared at her. <I could tell them about you. They'd hunt you down.>

<But you won't,> said the physic, <because now you don't believe anything the Book *says about the cursed. And once that nonsense is gone from your mind, it's gone.>*

Kira looked down at Berril's medallion again before tucking it into a pocket in her glove.

<You can never come back here,> Cyrrin warned her. <Never. It's too dangerous for us.>

<I understand.>

<You'll have to pretend he's really dead,> said Cyrrin. <Say it now. Make me believe it.>

The trees crowded in around her. Kira drew in a deep breath and threw back her shoulders.

<Trey Arregador is dead.>

Kira opened her eyes on the throne room, and for a moment could not remember in which direction she had been heading.

For three years after she'd lost Trey she had spun like a hollow top through a pointless round of feasts and hunts and tournaments. When she was not having to be present at some function or other, she shut herself up in her rooms with Aline. Then six months ago Gannon had come back from Thrakya and sought her out. Perhaps if she had put him off more firmly at the beginning; perhaps if he had been less attractive, less virile; perhaps if the attentions of the Scion of Norland had been less flattering to her vanity and less provoking to her self-appointed rivals, then perhaps Gannon would never have boasted of the witch's predictions and she would never have stuck her foot in the trap.

She could never go back to the life she'd led as Trey's wife. She couldn't leave Ravindal, not knowing he was still out there and needing to be warned if the witch turned her elixir-sharpened eyes his way. But keeping up the vapid courtier act was wearing her down. In the old days, when Trey had been out on one of his long campaigns with Gannon, she had turned to his brother Rho for company, frequently racing him to the bottom of a wine jug. Now Rho was gone too, and neither one of them was coming back.

She suddenly realized Aline had been anxiously watching her all this time.

<You can't keep on like this, my Lady,> Aline said. <It's making you ill.>

<Oh, I'm all right,> said Kira, shaking her head and shoulders to wake herself up properly. <I just need a little sleep.>

<They're going to find out, aren't they?> asked Aline. <About my sister, and Lord Trey?>

<If they do, we'll warn them,> Kira reassured her, heading for the throne room doors. <That's what all this has been about, remember? In any case, the witch hasn't said anything about them being alive, or in hiding. Maybe she *can't* see that. Maybe she means someone else entirely when she talks about the "cursed." What would she know about them anyway? I know she's been here a long time, but she's still a foreigner.>

Aline trailed behind her, still fretting. <But she did say the cursed would rise, just like it says in the *Book*.>

<The *Book*!> Kira said derisively, stopping where she was and spinning around. <Aline, you and I both know that everything *The*

Book of the Hall says about the cursed—and probably everything else, for that matter—is nothing but a pack of fear-mongering, self-serving lies. I'm sorry that you have to be burdened with the truth at your age, but there it is.>

<But the witch's visions have to mean something, don't they?> Aline persisted, staring uncomfortably down at the clasps of her wool cloak. <You said she's never been wrong—not ever. Can't you think what she might mean, my Lady?>

Kira closed her mind against the memory of the wretched yearning in Trey's words when he'd told her, *Lord Valrig wants to raise his armies and he needs my help.* He couldn't have known what he was saying; not after what he'd just been through. He wasn't cursed. There was no such thing. She clamped down on the panic swelling up in her chest until her breath came out in a thin, painful wheeze.

Then she reached out and gently took Aline's arm. <We'll just have to wait and find out, all right? Until then, we'll just have to go on as we are. Understand? Exactly as we are.>

Chapter 7

"You said you couldn't go without your medicine," said Mairi, glaring from the threshold of Lahlil's tent as she handed over the basic medicine kit she had just put together. "Give me a few more days."

"You wanted me to go."

Mairi shrugged, that Nomas gesture that meant whatever they wanted it to mean. This time it meant the healer was tired of explaining the obvious. "Not behind Jachi's back, and not when you're being such a stupid ass about it."

"I can't wait any longer. The trading here should have been done days ago. He's dragging it out on purpose." The dawn and twilight seizures were getting worse, outstripping anything she had endured before, but she had to get away, medicine or not. She could feel disaster gathering just out of sight, like a gang of bandits waiting around a bend in the road.

"You can't take Oshi," said Mairi. "How are you going to feed him?"

"I'll find a way." She was about to say more when she heard Jachad's jovial voice coming toward the tent. He had spent the afternoon in Wastewater, ostensibly finishing up the trading. From the sound of his hollering, his business had apparently been conducted in Wastewater's one and only tavern.

"Mairi!" he called out. "Lahlil! Where are you? Stop talking about me and come out here!"

A smile tugged at the corner of Mairi's mouth. "Jachi," she said, shaking her head. "He'll never grow up."

They came out of the tent to find him with his arm around Callia's shoulders, grinning broadly in a patch of moonlight, with his red hair mussed and his robe askew. "You *were* talking about me. Look, Mairi's blushing."

"That's right," the healer shot back. "I was telling her how you used to run across the decks of the *Argent,* naked as a fish, flapping your little—"

"Silence!" Jachad roared, drawing himself up and frowning, but his eyes still shone. "I am your king. You will afford me the proper respect." He grinned again. "I'm afraid I have terrible news."

"What news?" asked Lahlil.

"No, no," he said. "Such terrible news calls for a drink. A shock like this must be cushioned. You must all come to my tent."

He strode off without waiting for a response, leaving them to follow as they would. Lahlil checked on Oshi: he was sound asleep in his cradle and safe enough for a little while. She followed the others to Jachad's tent.

"What do you want to tell us?" Mairi asked, coming no further than the threshold. "I have things to do."

"First we need a drink." Jachad lifted the wine jug on the table, shook it and frowned. "Wait, I have more. Courtesy of the Shadari." He dived into the corner for his pack and lifted out a small wineskin marked with yellowish smudges on one side. The chalky residue rubbed off on his hand and he wiped it on his robe before pouring the contents into four cups and handing them around. Then he stood in the center of the tent and raised his arm. "To the Mongrel! Drink—come on, drink!"

He tossed back the wine. Mairi kept her cup lowered, scowling. Callia took a small sip, made a face, and set the cup aside on Jachad's desk. Lahlil drank steadily, readying herself for the battle she sensed was about to begin.

"Well? What about her?" asked Mairi.

"She's dead."

Callia turned around. "No, she's not. She's right there," she said, pointing at her.

Jachad gleefully recounted what he had learned while in town: a well-known mercenary named Josten Drey had claimed to have found her sick and hiding out in a hut in some tiny hamlet. He and his crew had cornered her, set fire to the building, then killed her when she tried to escape the flames. Drey had been traveling around with her body in a block of ice, collecting on the various bounties. People who had seen the corpse up close had sworn it to be hers.

"What does that have to do with us?" asked Callia. "It's not true, obviously. He faked it somehow."

"No, he wouldn't be showing off in that case," put in Mairi. "What would he do if she suddenly showed up somewhere? My guess is he bought or stole the body from someone else and really thinks it's her."

Jachad waved his hand, splashing a little shower of celebratory sparks into the air. "Who cares? It only matters what people believe—and now they believe the Mongrel is dead."

Lahlil stood her ground as he came to her. The scent of the wine on his breath overlaid the flowery musk of Callia's perfume.

"They're not wrong, either," said Jachad. "She *is* dead. Now no one will come looking for her, and now there's no reason for you to run off to the edge of the world, is there?"

Mairi drained her cup in one swallow and set it down on the desk with a decisive rap. "Well, I've heard enough," she said, and left the tent without another word.

"Me, too. I'm going to sit with Oshi," said Callia. "And that wine is terrible, by the way." She helped herself to a cake from Jachad's desk and moved toward the tent flap, but she paused on her way out to whisper something in his ear that even Lahlil couldn't make out. "Promise me," she said, as she swept toward the exit.

"I will not. Be gone, you little chit."

Lahlil suppressed a cough. Her throat was dry, but she set the half-full cup of wine down on the desk next to Mairi's. She needed to be sober for this.

"Let me guess," Jachad said, walking to the desk and sliding the fruit plate to the exact center. "You're going to tell me how this changes nothing."

Promises, assurances, vows . . . Those were things people said when they were too cowardly to face the truth. "I'll come back, if I can."

"I'm not waiting. Not this time." The words sounded as if he had chiseled them out of rock. "You can live your life alone if that's what you want, but don't expect me to do the same."

"I won't." She started to go, but something stopped her. At a loss, she fixed on the only question to come into her mind.

"What did Callia make you promise?"

Jachad folded his arms across his chest. "Her exact words?" he asked. " 'Amai's sweet flower, if you don't bed her tonight, I'll find someone who will. Anyone can see she's gasping for it.' "

Lahlil laughed; she actually laughed. Then she stopped laughing because Jachad had pulled her to him. His beard, softer than she expected, moved against her cheek and his lips brushed up against hers. The entire world condensed down to the points where their bodies touched and she brought her arms up around his neck as his came around her waist.

"Lahlil."

Her name sounded new, like she had never heard it before. She didn't know what was happening or what it meant and she didn't care. She felt his breath in her ear; his lips skimmed her neck. They kissed again, and her skin came alive under his touch like the chill of a fever: a terrible ache that she couldn't bear another moment. He hooked his finger under the cord of her eye-patch and tugged it down around her neck. His face blurred as her mismatched eyes fought each other: the brown eye, weaker at night, ruled over by Shof, and the silver eye taken by Amai. There had been a time, before her body became a battleground for the gods, when she and Jachad had sat side by side, gazing into the bonfire; when the cold desert wind had charged the night with possibility. His fingers traced the scars on her forehead, roved down to the crescent on her cheek.

Then he touched the scar pulling up the corner of her mouth and she flinched as the too-recent memory of pain from Nevie's cut licked down her spine like a tongue of fire.

"What's wrong? Did I hurt you?" asked Jachad, his eyes softening with concern.

She felt the moment slipping away and wanted to scream. "No," she told him, looking to drift away again into his sea-blue eyes, but finding only her own memories reflected back at her. "That scar reminds me of something."

"Reminds you of what?"

Lahlil remembered her face throbbing with pain, and the wound at her mouth trying to split apart when she swallowed. They had taken her eye-patch, and just like now, the double-vision had made it impossible for her to see very much. She recalled the faintly medicinal aroma tingeing the air, and even the feel of the fur rug beneath her fingers. She had woken other times before that one, feeling the same fur, seeing the same semi-darkness . . .

<You can stop pretending. I know you're awake.> A Norlander woman was standing stiffly by her bed, next to a man wearing what appeared to be an imperial sword. Thick scar tissue notched into his hairline above his right temple. He had his finger stuck between the pages of a book.

<Who are you?> Lahlil asked them.

<My name is Cyrrin,> said the woman. <I'm a physic. Does that blue bird belong to you? It's been hanging around here since we brought you inside. It could draw attention—if it doesn't go away soon, we'll have to shoot it.>

A Norlander physic: someone who could actually see the diseases and wounds inside her. Lahlil drew her shoulders a little further under the rug.

<Your leg is fine,> said Cyrrin, <but that cut on your mouth is a problem. It's going to leave a scar. Not your first though, is it?>

Lahlil said, <You know who I am.>

<Of course we do.>

<Then you know I need to leave.>

Something of significance passed between Cyrrin and the man with the sword, but she didn't understand it. <Then you weren't trying to find us?>

<I was going to Ravindal. I didn't know you were here. I didn't know you existed.> She hauled herself up and swung her legs over the side of the bed, which turned out to be made of several pallets of stacked fir boughs. Bolts of pain shot up both legs the instant she tried to stand, and something inside her chest fluttered. <What time is it?>

<The fits come on you every day at dawn and dusk, don't they?> Cyrrin asked, just as the pain wrapped its iron bands around her arms and legs and squeezed her lungs. <I was very careful to make sure you'd wake up just before dark.>

Lahlil lurched up anyway.

<Hold her, Trey,> Cyrrin said wearily.

The man grabbed her wrists and held them behind her back, but though she struggled, she wouldn't have been able to break the grip of a child in her current state. Cyrrin produced the silver flask Nevie had taken off the corpse of a duke after they had broken the siege of Bakkenresh—the one she kept filled with a cheap spirit that smelled and tasted like lamp oil. Lahlil tried to keep her lips closed as Cyrrin brought the spout up against them.

<It's medicine. I don't want to force it down your throat, but I will,> the physic remarked. <That cut has given me enough trouble already, and you're going to open it up again if you struggle. One swallow should be enough.>

<You can't cure me,> said Lahlil. <I'm not sick. It's the gods, fighting over me. Let me go, before it's too late.>

<The gods, eh?> Cyrrin's derision was palpable: a spattering of carmine. <Trey, pinch her nose for me. Onfar's eyes, I've treated feral marmonts who were more cooperative.>

Lahlil held her breath when they pinched her nose closed, but she couldn't hold it forever and the instant she gasped for breath, the healer tipped in the liquid, pushed her mouth closed again, then unexpectedly started stroking her throat so that she'd swallow before she could spit the medicine out.

The draft was cool, and tasted not quite sweet, not quite sour. She could feel it moving inside her—and then, a moment later, a heavy calm spread through her, like the stilling of a pool of water. An uncomfortable sensation pulled at her arms and legs, but it was nothing like she'd endured the past few years; it wasn't the pain with the force of a lightning bolt that sent her muscles into spasm and locked them hard as stone.

The man pushed her back down on the bed.

She took a deep breath, expecting the sickness to squeeze the air out of her lungs, anticipating the suffocating pressure that went on and on and on, trying to choke the life out of her.

It didn't come.

<You shouldn't be drowsy for long. I can make adjustments if it's too strong,> said Cyrrin as she patted the bandage on Lahlil's cheek back into place—there was no pain now—then circled her fingers around her wrist to feel her pulse. <So, who's Meena? You called out for her when you were waking up.>

Lahlil looked up into the void and saw the ceiling of her childhood bedroom pressing down on her; she heard the deep growl of the stone as Meena opened the secret door. She must have dreamed of her old Shadari nurse slipping into the hidden room to check on her, taking her wrist as Cyrrin did now, while she feigned sleep so she wouldn't have to explain the nameless panic that pinned her to the bed night after night. Lahlil shut her eyes now, feeling that panic threatening again, but helpless against the drowsiness pulling her down.

<My Shadari nurse. Her milk saved my life,> she answered, but she wasn't sure if she really said it, or only dreamed she said it.

<That black hair and dark eye,> Cyrrin mused. Lahlil heard her move away from the bed. <She'll sleep now. I know what you're going to say, Trey, so can we just pretend you already did, and leave it at that?>

<You have to believe it now,> said Trey. <The Mongrel—the greatest warrior of our time—turns out to be one of us, and Lord Valrig brought her right to our door. The time of the cursed is here; our army will rise. You can't deny it any longer.>

<No? Well, that woman, whatever her real name is, would be dead right now if I hadn't closed her wounds,> said Cyrrin. <Your imaginary god Valrig would have left her to bleed to death in the snow. Deny that.*>*

<He knew you would save her life, just like you did me and all the others, whether we wanted you to or not.> His emotions swelled up in angry hues of purple and black. <You know who she is. You know the things she's done.>

<I don't care what she's done. If she's one of us, she deserves a home just like me, you and everyone else here. Please don't make this something it's not. I've never regretted saving a life before. Don't make me start now.>

<You mean her life, or mine?> asked Trey.

<You?> asked Cyrrin. Something as warm as the fur blanket moved over Lahlil, but that warmth wasn't for her. <I mean both of you. You're both here now, and this is where you're going to stay.>

Lahlil made herself focus on the present, on the striped tent around her and on Jachad's searching blue eyes, still waiting for an explanation. He wanted her to have faith. Maybe this time, with him, it wouldn't all go wrong. Maybe this time, she really *could* stay.

Then she heard the panicked shouting outside and she knew the gods weren't through with her yet.

Chapter 8

Lahlil and Jachad rushed out of the tent to find the source of the sound and instantly ran into a throng of frantic Nomas wading through the puddles and trampling down the reeds in their haste to reach them.

Lahlil listened to all of them at once, trying to piece together the story from their overlapping accounts while Jachad was still asking questions and begging for them to calm down. Callia had collapsed in the street—it wasn't just an early labor; she had screamed that she could feel something wrong. Mairi had taken her into her tent and Callia was screaming and crying in there still. Mairi wouldn't let anyone else inside.

"She'll let *me* in," Jachad vowed as he charged off.

"She was taking care of Oshi," Lahlil said. "Where is he?"

But no one knew.

Lahlil followed, pushing her way through clouds of twinkling insects. She found a large, ominously quiet crowd clogging up the avenues around Mairi's tent. A few had brought lamps, and the way the lights bobbed up and down as the men paced made her feel like she was on a ship. She heard no screaming or crying now.

Behr had taken charge of Oshi and was rocking and talking to him with gentle enthusiasm. He had been with Callia when it happened.

"She said she wasn't feeling well," he told her. "I was walking with her to Mairi's tent, and she just . . . stopped. I don't know much about how they get here—babies. My wife had all three of ours on the *Windbourne*. Is this kind of thing normal?"

She almost laughed at the idea that she would know any more than him.

Oshi gurgled and he added, "Mine are so big now. I miss this a little." He was smiling up at the baby as he lifted him up high and jiggled him around. "They're so easy at this age. Do you want to take him?"

Then Mairi came out of her tent. One look at her face was more than enough, and the blood in Lahlil's veins turned to sand. Dead. The baby was dead. Jachad's successor; the half-brother he was to have raised to be the next king: Shof the sun god's son was *dead*.

"Callia?" someone asked.

"She'll be all right," said Jachad, coming out of the tent. Mairi dropped the cloth she was using to wipe her hands and staggered into Jachad's arms. She wept into his chest, gasping apologies and explanations as the others turned to comfort each other or go back and spread the news.

"This isn't right," Lahlil told Mairi. "I want to see the baby."

"What's the point now?" Jachad asked wearily, still stroking Mairi's hair. "Babies die. It's part of life. We all have to accept that."

"No son of Shof's has ever died before," said Mairi, lifting her tear-stained face from his shoulder. "You know that, Jachi. Let her look."

"But she—"

"Do it," said Mairi, looking up at Lahlil through pale eyes so swollen they barely opened. "I want you to see him. Poor little thing." The last word sent her diving back into Jachad's arms.

The lamp-lit tent was bright compared to the swamp outside. Many of Mairi's belongings had been pushed aside to make way for a large basin of ominously dark water and a basket of soiled linens. Callia was lying on Mairi's bed, just a vague shape huddled under several blankets. She looked like she was asleep, but Lahlil saw her shrink a little deeper into her coverings as she approached.

The bassinet, brightly painted with desert flowers and rolling dunes, sat on the floor against the surety of a happier outcome. A carefully folded blanket nestled inside. She knelt down beside it and pulled back one corner.

He was pathetically small, but perfect. She took inventory: two little arms and two little legs; a tiny head with a patch of dark hair; half-open eyes too small for her to see their color; ten fingers; ten impossibly small toes; a little chest, sunken and still where the beating heart should have been, and over it a strange black mark: a spot in the center with lines snaking out like a spindly anemone. She touched her finger to it and felt the cold flesh give under the pressure.

"Lahlil?" Callia called softly.

She kept her voice steady and calm. "Yes?"

"Do I still get to be queen?"

"I don't know."

"Will you ask Jachad?"

"Yes, I'll ask."

When she came out of the tent she could already feel the change, like the rustling of tinder before the spark. The ordered, routine world of the Nomas had just been burned away from the inside. The ash still held its shape, but the next breeze could blow it away.

"Did you see the mark?" asked Mairi, breaking free from Jachad's arms and careening toward her as if she intended to fall at her feet. Jachad walked away toward the swamp. Men turned as he passed, looking as if they wanted to speak to him, and then looked away. "Have you seen it before? Do you know what it is?"

"No," said Lahlil, watching Jachad walk away.

"No? Me neither." Mairi dried her tears and set her face into a grim mask. "It's *not* natural. I know what can go wrong with childbirth, but this . . . No, this is something else. Jachi knows it, too. He doesn't want to believe it, that's all."

Lahlil took a lamp from one of the men and followed Jachad into the swamp. He left the high ground and waded across a shallow pool, not altering his course until a stand of razor-grass blocked his path. The light from her lamp bounced off the water, creating ripples of luminescence, and moths beat their papery wings against the pierced metal until they fell away, dazed by the heat.

"Jachi?"

He turned to her. He was pale enough for her to see every one of his freckles, even in the lamplight, and she didn't like the way he had his hand pressed against his chest.

"Stay back," he said, raising his palm to her.

A cold breath of fear blew over her. "Why?" she asked, moving forward regardless.

"Stay back!" he shouted, raising both hands high into the air. Twin flames shot up, revealing the plants and creatures of the swamp around them as suddenly as a bolt of lightning. But then the flames sputtered and in the center of each twisted a thin spiral of black smoke.

The tension in his mouth, the creased eyes . . . That wasn't grief. It was physical pain.

"I felt it, when we were in my tent," said Jachad. "I didn't think it meant anything—"

She dropped the lantern onto the wet ground and leaped forward. Yellow and orange petals of flame scattered from his hands as she reached out for the front of his robe. He gripped her wrist and held it tight, squeezing until she could feel her own pulse throbbing beneath his fingers. They stood locked together, Jachad merely delaying the inevitable, stubbornly holding the line in a battle he'd already lost. Then his hold finally loosened.

She seized the collar of his robe with both hands and tore the fabric apart. The mark was there, over his heart: black vines, reaching out, pulling her down.

Chapter 9

Isa had exactly one thing to look forward to after the latest temple collapse: Daryan had announced a ceremony to open the Shadar's first school, despite the advice of Omir and nearly everyone else around him. For hundreds of years, the only people among the Shadari who had been permitted to read and write were the ashas and the daimon, and even for them, the store of the Shadari's knowledge had been reduced to nothing more than a few rote supplications to the gods. Daryan firmly believed his dream, to coax that knowledge out of the past, was as vital to the Shadar's survival as forging black-bladed weapons for themselves or finding those people who had the ashas' powers—the same powers as little Dramash. He was convinced that this would be the turning point.

Isa woke before dawn that morning to saddle Aeda. After an infuriating hour spent wrestling the massive saddle into place and securing it using all the one-handed tricks she had developed, she came back into the ashadom to wash and to get Blood's Pride. A lamp left burning on one of the makeshift tables—wasting lamp oil, as if it wasn't as scarce as everything else—illuminated a landscape of unwashed plates and cups, not to mention Herwald lying face-down on a bench with his arm dangling over the side. On the opposite side of the table, Tovar lay slumped over with his head on his arms. The rest had at least made their way back to their beds and would no doubt snore the day away until dusk, when they'd start over again, circling aimlessly through the monotonous days like a one-oared boat.

The humped back of the broken saddle separating her corner of the cave didn't afford much privacy, but she washed as best as she could in the basin of water, though nothing but a proper bath would scrub away the reek of straw, sweat and triffon's hide. She missed her big stone tub, along with the room to put it in and the cool water to fill it up.

<You have some place to go?> Falkar asked from somewhere on the other side of the cave.

A chill shot up Isa's spine, but she hid it as best she could. She scanned the darkness until she found him leaning back on the bench with his feet propped up on a nearby table. She pulled on her shirt as quickly as she could without making it obvious that he had unnerved her. The fabric stuck to her tacky skin and she wished she hadn't bothered with the wash.

<They're opening the school today and I want to be there.> She took up Blood's Pride and slung the belt over her head, rolling her shoulders back to settle the weight of the sword.

<They can build schools for people who don't want to learn, but they can't find us a place to live,> said Falkar.

<This is a place, isn't it?>

<Norlanders aren't supposed to live in caves and tunnels. It's in the *Book*.>

<We're not underground. It's no different than living in the temple.>

The front legs of the bench came down with a gritty crunch and Falkar leaned toward her.

<I should kill you.> His bloodshot silver eyes and flushed neck made it clear he was still drunk, but she wasn't stupid enough to dismiss him because of that. She could just make out his sword, Fealty's Strength, surrounded by dirty plates. <That's what I'm supposed to do, isn't it? That's in the *Book* too. The "all so afflicted" part.>

Isa curled her fingers into her palm until her untrimmed nails dug into her skin. <My brother ordered you not to interfere with me. He is still your commander.>

<What if the gods damned Lord Eofar for not letting you die in the temple?> His question jumped into Isa's mind with a plaintive lilt, but the anxious rhythm he tapped out against the hilt of

Fealty's Strength said something more dangerous. <What if they damned you for your arm, and Lord Eofar for not setting you out, and then us because we followed him into battle against Lady Frea? I feel damned. Don't you? Do you feel the gods hating you?>

<Yes,> she said, seeing no reason to hide her bitterness, <but that's nothing new. I've felt that way most of my life.>

<I could do it. I could kill you,> said Falkar. He got up from the bench and came around the table, carrying his sword with the hilt in his right hand and the scabbard in his left, ready to draw. She clenched her arm against her side, refusing to give him cause. She felt his strange compassion moving over her like the swipe of a damp rag. <At least you can die fighting. It's more than you deserve.>

<It wouldn't be a fair fight.> Isa rolled her left shoulder, poking the stump of her arm toward him so that the knotted sleeve swung in his direction. <You're too drunk.>

He stared back at her for what felt like hours, his wine-muddied feelings pulling at her like sucking marsh sand. Then his presence in her mind went foggy and the sword sagged in his hand. Isa left Falkar behind, her metal-tipped heels hammering down on the uneven floor as she walked straight past the stone table toward the entrance to the cavern. She grabbed her sun-proof cape without breaking stride and pulled it over her head as she marched toward the patch of gray framed at the end of the short tunnel. As soon as her boots hit the sand, she gulped down the cold early dawn air and fumbled one of the remaining pills out of her pouch, only to have it slip through her fingers as the pain ripped through her missing arm again.

They were all lost here: every one of them.

She couldn't go back in there; she couldn't live among those people any more. She had tried to make it work–she didn't want to burden Daryan with yet another problem—but she had reached the end. She would have to move into the half-built palace, even though it would make his supporters uncomfortable. There wasn't much room, but surely Daryan could set aside one tiny corner for her?

By the time Isa flew toward the city, the rising sun had squashed the houses into flat black cut-outs and compressed the people into streaky black lines. The new school building was on one side of the forecourt of the old castle, near a broken basin that had once filled the air with the sound of burbling water. The school was a typical dome-shaped Shadari house, distinguished by the gleam of fresh whitewash and an uncovered doorway which Daryan had insisted remain open for the ceremony. A gray cloth had been tacked up on the wall above the doorway, hiding the inscription Daryan had painted with his own hand. A large crowd—a thousand people, she reckoned—had turned up for the dedication.

Isa brought Aeda down to a spot on the far side of the palace where two broken walls met in a corner, providing a rare bit of shade. There was a stone trough there, kept filled with water for the triffon. Once she'd settled Aeda, she set off toward the little platform where Daryan and his supporters were gathered. She'd hoped for a moment alone with him, to tell him about Falkar, but she found him embroiled in an argument about the possibility of Binit interrupting his speech and they went right on arguing while she stood like a ghost outside their circle: one of those misguided spirits who had turned their backs on the doors to the After-realm to cling to a life that had already begun to forget them.

"Binit's kept the truce so far," said Daryan. "Anyway, he prefers going behind my back. He's not going to start something here."

"Binit doesn't worry me," Omir replied. "It's the resurrectionists."

"They haven't made any threats. You worry too much about them, Omir," Daryan said. "Listen, I'm not going to wait any longer. If someone starts trouble, we'll deal with it. Nothing is going to stop me from opening this school."

He left the group behind him and circled round to climb up to the platform. Omir and a few of the others followed him, while the rest—the red-robed armed guards—fanned out in front. Isa found her view blocked and moved back, shimmying between a clump of frowning men and a mother with a pinched forehead and a pair of fidgeting children.

She could see Daryan's head and shoulders rising above the throng, and heard the sound of his voice, saying the same things he had been saying to her for months: "Even if it's just an empty building now, it will remind us of what we're working toward. We're going to do more than just rebuild what we lost to the Norlanders; we're going to reclaim the knowledge that's ours by right, and then we're going to take our ore and make our place in the world. The worst thing we could do now is to condemn the next generation to the same ignorance handed down to us. The next time the Norlanders—or anyone else—tries to take our freedom from us, we'll be able to defend ourselves."

Isa moved a little closer, sliding between an old woman leaning on a cane and a young man who reached up to push a fringe of lank hair out of his eyes. He had open blisters on his fingers, dirt caked under his nails and a wide black band of filth marring the bottom of his robe, but it was the smell—the sweet smell of rotting things and the acrid tang of smoke, the smell of death itself—that gave him away. *A resurrectionist.* She had never been this close to one before.

Just then a gust of wind billowed out the cloth tacked up above the door of the school and it came loose on one side, flapping down to reveal a few words written in Shadari. People gasped and cried out, and most looked away or covered their eyes. Some even dropped to their knees or pulled their robes up over their faces. Only four people did not react: the resurrectionist, who folded his arms across his chest, and a little trio: a man, woman, and a girl of about twelve in a yellow headscarf, who were arguing in fraught whispers.

"I want to tell the daimon," Isa heard the girl tell her parents. She was a scrawny thing, with big staring eyes. "It's different now. I don't have to hide it any more."

"No, not after what they're saying about Namah and his. Six, all gone," said her father, looking about. His eyes rested on Isa for a moment, but her face was hidden beneath her cowl and he couldn't tell that she was watching them. And most Shadari still assumed she didn't speak their language. "Think about your brothers and sisters," he urged.

"We shouldn't be talking about this here," said the mother, taking her daughter's arm and urging her toward the back of the crowd.

"But we're supposed to come forward," the girl insisted. "It's not a sin. It's *not!*"

Then sand washed up over Isa's feet, covering the toes of her old leather boots and sifting back toward her heels, rippling out in tiny waves around the girl.

The mother clapped both hands over her mouth.

An asha. The girl was an asha.

"I'm sorry," said the girl, with tears streaming down her cheeks. "I didn't mean to."

"Come on! Hurry!" said the father, and the three of them hustled away with their heads down and the girl still weeping.

Isa suddenly became aware of a disturbance in the crowd, though she had no idea what had started it—maybe an altercation broke out somewhere near the front, or perhaps someone began running; all she knew was that the uncomfortable hush had given way to a restless muttering that was growing rapidly in volume and urgency.

Daryan held up his hands and begged for everyone's attention even as Omir's red-robed guards clustered together at the base of the platform to protect him. In the meantime, the girl in the yellow scarf was getting further and further away.

The people around Isa were jostling against each other and craning their necks to see what was happening; she would never be able to get through them to tell Daryan in time for him to intercept the family. She'd not heard any of their names, and the girl was hardly the only Shadari with a yellow scarf. If she lost them now, Daryan might never find them again.

She would have to follow them.

They had moved away from the palace and the crowds already, and now the father was propelling them through the rutted streets of the southern district. Isa stayed behind them as the sun peeled back the shadows and exposed a city sliding into ruin: refuse littering the scrubby garden plots and stinking waste piled up in the alleys, houses bearing the scars of old, inexpert repairs alongside more recent wounds. Her sun-proof cape weighed her down and the stale air beneath her cowl tasted like the grit kicked up by her boots, but she was determined not to lose sight of the girl and her parents.

The street flowed into a circular yard with a well in the middle and other streets leading away in several directions. Broken stuff too worthless even to loot had been piled up in charred heaps. All of the houses on the far side of the yard had burned down, leaving circles of blackened clay bricks. The neighborhood children were playing around one of the piles; a few of the boys had lashed sticks together to make swords. The family went into a house with a blue curtain over the door, and Isa heard the voices of children in several different registers as the heavy drapery swung to one side.

She turned to make her way back to Daryan, but winced as a shaft of sun found its way into her eyes. As she blinked away the tears, she heard the chink of a clay brick falling against another and when she was able to see again, she found two of the boys staring at her.

"Hello," she said to them.

"Hello," said the larger boy. The smaller one just sucked his lower lip in between his teeth.

"Do you know who lives there?" asked Isa, pointing to the house with the blue curtain.

"Sure," said the boy, but before Isa could ask anything else, a voice piped up from her left.

"You talk funny." A very small girl, disguised, lizard-like, in a robe and scarf the same color as the ground, sat right near Isa building a little city of stones and sticks.

"What are you making?" Isa knelt down beside the child.

The girl dragged her finger shyly through the dirt and shrugged.

A man came through the blue curtain and walked off down one of the streets across the way, tossing something aside as he went. Isa couldn't see his face, but he was too thin to be the girl's father. She stood up again and eyed the curtain still swinging from his passing. Smoke wound up from the house's chimney, but the noise of a large family moving around inside had vanished and the quiet gave her an uneasy feeling.

"Do you think they would let me talk to them?" she asked the boys.

"Don't know," said the older boy, flicking shadows at her with swings of his toy sword. The younger boy continued to stare silently.

Isa took a deep breath as if she was about to dive into deep water and then strolled across to the house. She brushed up against the curtain as if by accident, and then took a quick look through the gap she had created.

She pushed it aside and walked through.

Every nerve in her body screamed, but she couldn't move; she couldn't even breathe, or open her eyes. She stood there for a moment, paralyzed, waiting for the shock to subside and leave her in control of her own body again. She studied the image hanging in her memory very carefully, preparing herself, as if she even could . . .

When she felt strong enough, she opened her eyes.

The family had been about to start a meal. Crockery lay strewn around the room, some broken, and a pungent, unfamiliar smell hung in the air. The man nearest the doorway—Isa recognized the father—was lying on his back. The pulled-up rug and scratched floor around him meant he had been trying to reach the door when he died. She could even see bits of his broken fingernails in the dirt. A trail of bloody spittle ran from one corner of his mouth and down to the floor.

Isa was about to step over him when she noticed the black lines on his chest, clawing their way up toward his neck. She hesitated for a moment, but then knelt down and pulled his robe open. The mark over his heart could have been a splash of ink or paint, but nothing came away when she brushed her glove over his dead flesh. A tangle of black lines snaked out from the blotch and then dwindled away, looking like the tentacles of some malignant sea creature.

She raised her eyes to the rest of the room.

Two boys—both younger than the girl she had followed—were slumped against the wall with their mother in between them. She still had her arms over their shoulders, and Isa imagined her holding both of them as they died. An old woman with gray-streaked hair sprawled next to the firepit, lying in the bright spot of sunlight pouring through the chimney hole above her. The old woman had torn open her robe, presumably in pain, and her exposed breast bore the same marks as the man by the door. Isa had no doubt she would find them on all the victims if she looked.

The old woman had died next to a stand holding an open kettle that was still boiling over the fire. The bubbling water inside sparkled in the light. The pungent smell came from the pot. Isa could still see the steam rising up and feel the moisture on her face as she leaned over, but she saw nothing but water inside, and she still didn't recognize the scent.

Isa found herself irresistibly drawn to what looked to be the curtained-off sleeping chamber on the far side of the room. She drew back the heavy material and tried to make sense of the tangle of shapes in the dim light: there looked to be enough limbs for two people: one too big to be the girl, the other too small.

When she turned around, she saw the cradle.

The room spun as she stumbled back outside and fell onto her knees, retching. Her throbbing shoulder was agonizingly painful. With shaking fingers she shook a couple of the pills from the little bag. One dropped to the ground, but she left it there and shoved the rest in her mouth. She felt as if she had been in that death-house for hours; finding the same sun-bleached sky overhead came as a shock.

Insects surrounded her, drawn by the vomit; they managed to get into her cowl and buzzed in her ears. Nothing felt completely real. She looked at the piles of discarded household goods and the tenacious weeds growing in the rubble, staring at these images of the mundane and hoping they would bring her back to the normal world. Most of the shattered objects defied recognition, but she could see one small jug thrown aside so recently that liquid still darkened the inside of the concave shards, two of which, the larger pieces, were lying side by side. As she focused on them she could see marks on the outside, in a greenish-yellow chalk: writing.

She thought of the Shadari, averting their eyes from the sign over the school door. The Shadari didn't write anything, not *ever.*

The smaller of the two boys came shuffling through the dirt and stood next to her. "Are you sick?" he asked.

"No," Isa reassured him.

"You sicked up. You could have the plague," said the boy. "People die from it."

Isa hauled herself up on her quivering legs. "Do they?"

"People take them away when they do. I saw them. They cover up their faces so they don't catch it."

She had been about to head back into the alley when the boy's words sank in. "You *saw* them take people away?"

A woman came out from one of the other houses and emptied a dustpan into the street. On her way back in, she glanced up and saw Isa.

"Come inside, all of you," the woman called out to the children. "You've got chores. *Now,*" she scolded when they hesitated and they scattered abruptly, leaving Isa alone.

She forced a deep breath into her lungs and ran for the palace.

Chapter 10

Isa ran through the streets, hugging the patches of shade whenever she could find them. Nothing looked familiar; she felt like the houses were all crouching down, ready to spring at her as she ran past. Birds streaked by overhead, spying on her. Dirt clouds chased her heels and her cape felt as stiff and heavy as iron. By the time she reached the school, the fear and the heat and the exertion had completely sapped her strength.

Nearly everyone had gone, leaving just a few people roaming through the dirt or clustered together in little groups. Isa saw a scarf on the ground, and more ominously, a single shoe. Omir and some of his guards had gathered over by the platform. One of them tapped Omir on the shoulder and pointed at Isa as she approached and he came out to meet her, quickly covering the ground with his long strides. Rocks and sand crunched under Isa's feet as she slowed to a walk, gasping for breath and with a cramp in her side.

"Lady Isa," said the big man, his deepset eyes telling her nothing, "is something wrong?"

"Where—?" She couldn't get any more out through the dryness in her throat; she reached for her waterskin and drank before she could speak again. "Where's Daryan?" she managed at last.

Omir glanced over his shoulder to the open doorway of the school. She saw the shapes of stools and tables within the cool shadows. "Why? What's happened?"

"I want to tell him myself," she said, moving around him. She skirted the platform and went to the door, stepping over the heap of gray cloth that had been tacked up over the inscription. She looked up before she went inside. The swirls and dots were vaguely familiar to her—she'd spent a lot of time lying on her cot in the ashadom, staring up at the ceiling—but she had no idea what they meant.

Daryan was sitting at the back of the large, open room, with his arms resting on the table in front of him. A cloth-wrapped bundle lay between his hands: his manuscript of the history of the Shadar, which he had spent precious hours painstakingly recreating after the original had been destroyed in the temple. Wax tablets and slates had been set out on the tables in carefully spaced order, in readiness for students who had obviously not come. Daryan was all alone.

"Isa."

The disappointment in his eyes came close to breaking her heart. She wished he would lose control and give vent to his fury; that just once he would curse every setback and failure, rail against every disaster. Instead she had to listen to the dejection in his voice as he said, "I built them a school, and they ran away. I just can't seem to reach them. There has to be *some* way to make them understand."

"Daryan, I know why the ashas aren't coming forward," she said.

"It's obvious, isn't it?" said Daryan. The light dimmed as Omir stepped in through the doorway. "You heard what Binit said the other night. They're afraid. They don't want to change."

"No, that's not it—not at all." Isa swallowed. She felt like a bird's egg had lodged in the middle of her throat. "Someone is murdering them."

"*What?*" Daryan's stool fell over as he jumped up from the table.

"There was a girl—a girl with a yellow scarf . . ."

She told him everything she'd seen, and what the little boy had said about people with covered faces coming to take away the dead—and she described the broken jug with the writing on it. She expected Daryan to rush out and summon his guards, but the expression of alarm on his face slid into something else even before she had finished.

"You said you heard the family talking when the girl went

inside." Daryan frowned as he came around the table toward her. "How long after did you go into the house?"

"Not long. I only spoke to the children for a moment."

"And the man you saw leaving the house—he just walked away like nothing was wrong?"

Isa rocked back until she felt the edge of the table behind her against the back of her legs. "Yes. But I saw him toss something aside."

"It doesn't make sense, does it?" Daryan asked, glancing up at Omir as if looking for support. "How could anyone kill all those people that fast?"

"Poison. I told you," said Isa. "I smelled something in the steam from the kettle. The poison could have been in the jug I found outside. He could have poured it in the kettle."

"I wish you'd brought the jug back with you," Daryan said, pressing his knuckles against his lips.

"I didn't think of it."

"Still, if it was something in the kettle, and it killed everyone that fast, why didn't it kill the man who left?" Daryan asked. "Or *you,* when you went into the house?"

Isa couldn't answer because she was afraid she might cry.

Daryan's mouth twisted up as he watched her, but he said nothing.

"The resurrectionists." Omir spat, darkening a spot of the dirt floor to the color of Shadari blood. "We'll find them."

Isa remembered the young resurrectionist standing next to her at the dedication. She remembered his light hair and dirty hands, but mostly she remembered the smell of him. Even in the open air, the smell of old death—of wormy dirt and moldy cloth, of forgotten names and fleshless faces—had been strong enough to bring tears to her eyes. She had walked through that family's house and smelled sweat and unwashed clothes, cooking oil, and the baby's soiled wrappings, but she had smelled nothing like that resurrectionist, nothing at all.

"We have to go back there, right now," Isa said, appealing directly to Daryan. "Whoever did this may come to take them away."

"Even if any of this is true, they can't carry off all those people in broad daylight," said Daryan. "Omir, get some of our people together. Do you think you can find the house from what Isa told you?"

"Yes, Daimon," said Omir, and turned to go.

"Stop!" Isa cried out, infuriated by the inference that she did not know what she had seen. "I'll take you there myself. I'll prove it to you."

"Binit has been waiting for something like this," cautioned Omir. "If he finds out, he'll use it to get more people on his side."

"Damn Binit!" Daryan exploded. He ground the heel of his hand into his eye, as if trying to expunge any hint of tears. "But you're right. And if he finds out Isa was anywhere near this—whatever *this* turns out to be—he'll just have one more thing to use against us. Go on, Omir. I'll be right there."

"Daryan—" Isa began the moment he was gone.

"No," said Daryan firmly, "no, you're going back to the ashadom. I can't have you getting any more involved in this."

"I can't go back to the ashadom," Isa told him, straightening up and walking away from him toward the door.

"Why not?" asked Daryan.

"Falkar wants to kill me." A surge of pain ripped through the stump of her left arm as she stared out at the sand, straining to hold back the tears that would be the crowning touch to her humiliation.

Daryan made a guttural noise in his throat. "What happened? Did you do something? Did you say something to set him off?"

" 'Set him off?' " Isa cried, turning on him with anger burning like fire in her throat. "You think I had to do anything? He hates me for what I am—for my missing arm. They all do. They always have. They'll kill me if I go back."

"But Eofar made them swear to leave you alone before he left," said Daryan. "I thought you were fine there. Why didn't you tell me before now?"

"I didn't want to worry you."

"Worry me? Isa, are you joking?" Daryan cried, with an ugly little laugh. "You make me worry about you every day, all the time, when I should be figuring out how to keep my people from turning on each other. Every one of their grudges, every unpaid debt, every unhappy romance of the last thirty years is somehow *my* problem now."

"I know that—"

But he couldn't seem to stop. "You don't want to worry me? That day in the temple, with your arm . . . I can face just about anything, but not that, not again. I don't think you understand what it would do to me if something happened to you. I'm doing my best to make a place for you here and keep you safe at the same time, but I'm not going to pretend that anything you've done has made it *easier* for me."

A new kind of fear blossomed in Isa's chest. "Maybe it would be better if I wasn't here at all."

"Stop it. Just stop, please," Daryan pleaded angrily. "I know I'm being unfair. I know you have no place else to go."

Isa took out the folded sheet of paper she had been carrying in her pocket for weeks and tossed it down onto the table among the smooth tablets and unmarked slates.

"What's that?" Daryan asked stiffly.

She didn't answer but watched silently while he unfolded it.

"This is a map," he said, staring down in confusion at the lines and dots.

"King Jachad's caravan route," Isa told him. "I asked him to make it for me."

"I see," said Daryan, his voice catching. "Why?"

"So I would know where to find my sister." Isa felt a strange relief at no longer having to wait for the inevitable. "I'm leaving. I'm going to get Lahlil."

Daryan reddened. "What for?"

"We need her help finding whoever's killing the ashas."

"Finding them?" Daryan cried, pounding his fist down on the map and making Isa jump. She hated the scraping, straining sound of his words as he spat them out. "Do you have any idea the kind of chaos it will cause if Lahlil comes back here now? Do you understand how weak it will make me look? *Finding them?* I don't need your sister to help me find people who want me to fail. All I need to do is walk down any street, close my eyes and point."

"Daryan . . ." Isa said, then tailed off miserably.

The two of them remained stuck in the same postures, neither looking at the other. Isa could not make herself move or speak. Her mind had gone blank.

"I didn't mean all that," Daryan said finally, straightening up.

Isa wanted to respond, but she didn't know how.

"Now that I know why no one with the asha powers has come forward, I can do something about it myself. There's no reason for you to go, Isa."

She stared down at the ground, struggling to keep an avalanche of feelings from sweeping her away.

"You just need to give me more time. I am going to make the Shadar whole again, I swear to you. We will be together some day, without all the hiding and the lies. I'm going to make it happen."

"You won't," said Isa. "You can't, and you never will."

The words hung in the air between them. She wanted to take them back—her jaw ached to do it—but her blood was as sluggish as an ice-choked stream and she was too numb to do anything but listen to the slow thump of her heart.

"You've lost faith in me," said Daryan. His arms dangled limply at his sides.

Isa could not stand to be there another moment. She took the map back and walked out of the school.

The wind had picked up and was blowing around the building with an eerie whine. Men in fluttering red robes had gathered together on the far side of the yard and Omir was giving them instructions. The sun had just begun to cross the line of the peaks in the distance and the facing slopes had already taken on shadows.

Isa finally remembered to breathe.

Daryan followed her outside and she looked back at him just long enough to see the flush that had risen to his cheeks draining away. The pain in her arm surged back, even worse than before. She still had a few of the pills left and she dug them out while she walked.

He followed her around the broken walls to where Aeda waited, lying in the shade with her head between her clawed front feet, and stood behind Isa as she began the methodical process of checking the seams and buckles on the triffon's harness. From a stand of palm trees came the jeering cry of a jay, and the melodic sound of bricks being stacked up on the scaffolding around the new buildings. She had always liked that sound. Now she would have to think of the torment of this moment every time she heard it.

"Don't go, Isa," he said, coming around beside her and hanging on to the curved edge of her saddle. "All I need is one bit of luck, one victory: an asha coming forward, getting the resurrectionists on my side; more of the elixir turning up—"

"I can't wait for luck any longer," she said, grimacing at the foul taste of the words as they left her mouth.

He grabbed her cape. "You can't go. I won't let them take you away from me."

"Then come with me." Sudden hope stabbed into Isa's heart; her hand shook with it. "We'll go to the Nomas together. We can go anywhere from there. You gave the Shadari their freedom. You've done enough."

Daryan squeezed the fold of white cape in his fist. "You said we could never be happy together if I left. Remember?"

"I was wrong."

Daryan let go of her cape, but then he unfastened and refastened the bottom clasp, then the one above it, and on up until he came to the one at her throat. He stopped with his hands still gripping the two ends, staring down at them as if they held some mystery to be solved. Then he drew in a breath to speak.

"Don't say it," Isa begged him.

"You were right." He let go of her cape but stood close enough to her that she could hardly bear not to be touching him. His jaw tightened. "There isn't anyone else. I can't abandon them to the likes of Binit—I wouldn't be able to live with myself."

She dropped the leather straps and plunged into his arms. Her missing arm throbbed mercilessly, but the pain paled in comparison to the heat from his hands as they clutched the back of her neck, or the brand of his lips pressing against hers. The shock of it thudded through her as she closed her eyes and kissed him with all the rage and sorrow and love in her heart, kissed him until the pain swept it all into one great bonfire fueled by their passion.

She gave everything in that kiss: everything she had went into the flames.

The pain finally forced them to pull away from each other. Then Isa climbed up into Aeda's saddle, not trusting herself to say or do anything more; too afraid she'd fail to keep back the assurances she knew would be lies and the promises she would most likely not be able to keep. She strapped herself in and was in the air before she had even made a conscious decision to take off. She didn't allow herself to look back. She'd given that peaceful-looking city with its fishing boats and its little white houses enough of her cold, blood-betraying tears. It wasn't getting any more.

Chapter 11

Rho leaned back beside the half-open cabin door and watched the mist drift through the pools of lantern-light. He could still feel the sway of the ship beneath him, but the *Argent* wasn't going anywhere; she hadn't moved forward since they'd sailed into the infamous Barrels two weeks ago. The murderous storms for which he had braced himself apparently had somewhere else to be. No stars pierced the fog to provide any sense of direction, and he only knew night had fallen thanks to the ringing of the ship's bell. The air felt neither hot nor cold; he was beginning to feel like he was made of mist himself.

Eofar struck another hollow boom from the *Argent*'s immaculate deck as he ran through an offensive set, stomping every time he thrust the black blade through the fog. He wasn't drilling; he was fighting someone, someone with flesh and bone and sinews to be parted—Ingeld, maybe; or Frea, with her dented helmet crusted with barnacles and seaweed clinging to her wave-worn white cape, or—

—or maybe Rho needed to spend less time staring into the fog.

Eofar came off guard and grabbed the shirt he had left hanging from a spar to wipe the sweat from his eyes.

<Unless you've got some other shirt I don't know about, you might want to take better care of that one. We are still going to see the emperor, right?>

<I'm not planning on talking to him about fashion,> said Eofar.

He tossed the shirt back down and launched into the same set again.

Rho paced over to the port side of the ship where he could see Dramash and Yara and some of the younger members of the crew sitting in a circle, playing a game with spotted wooden blocks. Dramash flipped over one of the blocks in what was apparently the losing move, sending up a chorus of triumphant laughter from the rest of the players. Rho stiffened as he watched Dramash's face grow dark, then the boy looked around at his companions and laughed along with them as Yara scooped the blocks toward her to start the game anew. Rho had intended to have another go at making Dramash practice controlling his powers, but he hated to intrude on a moment when he was as happy as any ordinary little boy.

The other sailors were making similar use of the calm. On the quarterdeck just above him, Sabina, the tall second mate, was coaxing a succession of liquid trills from her little harp. A group of older women sitting together in the corner were passing around a clay pipe. The scent of the faint spirals of mauve smoke hanging in the breathless air above them reminded Rho of a spice market.

<Why don't you join them?> suggested Nisha as she leaned over the quarterdeck railing beside the wheelhouse. She wore her hair loose, and a belted gown of some crinkled fabric that looked as soft as the fog, and not much thicker.

<What's that they're smoking?> he asked, sniffing the air.

<It's medicinal.>

<What for?>

<Seasickness,> Nisha replied. Sabina snorted, then coughed behind her hand at the joke.

<Now you tell me, when this is the first time I haven't been sick since we left the Shadar.>

<It might help you relax. You really should stop watching the poor boy like he's a pot about to boil over. Sweet Amai, that's enough to make anyone jumpy.> Nisha yawned lightly and pushed her hair back with both hands. "I'm off to my bunk," she announced to her crew.

She went into her cabin and shut the door behind her. Rho waited for the music to start again, but when he looked up, he saw

Sabina loosening the last few strings on her harp and then rising with graceful ease. She strolled to Nisha's cabin and went in without knocking.

Rho spent a long time staring at the closed door with a sharp twinge of envy. Life never arranged itself that easily for him.

"What's the matter? Never seen a door before?" asked Grentha, appearing from behind the wheelhouse.

"Don't you ever sleep?" Rho asked her. He could have sworn she had been on the forecastle just a moment ago. She had a way of roaming silently around the ship and then popping out whenever he did something embarrassing, like tripping over a locker or tangling himself up in the ropes.

"When I'm tired."

<Only she's never tired,> said Hela, circling around toward him past the bit of deck Eofar had appropriated for his sword practice. <We tell the new cabin girls that she sleeps standing up, with her eyes open—like a burcapa. You should see their faces.> She laughed out loud, as the sailors often did even when they were speaking Norlander. Rho had grown accustomed to the incongruousness.

<It's not hard to believe.> He started back for his cabin, but Hela slid around him and stood in front of his door.

<Come up to the lookout with me,> she said. <There was a whole pod of selkwhales out there earlier. The babies have fur, did you know that? It doesn't fall off until they're about a year old. The Stowari hunt them, skin them and sell the fur. The 'whales are smart, though. They can tell a Stowari ship by its ironwood keel and they know to steer clear.>

<It's too dark to see anything.>

She cocked her head to one side. <Oh, come on, Rho. You're wearing down the varnish, pacing like that. It won't make the ship go any faster.>

He had run out of arguments so he followed her past the wheelhouse and Nisha's cabin and up the last short ladder to the stern look-out. He went to the little crook where the two railings came to a point and looked out, but he could see nothing but the rippling black silk of the water. Hela stepped up to the polished rail by his side. He could feel the heat of her body pulsing around her, and he could smell her hair: a blend of the salty sea air and the heavy mauve smoke.

<You're going home,> said Hela, as she turned around and leaned against the rail. The light from the lantern above dappled her honey-colored skin with purple shadows. <You must be happy about that. How long since you left Norland?>

<Three years.>

<Your family will be glad to see you.>

<I don't have a family.>

<You don't?> asked Hela. Even with her blunt foreign accent, he could feel her dismay. <Why not? What happened to them?>

<I ate them.>

<Rho,> said Hela, <I'm serious. It's awful not to have a family.>

<You never met mine,> said Rho. He leaned his elbows on the rail and looked down into the water, seeing the gleam of a ripple here and there and hearing the splash of what might have been Hela's selkwhales. <My father had four sons by his first wife, then she died, and he married my mother and *she* died when my brother Trey was still an infant. I don't remember her at all, so I never missed her. My older half-brothers spent their whole lives arguing over who'd got the biggest piece of meat at dinner, and scheming to take over my father's estate. When he died, they gave me and Trey our allowance and packed us off to Ravindal so they could murder each other in peace.>

<So what about Trey? Your little brother?>

<You mean you've never heard of Trey Arregador, the Hero of Redland?> He wondered if she could feel the bitterness burning in his chest. <He was the best person I ever knew, and the only person I ever really loved. He died three years ago.>

"Oh, Rho," Hela said aloud, turning her round-cheeked face up to him. <And no wife waiting for you? No girl counting the days until you sail back to her?>

He hadn't realized she was so small: the top of her head only just reached his shoulder. She wore a green shirt with the collar untied, and kept twining one of the strings around her fingers. The movement drew his eyes, then he stopped to linger over the curve of her breasts. She tucked a few tendrils of her light hair beneath her scarf and wet her lips.

<At least now I know you like girls,> she said. He could feel her sliding closer in his mind. <I was beginning to wonder.>

<Hela,> he began, formulating his refusal, but she let him get no further.

<I'm very persistent, Rho,> she said. <You might have noticed.>

<I have . . . > Although at the moment, he was noticing the way she was gently biting her bottom lip. He cleared his throat, even though they were still speaking Norlander. <If you're trying to win the bet, you can tell the others whatever you like. I won't give you away.>

Hela laughed again, softly this time. <I started that bet myself, idiot. I wanted a reason to flirt with you without the others pestering me about it.>

<Oh.> He should have figured that out on his own. <Trust me, this isn't a good idea. You don't really know me.>

<I know enough. I can see how much you care about Dramash. And I know you're lonely. I like lonely people.> Hela put her head to one side and regarded him for a moment with serious eyes. But then her sly smile returned and she reached out and ran her fingertips along the back of his hand and up his wrist, a feather touch which sent a blaze of heat shooting up his arm. <But mostly I'm curious. I think you are, too.>

Rho struggled to keep his breath from quickening. <But the cold—>

<Oh, I know it will hurt. Pain and pleasure, they're two ends of the same rope. That's what we Nomas say. Well, I say it anyway.>

Rho pushed his hair out of his eyes, only to have the breeze blow it right back again. He wanted her. There was no denying that he wanted to grab her and kiss her, right there on the deck, kiss her hard enough to make her cry out. He wanted the pleasure they could give each other, but she was right: he wanted the pain even more.

He reached for her, but Hela spun suddenly and backed up against the rail. "Did you feel that?" she asked, her voice thrumming with excitement. She pointed at the sails that had been hanging like neglected washing for the last two weeks. From the light of the lantern in the crow's nest above he thought he saw the top sails' belly, just the tiniest bit.

The clang of the ship's bell rang out over the deck and Grentha appeared on the roof of the wheelhouse, already bellowing out orders. The women on the deck scrambled for their posts and others came up from below decks. Hela gave Rho a crooked smile of regret and slid down the ladder. Nisha and Sabina emerged a moment later, both dressed in their regular clothes.

"Here we go, girls!" called out the captain. "Look sharp!"

The Barrels had no intention of letting the *Argent* go without living up to its reputation, and the raging storm was worse than anything Rho could ever have imagined. The wind came at them in a constant scream. The waves were so high, the troughs so deep, that Rho and his companions were forced to lash themselves to the struts to keep from being tossed around like Dramash's ragdoll. So loud was the creaking of the tortured timbers that Rho was sure the ship was about to break apart, and it was too dark to see a thing—there was no point trying to light the lanterns, not when the heaving of the vessel continually knocked over the candles into the sand on the bottom. After one attempt to open the cabin door, which resulted in an inch or more of freezing water cresting over the raised threshold and washing across the floor, Rho resigned himself to staying put—not that he would have been any help to the Nomas; he felt so ill that he began to wish the ship would capsize so he could drown in peace.

He was relieved to see the storm's ferocity didn't bother Dramash, except for the personal inconveniences it caused. After falling off the stool he'd pulled over to the porthole so he could look out at the waves, he complained that he didn't like having only ship's biscuits to eat, though there was no way anyone would be able to keep a cookfire alight in the galley. Then Dramash found Eofar's sword, Strife's Bane, in one corner of the cabin and settled down in Rho's hammock with the hilt in his lap. The boy sat there in the dark, stroking the silver triffons and whispering secret commands that Rho strained to hear over the noise of wind and rain and straining planks. Rho wondered if Dramash was trying to find the right words to bring the creatures to life. Sometimes, instead of murmuring his incantations, he sang to himself: a song of nonsense words, maybe something his mother might have sung to him when he was a baby.

Rho tried very hard not to remember the last sound Dramash's mother had made: that wet little gurgle as he cut her throat . . .

Rho was more worried about Eofar. The storm didn't frighten him either, but he had traded the intoxication of wine for the visceral violence of the weather. His emotions mimicked the waves: dark troughs of anger swelling up into white-capped swells of mad euphoria. The rain was merely the sky, weeping for a wife and son taken from him; the wind was his scream of fury. Rho began to worry that Eofar's sanity would be washed overboard with everything else before they even reached Norland.

It took four long days for them to come out the other side of the storm.

The sailors took stock of the damage. Two crew-members had been lost: Arva, the bursar, had slipped over the side, and Katie had broken her neck after courageously climbing the rigging to secure one of the sails which had ripped loose. Almost everyone else was injured, including Leth, the cook, who had taken the worst of it when the foremast splintered off and smashed through the galley. Sabina had a deep gash in her arm that was already looking infected, and even Dramash's friend Yara, the little cabin girl, had a broken wrist. Sheer exhaustion and four days of constant freezing wind and rain had put a quarter of the crew down with a fever, including Mala, the ship's healer, who dosed herself up and dragged herself around to tend to the others.

The *Argent* herself was in equally bad shape. As well as the loss of the foremast and the galley, most of the sails were damaged, and all sorts of important things had been lost or broken beyond repair, including one of their two landing boats. Still, the mainmast had survived in one piece, and the keel was in pretty good shape.

From the way the sailors kept repeating those two facts, Rho realized they were lucky to still be alive and afloat.

And somehow, through all that, Nisha and Grentha had kept them on course, and not even a week later, the *Argent* glided into the harbor at the lower town of Ravinsur.

Everyone who could stand upright put on as many layers of clothing as possible and came out on deck to watch. They'd cut down a fur coat for Dramash and then used the offcuts to make mitts and a hood in the Norlander style that covered his whole head except for his eyes. Even under the circumstances, Rho was amused by the sight of the boy trundling across the deck like some rotund little forest creature.

A heavy mist drifted over the dark water and every sound had a muffled quality, like someone had wrapped it all up in rags. Even the *chunking* of the ice floes as the *Argent's* prow nudged them aside had a dream-like distance to it. It was a Norland silence, and Rho hadn't realized how much he'd missed it until it settled over him again.

Eventually Ravindal's crowded towers started to appear, the black shapes barely visible through the mist. Their upper stories were further hidden by a perpetual ring of wood-smoke from the city's streaming chimneys. Torchlight and firelight glowed behind green-glass windows offset in the thick stone towers and watch-fires leaped in great braziers on the city walls. Rho had once patrolled those walls as an Arregador guard, alongside resentful mid-clan comrades and other high clansmen too young or lazy to go soldiering. Steam from the warm springs beneath the castle shrouded the immobile waves of the frozen waterfall tumbling from the cliffs. The buildings of the lower town of Ravinsur rose up in a series of steps from the docks, separated from Ravindal by the wide, sharp ascent of the Dock Road. Ships jostled each other in the deep harbor, and through Nisha's spyglass Rho could see the usual collection of stevedores, dock-wardens, merchants' scribes, children and dogs congregating on the docks. Dramash nuzzled up beside him, asking an endless series of questions through his fur hood. Rho answered every one he could understand.

Not everything matched his memories. The last hours before dark usually had a certain quietness to them as the lower clans prepared the evening meal and the nobility prepared to eat it. Now he had counted at least a dozen triffons coming and going in just the short time he'd been watching, and there was new scaffolding around sections of the walls and towers which were swarming with activity, apparently repairing or adding to the fortifications—but Ravindal had not come under direct attack since the end of the Second Clan War a century ago.

Nisha gave orders to drop anchor and lower their remaining landing boat; Rho paced the deck as the sailors hurried to furl the sails. A few moments later he heard the weighty clanking of the chain as four sailors walked the capstan round, but they walked in silence instead of singing the cheeky little song that had been Rho's favorite. The captain came up onto the foredeck to stand beside him at the rail and started scanning the expanded docks.

<Are they preparing for something?> Nisha asked after a moment.

<Orders from the new emperor, maybe,> Rho conjectured, looking away to the shore. <Making changes for the sake of it.>

<But you don't believe that, do you?>

<No.> A sense of expectation hung over the city that might have been dread. Maybe Rho was imagining it. Maybe he was bringing the dread with him.

<What do we do now, then?> asked Nisha. Her feelings, slippery things that normally tripped by so nimbly, now eddied like a muddy stream. <I could take a few girls ashore, ask around, find out what's happening.>

<You have to ask Eofar,> said Rho, pitching his words across the ship. <He's in charge.>

<I'm going myself,> said Eofar, stomping across to them. He cut an imposing figure with his hood down and his cowl up. Even the hilt of Strife's Bane looked less gaudy in the colorless light. <But Rho's past connections would be useful.>

<I doubt it, unless you want a ranking of Prol Irat brothels,> said Rho.

Eofar waited for more.

<All right,> he said at last, <there's a tavern I know. If the keeper's still there—well, he could talk the hind leg off a triffon. We should be able to get the latest news out of him.>

After arguing for a while longer about who should make up the landing party, Rho ended up in the boat with Dramash next to him on the middle bench, Eofar in the back, and Grentha to row them all to shore. Unlike the rest of them, the first mate wore a hat instead of a hood—the cold didn't seem to bother her.

"I fell asleep once, on watch," said Grentha. Her leaden eyes touched his for a moment. "I was mate on the *Lady Bright*. We hit a reef—tore a hole in the keel. Four girls and two babes drowned."

Rho just stared at her.

"Want to know their names?"

"Their names?" he asked, still confused.

She rattled them off: "Cari, Lora, Embeth, Fen, Josep, Kelli." The oars slid into the water and out again. "No other captain would have me after that, save for Nisha. Said she'd rather have someone who knew what a mistake felt like than one as never made one."

Rho, not knowing what he should say, said nothing.

Grentha gave a dry laugh and kept up the rhythm, moving the blades of the oars in and out of the water, periodically spattering them both with icy spray.

The town of Ravinsur climbed up the rocky steps beyond the docks, its structures looking like they were huddling together for warmth under a riotous blanket of thaw-vine. Most roofs had green-glass wedges set on top, designed to keep the snow from piling up and caving them in, and canopies of the same durable ice-glass arched over the narrow streets where the more prosperous mid-clansmen lived. The docks were divided into dozens of little craggy berths and ice crept up the hulls of the moored boats. No one paid any attention to their boat as they landed, and Rho began to understand why as he got a closer look at the crowd: there were soldiers everywhere.

Eofar climbed out onto the ice-slicked dock and said, <Come on, then. What are you waiting for?>

Rho had finally come home, after three long years, and yet all the voices in his head were telling him not to get out of the boat; to go back to the *Argent*; to just keep drifting.

Chapter 12

Rho led them past filthy snowbanks and heaps of rubbish—ice chunks, broken boxes and other trash—to the steps leading up into the cramped little town of Ravinsur. No one gave them more than a passing glance except for an old man shuffling along with an equally old dog at his heels, who stepped into a vine-covered alley so they could pass.

<Is it always this crowded?> asked Eofar as a group of four soldiers in Vartan tabards barged past, all talking at once.

<No,> said Rho, watching those four imperial swords heading down the street and keeping Dramash as close as possible. His lungs, long used to the desert's furnace, already ached from the cold. <I guess we're just lucky. Let's get off the main street at least.>

The alley he led them into split off in several directions, each one sliding gradually into darkness as it ended in a blank wall or sharp turn. Melting snow marked out a steady patter as it dripped through the warm thaw-vine branches and salt and gravel crunched under their feet, but little else broke the stillness. Rho could almost feel the silence weighing him down, just like the furs piled up on his shoulders. Even Dramash was affected, twisting around to look at the exotic sights all around him, but rarely speaking. The boy looked wrong trudging along beside him, away from the sun and surrounded by gray: gray ground, gray walls, gray sky.

Rho had once ended up drinking with a Ranjarian who believed that after you died, you walked backward through your own life as an observer, all the way back to the day you were born. He thought at the time that he might have lived his life differently if he had known he was going to have to watch himself slum away his evenings down here, enduring tales of how General Gannon had crushed yet another kingdom into oblivion with the fearsome warrior Trey Arregador by his side.

They entered a wider street lined on both sides with two-story warehouses and busy with carts coming and going. Glow-globes imported all the way from Angor lit the doorways, even though Norland didn't provide enough light for the living algae inside to keep them working for more than a few months. Green-glass statues guarded the doors and lined the walls: some of Onfar or Onraka, a few of the progenitors, and a great many more of generic naked men and women in improbable if entertaining postures. There were even green-glass windows in a few of the newer buildings, obviously owned by those rich enough not to care about the fuel they wasted in exchange for that little bit of light.

<Wait,> said Eofar, stopping in the middle of the street and standing there, immobile, as a low-clan woman with a handcart piled high with kindling tried to get past without knocking into him. Dramash pulled his hand out of Rho's and ran to stroke the smooth leg of the nearest statue. <This place is a maze. Do you even know where you're going?>

<It all looks different when you're sober,> said Rho, hurriedly retrieving Dramash and warning him once again to stay close. <If we don't find it soon, you can try spinning me around until I'm dizzy enough to fall over. That should jog my memory.>

As they walked a few more yards the houses became less grand and they found themselves in a district of taverns, run-down shops and single-story houses. Finally they came out into a tiny square with an old stone statue of an ursa in the middle. It had obviously once been part of a group, moved here from someplace else, but Rho had always liked it; he thought it had more power in its simple lines than all the curlicues and flourishes of the modern green-glass beauties. People dressed it up from time to time, just for fun; right now its blocky, chiseled head sported a tall mummer's crown left over from Eowara's Day.

<Almost there,> he told Eofar. <The Red Tower's around that corner.>

They left the square and climbed yet another set of steps, then turned the corner and there was the black door with the red tower painted over it, right where it was supposed to be.

"Dramash," said Rho, crouching down in front of the boy until he could see his eyes, "you can't talk in there. Do you understand? We don't want anyone to know you're from the Shadar. Not yet."

Whatever Dramash said in reply was unintelligible but at least he nodded. Eofar pushed open the door and stepped across the threshold before Rho could add anything else from the long list of warnings he had been compiling.

The elapsing of three years had not touched the Red Tower. The heavy beams overhead, the pitted stone floor underfoot and the surrounding walls hung with ancient furs were all just the same. The ursa head over the mantle still glared down through lifeless glass eyes. Barrels of cheap wine were piled up in the dark corners and the tavern's unique aroma of sour wine, resin, salt, grease and damp fur hung in the air.

The place boasted a decent crowd for the time of day, but no one did anything more than look up briefly before turning their attention back to their companions. Five mid-clan merchants were crowded around a corner table, and eight soldiers in a mix of Aelbar and Eotan colors had pushed two more closer to the fire. Two women sat by the wall with their heads close together, talking earnestly and pushing a scrap of paper back and forth between them. The general attitude was unusually somber for friends drinking together in a tavern, and Rho thought he detected an undercurrent of tension. He also counted at least eight imperial swords, not including Strife's Bane.

Then Old Peel came out from the little storeroom in that same leather coat, just a little more worn down at the elbows. His hair still brushed his shoulders in the fashion of a decade ago, only a little grayer now. Rho relaxed a little for the first time since they came into the harbor.

<Don't I know you, my Lord?> Peel asked, coming forward to wipe the table down for them as Rho lowered his cowl and took

off his hood. <You used to come here, years back, didn't you? Called back from campaigning, like everyone else?>

<That's right,> Eofar answered, before Rho could get a word in. Rho pulled out a stool for Dramash and lifted him onto it.

<Well, this should help you get used to the cold again,> said Peel, taking a jug from the shelf on the wall and two cups, then adding a third after an uncertain look at Dramash, keeping his questions to himself.

"I'm hungry," said the boy through the layers of fur.

Rho put his finger to his lips, but not before Peel had stepped back in surprise. <And a couple of goat sausages,> Rho said to the innkeeper, who had composed himself almost immediately. <The spiced ones.>

<More soldiers coming back every day,> said Peel, transferring two sausages to one of the Red Tower's battered metal plates. <Castle warden says he might have to start billeting down here—we all have to be ready. It's for our own protection, he says.>

<Protection?> asked Eofar, as he pulled the jug over and began pouring out the wine while Rho helped Dramash take off his gloves and hood so he could eat. Peel watched as the boy began tearing at the meat with his small teeth, his growing curiosity giving Rho another reason not to stay any longer than necessary. <Protection from whom?>

<What, you mean no one's told you?> asked Peel. The attention of the merchants in the corner shifted over their way at his raised tone. <The cursed are about to rise—Lord Valrig's army, just like it says in the *Book*. That's why Emperor Gannon's called everyone back. We're getting ready for war.>

The little warmth Rho had absorbed since coming inside drained out of him all at once, leaving him as cold as the green-glass statues outside. Eofar downed his wine and poured another one, ignoring Rho's silent growl of warning.

<The cursed?> asked Rho, forcing some jocularity into his mood as he lifted his own cup and leaned back on his stool. <This some new joke you're playing on folks who've been away? The army of the cursed? Really? Do we look that gullible?>

<Not a joke, my Lords. Not a funny one, anyway,> said Peel. <Emperor Gannon knows all about it.> He pitched his voice lower

so only they would hear, and his words bubbled with relish. <No one's supposed to know, but it's that witch he's got up there, the Shadari witch, up in the tower. She can see the future—they say she's never wrong. Old Emperor Eoban swore by her. No one can stop it now, they say. And not just that, but you'll never guess who's going to be leading the army of the cursed.>

<Who?> asked Eofar.

Peel's relish rose to new heights, but he spoke with solemn reverence. <*The Mongrel.*>

Another customer summoned Peel away before they could ask him any more questions, and as he left Rho felt Eofar's anxiety rising like bile in his throat. <This can't be happening,> Rho said, setting down his untouched wine. <Is there some other magical elixir that curses you with bad timing? Because if there is, then someone's been dosing my drinks.>

<Lahlil is supposed to be with my son.> Eofar was worried.

<And she is,> Rho assured him, watching Dramash. He had finished one sausage and was working on the other; he wouldn't sit there quietly much longer. <Trust me, more people have claimed they've killed the Mongrel than I've had hot baths, and this time is no different from all the others.>

Eofar's silver-gray eyes grew a little brighter behind his white lashes. <What do you know about this witch?>

<Nothing, really,> said Rho. He flinched, remembering Frea's strong, cold fingers wrapped around his wrist as she asked him the same thing, that night in the Shadar. <Just rumors.>

<The innkeeper said the Shadari witch could see the future,> Eofar reminded him. <Do you think she has divining elixir?>

<I don't know. Maybe. Sounds like it.>

<And she predicted the army of the cursed would rise.>

<If it is the elixir, then you know those visions could mean anything,> Rho said. <So what does it matter?>

Eofar turned his attention back to his wine. <The cursed. Monsters under the ground; child-eaters; something good, brave Norlanders like your brother would die rather than become. And then there's my family. First Lahlil and now Isa.>

<Isa is no monster,> Rho shot back, trying very hard to keep his temper. <And in case you forgot, *you're* the one who cut off her

arm. If you really believed the *Book,* you would have killed her instead.>

<Daryan convinced me to save her. If he hadn't been there, I would have put my sword right through her heart.>

A chill ran down the back of Rho's neck, even though the tavern was starting to feel uncomfortably warm. Eofar said nothing more, and when Rho reached out to his mind, found only the darkness.

<Eofar, what are you thinking?>

<Only that our timing might not be so bad after all.>

Dramash pushed his empty plate across the table. "I'm still hungry," he said, and every single person in the tavern turned at the sound of his voice.

Rho bent down to him so he could speak as quietly as possible. "We'll find something for you," he said, before turning to Eofar. <Let's get out of here. We got what we came for.>

Eofar lurched up and reached into his coat. <Can't leave without paying the bill,> he said, drawing out a single imperial eagle—at least ten times what they owed—and tossing it down on the table. Rho watched it land on its edge and spin, flashing in the firelight with each revolution until it slowed, wobbled, then fell over with the eagle side up. The gold took on a ruddy hue in the firelight, like—

Rho slapped his hand down over the coin, but not soon enough. Dramash had already locked his eyes on it. The hilt of Eofar's sword rattled against the top of its scabbard.

"Dramash," said Rho slowly, sliding the coin from the table with his hand still covering it. "It's all right." The last golden eagle Dramash had seen had been the one covered in his mother's blood. That coin—retrieved, kept secret, held back like a notched arrow—had triggered the temple collapse and all of the death that had followed.

The soldiers around the table jumped up, reaching for their quivering weapons, reading the build-up of emotion at the other end of the room.

"Dramash!" Rho said again.

Then the front door flew open and startled Dramash out of his distress. A soldier in an Arregador tabard straddled the threshold, yellow flares of excitement shooting out of him. <He's here!>

called the soldier, addressing his friends by the fire. <Josten Drey. They're bringing her up to Ravindal right now!>

He'd barely finished speaking before everyone else in the tavern was grabbing their outerwear and rushing for the door. Eofar snatched at the coat of one of the women before she got away.

<Wait!> he cried. <What's going on?>

The woman's incredulousness hit them like a punch. <It's the Mongrel—Josten Drey's brought her body here to collect the bounty. He's taking it up to the emperor.>

Eofar dropped her sleeve.

<The Mongrel isn't dead,> said Rho.

<The emperor won't be pleased if she is,> said the woman. <She can't lead the army of the cursed if she's dead, now, can she? If that's her body, then the witch's prophecies are wrong.> She ran after her friend, slamming the door behind her. Rho stepped in front of Eofar to stop him from running out after the others. <You need to stay calm. It's not her. It can't be.>

But Eofar walked around him and out the door. Rho helped Dramash back into his mittens and hood and followed after him, pausing briefly to place the coin on the bar.

Night had fallen in the short time they'd been inside. People were running through the streets, many of them still pulling on cloaks or hoods or gloves, all heading toward Dock Road. The excitement of the whole city pulsed around them.

<Where are you going?> Rho called after Eofar.

<To the emperor.>

<Are you insane?> asked Rho, picking up Dramash and carrying him in order to keep up.

<This is our chance to get the emperor on our side,> said Eofar without waiting. <We might be the only two people in Ravindal who can swear to him that whatever body they're bringing him is not genuine.>

Having just convinced Eofar that the body could not possibly belong to Lahlil, Rho found himself in no position to object.

"What's happening?" asked Dramash. "Where's everybody going?"

"To Ravindal," Rho told him, "and so are we, apparently."

Chapter 13

Rho kept a firm hold on the back of Dramash's coat like he was carrying a kitten by the scruff of the neck as they joined in the unruly procession heading up the wide road. Everyone was pushing to get a closer look, and one enterprising youth even climbed up onto the back of the bulky, slow-moving marmont pulling the cart before the guards plucked him off and tossed him back into the crowd. Through all of the excitement Rho could feel the same undercurrent of anger he had felt in the tavern. He and Eofar might be the only people in Ravindal besides the emperor hoping that whatever was frozen in that block of ice was *not* the Mongrel's dead body.

"There's a dereshadi," said Dramash excitedly, "no, look! Two, no, four!" The triffons swept low over the crowd, then met up with two others. A full wing, thought Rho; someone must have been worried about the crowd getting out of hand. The cart and its frozen trophy bounced up the last steep rise to the South Gate and was immediately admitted by the guards. Everyone else was kept back, and the crowd, muttering, spread out across the ledge. Rho stopped for a moment to catch his breath. He couldn't decide if the pain in his side was real or imaginary.

<Oh, look. They've run out of spikes,> he said to Eofar, looking at the line of severed heads above the gate in Traitors' Row. <Traitors must be thick on the ground in Norland these days.>

"Why are we stopping here?" asked Dramash.

"No reason," said Rho, pulling his eyes away from the blood-and-frost-stiffened hair and gaping, snow-filled mouths. "I just thought I saw someone I knew."

<How do we get in?> asked Eofar.

<You're an Eotan and I'm an Arregador,> said Rho. <We walk in.>

They forced their way through the crowd without apology, hardly slowing when the guards moved out to block their way. The bejeweled hilt of Strife's Bane was enough to open a channel toward the small side gate and they walked straight through.

The cart acquired a new and much better dressed crowd of followers as it rumbled on through the upper city's streets. Rho found himself surrounded by familiar walls of black-streaked stone, with torches set high up so as not to burn the people crowding through the narrow concourses. They mixed in with servants in thick woolen capes carrying bundles or escorting their masters, and mid-clan soldiers in high-clan colors. He felt the presence of people who might once have been his drinking buddies: the high-clans' lesser lights who would never bother to hold a breach, or sit out a siege, or ride a triffon into a volley of flaming arrows. They wore silver ursa or lagramor or striped crag-cat fur, and every one of them had a black-bladed imperial sword strapped to his or her back. The kind of damage Dramash could do here made Rho's head spin.

"That's Arregador House, where I used to live," he told the boy, walking a little faster. "Each clan built its own house here after the Clan Wars ended. See that bridge up there? Someone dared my little brother Trey to climb it when he wasn't much older than you, and he did." And then, "Through there, all the way back, that's where the triffons—the dereshadi—sleep." He regretted this last one, because of course Dramash immediately grabbed his sleeve and tried to pull him in that direction, but luckily, the crowd blocked their way and he was able to pull Dramash past, saying, "We can't see them now because they're all going to sleep soon."

Rho had assumed the cart would be unloaded once it reached the Front, but instead they unhitched the marmont and pulled the cart straight through the gates and into the castle. Rho kept Dramash as close against his side as he could as they followed the cart bumping up the shallow steps toward the throne room. He found himself looking for Kira in spite of himself, but there was no sign of her—but of course, she had probably left Ravindal altogether by now, especially if she thought war was coming. She was barely competent with a sword, and he remembered joking with her that if she ever went to war, she should go as a spy. She had taken the remark more seriously than he had intended, assuring him that she would have made a very good spy.

<Get out of the way,> Eofar called out, pushing closer and closer to the cart. <Make way. We need to get through. Make way!>

By the time they entered the throne room, they were right behind the cart. A woman in the uniform of captain of the Eotan guards led a phalanx of her command toward it. Rho briefly wondered what had happened to old Kurt, the nemesis of Ravindal's children for as long as he could recall—he and his friends had victimized the man by throwing nuts at him, trying to make them ping off his helmet.

He could feel the presence of several people at the back of the room, back by the throne, but the torches had not been lit at that end and all he could make out were a few glowing shapes.

<You need to let us see that body,> Eofar told the new captain as the guards tried to herd the crowd back with limited success.

<Why is that?> she asked. Her gritty presence scraped like the bottom of a boot. He couldn't imagine anyone throwing nuts down on her.

<Because we've stood as close to the Mongrel as we are to you now,> Eofar told her. <Do you want to know if it's really her, or not? How do you know Josten Drey isn't playing the emperor for a fool?>

She didn't trust him, but Rho could feel something deeper underneath, something naked and a little bit desperate. The moment she stepped out of the way, Eofar strode toward the block of ice while the guards kept everyone else back. Rho had little choice but to pull Dramash along after him.

The frost had been scraped away and the ice was remarkably clear. Inside lay a woman with gray skin, black hair and an eyepatch. She had the long, muscular limbs of a Norlander, and a revolting collection of scars on her face and one of her bare arms.

<It's not her,> Eofar announced. <It's well done—very well done—but that's an imitation. That is not the Mongrel.>

Rho could feel the outrage of the assembly behind him like the yowling of cats thrown into a sack. A chorus of denials and demands for Eofar to prove it battered into his head.

Eofar went over to the wall and grabbed a broad-axe from a display of weaponry.

<Stop!> commanded the captain, drawing her sword and running forward to stop him.

<What the hell are you doing?> Rho asked as Eofar sprinted back to the cart. <It's not her. You already told them.>

<I obviously have to prove it.>

<Stand down, Captain Vrinna,> said the emperor from the distant throne and she stopped dead, raising a hand to halt her guards as well, but they kept their black-bladed swords pointed at Eofar. Rho heard the sound of claws scrabbling against the stone flags just before two drooling hounds with flaring, black-rimmed nostrils melted out of the darkness and loped toward them. Rho pushed Dramash behind him.

Eofar pulled down the back of the cart and leaped up onto the platform, then he swung the broad-axe and sank the blade deep into the ice until it stuck fast. Chips flew into the air as he worked it free again, then he struck at the block once again, twice, three times . . . By the last stroke he had chopped out a wedge close to the corpse's neck. He changed the angle and struck sideways. A chunk broke away near her face and he stopped and rolled his shoulders, giving his arms a moment to recover.

As the emperor came toward them out of the darkness, his dogs bounded back to him and craned their necks up for a scratch from his bejeweled fingers. Rho had not seen him since before Trey's death, but he had pictured "Emperor" Gannon many times since then: covered in his brother's blood as he walked away through the trees.

<If you had killed the Mongrel and you intended to cart her frozen body around to prove it . . . > Eofar tailed off as he drew his knife and chipped away near the face, bit by bit, until he could reach in and pull chunks away. Her flesh had stuck in places and came away with the ice. <Why would you,>—he slashed through the cord of the eye-patch and slowly peeled it back, as if he was paring the loose skin from a piece of ripe fruit—<leave her eye-patch on?>

Two silver eyes, both the same. Eofar slammed down the axe into the block of ice one final time and left it there.

<What did I tell you, Captain Vrinna?> said Emperor Gannon, slapping the woman on the back and radiating a sense of triumph as hot and bright as a burning bridge. <My witch hasn't been wrong yet, has she?>

<No, your Majesty,> said Vrinna.

The guards at the front of the cart moved out of the way for the emperor as he circled around it. The dogs paced behind their master, panting and slobbering, but no one else moved. Suddenly Gannon put his shoulder under the shaft and tipped the front of the cart up. The wood creaked and the ice-block slid off and crashed to the floor, scattering people out of its way as it shot forward like a runaway sledge. It finally smashed into the doorframe and the ice cracked in half along the fault Eofar had already made. The imposter's frozen flesh cracked along with it, splitting apart until bone and muscle came poking out.

<That's that, then,> said the emperor, sweeping them all up in his churning, grasping eagerness as he pulled the axe from the ice. <Some cut-rate cut-throat thought he could cheat me out of my legacy.> He brought the blade down with more force than Eofar had been able to put behind it and dug another cleft into the unknown woman's torso. Jellied blood stuck to the axe when he pulled it back. He brought it down again, and again, until he had hacked the body in half, and then he turned his attention to the head and neck, striking over and over again until he had mashed them to a pulp. Finally sated, he threw the axe aside and the ear-splitting clang of the heavy blade striking the stone floor startled the crowd as if from a trance.

The guards pushed them back and out of the throne room until they were able to close the doors on them.

<I told you, my day of glory is here; the army of the cursed is on its way,> the emperor told the captain, sending ice shards spinning away over the floor as he stalked back to her. <I want Eowara's tomb opened tomorrow. Tomorrow, understand? Arrest anyone who tries to interfere. The gods want me to take Valor's Storm. I must have it before Valrig rises. Rho Arregador.> The imperial

notice swung at last to Rho, as heavy as the axe he had just wielded. <You're back from the Shadar.>

<Your Majesty.>

<You look more like your brother than I remembered. What do you think, Kira?> he asked as another figure swept forward out of the darkness. <Looks like Trey, doesn't he?>

<Very like, your Majesty,> Kira answered. <So alike, I didn't even recognize him.>

Kira.

Rho's memory had been kinder to her than she deserved. Her eyes sat further apart than he preferred, and her neck wasn't nearly as long or as graceful as painted by his imagination.

<Shame Trey had to die like that,> said Gannon.

Rho bit back his first thought: that it was a shame they'd never know if Trey would have lived if they'd brought him to a physic. The emperor's attention had already turned to Eofar anyway.

<I don't know that sword. Who are you?>

<Eofar Eotan, your Majesty.>

<Eonar's son? From the Shadar?> Gannon studied him. <You have the Eotan face, all right.>

Rho watched the white fur of Kira's robe move softly against her arms and throat as she drifted toward him. The torchlight lent a warm glow to her deep-colored jewels. She looked different, but that wasn't all; the more startling change was the hollow core where her heart had been. She was like green-glass, glittering and prettily wrought, but with nothing at the center; put her close to a flame and she would melt into nothing. He pushed deeper, trying to peel back that shiny veneer of affectation and found nothing but more of the same.

<What's that furry thing you're hiding behind you?> Kira asked, referring to Dramash, who was still squashed up against the back of Rho's legs. <Is it a person, or an animal? Oh, it's a boy. At least, I think it is. That coat makes him look like he's been swallowed by an ursa. Oh, this can't be the boy who destroyed the Shadar, can it? But he's no bigger than a mouse!>

Her knowledge of events caught Rho off-guard, as did her flippancy. <You already heard what happened in the Shadar?>

<Deserters from your garrison,> the emperor informed him. <Why did you bring the boy here?>

Rho waited with his heart pounding, hoping that Eofar had worked out what he wanted to say. They would never get a better opportunity than this one.

<A gift, your Majesty,> said Eofar. <He's my gift, to you.>

<What? What are you doing?> Rho asked Eofar in dismay, only to have a mental door slammed when he reached into his friend's mind to find out what he was thinking.

Eofar went on with hardly a pause. <I came to ask for troops to retake the Shadar from the rebels who killed my sister Frea and burned down half their own city. I won't need very many. The Shadari are a cowardly people for the most part, and very poorly armed. All they really had was the boy.>

Rho felt like he was going mad. He must have hit his head somewhere; or this was another nightmare and he would wake up to the sound of his hammock scraping against the iron rings.

<Let's see him,> said the emperor, rubbing his hands together like he had just been served a meal. <Make him do something.>

Eofar came and knelt down beside Dramash. "That man is the emperor, Dramash. Just stay quiet and calm and do what I tell you."

<What are you doing?> asked Rho.

<Trust me,> said Eofar, drawing his sword and laying it on the ground in front of Dramash. "Move the sword."

"No." The boy looked up over his shoulder at Rho. "I can't."

Rho swallowed. "You only need to move it a very little."

"No," Dramash said again, shaking his head at Eofar. "I don't want to. You can't make me."

<Problems?> asked Gannon, and motioned two of his guards forward.

<Eofar,> Rho warned as he grabbed the back of Dramash's coat. He wanted to draw, but Fortune's Blight would be no good against a dozen or more imperial swords. <Eofar, *do* something.>

The first guard flew thirty feet across the room and smashed into the wall. Then the sword ripped out of the second guard's hand and fired straight up to the ceiling as if shot from a bow. Rho pulled Dramash back as everyone else jumped to avoid the tumbling blade. The rest of the guards darted forward to surround them, but Dramash ripped every one of their swords away the moment they came close. The guards shook their stinging hands in shock and watched speechlessly as their weapons slid out of their reach.

Captain Vrinna charged forward, but her sword pulled her hand down as if its weight had increased ten times. She managed to force herself forward a few more steps before falling to the ground along with her weapon.

"Dramash," Rho said, but he wasn't sure the boy could even hear him. Tears were running down his cheeks, wetting the fur into clumps. Rho dropped to his knees and raised his voice until he could feel the burn in his throat. "Stop, Dramash. Stop now."

Emperor Gannon drew his own sword, only to have it whip his arm around in the opposite direction. He hung on doggedly, but he looked like he was trying to drag a lagramor out of its hole by its tail.

"Dramash," said Rho, "it's all right. No one's going to hurt you. You can stop now." Then he saw two guards armed with steel swords—not imperial swords—rushing toward them.

<No! Stop!> Rho shouted to them, but of course they weren't listening to him; their only purpose was to protect the emperor at all cost. Rho did the only thing that he could think of. He stripped off one glove and pressed his bare hand down on Dramash's neck.

The boy screamed in pain and Rho felt it like a spike straight through his head: a single, sharp pitch that made every Norlander in the room double over and clap their hands over their ears. He kept his hand on Dramash's skin, telling himself that the flesh of his palm was *not* singeing and peeling away—which was how it felt—and that the pain would stop when he finally pulled his hand back.

Dramash slumped to the floor in a dead faint and Rho staggered back with his stomach heaving and his hand on fire, struggling to keep from joining him on the floor.

<Get that boy out of here,> the emperor ordered. He sheathed his sword while the stunned guards scrambled to retrieve their own weapons. <Send him to the tower with the witch. Tell her to get him under control, or I'll make her sorry.>

Rho did nothing to stop the guards as they picked up Dramash and took him away. He didn't even watch them go, and he couldn't look at Eofar either. Instead, he bent down to pick up the glove he had dropped and carefully pulled it back on. Kira had taken shelter on the far side of the cart. Despite her heaving chest, the emotions he sensed from her still had no depth; she remained the same shallow, reflective puddle she had been from the start.

<Your Majesty,> Rho said to Emperor Gannon, <if you don't need me any longer, I'd like to see my brother's tomb.>

<You can go,> he said, waving a hand, already turning away. His coat—hundreds of lagramor pelts, like a whole swarm of the vicious little beasts—billowed out behind him as he headed for the doors to the throne room. The dogs were summoned back from where they had been chewing on the mangled body, clicking into step behind their master's heels. <Come with me, Eofar. You can tell me more about how you lost my most important colony to a bunch of sweaty miners.>

Rho pulled up his hood and went back out into the gallery, down the steps and outside, drawing no attention at all from the crowds still lingering there. He had expected to be followed, and he had expected someone to call to him as he headed down the steps to the Front, but he did not expect the hand now on his shoulder to belong to Eofar.

<What have you done?> Rho asked him, seizing the front of Eofar's coat.

<I had to—you saw the way Gannon hacked up that body. You heard him talk about fighting the cursed. He thinks he's the new Eowara. The Shadari's powers won't stop someone like that from trying to get back the colony; he'll just want to fight them that much more.>

<All right, so maybe that wasn't so stupid,> Rho admitted, releasing him. He walked down a few more steps, then stopped and asked Eofar, <So, what now, then?>

<I'm going to be Eofar Eotan for a while. I want to find out more about this prophecy before we go any further. I'll find a way to get Dramash back.>

<You're going to talk to Gannon and the other Eotans?> Rho asked. <Without me?>

<Yes,> said Eofar, raising himself up. Now he was more like the

haughty governor's son Rho had known in the old days and less like a used bar towel. <I am still an Eotan and you're merely an Arregador. Plus, I don't think our new emperor likes you very much. Is there a problem?>

<No,> said Rho, even though he did have a problem; he just couldn't articulate it.

<Is there some place you can go?>

<Arregador House,> said Rho. <They'll give me a room—and enjoy adding it to the bill I left unpaid when I went to the Shadar.>

<I'll come and find you there,> said Eofar. <Just promise me you won't do anything stupid in the meantime, like trying to rescue Dramash.>

Rho looked out over the black Front, at the cracks in the rock glowing faintly from the mists far below. <I won't. I wouldn't even know how.>

<Just trust me,> said Eofar, before he trotted up a nearby set of steps and strolled into Eotan Castle as coolly as if he had been walking in and out of those iron-banded doors every day of his life.

Rho realized his biggest problem was the degree to which he trusted Eofar. Which was not at all.

Chapter 14

Kira found Aline waiting in the gallery, holding her cloak.

<What happened?> Aline asked as they made their way outside and down onto the Front. <They're saying it's not the Mongrel after all.>

<It isn't,> said Kira, pulling her gloves straight as they headed back through the crowded streets toward Arregador House. <Josten Drey lied, or was tricked. He's probably dead by now; I would guarantee Vrinna saw to it personally.>

<Then there really is going to be a war with the cursed?> Aline blanched. <*Our* cursed?>

<I don't know. I can't make myself believe the cursed are really going to rise out of the ground like a bunch of raggedy mummers.> She stopped at a crossing to let a cart rumble past. <If it does have something to do with our people, I can't warn them now. Vrinna will be watching me even more now that Rho's back. I don't know what to do next.>

<Why would Lord Rho change things?> asked Aline, shivering under her wool cloak.

<That sounds like the beginning of a riddle,> said Kira. <Well, for someone who can't be bothered about anything, he has an uncanny knack for turning up at exactly the wrong time, blundering into the middle of things that have nothing to do with him and blithely ruining everything for everyone. But the real reason is that if he starts hanging around me, Vrinna will undoubtedly

try to make Gannon think that Rho and I are lovers. Come to think of it, I *do* know what to do next. We're going to Trey's crypt. We're going to rid ourselves of Rho Arregador, and right now.>

They walked down the curve of Vine Street and through a series of little courts where the green-glass casters, book-binders, goldsmiths, stonemasons and other artisans occupied themselves adorning and amusing those of her station. People gathered inside and in front of the workshops, but few were working, or even pretending to work. Kira lifted her chin as she felt them staring at her and added a little sashay of unconcern to her walk. She needed Rho to meet the same person he had just met in the throne-room: the emperor's empty-headed mistress, unconcerned in anything outside of her own shallow interests. She had played her role well enough to fool these people; after three years without a word from him, she was certain she could fool him as well.

The green-glass statue of Arregador, complete with pine-bough wreath and an armful of drooping branches, watched them approach from a niche above the entrance of the crypt. Kira glided up the steps behind Aline, her feet already numbed with cold. A supply of tapers waited just inside the entrance, but a light was already flickering far back in the corner, near Trey's tomb. The crypt wasn't very large—the building itself dated from just after the Stonewood Treaty, like most of the buildings in Ravindal, and had been intended only for those few Arregadors who, for whatever reason, could not be buried in the crypts on their family estates. Even so, the Arregadors couldn't stop jostling each other out of the way in the service of their ambitions, and in angling for the most prominent positions, the placement of their tombs made it look as if someone had dropped them in this haphazard way and then forgotten to come back and arrange them properly.

They made their way inside, winding slowly around pillars, tombs and sarcophagi, breathing in the smell of cold stone, frost and lamp-oil. Kira let her fingers slide over a stone arm here, a carved cheek there, noticing how the decorated lids became less and less ornate the further back they went.

<Wait here,> she told Aline as she stopped next to a plain, square tomb where a husband and wife slumbered sweetly with their

arms around each other's waists. She went on alone until she walked into the circle of light from Rho's lamp, which he had set down on the crossed hands of the effigy on the next tomb over.

<Did you have a funeral?> he asked her, without lifting his eyes from the face of the effigy on his brother's tomb.

<Oh, yes. Gannon paid for it, and for the tomb, too.> Kira took off her gloves and hood and tossed them down by the lamp. <We had a procession all the way up from Ravinsur. Everyone came out. Well, nearly everyone. You know how *some* people just can't be bothered, don't you?>

<It's a rotten likeness,> said Rho.

<Well, the sculptor did the best he could,> Kira said, loosening her coat at her throat, even though cold bled from the stone all around her. <I've never been much good at describing things. Now if *you* had been there, you could have done it much better. You would have remembered what Trey looked like before the accident. I could only imagine how he looked the last time I saw him.>

<It doesn't matter, since it's empty anyway,> said Rho. He leaned against the lid and dug out a bit of dirt from a crevice with his fingernail. He was pretending to be the same old Rho and was apparently unaware of how miserably he was failing. She had already noticed the circles under his eyes in the throne-room, and the sag of his shoulders looked more like fatigue than his former indifference. <I know we both have regrets about what we did, but—>

<How perceptive of you, to know *my* regrets.> Kira walked toward the wall past the foot of Trey's tomb and looked up at a blackened torch in an icicle-bejeweled bracket. <I had to guess at yours, but since you were already on a ship heading to the other side of the world by the time I woke up the next morning, it wasn't too difficult. Unless you discovered them through my letters? You did receive my letters, didn't you? I'm sure you did, though I expect your weighty duties in the Shadar kept you from answering them.>

<Did you tell Trey?> asked Rho. She could feel him shrinking behind her until he was little more than a floating point, like a beacon in the far distance.

<No. I didn't think it was important,> said Kira, still facing the wall. <We didn't exactly invent infidelity, did we? It happened. It was over. You were gone.>

<Then Trey never knew why I left Norland?>

<I said I didn't tell him,> said Kira. Trey's words came back to her, slippery with his wet blood: *I think you owe me that much.* <I didn't say he didn't know.>

For the first time she felt Rho's true grief, and how desperately he wanted to keep it from her. She turned back around and saw him standing with one hand braced against the tomb, holding it back, as if he expected it to slide right over him and crush him. Already she could feel him seeping back into the Rho-shaped hollow he had left behind: an older, sadder version of Trey. The trapdoor keeping her secrets hidden away strained against its latch, but she layered it over with frivolity—banquets, blouses, pelts, perfume—until she felt ill, like she'd eaten too many sweets.

<So, are you and your Eotan friend going back to the Shadar?> asked Kira. <I would, if I were you. All anyone here cares about is the cursed. Every day it's something new. Now Gannon thinks he has to open up Eowara's tomb and get Valor's Storm. Ravindal is no fun any more.>

She clung to the grooved edge of the tomb as he straightened up and came around toward her. The change in him showed even more from close up; either he had aged more than he should have in the last three years, or he had been through something truly awful.

<Why are you talking like that?> Rho asked her. <Are you playing some kind of game with me? Are you trying to punish me?>

<I don't know what you're talking about. I'm just trying to give you some sisterly advice.>

<You're not my sister,> said Rho, but he backed away again to the corner of the tomb. <You and Gannon—is that true? I never pictured you with someone like him. I didn't think he was your type.>

<What do you mean: rich and powerful?> She ran her fingers along the line of the necklace at her throat as she wandered away among some of the nearby tombs. <Yes, it's past understanding, isn't it?>

<Is that why you're in such a hurry for me to leave?> asked

Rho. <You must be afraid I'll get in your way. You've moved on. Is that it?>

<Me? I haven't moved anywhere. I'm right here where I've always been,> said Kira, standing up a little straighter and adjusting her coat over her shoulders to hide the flush crawling up from her neck. Her chest burned like all the air had rushed out of the room.

<Stop it, Kira.> Rho came straight at her, and it felt as if the tombs shifted out of the way to let him pass. The movement brought the scent of him—unremembered until this moment, but now perfectly recalled—along with a hint of the sea, and something else, something hot and threatening. <I don't know why you're acting like this, but you're not fooling me, so just stop it, because I don't think I can stand it any more.>

<No one asked you to,> Kira shot back. <Just the opposite, in fact, so why don't you go, and leave us to get on with things here?>

<Things like this?> He hooked his fingers underneath the collar of her coat and pulled out her necklace. It was the only one of Gannon's presents she genuinely liked: red calipsets surrounded by emeralds. Aline had warned her about the clasp just that morning and now a broken link pinged to the floor and bounced out of sight, leaving the necklace dangling from Rho's fingers like a bird with a broken neck. <I'm sorry. I didn't mean to do that.>

<Never mind,> said Kira, backing away from him so she could circle around the tomb in the opposite direction. She could still feel the touch of his fingers against her throat and suppressed a cough. <It's not important.>

He worried the links of the necklace between his fingers for a while before answering her. <I want to go. I can't wait, to be honest. But I have to get the boy back first.>

<That little Shadari boy? Do you need his powers for something?>

<No. I . . . I killed his mother.>

<His mother?> Kira started, genuinely confused. <What, in battle?>

<No. I mean I murdered her,> said Rho, facing her across the tomb. <I cut her throat, for no reason that's worth explaining now. But I'm responsible for Dramash, and I can't leave without him.>

<Rho, you *murdered* someone? I don't believe it. You're the last person who would do something like that.>

<Then I guess there are a lot more murderers out there than you thought,> said Rho, pacing away toward the main part of the crypt and leaving a sickly swathe of remorse behind him.

She couldn't swallow past the sudden lump in her throat. <Then you should get the boy and go. You don't want him here when the army of the cursed attacks.>

<There is no army of the cursed,> said Rho, stopping between the tombs just inside their circle of lamplight. The darkness was creeping up on his heels. <I don't know what Gannon really saw, but you can trust me on that.>

<Why do you say that?> asked Kira.

<Because there's no such thing,> said Rho.

<Oh, really?> Kira asked archly, hoping to disguise the sudden pounding of her heart. <Have you been reading a different *Book* from the rest of us?>

<No. I don't really care what it says in the *Book*. I know someone who lost her arm in the Shadar after they tried to burn her to death. She would have been set out if we'd been in Norland. When she showed me her wound after it had healed I knew what I was *supposed* to feel. I just didn't feel it. I *knew* she wasn't cursed. She's no different from anyone else, except that she has a lot more courage than just about anybody I know; and that includes Gannon Eotan.>

Words scrabbled around inside Kira's head like mice in a sack, climbing over each other and gnawing at the seams to find their way out. Telling Rho about Trey was not an option; something not even to be considered.

<Where are you going?> asked Rho, as she took up her gloves and hood.

<Oh, I'm not leaving because of what you said,> she said, putting her back to him so he wouldn't see her hands shaking as she put on her gloves. <It's dinner time.>

Aline slipped out of the darkness as Kira came past and they retraced their steps through the crypt and out into the dark gray of the Norlander evening. Kira walked along in a daze, trying to blank that distressing conversation out of her mind, at least for the time being, until she had time to think through what it all meant. The task of *not* thinking required so much effort that she saw nothing except Aline's back until they walked around to the front of Arregador House and came up against a group of people blocking their way.

<I don't want to speak with anyone right now,> she told Aline, even more adamant when she recognized the lofty personage of Exemplar Orina and the smug members of her retinue, newly returned from the forests, judging by their bloodied hunting clothes. <Just keep going.>

<Lady Kira,> Orina called out as they passed. <Just the person I wanted to see. Can you come to my quarters, please? There's something I need to discuss with you.>

<If you don't mind, Exemplar, I'm not feeling very well.> For once, pretense and reality matched seamlessly. <I suspect it was lunch. What was that horrible yellow stuff? Oh, never mind, I forgot you weren't there. I'll join you as soon as I've quite recovered.>

<It's *important,* Lady Kira,> Orina pressed.

<Then I certainly want to give you my full attention,> said Kira, angling herself closer to the door, <which I'll be able to do much better after a little rest. Don't bother sending someone for me. I'll trot on up in a little while.>

The door-warden opened up at her knock, and she avoided speaking to anyone else as she and Aline swept through the halls into their poky little corridor. Aline opened the door for her.

<Where's your necklace?> asked Aline, as she whisked off her coat and other things. <You were wearing the red one. Did the clasp break?>

<Yes. You warned me about it, too. I should have known better.> Kira crossed to her dressing table and dropped down onto the stool, but she shut her eyes when her wavy reflection in the glass made her feel dizzy.

<You're not well, my Lady,> said Aline, hurrying over. She began pulling the jeweled pins out of her hair, and Kira felt the gentle thump of the braids uncoiling down her back. <You should get into bed. You need to rest.>

<I can't rest now,> said Kira, even as her body felt like it was pulling her toward the bed. <I have to think. I can't go back and warn Trey, not with Vrinna on top of me, and I'm going to have a hard

time staying close to the emperor if Rho keeps making a nuisance of himself. Everything's gone wrong at once. I wish we could go back to the way everything was before he got here.>

<Nothing was very good, then, either. Remember?> asked Aline.

A knock came at the door. Aline hesitated, but she left and came back a moment later with a note. Kira took it from her and tossed it down on the table without opening it. She didn't need to read it. Gannon's interview with Eofar must have ended satisfactorily, so now he was whistling for her as if she was one of his smelly hounds. And like them, she would obey. She had allowed the collar to be placed around her neck of her own free will; whingeing about it now would not loosen it.

She handed the pins back to Aline and straightened up to have her hair re-dressed.

<And you'd better bring me a different necklace,> she said. <The orange one, I think. It's his favorite, after all.>

Chapter 15

Isa stared blankly down at the lines and shapes on the Nomas' map, then rotated it until the waves of blue—the most obvious landmark—lined up with the sea sparkling to her left. She had always imagined that when she left the Shadar it would be over the sea, sailing toward the gray Norlander horizon. She had never once imagined going the other way, into the desert. The desert meant death for people like her.

Bitter anger kept her going at first, and she embraced its dark vigor. She hated Falkar. She hated Binit. She hated Daryan for letting her leave, but she hated herself more for going.

The landmarks on her map were few and far between and the glare made her eyes water, but if she missed one rock formation, trench or crude shelter, she'd be flying into a barren death-trap. Soon everything hurt. She felt like a piece of fruit bruised past wanting and then tossed aside. At the first oasis, which was little more than a circle of stones around a deep well, Aeda flopped down in the hot sand and whimpered so pathetically that Isa nearly gave in and turned around. Then she thought of the humiliation of crawling back now and got the triffon back in the air.

She flew on and on, fighting sleep as the sun sank slowly toward the horizon. She might have even nodded off at one point, because the second oasis never appeared. She tried to ignore the panic raking its claws through her chest as she checked the landmarks on the map, but the landscape would not arrange itself to match. She was on the verge of retracing her flight path when the smudge of color she had been watching in the distance eventually resolved itself into a stack of huge red boulders sheltering a tiny oasis. She *had* missed the second one, but miraculously, she had found the third. They landed by the bank of the spring-fed pool and after Isa fumbled her way out of the straps and buckles, she stumbled to the water and finally collapsed, lying there soaked to the skin until the sand turned gray and the air chilled around her.

Aeda had made herself a meal of something feathery by the time she dragged herself out of the water. She found the stores the Nomas had buried underneath a marked rock, but she couldn't make herself eat. She put a box of journey-biscuit and some dried meat into her saddlebag, and returned the rest.

She had already taken her last two pills, though she didn't even remember swallowing them.

Her wet clothes stuck to her skin as she looked up at the stars. She had spent many dull hours in her cot in the ashadom staring up at the dots on the ceiling, but no meaning had ever emerged. Even the Shadari no longer remembered the names of their gods, so how could she have hoped to make any sense of their markings? She listened to the silence of the vast desert around her and imagined how little trace she would leave if she were to die here: just bones in the sand.

She slept heavily and without dreaming, but the world she woke into felt less real than most dreams. The air had no scent. The light had no color. The textures of the water, the sand, the rocks, and the tall grasses were indistinguishable from each other. She had left her senses back in the Shadar, along with everything else she had ever cared about.

Two more days passed the same way, flying from oasis to oasis under the constant fear of losing her way. A thin scab had formed over her heart by the third day so that she was no longer in danger of bleeding out with every breath.

At sunset on the fourth day she caught up with the caravan. From the air, she could see nothing of the town except a fuzzy haze and a few shining spots that turned out to be little ponds reflecting the setting sun; as she got closer, the haze resolved into the town of Marshmere: a collection of crude wooden buildings clustered together at the mouth of a slow-running river. The Nomas had set up camp a little way from there, on the edge of reed-infested marshland. She brought Aeda down at the edge of one of the ponds, crushing the tall grasses and startling a flock of spotted brown birds into flight, but she just sat in the saddle, lacking the volition even to pull herself out of the harness.

She braced herself for a mob of Nomas men bristling with difficult questions, but the few who came out to meet her said little, and took charge of Aeda without being asked. Maybe they felt the invisible barrier wrapped around her, separating her from everything except the pain in her arm. She fumbled under her cloak before remembering her pouch was empty.

A large man with shaggy blond hair came forward as she swung down from the saddle. Four days of constant riding had stiffened her so much that the sand pulled at her feet like cement.

"You probably don't remember me, Lady Isa. My name's Behr," he said, speaking Shadari; many Nomas did not speak Norlander, and the rest only did so when they had no choice. He bent back the reeds so she could come out onto the path. "I'm the wagon-master."

"Is Lahlil here?" Isa asked.

"I think she's in her tent," said Behr. "I'll take you to her."

A few of the men nodded to her as the wagon-master led her through the tents, but no one asked any questions. The camp had a hush to it that matched her mood so perfectly that she began to wonder if she had brought it with her. Men walked together with their arms over each other's shoulders, or stood in small groups besides the stands of stiff reeds, but hardly anyone was speaking, and not a single child ran through the streets between the tents.

"In there," said Behr, pointing her to one of the striped tents, and left.

Isa didn't want to go in. She didn't want to tell Lahlil or anyone else what had happened, because telling would make it more real, and right now she wanted to believe she had dreamed it all and could still wake up.

She heard someone huffing loudly behind her and stepped aside. The Nomas woman's eyes were swimming with tears and her face was so blotchy from crying that at first Isa didn't even recognize her. But Mairi didn't notice her either; she walked right past her and pulled the tent flap aside with enough force to shake the whole structure on its supports. She left it open just wide enough for Isa to see inside.

"What are you doing here?" Mairi demanded, directing her words to the shadowy figure inside the tent. Lahlil had her back to the entrance and was methodically placing the items laid out on the bed into a large traveling pack. It looked like the possessions she had excluded from consideration had been flung all around the room, and some of them had been smashed or torn up, maybe deliberately. A cradle sat in the corner next to a rocking chair, but both were empty. Lahlil looked better than Isa had ever seen her—the loose sleeves of the Nomas blouse hid the mess on her arm, and the new eye-patch was a definite improvement over the old black one—but the invisible bandages wrapped around her emotions had come loose and released something jagged, like a snapped bone poking out from a broken leg.

Mairi said something in Nomas; Isa spoke little of the language, but thought it was something like, "*Now* you're leaving?"

"Not yet," said Lahlil.

"You should be with him. He wants you."

"What are *you* doing here?" Lahlil returned with just as much force. The sound of her voice scraped at Isa's throbbing nerves like sandpaper. "You should be with him, trying to cure him."

"Cure?" Mairi's mouth hung open. "Sweet Amai, I thought you understood. I can't cure this. I've never seen anything like it in my life."

Isa wasn't understanding much; she had no idea what they were talking about.

"There has to be something you can do," said Lahlil. She ran a knuckle along the scar at the corner of her mouth. "All those things you have, all those medicines. They must be good for something."

"I know how to splint legs, deliver babies, take fishing hooks out of arms. If there were any Norlander healers still in the Shadar, I'd say take him there. They could at least see what it's doing to him. But the truth is, I don't even know where to start."

"It's killing him," said Lahlil. "Start there."

"You're not listening—"

"You're just not trying hard enough. You—"

Mairi slapped Lahlil's face as hard as she could, but Lahlil didn't move, not even to raise her hand to the burning spot on her cheek where the healer's fingers had marked her. Isa could feel the ache of it pulsing through her.

"Don't you dare—*dare*—say that to me," Mairi said with her teeth clenched tight. "I grew up with Jachi. He's as near a brother to me as anyone, *and* he's my king, and you—" Her mouth twisted up and she swallowed hard, apparently unable to continue. Then she left, holding her breath as if she couldn't bear the stench, again walking right past Isa without noticing her at all.

Isa went into the tent.

<Isa,> said Lahlil, looking up as she entered. She went back to packing as if Isa's presence had hardly registered. <What are you doing here?>

<Is something wrong with Jachad?> she asked.

<Some kind of sickness.> Lahlil placed a small stack of folded cloths in the bag. <He came down with it yesterday.>

<Is he going to be all right?>

Lahlil's emotions burst out in a single flash of white flame and immolated the tent and everything in it, including the two of them, to an ash so fine that it hung in the air like a cloud. Isa wet her lips as if she could feel the ash settling on her face.

<No,> said Lahlil, and placed a wooden spoon in the sack.

<What kind of sickness?> Isa asked, watching her sister thrust in items one after another.

<No one knows,> said Lahlil. <He has a black mark over his heart.>

The tent's stripes appeared to undulate as Isa reeled and she looked for something to hold on to before she fainted, finally shaking the whole tent when she grabbed hold of one of the supports.

Lahlil looked at her at last. <What's wrong with you?>

Isa said, <I know what it is.>

The pack in Lahlil's hand dropped to the bed. <*What?*> Then, <What did you say?>

<It's poison—someone in the Shadar has been poisoning ashas the same way. That's the reason I'm here.>

<*Poison.*> Lahlil repeated the word as if it meant nothing to her. <What do you mean, "poisoning ashas?">

<I mean, I think it only works on them, otherwise it would have killed me too.>

Isa drew back as Lahlil threw the pack aside and ran out of the tent, leaving her to follow behind in an exhausted, stumbling run as her sister loped down the sandy paths. The stricken looks and aimless pacing of the Nomas made sense now, as did the crowd Lahlil forced her way through to get to Jachad's tent.

"Where is it?" Lahlil shouted to the people inside. No one paid Isa any heed as her sister barged around, bending down to look under the little table, then bumping into the desk with her sword and knocking the scrolls to the floor. Then she turned to the desk, and when she still didn't find what she wanted, she darted to the corner and began rummaging through the neatly piled bags and trunks.

Jachad sat propped up in bed with a loose tourniquet circling his left arm and his hand supported by cushions, while blood dripped down from his forearm into a wide bowl. Mairi had just come back in herself and was pulling a stool up to the bed. A lancet glinted from the folds of a cloth in her hand.

"The wineskin," said Lahlil, "the one we drank from yesterday—where is it?"

"What's going on?" asked Jachad, trying to sit up until Mairi pushed him back into the cushions.

Lahlil continue to rummage, ignoring the stream of golden lentils pouring from a sack she'd tossed aside. Finally she uttered a strangled cry and turned around with a small wineskin in her hand. A smudge of yellow chalk marked one side.

<I know that mark,> said Isa, stepping forward. <It's the same.>

"Isa! Sweet Amai, girl, where did you come from?" Mairi cried.

"The wine was poisoned," said Lahlil. "Magic users—it only kills magic users. Someone in the Shadar has been using it to get rid of the ashas. You see? *That's* why it affected Jachad and Callia's baby, but not Callia or me."

"Lahlil," said Jachad. He began to rise, but the moment he swung his legs over the edge of the bed his eyes rolled and he crashed back down again. His elbow caught the edge of the bowl and flipped it over, splattering the striped tent wall with his blood.

Mairi cried out and jumped across to him. “Everybody get out!” the healer screamed at them.

Isa grabbed her sister’s arm and hauled her outside.

<You have to come with me back to the Shadar,> said Isa, ignoring the stares of the Nomas men all around them. <We have to find out who’s doing this and stop them. Daryan can’t do it alone. He needs our help.>

<Stop them?> Lahlil’s words flew at her with the flaying force of a sandstorm; in the middle of the whirlwind Isa saw the flash of revolving steel and the answering spray of blood: so much beautiful destruction. <There’s nothing to stop. They’ve already done it.>

Mairi came out of the tent, fists clenched, eyes aflame. “What was that all about?”

“Get Jachad ready,” Lahlil said to her. “I’m taking him to Norland. There’s a healer there, someone I trust . . . she can cure him.”

Mairi just stared in shock as Lahlil turned to Isa. <You came on a triffon, didn’t you?>

<You can’t fly a triffon all the way to Norland,> said Isa, <and you can’t have Aeda. I need her to get back to the Shadar.>

<I only need to get to Prol Irat—I know someone there who can take us the rest of the way. A strider.>

<But the striders are all dead,> said Isa. <You killed them all. Everybody knows that story.>

Mairi shook herself and, deliberately switching the argument back to Nomas, said, “Then go and get your healer and bring her back. You’ve got your brains in a knot if you think Jachi can go anywhere in his condition.”

“It would take too long,” said Lahlil, seething with impatience. “It’d be at least a week, if I could get her to come at all.”

“If you’re going to shout at each other out here,” said Jachad, appearing in the doorway of his tent with a fresh bandage on his wrist, “do you mind if I join you? It’s a little hard for me to hear from in there.”

Mairi and Lahlil glared at each other.

“How long do I have, Mairi?” Jachad asked her.

The healer twisted a lock of her tangled blonde hair. Then she said, “If we keep bleeding you . . .”

"Days? Weeks?" Jachad persisted. The forced jauntiness in his voice made Isa's throat ache.

Mairi's face screwed up. "Jachi, don't . . ." He said nothing, only stood waiting patiently. After a moment, she rolled her shoulders and wiped her red eyes with her sleeve. "A few days, if we keep bleeding you. And I might be able to make up a draft to help you breathe better. But this is ridiculous—I won't allow it, Jachi."

"Do we have any other ideas?" His voice rose as the cracks began to show in his brave façade. "Because I don't really want to die, to tell you the truth, and if I can't avoid it, I'm guessing Prol Irat or Norland is just as good a place for it as Wastewater."

"Well, you're my king, so I can't stop you," said Mairi. "You can do what you like, even if it means dying in some frozen ditch somewhere, away from everyone who loves you—" She squeezed her eyes shut and lowered her head for a moment, but when she raised it again her face blazed with anger. "What about Oshi? You can't take him with you, Lahlil. I won't let you."

"I know. I'll take care of it," said Lahlil. "Moonrise—we can't wait any longer, or we'll lose the light."

"What do you mean, you'll take care of it?" Mairi demanded.

"Mairi," said Lahlil, much too quietly, "leave it alone." She took off back down the sandy path, Isa in hot pursuit.

<Wait, Lahlil. You can't go to Norland.> Isa darted around a spindly dead tree and stood in front of Lahlil, ignoring the stinging insects landing on her hands and buzzing in her ears. <Come back to the Shadar with me. We'll find out who gave Jachad the poison and make them give us the cure.>

<There's no time for that,> Lahlil told her, trying to brush past.

<You're coming with me!> Isa felt any chance she might have had for reuniting with Daryan slipping through her fingers, and in desperation, she slammed her palm into her sister's chest and shoved her back. <I swore I would bring you back. I *can't* go back to the Shadar without you, do you understand?>

Lahlil's left hand curled into a fist and her right hand slid in toward the hilt of her knife. Isa stepped back in a cold flush of fear. Her sister could end her in a heartbeat. But then Lahlil gave a weird little shudder, like someone just waking up, and looked at

Isa with her head cocked to one side as if she had just recognized her.

<You left Daryan?> asked Lahlil.

<I had to do something,> said Isa, freezing the tears behind her eyes before they could fall. <Things have been bad there. He's been having a hard time keeping everything under control. Now someone is murdering the ashas—the Shadari are defenseless without them, and there's nothing Daryan can do.>

<Why come to me?> asked Lahlil. <Why didn't you stop it yourself?>

<They're already using me to tear him down,> said Isa, <and they don't even know what I am to him. The Shadari might love me for killing Frea, but they still hate me for being a Norlander. If I can fix this—if I can save the ashas—they'll have to accept me, won't they?>

<Unless the ashas are already dead,> said Lahlil bluntly.

<That's correct,> Isa shot back, refusing to be daunted. <I can save them, if they're still alive.>

<No. There's another way.> Something snaked through Lahlil's words that made the hairs on the back of Isa's neck stand up. <I'm not going back to the Shadar, and neither are you. You're coming with me to Norland.>

Norland. The word came at Isa as hard and bright as a polished blade, and it cut right into her. The stump of her left arm flinched, and hot shame bubbled up from inside it.

<You know I can't go to Norland,> she said.

<You need ashas and I know where to find one,> said Lahlil. <The Shadari who first brought the ore to Norland—she's still there. The emperor's kept her locked up all this time.>

Isa sucked in a breath of the marshy air. <How can you possibly know that?>

<She's the one who gave me the divining elixir. You can rescue her and bring her back to the Shadar.>

<You think she could help Daryan?>

<Help him,> Lahlil said slowly, <or replace him.>

Replace him. He would be free. They would both be free. <But my arm—>

<—won't be a problem, not where we're going. You'll soon see you're not the only Norlander with scars.>

Isa stood very still, listening to the hiss of the reeds brushing against each other in the breeze.

<I'm going to get the supplies we need from Behr.> Lahlil started off down the path. Without turning back, she repeated, <We leave at moonrise.>

Mairi came out of Jachad's tent carrying a bowl full of blood-stained bandages. She kept her head down and would have walked past again if Isa hadn't stepped out in front of her.

<I need more pills,> said Isa.

<Your arm?> asked Mairi. Her eyes narrowed. <You shouldn't be in pain still.>

<I can still feel it burning.>

<Show me,> said Mairi, unbuttoning Isa's cloak. Isa had left in her old shirt, and now Mari undid the knot on her sleeve and pushed it back until the stump was exposed. She turned away from the sight of the violet, puckered flesh.

<No infection.> Mairi muttered something to herself in Nomas that Isa didn't understand. <You say you're still experiencing pain—and the pills were helping?>

<Yes,> said Isa. <Can you make them stronger?>

<I'll try.> Mairi buttoned her cloak back up. <I'll make you up some more before you go. You should get some rest in the meantime. You've got a long journey in front of you. I don't envy you, I'll tell you that. I think you're all heading straight to perdition.>

Isa didn't mind going to perdition; the sooner she got there, the sooner she could come back.

Chapter 16

Lahlil walked through the camp looking for Behr, but every time she tried to think about the supplies they would need for the journey to Norland, the memories of that last argument with Cyrrin locked up her mind like rust on a wheel's axle. She had been living in Norland with the other outcasts for five months: that was already longer than she'd stayed in any one place since she'd left the Nomas . . .

The clearing was only a short way through the tunnel in the briar, but ice had already stiffened her fur coat and the cold was scorching her lungs. She paced around the ancient statue, cataloguing its particulars: a sexless body, a mound for a head, twin pits for eyes. Snow filled the basin where people had once burned their sacrifices.

Trey was waiting for her answer. Heavy snowflakes fell around him and settled on the hood and shoulders of his patchwork furs and on the shining hilt of Honor's Proof. Darkness drifted from him: smoke, and storm clouds, quiet as the forest around them.

<You have forty-eight people,> said Lahlil, watching as the snow blurred the jagged crenellations and broken towers of their mutual home. <Five can't walk; three can't see; seven are low-clan and have never even held a sword; five are too old to fight; three are children. You have one archer with a bad bow and worse arrows.>

<We have you,> said Trey. <Lord Valrig's army will rise if you'll lead us. I know it.>

<I don't serve Lord Valrig.>

He took out the copy of the Book *that he had been carrying when he was injured; he never went anywhere without it. Lahlil had watched him pore over it for hours when it was their turn to wait at Onfar's Circle for new outcasts to bring to Cyrrin. Now she watched him flip the blood-stained leaves to a particular page.*

<I don't need to see it,> she said.

Trey gripped the book with one hand and tore the page from the binding. She knew how he felt about the Book*; she might be jaded, but for him it must have been like tearing off a fingernail.*

<Here,> he said, pushing the page into her hand before the snow could wet the ink. <Take it. Keep it with you. You know what it says. He's claimed you, whether you like it or not. You have no choice. That's why you didn't die. Why I didn't die.>

She folded the page and slid it into the sleeve of her coat.

<We can't go on like this,> said Trey, as the grachtel swooped by him and alighted on the top of the statue's head. <You know it. You can see this place for what it really is, can't you?>

<Trey—>

<Can't you?>

<You know I can,> said Lahlil, staring down at the statue's faint shadow. <It's a prison.>

They sensed Cyrrin coming even before her approach flushed a flock of silver birds from the treetops and filled the air with cries like a chorus of rusty hinges.

<I knew you'd be out here plotting,> said Cyrrin, leaning heavily on Berril's shoulder. Scarlet pain bled through her words, staining the snow at her feet.

<You shouldn't have followed us,> said Trey. <There's no point. You weren't born high-clan—you were never a warrior. You can't understand what it's like.>

<This is all her fault,> Cyrrin said, as if Lahlil wasn't standing right there. <You were here three years before she came, without any of this. You were doing better. You were settling in.>

<I was dying. You just didn't want to see it.>

Lahlil swallowed back the taste of blood: the cut on the corner of her mouth had cracked open again. <I'm not going to attack Ravindal,> she said firmly. <I'm not going to lead an army of the cursed, or any other kind. I'll fight to protect the people here if it ever comes to that, but that's all.>

Trey fixed her with his silver eyes. <But protecting people isn't what you do, is it? People hire you to destroy their enemies, not protect them. Destruction and death: that's what you were made for.>

<Stop it, Trey.> Cyrrin rocked in the snow and nearly fell, but Berril locked her skinny arms around her, brace and all, and held her up. <Dress it up in your pious nonsense all you want but what you really want is revenge: common, ugly revenge.>

<What I want is to pull it all down,> said Trey. The words snapped off one by one, like icicles from a ledge. <I want to pull it down and see what crawls out of the rubble. I want to see what happens when everyone *has scars. So do you, Lahlil. I know you can see it, too. That's because it's part of you.>*

He was right: she could see it. She could see the towers and walls crumbling and sending an avalanche of stone through the streets of Ravinsur and rumbling through the warehouses, mansions, and towers. She could see the beacon toppling, scattering fire across the Front as it fell, and the plundered wealth of a hundred nations trammeled underfoot by the panicked mobs. She could see ten thousand mangled bodies groaning beneath the rubble, begging for the mercy of death.

She could do it. She could pull it all down. She was the Mongrel.

<Trey,> said Cyrrin, <leave us alone.>

He hesitated for a moment, then he dropped his gaze, crossed the clearing and disappeared into the briars.

Berril helped Cyrrin walk up to the statue, where she looked up into its staring eyes. She scooped a bit of snow out of the basin and let it fall in a wet clod at her feet. <What do you think those long-gone Norlanders expected to get for their sacrifices? Death for their enemies? Favors? Protection?>

<I don't know. Whatever they wanted, I guess.>

<I used to want things,> said Cyrrin. <At least, I remember wanting things. Now I just want to survive until tomorrow, and keep as many of these people alive as I can. I've only ever wanted one thing for myself since I came here. One thing.>

The grachtel took off into the trees.

<I thought you just needed more time,> said Cyrrin. <I thought you'd find something here to live for, the way the others have. But you . . . you're tearing us apart, Lahlil. I've pretended not to see it for too long. You're not like the others; you can survive out there. If you want to go now, I won't stop you.>

Lahlil felt an unfamiliar pull in her chest. <I never said I wanted to go.>

<You know what else you never said?> asked Cyrrin, her words as brittle and sharp as broken glass. <"Thank you.">

Lahlil found Behr over by the goat pens and gave him a list of what they would need. He listened attentively, suggested a few substitutions, and recommended a few more things they might find useful. Then she headed back through the silent camp to finish her packing. No one plucked a harp or puffed pipe smoke into a wedge of lamplight. No voices bubbled up in laughter or song or impassioned conversation.

She found Callia in the rocking chair. She was still very pale, but she had put on a clean dress and had brushed her hair into its usual glossy waves. She had Oshi in her arms. Something about the way she was holding him reminded Lahlil of someone in a swollen river clinging on to a tree root to keep from being swept away.

"He's tired," Callia warned her as she came closer. "That's why I brought him back. I'm just trying to get him to sleep. Then I'll go."

"Let me have him," she said, and Callia took a moment to fuss with his blanket before handing him over. He started to cry as Lahlil cradled him against her shoulder and she gave him her finger to clutch in his tiny hand. An ember not quite dead somewhere inside her glowed as he fit snugly into the space in her arms, but Callia looked small and lost without him.

"I'll go back to my tent now." Callia tilted her head and stuck out her chin, like always, but her dull eyes had none of the playful mischief Lahlil had grown accustomed to seeing there. "Or did you want something? You're looking at me funny."

Lahlil stood still for a moment, just breathing. "When a Nomas takes something from someone else, they're supposed to pay it back, aren't they?"

"I don't owe you anything," said Callia with a dismissive wave. "The only thing I ever got from you is your bad temper, and you can have it back any time you want."

"I meant it the other way."

Callia pursed her lips. "You don't owe me anything. What happened wasn't your fault. Everybody says so, even Mairi."

"I know they do. I'm just not as sure."

"Of course you would think it had something to do with *you*." Callia snorted a little, a bit more like her old self, and rocked back in the chair. Lahlil found the sound of the runners hissing against the carpet oddly soothing. "Everything always has to be about you. You're like a little sprat who thinks everyone else disappears when she shuts her eyes. We don't, you know. I'm sure you'll be surprised to know that our lives go right on happening, even when you're not around."

"I'm going away."

This took Callia back a little. "So you finally made up your mind. Where to?"

"Norland. I'm taking Jachad to a physic there."

"Norland? What about Oshi? Don't tell me you're taking him with you?" asked Callia.

"I'm not."

"Then what–?" she started, then tears started pooling along the lower lashes when she finally realized what Lahlil was trying to tell her. "Oh." A long silence stretched out before Lahlil took Oshi from her shoulder and knelt down beside the rocking chair.

"I'll look after him properly," Callia said as she took the baby from her arms. "You don't need to worry. He'll be fine until you get back."

"I know."

Callia suddenly reached out and put her delicate hand on Lahlil's leg. "You are coming back, aren't you?"

The easy lie was right there in her mouth, like ashes on her tongue, but she couldn't get it out.

"Well, you'd better," said Callia, turning away. "I have a lot of limericks to teach you before the sea calls me back again."

By the time the moon rose over the swamp, Aeda's saddlebags had been loaded and they were ready to go. Lahlil waited outside Jachad's tent while Mairi fussed over him. When he and Mairi came out, the healer had hardened her face into a glare that reminded Lahlil of the little stone fetishes the Thrakyan soldiers carried around in their pockets to ward off evil spirits.

He's dying. No matter how many times she said it to herself, the words still didn't make any sense. Dying happened suddenly, with screaming and crying and pointless appeals. Jachad smiled at her, and his blue eyes held all of the things he wasn't saying. Whatever was left of her own stoicism crumbled away, leaving her fear exposed in all its stark shapes: shadows etched by lightning.

"You're sure about this?" Lahlil asked him.

"No," said Jachad, giving her a crooked grin. "Not even a little."

Mairi handed over the bag of medicines and repeated the same instructions she had given to Lahlil three times already.

A corridor of men led from Jachad's tent to the waiting triffon, and most of them tried to smile and offer words of encouragement as they passed. Hands clapped Jachad's shoulders as children crowded around their fathers' legs, sat on their shoulders or rocked in their arms. They had no idea what any of this meant, but their faces betrayed the anxiety their fathers were trying so badly to conceal for the sake of their king.

Jachad teased and joked with them, blithely agreeing with all of the happy plans and celebrations proposed for when he returned and promising to bring back snowballs and icicles. His courage made Lahlil so angry that she could have spat vitriol up to the heavens, at Shof himself.

"Please bring him back to us," Behr whispered to her. "I don't know what will happen if we lose him. We've never been without a king before—never. How could Shof let this happen?"

Callia had come out too, and was waiting near the triffon with Oshi in her arms. Jachad kissed her round cheek, then kissed the baby's head.

"Take care of each other," he told them.

" 'Said the deluge to the dewdrop,' " Callia said with a wink.

Isa waited in the saddle, already strapped in and impatient to go. As they walked toward the triffon, Jachad leaned closer to her and said, "So that was the elixir's prediction—that's why you took Oshi, so you could give him to Callia. That's it, isn't it? It's all over."

"Yes," said Lahlil, as something inside her quietly shattered, "that's all over."

Chapter 17

Rho sat in a chair in his room in Arregador House. It wasn't a comfortable chair, but he had fallen asleep in it anyway. He dragged his eyes open to see a glowing fire and a small boy curled up under a blanket in front of the hearth. The boy appeared to be sound asleep. Something inside Rho that had been pulled as tight as a fishing line went slack, and he closed his eyes again, allowing his body to sink back into the chair's fragrant pine-needle cushions.

Dramash was safe.

Just a little more sleep, and then in the morning they would go back to the *Argent* and sail away—but not back to the Shadar. They would go somewhere peaceful; somewhere where Dramash's murdered mother wouldn't bleed into Rho's dreams.

When he woke up properly a short time later and looked at the hearth, he found his dirty woolen cloak piled up in front of the firescreen. If he squinted and turned his head to one side, it *almost* looked like a sleeping child.

Rho bolted up out of the chair, cursing his stiff muscles as he limped to the window—typical Arregador ostentation, putting a window in a poky little closet like this—to see how long he'd slept. They'd given him a room at the back of the house with a commanding view of the slopyards, topped by the snow-dusted wall of Garrador House just to the north. He could see a flicker of light: the smiths were building up their fires, so dawn couldn't be far off, then. He had wasted the whole night waiting for Eofar, and he still didn't know if Dramash was all right—he was probably hungry and cold and frightened and confused.

The change of clothes the Arregador house-warden had given him lay on the untouched bed. He stripped off his ship-worn rags and after breaking the thin crust of ice in the ewer he scrubbed himself down, hoping to shock his mind awake with the cold water. He dried off in front of the fire and dressed as quickly as he could.

When he dragged the chair closer to the fire to pull on the borrowed boots, Kira's broken necklace slid across the seat cushion. He caught it just before it hit the floor.

No one had called him "my Lord" in three years. He had not had a real bath, or eaten meat fresh from the hunt, or drunk decent wine, or walked across a room without breaking into a sweat in all that time. He had almost forgotten that particular Ravindal scent: the deep notes of woodsmoke and furs, cut through with the sharp tang of the hot springs and the pungent sap of the thawvine. For three years he had not slept on a pine-needle mattress, or worn fur, or spoken to a servant without opening his mouth like a gasping fish—and now all he wanted was to take Dramash and get as far away from Norland as possible. He tossed Kira's necklace down onto the table, only to find that he'd been squeezing it so hard it had left its impression in his palm.

He jumped as a knock sounded at his door, and it swung open and banged against the wall before he had a chance to ask who was there.

<Finally,> said Eofar. <All these hallways look the same.>

Rho grabbed his arm and yanked him into the room with so much force that Eofar spun like a top across to the other side and crashed into the wall.

<Where have you been?> Rho demanded, slamming the door shut again. <I've been waiting for you all night.>

<I'm so cold.> Eofar dropped his hood and gloves onto the table and moved closer to the fire, tracking dirty slush across the floor. <Why didn't you tell me it would be so cold here? It feels like my bones are cracking.>

<You're drunk again.> Rho shut his eyes for a moment, trying to stay calm.

Eofar held his hands out to the flames. <I've been with the Eotans.>

<All night? Did you meet every one of them individually? What about your tainted bloodline?>

<Yes, about that.> Eofar's silver-blue eyes glowed a little brighter, but blackness dripped out of him like tar. <That was all just court politics, just like Frea said. My father's ambitiousness apparently worried Emperor Eoban, who decided to send him away. Eoban told my mother that story about our tainted bloodline to keep him in the Shadar. They were very surprised she even believed it. Some of them thought that was very funny. Emperor Gannon, for instance.>

<So the story that destroyed your family and drove Frea to madness was all someone's idea of a joke,> said Rho. <Yes, that's very funny. Exactly the kind of harmless little prank I'd expect from the Eotans.>

Eofar slouched in the corner and closed his eyes.

<Here, come away from there,> said Rho, pulling at him and wincing as the wings of Strife's Bane's silver triffons scraped along the wall. <When can we get Dramash and leave? This whole trip was obviously pointless. We're not going to be able to stop Gannon from invading the Shadar. Let's go while we still can.>

<We can't leave now,> Eofar protested, falling into the chair Rho had pushed in front of the fire. <The cursed are coming.>

<Not you, too? You can't believe that story. Not after what you know, and what you've done. In any case, the Mongrel—Lahlil—isn't coming to Norland, not in a block of ice, nor on a triffon, nor riding a chariot made of pudding. She's with the Nomas, taking care of your son.>

<Well, Gannon believes it.> He stroked the ruffled silver fur on his sleeve back into place. <Now that he knows the Mongrel's body is a fake, he's going to open Eowara's tomb and get Valor's Storm. He said we would all go and "knock on Valrig's door." I've noticed he's not a patient man.>

<The exemplars will never let him open that tomb,> said Rho. <Going down into the deep places goes right against the *Book*.>

<Yes, they will. Everyone else is so afraid of looking like a

coward in front of Gannon that they're lining up to go down there with him. I might go myself.>

<That's a very bad idea,> said Rho instantly.

<Who are you to be squeamish? High-clan or not, you were a guard in the Shadari mines once.>

<Not *in* them,> Rho pointed out. <That's why we had overseers, so we wouldn't have to go down there ourselves.>

<That's right,> Eofar remembered, <we gave them quotas, and if they didn't meet them, we beat them. Sometimes they died, but that was all right, because it taught the others a lesson. Now I can look around here with pride and think about everything my family did to help build all this.>

His false levity was underscored with a bitterness that turned Rho's stomach. <If we're not leaving and you won't let me rescue Dramash, then what *are* we going to do?>

<You know how the succession for the throne works, don't you?>

<Of course I do,> said Rho. <The highest-ranking Eotan in Ravindal takes over until someone higher comes back to challenge them. That's why that pompous ass Betran Eotan is always here instead of out campaigning. He thinks he owes it to Norland to be here while Gannon's children are gone, so the throne doesn't fall into the "wrong hands.">

<I told you Eoban wanted my father out of the way because he was too ambitious, didn't I?> Eofar went to the table and picked up his hood and gloves. The steadiness of his walk made Rho wonder if he was drunk at all, and that worried him even more.

<Yes, I remember. So?>

<So, do you want to know what I kept thinking tonight while I sat in the Great Hall of Eotan Castle with my fellow clansmen, under the ribs of the leviathan killed by Lord Onfar himself?> A blue flush crept up Eofar's neck as he pulled his gloves back on. <"This is what I always wanted." All of us, really: Isa, and Frea, of course. Maybe even Lahlil. I finally have what I've always wanted. I can drink all night and complain about how useless the servants are because they take too long to carry hot water up three floors to fill my bath. I can spread rumors to destroy another family because they lent me money I can't pay back. I can tell stories

about the funny, stupid foreigners, like how during the siege of Castastan, the women threw their babies into the moat so they wouldn't have to watch them starve to death. It's all just like I dreamed of when I was a boy.>

<Eofar, I have no idea what you're talking about,> said Rho, trying to swim up through the noxious pool of emotions. <What's your plan? Do you even have one? What about Dramash? We can't let him stay a prisoner—he's just a little boy.>

<I'm working on a new plan that will solve all our problems,> said Eofar, pulling down his hood. <Just stay clear of me for a little while and let me do what I need to do.>

Rho watched Eofar leave, rudely leaving the door open behind him, before he could finish sorting through all the objections that were piling up in his mind. He shivered as he stood regarding the blank stone wall across the way until Eofar's meaning finally cracked its way through his thick skull: if the ambitions of Eofar's father had worried Emperor Eoban enough to prompt that underhanded banishment, then he must have been much closer to the throne than anyone in the Shadar ever realized . . .

<Eofar? Wait!> he called out, dashing to the door, <I know what you're thinking—>

<My Lord, can I speak with you?>

Rho stumbled in mid-stride and then adjusted his shirt over his shoulders to reclaim a little of his dignity. He found a small woman—a girl, really—standing in the hall. He had the impression she'd been waiting there for some time.

<Who are you?>

<Aline, my Lord. Lady Kira's hand-servant.>

<Oh, I see.> He checked over his shoulder, but Eofar had already disappeared into the darkness. <What does *she* want?>

<Please, can you come and see her?>

<See her?> Rho echoed, walking back toward her. <What, right now? It's not even dawn.>

<Yes, my Lord.> Aline lowered her head and moved a little closer to him, like she wanted to tell him a secret. <She needs you.>

<She told me to stay away from her.>

<She didn't mean it.> Aline said it as a statement, but he caught a little tail of doubt toward the end.

<I think she did. She practically spelled it out in the snow with sacrificial entrails.>

Aline said, <She changed her mind. Please come, my Lord.>

Rho looked over his shoulder. Eofar was probably halfway back to Eotan Castle by now. He'd never catch up with him.

<All right. I'll come,> he told Aline, and started down the hallway in the direction of Kira's spacious apartments in the north wing before she called him back.

<It's this way, my Lord,> said the servant, gesturing in the opposite direction. <I'll show you.>

Rho had to walk fast to keep up with Aline's quick steps. He paused for a moment when they reached the gallery that overlooked the hall below, where he and Trey had always come when the feasts below grew dull, or the fire too hot. No fire burned now, and the tables and benches had all been pushed to one side. Torches burned on four of the pillars, throwing off just enough ruddy light for him to see Eofar striding down the length of the hall to the door that the door-warden sprang up to open for him. He had told Rho to stay clear, and he was in charge.

<My Lord?> Aline called urgently, turning back to him.

<Sorry, I'm coming.>

She led him onward, though he was surprised when she pushed on past the posh apartments in the main part of the house and into the same sort of utilitarian wing where Rho had lived alone after Trey and Kira had married. They had just turned into a cold, plain corridor when Aline suddenly stopped and motioned him back.

<What–?> he began, but she cut him off with a wordless warning. A woman in Arregador colors was waiting by the third door along.

<That's Exemplar Orina's hand-servant. She must have just come,> Aline fretted.

<Then I should come back later.>

<No!> Aline said, forgetting herself and seizing his sleeve. <No. Come this way instead.> She pulled him back a few paces and opened a door he had never even noticed, then led him down an exceedingly narrow passage, around a corner and then into

another cramped hallway with doors on either side. Four doors along, she pushed the handle and led him into a dark little room with a bed and not much else. In the opposite wall was another door, shut tight.

<Aline—>

<The exemplar won't be here long,> Aline promised. <My mistress will take care of that.>

She waited a moment to collect herself, then went out into the main room, leaving the door partially open behind her. Rho could feel Kira's presence as she took note of Aline's entrance, and then she found him there, brushing by his mind with a wordless warning to stay back. He remembered Orina; he had always found the exemplar to be a haughty, self-righteous bore.

<But Exemplar,> Kira said to her guest, her tone implying no hint of anything amiss, <you over-estimate my influence on the emperor. I can't get him to do *anything*. I can't even get him to keep those smelly dogs of his out of the bedroom—there's nothing quite so bad as an old, unwashed animal too close to a fire, is there? Speaking of which—you're not too hot there, are you, Exemplar? Aline, why haven't you brought the exemplar any wine?—and you expect me to convince him not to open Eowara's tomb? He was buzzing about it all night, like a boy on the eve of his Naming Day.>

<But surely *even you* can understand how all of this is hurting our clan?> Orina asked. <He's brought back most of our troops already and he's left the mercenaries in charge. Order is breaking down in all the colonies. We'll either lose our holdings completely or we'll have to invade them all over again. It's a catastrophe.>

<Oh, yes, I can see how that would be terrible for you. If those people in the colonies start dying again, you won't be able to tax them. No, no. I wish I could help; I really do.>

<Maybe Lord Rho can assist you?>

<Rho?>

<Yes. Weren't you with him last night?>

<Rho? Last night? Oh, you mean in the crypt. I remember now. More like evening than night, because I remember wondering what we'd be having for dinner.> Kira's bland concern and vapid curiosity even in the face of such an obvious threat couldn't

possibly be real, but Rho kicked himself for not leaving the tomb the moment she turned up. He knew how rumors started, and this one would be very bad for her if it got back to Gannon. <Is there something odd about me visiting Trey's tomb with his brother? Other than the fact that it's empty, of course. Maybe that's odd to you, but I don't see the difference. It's not like anyone ever looks inside them. Your husband is dead, too, isn't he, Exemplar? You've never looked inside his tomb, have you? He might not even be in there, for all you know. Maybe it's empty. Maybe there's someone else in there! Wouldn't that be funny?>

<Lady Kira—>

<Anyway, if we send all the soldiers back to the provinces, what happens when the Mongrel and the cursed come for us? If there's no one here to fight them, we'll all be chopped up and roasted. Don't the cursed eat people? Or is that the Scathrings?> Rho couldn't see from where he was hiding, but he heard a great deal of rattling. <I'm sorry, Exemplar, but I haven't had my breakfast yet and I'm famished. Cake? No?>

<Not everyone believes the cursed are coming at all,> said Orina. <Some people believe Gannon is so nostalgic for the glory of the battlefield that he's finding signs where there are none. He may be destroying the empire for no reason at all.>

<In that case, all you have to do is find someone to kill Gannon.>

<What?> Orina's shock sliced at Rho straight through the wall of Aline's room. <That's not what I meant!>

<Oh, I know,> said Kira, <but of course you're right. If Gannon really has invented this whole business with the cursed just to give himself something to do, then killing him will stop it, yes?>

<Lady Kira, you shouldn't—>

<Oh, but I just remembered, if Gannon dies before his daughter gets back—she's still stuck on those islands, apparently, what are they called? Beetlehead? Bucklehead? I don't remember—or his son, then Betran Eotan will be the next emperor, and he's one of those people who thinks the Stonewood Treaty was the worst thing that ever happened to Norland. Onraka's elbows, can you imagine what would happen if he were emperor? He'd kick everybody out of Ravindal except the Eotans and start the clan wars all over again.>

<Betran *was* the next in line,> said Orina. <I heard that drunkard who arrived yesterday from the provinces—Eofar Eotan—is next in line now.>

Of course, gossip like that would have spread like a mattress fire, and yet Rho had still been the last to know. He would have banged his head against the wall if he hadn't been so afraid of making a noise.

<No!> Kira cried in astonishment. <Eofar? Well, then that's perfect. You and the other exemplars should have no trouble controlling a provincial rube like that once you've killed Gannon. You're not leaving already, Exemplar? You're sure you don't want any cake?>

Orina declined and rattled off some obligatory words of thanks for the interview. Rho saw the big emerald ring on her finger flash as she headed toward the door.

<Well, good night!> Kira called after her. <I mean, good morning! I'm going to bed now, so for me it's either, or both, really. Goodbye! Yes, that's better. Goodbye!>

Kira collapsed into her chair as soon as the door closed and Rho felt her weariness like a weight on his chest.

<I knew they were thinking about assassinating Gannon,> she told Aline. The complete shift in her tone and manner stopped Rho with his hand against the door. <I wonder who they were going to get to do it? I can't imagine any Norlander willing to face the punishment that would come in the After-realm for murdering the emperor. Maybe they were going to use the Mongrel, since she has the impertinence to be alive and breathing. Gods, that would fit the prophecy, wouldn't it? Well, let's hope I've put them off. I've always suspected Orina to be a bit of a coward, anyway; she won't do anything if she thinks it'll blow back on her. Rho, are you going to skulk around in my hand-servant's closet all morning, or did you have some other reason for coming? What is going on here today? Did I leave a sign outside announcing new visiting hours?>

Rho came through the door.

<What are you doing here?> asked Kira.

<What am I—? You sent for me.>

<No,> said Kira, <I most certainly did not.>

<Then you didn't send Aline to get me?> he asked, with the familiar sinking feeling of having been duped.

<No, I didn't.> Kira pushed herself up out of the chair to face her servant. <Aline, not that this isn't cozy, but would you be kind enough to explain what this is all about?>

Rho could feel the defiance leaking out from between the cracks of the girl's modest demeanor, though what she must once have considered a good idea had apparently lost some of its luster.

<I was just . . . > Aline tailed off and twisted her hands together.

Kira went over to her and patted her back. <It's all right. Whatever you were thinking, I'm sure you meant it for the best. Just tell us.>

Aline pointed at Rho. <Since he's already a murderer,>—the girl stopped and took a deep breath, looking at her mistress with determination—<I think he should kill the witch.>

Chapter 18

Kira felt Rho's horror on the other side of Aline's pointing finger and wished the ceiling would just fall in and crush them all.

<You've made a terrible mistake, Aline,> she said, stepping in front of Rho and pushing the girl's finger down. <Just don't say anything else. Lord Rho has better things to do than worry about our petty little problems. I have everything in hand.>

<What is she talking about?> asked Rho.

He looked like he hadn't slept at all, and he stood in the middle of her carpet like an ursa who'd been pulled from his cave in the wrong season.

<He already said he murdered someone,> Aline said again, ignoring Rho. <He's already damned in the After-realm, so it won't make any difference to him. When the witch is dead, we can get Berril and leave Ravindal, just like you promised.>

<You told her about Dramash's mother?> asked Rho, in a voice like a pinprick.

<You did that yourself, idiot,> said Kira. The floor shifted back and forth under her feet, as if the whole house was a stack of plates about to topple over. <She was outside Trey's tomb when we were talking last night. I didn't know you'd be blurting out confessions.>

<And now you want me to murder someone *else* for you? Of course. Why not? Just one person, or do you have a list?>

<Stop it,> she snapped. <This was an error of judgment on Aline's part, that's all.>

<At least you've stopped pretending to be that simpering moron. Now are you going to tell me what's really going on?>

<No, I'm not,> said Kira, trying to hide her panic. <I'm going to ask you to get out of my room.>

<Please tell him, my Lady,> said Aline. <You heard what he said last night. He should know.>

<Aline, please, don't say any more.>

<Lord Rho's his brother,> the girl went on insistently, ignoring Kira's frank dismay. <What if you had never told me about Berril?>

<Did you say my "brother?"> Rho backed up until he collided with her dressing table, making the little things on top rattle. <Kira, I swear to Onfar, if you don't tell me what is going on *right now*—>

<It's better that you don't know.>

<Oh, is it? So, I'll just leave then,> said Rho, folding his arms.

<Your brother—> said Aline.

<No! Aline, what—?> Kira looked at the girl standing there, flushed, with one hand clutching the wooden pendant Kira had brought back to her, the one she had taken from little Berril's maimed hand. <All right. All right, I'll tell him, since you've left me no choice. Go over to Eotan Castle and find out when they're going to open Eowara's tomb.>

<Midday, is what I heard.>

<Well, please go and find out for certain.>

<Yes, my Lady,> said Aline, and shot off as if she was afraid Kira might change her mind.

Kira waited for her to leave, with Rho staring at her as if he expected her to burst into flames. As soon as the door closed behind Aline, he went to the little table where her half-eaten breakfast had yet to be cleared.

<So, there's something you want to tell me about Trey,> said Rho, <and whatever it is will explain why you and your hand-servant want me to murder a witch. Something tells me I may need a drink.>

<You never answered my letters,> Kira told him, sitting back down. <I wrote to tell you that Trey had died and you never responded. Not a word.>

<I did write a letter . . . but I threw it on the fire.> Rho lifted up the wine jug and turned it around for a better look. Trey had sent it back from one of his campaigns. It had a decorative spout made to look like the head of some goat-like creature with whimsically curled horns. <That was one of my better decisions, actually. I wasn't in the best frame of mind when I wrote it.>

<I'm not blaming you. I only want you to understand why I didn't tell you before now. And besides, I swore an oath.> Kira tented her fingers and watched the glow at the center of the fire. <I've never broken my word before. I'll just have to hope he forgives me.>

<I'm sure he won't care.> Rho poured the wine into one of her dainty little cups. <He's supposed to be cavorting in the After-realm with Onfar and Onraka. Why should he care what we do now?>

<Trey isn't with the gods in the Celestial Hall.>

<No? You think he went to the Under-realm after all?>

<He's not in any After-realm.> She waited while he took a sip of the wine, and then watched him lift up the jug for more. <Rho, I'm trying to tell you that Trey is still alive.>

He made a noise—it was a small noise, but she had never heard any Norlander make any sound like it before. He set the cup and jug back down very deliberately, then his distress swept through the room like black smoke flooding in from behind a newly opened door. Kira couldn't breathe; she hunched over in her chair and tried to wall herself off from him, but she couldn't escape the crushing pressure of his shock.

<Tell me,> said Rho at last, his hand still gripping the handle of the wine jug.

She told him what had happened that day in the forest; about how Trey had begged to be left to die with whatever honor was left to him, and how Gannon and the others had dragged her away. Then she told him about going back. Rho stayed at the table, saying nothing. He didn't move when she finished. He just stood there with his fingers moving over the glazed pottery, wiping up a few beads of wine that had dripped down the side.

<So you left him in that place and pretended he was dead,> he said at last. <You never spoke to him again.>

<I swore to that woman—Cyrrin—that I would never go back.>

<That was three years ago,> he pointed out. <You don't even know if he's still alive. What are the chances he could survive out there, living like that?>

<He's still alive. I'd feel it somehow if he wasn't. Or they would find some way to get word to me.>

The dishes rattled as Rho pushed himself away from the table. <You're going to take me there.>

<No.> Kira shrank back in the chair as he came forward and loomed over her. <That's one of the reasons I didn't tell you. I can't take you there.>

<I need to see my brother. I don't care whether or not you come with me. Just tell me where to find them.>

<Rho, please don't,> she said, standing up to push him back. <Don't do this to him.>

<To *him*? To *him*?>

<He doesn't want anyone to see him, not the way he is now.> His incredulity splashed over her like scalding water, dissolving her skin and leaving every nerve exposed. <Can't you understand? Would you want him seeing *you* like that if your situations were reversed?>

Rho stepped back away from her and she could feel him trying to leash his emotions, but he kicked the leg of the dressing table with enough force to send the items closest to the edge tipping over and rolling onto the floor.

<You just left him there?> Rho said again. <Three years—three years he's been out there, and the whole time you were here, just a few hours' ride away?>

<What else should I have done?> asked Kira. <Go ahead, tell me: what would *you* have done, O Great Rho Arregador? I'd love to know, since of course I didn't have the benefit of your wisdom at the time. I'm eager for your advice now that you've decided to take an interest.>

<I may not be wise, but I told you, I went through nearly the same thing with someone I cared about. I didn't tell her to go hide in a cave and never come out,> said Rho. <You could have found some way to help him. You could have gone somewhere with him.>

<Oh, of course! I never thought of that. I could have taken him

to some hut in the middle of nowhere, where he could spend the next fifty years listening to the wind blow.> She could no longer stand the sickly taste of her own sarcasm. <For Onfar's sake, I'd have put my own sword through him first and let the gods praise me for it. You've never really known him at all, have you?>

<Or you, apparently,> said Rho.

Kira rode out the pause, pretending to wait for him to say something more. <Am I supposed to infer something from that remark?>

<So what *was* your solution exactly? Did it have something to do with jumping into bed with Gannon? How long has *that* been going on, anyway? Is that ninny act of yours for his benefit?>

<I have my reasons,> Kira shot back.

<That's no surprise. I'd love to hear them.>

Kira's jaw was beginning to ache from clenching her teeth. <The witch has a potion that lets her see the future—>

<Shadari divining elixir,> he broke in. <I know all about it. I've seen it at work in the Shadar.>

<Then you know that one of these days she might see something about Trey and the others, especially now that Gannon has become obsessed with the cursed. That's why Aline wanted you to kill Ani, to stop anyone from finding out.>

<What does that have to do with you bedding Gannon?>

<I needed a reason to be close to him without him being constantly on his guard,> she said. <If Ani said something, I could warn Trey and give him time to get away. Not that it matters much now, since Gannon no longer seems to care *who* knows about the witch and her visions.>

<Well, you seem to be enjoying it, anyway. This little act of yours.>

<Oh, I am.> Kira watched him pace, feeling each step pounding in her head. <You'd be surprised how much you can get away with when people think you're an idiot. I haven't fooled them all, but as long as I pretend not to understand them when they insult me to my face, they can't prove otherwise.>

<I see,> said Rho, apparently more interested in the tapestry on the back wall than in the topic he had raised.

<But I was also lonely,> she drawled, using her own shame as a weapon against him, <and Gannon is an excellent lover. I hated

him, of course, but I hated myself just as much, so that wasn't much of an obstacle.>

Rho paled and then flushed in quick succession. <I shouldn't have said anything about Gannon,> he said. <It's none of my business whose bed you rumple.>

<Maybe this is what I should have done, instead.> Kira jerked her jeweled knife out of its sheath as she swung over to the dressing table. She swept her arm across the littered surface, scattering the jars, bottles, combs and pins to the floor. She tested the blade on the silk covering of the dressing table before raising it to her cheek. <It wouldn't take much; just a cut, left open to fester. Then I'd just have to wait for them to strip me and set me out, and hope that Cyrrin's people found me before the cold got to me, or before the wolves caught my scent.>

Kira stopped. It really would be that easy. Anyone with an ounce of real courage would have done it from the very beginning. Her own image stared back accusingly from the mirror: flushed, wild-eyed, hair askew. She had abandoned her husband to the care of strangers and then gone right back to her safe, comfortable life. She wasn't protecting Trey; she was keeping him trapped like a fish in a bowl so she could have some way of living with herself. The blade flashed in the firelight as she pressed the flat against her sharp cheekbone, and then pressed down harder until blood welled up in a single fat drop. A heartbeat later, a quick flash of pain burned across her face and she gasped.

Rho's dark shape streaked by in the mirror and he seized her forearm with enough force to yank her up out of the chair, then he dug his fingers into her wrist and twisted until she had no choice but to drop the knife. She sank back down onto the floor when he finally let her go, feeling the drop of cool blood running down her neck and under the collar of her shirt.

He sat down across from her, heavily, as if his legs had given out, and tossed her knife away. The perfume from a broken bottle laced the air between them with the scent of some exotic flower. Neither of them moved at all until a loud snap from the fire made them both jump.

<You weren't really going to do that,> stated Rho, as if reassuring himself.

<I don't know,> Kira responded. <If I thought he wanted me . . . But he sent me away and told me not to come back.>

<Well, you'd better take care of that cut or it will get infected whether you want it to or not,> said Rho, getting to his feet. He went over to the table and found a clean napkin, then twisted it up and dunked one end in the water ewer. He came back and knelt down beside her, close enough for her to see the beginnings of a beard on his jutting Arregador chin, and for a moment she thought he was going to clean the wound for her. Instead, he only handed her the damp cloth. <Here. If you clean it, it should heal up in an hour or so.>

She took the cloth and dabbed at the cut as he moved back to the other side of the room. The cold water stung more than she had expected.

<If you really want to protect that boy you need to get him out of here,> Kira told him.

Rho walked to the door and stared at it for a few moments. <How would I even do that?>

<Gannon is going to open Eowara's tomb today to look for Valor's Storm, so he can be the great hero the *Book* says will come forth to fight the cursed,> she said, <and provoke the cursed into attacking. No one's been able to talk him out of it. The Front will be filled with soldiers from all the clan regiments, and everyone else will either be going into the tomb or outside watching to see what will happen. It will be the perfect time for you to get into Eotan Castle. They keep the Shadari witch in the southwest tower. I can tell you how to get there through the servants' corridors. She does have a guard, though, and he has an imperial sword. I don't know how well you'll do with that old relic you're carrying.>

<If I can rescue Dramash, then I can take Ani too,> Rho offered, as she went to her writing desk to sketch out a little map for him. <She can go back to the Shadar with us.>

<Take Ani?> asked Kira. A little giddiness tickled through her at the prospect of an end to all of this, but it quickly faded. <Gannon relies on her to take the elixir for him. He'll spend his last eagle and his last breath hunting you down.>

<Why doesn't Gannon just take the elixir himself?>

<He's afraid it will kill him. He tried it on a half-dozen "volunteers" Vrinna provided for him. They all died in agony.>

Rho's bewilderment caught Kira by surprise. <That doesn't make sense. Eofar took the elixir himself. It made him a little sick for a while, but that was all.>

<Well, that's what Gannon told me,> Kira said, blinking as the lines on the paper began to run together. She felt like she hadn't slept in three years; she probably looked like it, too. <No, take Dramash away if you can, but don't try to take the witch.>

<If you say so,> said Rho. <But what are you going to do?>

<Me?> She picked herself up out of the chair and handed him the map. <I'm going to get some sleep.>

He had more he wanted to say, but all he managed was, <I'll bring your necklace back before I go.>

<You can keep it,> Kira said sincerely, as she moved the cushions around on her bed. <Judging by all the girls pining around here after you left, I'll bet you've no shortage of soft necks to put it on. Or you could sell it. It ought to be worth at least passage for two to the Shadar.>

Rho hesitated for a moment, and then walked out into the entrance hall. Kira waited until she heard the thump of the outer door closing, then she dropped down on the bed, pulled her boots off and tossed them aside. She closed her eyes and tried to think of something pleasant, but she kept imagining walking down into Eowara's tomb, going down, down and down, until she finally let the black swallow her up.

Chapter 19

After three days spent flying toward Prol Irat, Isa's skin had been chafed raw by her harness and her muscles were in knots from sitting in the same position for hours on end. Lahlil had put Jachad in the middle, where he would be safest, and taken the reins herself, leaving Isa to sit in the rear. Having nothing to do except to stare at Jachad's back made the burning pain in her stump that much more difficult to ignore.

They stopped every few hours to rest and for Jachad's prescribed blood-lettings. The Nomas king tried to make the journey cheerful, teasing them about being dull traveling companions and telling them ridiculous stories of things he claimed to have witnessed or experienced on his travels. Mairi had given him something for the pain; he used the mixture sparingly, but when he drifted off into a daze and Lahlil took the brown glass bottle from his hand, his steady decline became all too apparent.

When she wasn't watching Jachad, Isa watched the landscape racing along below. The marshes around Wastewater had given way first to plains of cracked, baked earth interspersed with islands of dead-looking grasses, then to brown crinkled hills before flattening out again to cultivated lands where tiny figures worked in vegetable patches and fields of grain. Lahlil steered clear of the prosperous port towns—they were either Norland colonies or allies—and instead took them inland where there were fewer settlements. The imperial armies had reduced many of the towns below to ruins, but people worked the scorched fields because they had no choice, and children played in the burned-out homesteads because they had nowhere else to go. This wreckage below her: this was the glorious Norland Empire. Her family had worked countless Shadari to death in the mines to make it all possible. How could she blame them for hating her?

She could make it better, though. She would rescue that asha imprisoned in Ravindal and bring her back to the Shadar, and together they would make up for the past. They would heal the old wounds, and Daryan would be free.

A storm began just after noon on the third day and showed no signs of stopping. Isa huddled in her borrowed woolen cloak and tried to keep the driving rain from getting underneath it and soaking her shirt. Despite the discomfort, her endlessly racing mind had swept her into a semi-conscious daze before a tongue of lightning sizzled across the sky, illuminating the world in one stark white flash. She was still blinking away the glow when a deep rumbling rolled through her, followed by a crack like someone had split a board just behind her head.

Aeda dipped down toward the ground and her stomach flipped. Jachad hunched over as Lahlil stood up in the stirrups and hauled on the reins, but Aeda tossed her head and reared, jerking them all backward. A cold sweat crawled over Isa's skin and she clenched her stomach muscles tight.

<It's no good. I'm taking her down,> said Lahlil, slackening the reins.

<We can't stop here,> Isa protested. She didn't dare take her hand off the saddle to slap away the hair clinging to her face. Another flash of lightning turned her sister into a stark silhouette and a gust of wind blew a sheet of cold water over her. <You said we'd reach Prol Irat before dark—we have to keep going.>

Lahlil said firmly, <We can't fly through this.>

Aeda banked and turned northwest, and as the lightning flared again Isa could just make out the treetops whipping around in the wind beyond a desolate meadow. A black ribbon snaked through the trees in the distance: the Truant River, one of the three that fed into the lagoon at Prol Irat. She expected Lahlil to follow it, but instead they spiraled down to a field where tall purple weeds crowded up to the blackened foundations of what had once been a farmhouse, landing near a stone well with a rusty bucket still hanging over it.

Lahlil jumped down from the saddle, then helped Jachad with his harness. Isa slid back the buckles on her own straps until she could wriggle out and drop down into the mud. The field had a dank smell that reminded her of an old washrag. She had taken no more than two steps before her shins cracked against the remains of a cart hidden in the tall grass. A blast of wind flattened her sodden cape against her body and bent the grass down to the ground just before another flash split the sky and ushered in another heavy roll of thunder. Aeda bellowed deep in her throat and sidestepped away through the grass.

<Get the packs,> Lahlil called to Isa as she rummaged through the saddlebags and tossed some supplies down to Jachad.

<Why do we need the packs?> Isa asked. <We're not—>A bolt of lightning streaked down toward the trees on the other side of the field and the great *bang!* that followed shook the ground. Aeda reared and stretched out her wings. Isa ran forward and tried to grab her bridle, but the triffon rolled her blocky head and then charged forward, forcing Isa to leap out of the way as the frightened beast flattened a wide swath of grass.

<I can't hold her,> she called to Lahlil. <What are we going to do with her? There's no shelter out here, and she's afraid of the storm.>

Lahlil hooked the packs over her arm long enough to wipe the water from her eyes. <We'll have to let her go.>

<Go?> Another gust of wind roared through the trees and swept across the field. Aeda crouched down and Isa could see the fear in her black eyes. She pulled the cloak more tightly around her, wishing she could block out the realization that her sister was right.

<We couldn't have taken her into Prol Irat anyway,> Lahlil said. <They have patrols.>

<What'll happen to her?>

<They usually go back where they came from when they're set loose.>

Isa approached the triffon slowly and stroked the bristly fur on her side, trying to imagine her flying back to the Shadar and landing on her favorite spot on the mountainside to dry off in the sun. She could go and live with the other triffons now and she'd be free . . . but not with her saddle on. Isa drew Blood's Pride and sliced through the straps holding the saddle in place, then shoved with her good shoulder until it slipped over the other side and rolled off into the weeds. The moment she was free, Aeda sprang into the air and almost immediately disappeared, hidden from sight by the driving rain. Isa was glad of the downpour. She didn't want Lahlil to see her crying over a triffon.

<Can we get out of this storm?> asked Jachad, speaking Norlander so he wouldn't have to shout just as more thunder swelled in Isa's ears. Another bolt of lightning whizzed overhead and she braced herself for the sound, then flinched anyway when it came. The rusty bucket rocked back and forth in the wind, squealing on its iron rod.

<This way,> said Lahlil, hoisting up the packs and leading them into the trees.

Isa forced her stiff legs to move and they formed a line with Lahlil in front and her at the back. Branches pulled at her cape and dragged across her face, sending cascades of cold water down over her every time she pushed one away. She had never been in a forest before and her inability to see more than a few yards in any direction was beginning to make her feel like the trees were closing in on her. She found herself holding her breath, waiting for them to break out again into the open, but they never did.

<See that?> asked Lahlil, stopping finally and pointing toward some rocks a little way ahead. There was an overhang, deep enough for one or two people to shelter under; it sat just under a run-off where water poured from the rocks above. <You two wait there. I need to check up ahead.>

<That will just take longer,> Isa said. <We should all go.>

<Isa, just do what I tell you.>

Isa would have continued arguing if she had not suddenly noticed Jachad swaying dangerously; instead, she took his arm and they trudged through wet leaves to the relative shelter of the rocks while Lahlil went off through the trees. She dived under the overhang, but Jachad just stood there with the rain pouring down on him, ignoring the stares of the grotesque faces that her imagination had carved out of the black trees' knotted bark. Then, finally, he let himself break down.

She had seen Daryan weep in a quiet, controlled way, but she had never seen anyone let go the way Jachad did now, as if everything he had been holding back was flowing out of him all at once. The force of his pain stopped Isa's breath, and she realized his physical strength wouldn't hold out for long; when it did overtake him she caught him, just before he fell, and half-carried him under the overhang. She sat him down in a sheltered spot where the waterfall didn't spray back, and as soon as he could manage it, he took out the brown bottle.

<It's not much further to Prol Irat,> she told him. He pushed his cowl back, panting as if he had been suffocating beneath it. His skin was pale enough that he could have been mistaken for a Norlander. <We'll find the strider soon, and then we'll be in Norland.>

Jachad gave her a tired smile. <You don't need to do that.>

<Do what?>

<Comfort me. Keep my spirits up.> He ran his fingers through his wet hair until it stood up. <I know I'm going to die—I've known it from the beginning, as soon as I saw my little near-brother lying in his basket. There's no cure for this—whatever it's doing to me can't be undone. I can feel it.>

<Then why come?> Isa asked. <Why put yourself through this?>

<If I didn't go, she'd have gone without me.> Jachad reached his hand out into the waterfall and let the water run through his fingertips. <Don't say it isn't true, because you know it is. What's easier to picture, her sitting calmly beside a sickbed, or charging off to some impossible place for a cure? If I only have a few days left, well . . . you know.>

<Why didn't you tell her?>

He responded with a little laugh, but said nothing else until Lahlil came through the trees up ahead. Just before she came close enough to hear, he said, <Please don't tell her what I said.>

<I won't.>

They got up again and followed Lahlil past a tiny weed-choked pond, over a swollen brook and then back into more woods so thick that Isa didn't even see the tower until they were on top of it. Not that it had been much of a tower for a long time, but the rectangular shape of the surviving story and the dressed stone blocks lying all around made its origin clear. Vines with brown fan-shaped leaves had obviously continued the work of pulling it all down, with tendrils insinuating themselves between the blocks until chunks had just crumbled away. The whole structure gave her an uneasy feeling. There was no roof.

<How is this a shelter?> she asked.

<Trust me,> said Lahlil, and led the way through a high-arched doorway with the hinges still dangling from the masonry, then around a corner to another doorway. This one had an iron-banded door, much newer than the stonework around it, which stood open under a makeshift porch to reveal a flight of steps already marked with Lahlil's wet footprints.

Isa halted. <Down there?>

<It's dry,> Lahlil pointed out.

"What is this place?" asked Jachad in Shadari, the language they had most in common. Isa guessed that the mental effort of speaking Norlander had become too much for him.

"Just a ruin," said Lahlil. She went halfway down and then stopped to adjust her sodden eye-patch while water dripped down from the hem of her cloak and speckled the layer of dust around her feet. "I know someone who can help us. He lives about an hour's walk away, right on the Truant. He should be able to take us to Prol Irat by boat."

Isa followed Jachad to the doorway, then the musky smell of an animal's den stopped her again. "I don't think we should wait—if it's only another hour we should just keep going."

Lahlil turned back to her. "Jachad needs to rest. You can stay up here if you're afraid to be underground."

"I'm not afraid," said Isa. She went down the first two steps, then turned and slammed the door behind her. Lahlil had left a candle burning below, though the flicking flame did little to dispel the blackness. "I just don't want to waste any time."

Lahlil took her pack and put it with the others she had brought down earlier. The space was large and divided into two rooms by a wall with a dark doorway leading from one to the next. Animal nests—mostly just bundles of sticks and leaves—took up the corners, but the creatures didn't show themselves. Their party obviously wasn't the first to take shelter there, either. There were some bits and pieces of crockery, mostly broken, a cracked knife-handle and a supply of rags smeared with some kind of oily black substance lying around.

<What is this place?> asked Isa, repeating Jachad's question as she walked out into the middle of the room, revolving slowly so nothing could creep up behind her. <Have you been here before?>

<That's not important,> said Lahlil.

Jachad had already stretched out on the floor. He pulled over one of the packs to use for a pillow, too exhausted even to put down a blanket. Isa took off her wet cloak and spread it out on the floor to dry, then waded into the vaguely reassuring pool of candlelight as her sister started rummaging through the packs. With the door to the outside shutting out the rain, she could hear every one of Jachad's painful inhalations.

<If we have to be stuck here,> said Isa, <you might as well tell me more about Ani. I've been waiting for the whole story since we left Wastewater.>

<Later.>

<What's wrong with right now?>

<Let it alone, Isa. I don't want to talk about it now, that's all.>

Isa watched her take out the lancet and the bowl, and the thought of the cuts already hashed into Jachad's forearms made her empty stomach squirm.

<Why won't you talk about it?> she pressed. <Is there something you don't want me to know?>

<There was still an open contract on the emperor's head when I left Cyrrin, so I went to Ravindal. Ani knew I'd be coming and had her guard intercept me. She gave me the elixir and I saw what I needed to do in the Shadar. Then I left.>

<And that's all?>

Lahlil began rolling up a bandage that had come undone.

<I can tell you're keeping something back,> said Isa. <The less you say, the more there is to know. There's something important you're not telling me. What is it? And don't tell me to drop it, because you know I won't. I'll hound you from here to Norland.>

<It wasn't important, just strange,> said Lahlil. An uncertainty emanated from her, something Isa had never felt from her before.

<She said I was part of something—that everything that had happened to me was leading up to something. Then . . . she told me she loved me.>

<Did you believe her?>

<Yes.>

Isa walked toward her shadow on the cellar wall, watching as it got larger and then disappeared into the general blackness. Bristly things stuck out from between the stones in no particular pattern. Isa touched one: a tree root? <Well, I don't believe it,> she said, tugging at the root and loosing a sprinkling of mortar. She turned back to Lahlil, who had gathered their waterskins and was checking them for leaks. <I don't believe there's any reason for anything. The Shadari girl who burned my arm didn't do it as part of some great plan. She did it because she was jealous and half-mad, and because I was stupid enough to let her get behind me. We make our own decisions; the gods don't make them for us.>

<How would you know the difference?> asked Lahlil.

Isa ignored the question. <The same goes for you. I don't want you making any more decisions for me; not now, and not when we get to Norland.>

<My decisions will be about what's best for Jachad.>

<As long as you know that if I see an opportunity to rescue Ani, I'm going to take it.>

<Ani has been a prisoner for forty years, Isa. She's not going anywhere in the next few days.> The waterskins clunked together as Lahlil swung them over her shoulder. <Just remember, it's Norland: you won't be able to go off on your own. You need to remember how they feel about people like you there.>

<People like *us*, you mean?> Isa stalked back across the room, watching the shadows jump as the candle fluttered. <Their hatred is what you've been fighting against all this time, ever since Father tried to set you out, but you've got it all wrong. You can never win, because no matter what you do, it will always be *their* game. As long as you're playing it, they've already beaten you.>

<Three months has taught you that?> asked Lahlil. Isa felt the shove of her disdain, like the opening move of a brawl. <I'm impressed.>

<I'm not going to let anyone else decide whether I'm worthy or

not, and I don't need anyone to heal me,> Isa declared a little too forcefully, trampling down the flush of shame she could feel crawling up her skin. <How many people has Lord Onfar healed and sent back, Lahlil? Have you ever met one? Have you even heard of one—just one—he's ever found worthy?>

<Then why put it in the *Book*?> Lahlil asked, and Isa started at her sincerity: it was the first question her sister had ever asked her that wasn't rhetorical.

<So they can blame us instead of themselves,> said Isa, seeing it all in a flash of clarity. <It's not *their* fault when we die after they've set us out: it's *our* fault for not being worthy enough to be healed.>

Lahlil just stood still, shutting Isa out with her silence. Isa turned her back and went to sit on the ground next to the candle. She watched a pool of creamy wax break over the top and slide down, hardening as it went.

<I'm going to fill these up,> said Lahlil. Isa didn't turn around, but she heard the sound of her sister's footsteps as she headed for the stairs. <Nothing's ever that simple, Isa. I've seen a lot more than you, and I can tell you what every back-alley swindler already knows: you have to let your mark win some of the time.>

The sound and smell of the rain swept in through the door as Lahlil opened it and left with the warning still hanging in the silence.

Chapter 20

Lahlil braced her back against a thick trunk and drove the soles of her boots into the tree in front of her, kicking off strips of the rough bark as the spasms had their way with her. The filled water-skins lay nearby where she had dropped them. She pushed back with her rage as the pain tried to suck her into oblivion, screaming her refusal in a silent explosion of determination. She *had* to get through this: Jachad needed her. Once he was safe, the attacks could pull her into pieces, drown her, burn her until her bones turned black, but not now; *not* now.

The fit passed.

She fell onto the wet leaves between the two trees, then pushed herself up and moved the eye-patch over. She picked up the water-skins, ignoring the fact that her hands were still shaking. The worst of the storm had ended, but water still pattered through the leaves and a ground fog limited her view to twenty paces in any direction. She meant to go back inside, but instead she found herself picking up a stick and seeking out a certain pattern in the fallen stones, then kneeling down beside them to dig. She continued gouging into the dirt even after Jachad appeared around the corner of the wall. He was hanging back, clearly thinking that she hadn't seen him even though his red hair blazed through the dripping greens and browns. She went on digging under the rock until she found the oiled-cloth pouch, then clawed it out the rest of the way with her fingers.

"Just doing a little gardening?" asked Jachad, coming forward.

"You should be resting."

"You were a long time coming back with the water. You keep telling me you have a lot of enemies. I was worried you'd been abducted by a gang of vengeful squirrels." He brushed the leaves off a nearby block of stone and sat down, ignoring the way the damp immediately started soaking into his clothes. She saw the way he tucked his hand under his thigh to resist the temptation to press it against his heart, and how he angled his body away from her so she wouldn't notice how he was straining just to breathe regularly. "So, what is it about this place that makes you hate it so much? It's obvious you wouldn't have come here if you'd had any other choice."

"This place." The ground wasn't solid enough for Lahlil's liking. She could see right through down to the cellars below, and through time as well: people slouched against the walls and lying in messy beds on the ground; glassy-eyed people dressed in scraps of stolen or out-lived uniforms, groping about in the dark. "You don't want to know."

"No, of course not; that's why I asked," said Jachad. "Since it's getting late, why don't we skip over the bit where I ask you again and you say you don't want to tell me, and then I make bad jokes until you tell me anyway?"

A laugh tugged at her mouth, but got no further. "It was a flop for mercenaries, back when the empire was pushing through all around here. I came here after I left the desert."

"I see," he said. "And that bag you just dug up?"

The knot was too tight for her muddy fingers, so she drew her knife and sliced through the string. She tipped the pendant into her hand, then looped her fingers through the chain until it hung down for him to see: a flat gold image of a flaming sun.

"I remember that," said Jachad. "I remember when old King Tobias gave it to you. Why did you bury it here?"

"I wasn't the person he gave it to any more."

"Why not? Because you were a mercenary?"

She shook her head. "We weren't just mercenaries, we were the lowest kind, the vultures. We took the jobs the regular mercenaries wouldn't do. We stole, cheated, robbed the dead and left our own dead to rot on the field."

"I see. So, this is where the Mongrel was born, is that it?"

Lahlil walked away toward the tower wall, kicking up the smell of mold from the wet leaves. The medallion swung from her hand like a pendulum.

"You were on your own," he said. "You had to survive."

"Don't make excuses for me," said Lahlil. "There was no excuse. You can't paint over the past, Jachi. It always bleeds through."

"This does look exactly like the kind of place you'd expect someone to get mystical fighting powers." He got up and followed along behind her, looking around at the broken stones, and not even pretending he hadn't deliberately changed the subject. "So, what was it? Magic mushrooms? It's damp enough for them. A gateway to a demon realm behind those trees over there?" With no warning, he coughed and fell against the tree-trunk next to him, cringing in pain.

"Jachi!" The ground whisked out from under her as if someone was pulling it up like a carpet. She held out her arms to catch him, but he put his hand up to keep her back.

"I'm all right," he said, in a spluttering voice. He coughed again, but then sucked in a deep breath. "I'm all right," he said again, a little more believably. "Sorry. Everything just stopped there for a moment. I'm all right now."

"Where's that bottle Mairi gave you?"

He pulled it from his pocket and took a sip. "I think she made this stuff out of spiders," he said, wiping the taste from his lips after he put the bottle away again, "and she didn't take the eyes out, either."

"You need to get back inside."

"Not yet," he said. She saw the way his knees were bent and knew the tree was supporting his weight. He didn't trust himself to walk yet and he didn't want her to know it. "You still haven't told me how you came to be the great warrior everyone dreads. It didn't happen skulking around in that cellar. So what's the secret?"

She leaned up against the trunk next to him and listened to the rain dripping through the leaves. "I'm not the one who made up those stories about magic and demon pacts and eating babies' hearts. No one ever wanted to know the truth."

"Which is?"

"I practiced," she said, dropping the pendant into the palm of her left hand. "That's all. When everyone else was getting drunk, I practiced. When I couldn't sleep, I practiced. When I was hungry, or tired, or angry, I practiced. You can get good at anything if you do it enough."

"I see," said Jachad. A group of nondescript birds abandoned a nearby treetop and scattered on the ground by the wall, pecking at the dirt. "Then why not get good at something else?"

"You know why," she told him.

"I want you to tell me."

"Because I liked it," said Lahlil. The truth burned in her throat like cheap drink, but she made herself talk through the pain. "I liked it. I liked the way I stopped being me when I was fighting. I could be the sword. I could be death. That's why I didn't care who I fought for, or why. I just wanted to keep fighting."

The moment for him to respond came and went and the silence that replaced it roared in her ears. He plucked one of the broad leaves from a vine that had wrapped itself around the tree and tore it in half. She could taste its foul scent on the back of her tongue.

"I was thinking," said Jachad, "that we might want to stop here."

A new fear jabbed her in the stomach. "Stop?"

"You were out of this life—really out—and now you're diving back in because of me. Remember what you told me, about how you don't get to stop being the Mongrel just because you want to? You have to practice that too, and this sure as shit isn't the place to do it."

"I can handle it. You were right. I've changed."

He caught her in his blue eyes. "Have you changed enough?"

"I'm not talking about this any more, Jachi." Lahlil didn't realize how hard she was squeezing the medallion until she felt the sharp points digging into her palm. "You're tired. You need to rest."

"What about Oshi?" he persisted. "What if you go too far to find your way back to him?"

"That's all over. I told you that at Wastewater."

"Is it? Because I think you would have said anything to make sure I got on that triffon." Jachad finally pushed himself away from the tree and pretended to stretch to hide another grimace of pain. "Besides, I'm not looking forward to getting tossed around in some leaky little boat, or my ears freezing off in Norland."

She followed him as he moved away toward the wall, catching up with him underneath a tangled canopy of ivy. "I'm not talking about this. I'm taking you inside to bleed you again before we start."

"The worst part is thinking about what's going to happen to you when I'm gone." The fog was getting thicker by the moment, crowding in on them, making their little patch of ground an island in a sea of gray. He reached out and found her hand among the wet leaves. "I can't stand to think of you alone again. I really can't stand it."

"Then stop talking about giving up," said Lahlil.

He seized her shoulders like he wanted to shake her, but instead he pressed his lips against hers like a challenge and kissed her, even more forcefully than he had that night in his tent. His fingers dug into her back and brought up the darkness churning inside her and this time she matched his ferocity, sliding her hand into his hair and yanking him closer. Some feeling she couldn't name blistered across her skin. The fog and the vines wrapped around them as they clung to each other: not for comfort, but as conduits for each other's fury.

She pulled away when she felt him weakening, wishing she could give him just one drop of the frantic energy coursing through her. "I'm not going to let you give up."

"I know," he sighed, keeping hold of her hand, "but you have to promise me something."

"What?"

"You won't let us be separated, no matter what happens."

She froze. "I can't promise that. I don't—"

"You have to say it, or I won't go another step. For Shof's sake, I don't even care if you mean it. Promise me you won't go off on your own, even if you think it's the only way to save me. Promise me: *we stay together.*"

The air in her lungs had turned to iron, but she pushed out the words. "I promise."

"All right, then. Let's go back inside."

She watched his mouth, expecting it to twitch into a smile, and waited for a gentle rejoinder or a clever retort. She didn't get either one, but before she followed him around the corner she put the pendant around her neck and tucked the gold sun into her shirt.

When they got back to the cellar they found Isa sitting in the shadows with her back up against the wall and Blood's Pride across her lap. She was asleep. Lahlil piled up the packs into a little couch and got the instruments ready while Jachad lay down.

"Do we really have to do this? I don't think it's helping."

"It's helping." She dabbed on the ointment and Jachad closed his eyes, trying not to think about the lancet coming next. She got the wide bowl ready in his lap and tied the tourniquet, then gripped his wrist so he wouldn't flinch and found a spot that she hadn't already cut into. He gasped and clenched his arm as the lancet found the vein, but he was careful not to jerk away. She slowly loosened the cord until she could hear the slow drip of his blood into the bowl, then she cleaned the lancet with the eye-wateringly pungent solution Mairi had given her for the purpose.

"Tell me a story," he said. His eyes were still closed.

"I just told you one."

"Tell me how we can be going to meet a strider, when everyone knows the striders are all dead."

"I can't talk about that," said Lahlil.

"You have to," said Jachad. "I'm dying. I get whatever I want. Those are the rules."

She watched the bowl carefully. "Emperor Eoban wanted the striders to work for him. When they wouldn't, he put out a bounty on their heads. *All* their heads."

"I know that part already. Where do you come in?"

"When there weren't any more battles to fight, I put a crew together—people who were good at what they did—and we took whatever jobs we felt were worth our time." The bowl had nearly filled to the little mark she had made with her knife. She used a little pressure to close the wound, then dabbed it with Mairi's salve and tied a clean bandage over it.

"The striders?"

"No. The bounty wasn't big enough for the time it would have taken to track them—and that got worse once they knew they were being hunted. If they saw anyone coming, they just strode away."

"Good for them," said Jachad.

She tied the bandage a little tighter.

"We were near Seabright when we found out eight of them had holed up nearby. It seemed like a good opportunity. We thought they'd try to stride away, but they didn't; they tried to fight us. Then we found out why."

"They were protecting something," Jachad conjectured.

"Abroan children can't stride, not alone, until they're thirteen or fourteen. They had forty children younger than that—orphans, mostly—packed into the back of that house."

Isa had woken up now. Lahlil thought about stopping, but pressed on anyway. "My crew was split over what to do with the children. Some wanted to kill them—the bounty was the same for adult and child—but the others wanted to let them go." She moved the instruments aside and sat beside Jachad with her back against the wall, listening to his breathing. It sounded steadier than before, but they had a long walk through the forest to Dredge's house. She wasn't sure he could make it. "We compromised: we let them live—for a price—and faked their deaths so people would stop hunting them. Then we collected the emperor's bounty on top of it."

"So that's the answer to how you lured them all into that field?" asked Isa, sitting up. "The massacre never actually happened?"

"We had the Abroans dig up their dead and bring them to that field, then we started the fire and burned the bodies," said Lahlil. "Instead of inventing some story that could be disproven, we just wouldn't say how we'd done it."

"Then where did all the striders go?"

"Nowhere." She leaned her head back against the wall and shut her eyes. "Striders are just Abroans if they don't stride. We told them if they ever strode again, we'd find them and kill them. I caught one of them at it, but I let him go. I thought I might need him someday. Now I'm calling in the debt."

Jachad's breathing had slowed a little more. She touched her fingers to his wrist as gently as she could. He didn't move, but his pulse was racing like a bird's and he was still awake.

"What happened to your crew?" asked Isa.

"I broke it up," she said. "I couldn't see any point in going on with them. They had disappointed me. I thought they didn't care about anything, but it turned out they still had some feelings left in them and that made them no good to me."

"But you're the one who wanted to let the striders go."

"No," Lahlil said. Out of the dark corners of the room, she saw Nevie forever walking toward her through the snow: Nevie, the only person in her crew who had been on her side that day. "I was the one who wanted to kill them all."

Chapter 21

Lahlil tried not to keep turning back to check on Jachad as she pushed through the woods later that evening, but she couldn't help it. She had let him rest as long as she could after the bleeding, but now he stumbled along behind her, rag-doll limp and barely able to keep the pace, while insects swarmed around the bloodstained bandage and roots trolled the ground as if purposefully snatching at his ankles. He had not mentioned the striders, not even once, but the way he avoided her eyes made her wish she had kept her silence. She had warned him before not to make excuses for her. Now she wished he would say something, anything. As for Isa, when she wasn't plaguing Lahlil with questions about how far they had to go and how long it would take to get there, she disappeared behind a chilly curtain of condemnation.

The rain was holding off, but the darkness was making navigation difficult. It didn't help that she'd avoided this area for so long. She tried not to let the others see her relief when they came into a clearing ringed by tree stumps.

"What's that noise?" asked Jachad.

"The river," said Lahlil, listening to the rushing sound beneath the forest's relentless insect drone. "This way."

The trees thinned out about thirty paces further along. A simple cabin with shuttered windows and a stone chimney sat in a cleared yard next to stacks of logs and a fenced-in coop. No light slipped through the shutters but she could smell the woodsmoke, even if she couldn't see it against the cloudy sky. The land sloped down to a muddy bank and the sound of the Truant flowed into her weariness like some insidious lullaby.

She wanted there to be some other way. She knew what it would be like for them to have her appear on their doorstep, as callously indifferent to what they had built here as a forest fire. She was a walking catastrophe.

<That doesn't look—> Isa began, and then a twig snapped behind her.

Lahlil slid out of her pack and drew her sword. She didn't see a man at all, at first; all she saw was the momentum of the axe swinging out of the darkness toward her. It was a woodsman's axe and not a battle-axe, but that didn't make it any less dangerous. She threw her cheap sword aside—it would never have withstood that blow without breaking—and dived onto the wet leaves. Isa had drawn her sword as well, but at Lahlil's hasty order, she placed herself in front of Jachad instead.

Their attacker swung through his missed blow and then used the momentum of the upstroke to turn around so he could come at her again.

From the corner of her eye, she saw Jachad spark both hands into flame.

"Jachi, no!"

But her warning came too late and he collapsed backward against the tree, clutching at his chest with his fingers still dripping blood-red sparks and his head rolling to one side.

<Look out!> Isa cried.

Lahlil threw herself at her opponent's legs as he came at her—big legs, like columns, attached to a big man—and tackled him to the ground. He fell hard enough to knock the breath out of him, and she made sure to pin him with her upper body before he could get it back. Only then did she stomp on his wrist hard enough to break his grip on the axe. She rammed her knee into his gut, forcing out the breath he had just gulped down, then snapped her knife from her hip and pointed it at his throat.

She waited for him to try to throw her off, but instead he just lifted up his curly-haired head and glared at her.

"General," he said finally. He'd meant it to be the low, warning snarl of an animal defending its den, but he couldn't quite disguise the edge of panic. "You can't be here. You're dead. Josten Drey's carrying your body around on some crazy bounty-collecting tour."

"Dredge." Lahlil pushed her knee a little harder into his chest. He'd gained weight and cut his beard, and he had a scarf around his neck covering the Stowari prison tattoo. She might not have recognized him if she'd passed him in the street. "Anyone else out here? Don't lie."

"Just me."

"Where's Jaspar?"

Dredge's lip jutted out as he considered lying to her despite her warning, but then he thought better of it. "Inside."

"How did you know we were out here?"

"Trip-cord in the clearing. Old habits. You know how it is." His slightly hooded eyes still had the steady, perspicacious gaze of a hunter. He didn't acknowledge the others, but Lahlil knew he had already sized them up. "What do you want, General?"

"I'm calling in the favor you owe me."

"*Favor?*" Dredge tried to sit up, but she moved the knife closer to his throat. "I was only in that jail because Alack's fancy lock-pick didn't work, that little shit. He owes you the favor, not me."

"Alack can't help me."

Dredge craned his neck up a little higher. "Why not?"

"Because he doesn't live upriver from Prol Irat," Lahlil told him, "and because he's dead."

The Stowari stared at her from under his heavy eyebrows, square jaw clenched. "How?"

"Bar fight, a year ago. Somewhere in Uln."

"A bar fight? That doesn't sound like Alack."

"The fight was supposed to be a distraction. He was robbing the tax collector next door."

"*That* sounds like Alack," said Dredge, and then added respectfully, "Greedy little bastard got what he deserved."

"I don't have a lot of time, Dredge."

"I don't do those kinds of jobs any more. Your kind," he reminded her, speaking just a little too quickly. He must have thought the darkness would hide the hand creeping toward the spot where he'd let the axe fall. "I've fixed this place up. Jaspar's back for good now and we live here just like regular people. We don't—"

"Try it if you want," she told him, gesturing to the axe. "You might get lucky."

"Lucky?" Dredge's voice dropped down into his chest as he spat the word back at her. "I'd be luckier dead than back out there with you. I don't have much to lose."

"Don't you?" asked Lahlil. She went to retrieve her sword, backing up to keep him in sight. He sat up, rubbing his wrist where she'd kicked him. A sick feeling churned in her stomach as she saw Jachad and Isa watching her, but she had only this one option left and she had to make it work. "I don't need to kill you. I can leave you alive—just alive enough for you to watch me drag Jaspar out here. Just like Bakkanresh. You remember Bakkanresh."

Dredge looked her up and down and for a moment she was afraid he would know she was bluffing. She didn't admit to herself the possibility that she wasn't.

"You're a monster, you know that?" Dredge said. He lurched to his feet and brushed the wet leaves from his trousers. With the extra weight on him, he looked as massive as the trees behind him, but she knew his blustering was just compensation for the fact that he still feared her. "Jaspar only came back because I promised him I was through with this life, and with *you*. General—for once, *please*—just do the good thing and walk away."

"Prol Irat," she said again. "We need to get there. You must have a boat."

He stood there for a moment longer, grinding his teeth together. Somewhere in the woods behind them an owl hooted and shot down through the leaves.

"I have a boat," said Dredge at last. "It's around the other side of the house."

"You're going to take us to the edge of the city."

"Then what?"

"Then nothing," said Lahlil. "Then you can go home."

Dredge's eyebrows arched. "Is this a joke? That's what all this is about? A ride?"

"We have to leave right now."

"Can't I even—?"

"Now."

Dredge stomped away down the sloping ground, leaving the

rest of them to follow as they would. Lahlil sheathed her sword and turned back to Jachad, bracing herself for what she would find. The way he listed on his feet reminded her of the times she'd been so drunk she'd forgotten how to fall down, but he was still conscious, and capable of taking another swig from the brown bottle.

"He'll take us," Lahlil told her companions, since neither of them spoke Stowari.

<I don't trust him,> said Isa.

<No one's asking you to.> Lahlil waited for her to start down toward the house and then went to get Jachad, who hadn't moved.

"I can't walk by myself," he admitted.

"I know." She put his arm over her shoulder and helped him slowly down the slope toward the water.

"You said something about Bakkanresh," said Jachad.

She scanned the ground up ahead, making sure there was nothing that might trip him. "I've told enough stories for one day."

"I already know the story. The duke opened the gates to the Stowari after they—after *you*—killed his wife in front of him and the whole court and threatened to do the same to his children."

"Yes," said Lahlil. The word felt like a stone hurled straight at him, but she had gone too far now to allow herself to soften it for either of them. "It ended the siege."

"And then the Stowari sacked the town."

"We were hired to get the gate open. We weren't paid to care about what happened afterward." Something hard bumped against her knee and then rolled away through the rustling leaves. She bent down to search for it.

"Don't bother," said Jachad. "It was empty."

They came over a little rise and saw the boat sitting in a trench dug out from the bank, upside-down. Dredge was just in the process of flipping it over. It was a simple boat and not very big, but it had three benches besides the one in the stern for the pilot. Lahlil took what felt like the first breath she had taken in days.

"How long will it take to get there?" she asked as she helped Dredge drag the boat down to the trench.

"River's fast from all this rain. Around dawn," he said shortly, stopping to catch his breath; he was getting soft. He leaned in toward her with his hand on the rail while water lapped at the bottom of the boat. "You know, getting away from you was the only good decision I ever made. You made it seem . . . normal, somehow, like it was just what people did. It's not, you know. I thought somebody as smart as you would have figured that out by now."

Isa climbed in while Dredge lit a lantern and hung it from a hook on the prow. Lahlil helped Jachad in and then tossed their packs aboard before climbing in after him. Isa took the bench in the prow. Dredge loaded the oars—he'd need them to get back upstream—and pushed the boat out into the water. Then he hauled his boots up out of the muck and jumped in himself, bringing the murky scent of the river bottom along with him.

"You can sleep for a while now," she told Jachad, balancing in front of him as he sat hunched over on the middle bench. He didn't look up at her, and when she leaned over she saw a distant look in his eyes that she didn't like at all. "What is it?"

"I thought I smelled the sea . . . but it's gone now," he said, slurring his words. She tried to blame it on the medicine, but she couldn't make herself believe it. "I like this boat. Reminds me of my hammock on my mother's ship, rocking, like when I was a boy."

"Lie down," she said, guiding his shoulders down until he was curled up on the bench with his head resting on his pack. She adjusted his cloak to protect him from the damp air and saw that the clasp at his neck had come undone, exposing a patch of freckled skin just below his throat. She pressed the collar of his shirt between her fingers.

"Don't look," he said, taking her hand even though his eyes had already closed. "I don't want to know how bad it is."

"I won't if you don't want me to," she said, tucking his hand back beneath the cloak. "Try to sleep."

She sat down in the stern where she could watch Dredge at the tiller. The banks streamed by as the swollen river bore them along, but she felt like they were standing still. Breaks in the clouds showed monotonous stands of colorless trees and the occasional drowsy homestead perched up on higher ground. Normal people lived there, with normal lives, like the one Dredge and Jaspar were trying to have.

"So, this is your new crew," Dredge said, startling her out of a half-sleep. "Sounds like the beginning of one of Bartow's jokes: a one-armed Norlander, a ginger drunk and the Mongrel all get into a boat for Prol Irat . . ."

"I don't have a crew any more."

"No?" he asked, leaning over to get a better view as he guided the boat around a bend, then mumbled to himself, "Pengar's hairy balls, it's a dark night."

"I quit, like you."

He took his eyes from the water for the first time. "You, General?" He gave a curt shake of his head. "You're yanking me. You'll never leave the life. Not like that, anyhow."

"How, then?"

"You know what I mean," said Dredge. "I'd watch you sometimes when some stupid kid tried to take you on—trying to prove something—and think, 'She's gonna let him do it.' I guess we all had days like that, when we just wanted it to be over."

Lahlil didn't have the energy to lie to him, or the courage to admit that he was right, so she said nothing.

Dredge said, "Josten Drey lied about killing you, then. That means there's still a price on your head: a big, fat one."

"I know."

"I could make a fair bit of money just telling people I've seen you." The tendons in his wrist hardened as he tightened his grip on the tiller. His size and strength would be better than any sword in a fight on a moving boat. "I've been thinking, you might be planning to kill me when we get to Prol to stop me from talking. And now I'm thinking I might stand a better chance if I steered us into the bank right now. I'm a good swimmer, and I know this river. I don't know about you, but I'd say the rest of your 'crew' wouldn't stand much of a chance in the water."

"I'm not going to kill you. You can tell anyone you want where I went."

The boat rocked hard as he cut into the current, taking them around another bend. "Staking out a cold trail, is that it? Draw everyone to Prol Irat looking for you while you're off somewhere else?"

"Something like that."

The river straightened out again and he leaned back against the rail. The shadow of a large moth flicked over the boat as the insect courted their lantern. "You remember that time in Volifer," he said, "when they set fire to that barn because you tricked them into thinking they'd trapped us all in there, and then we went back to their castle and beheaded that asshole Prince Burton while his bodyguards were still standing out in that field, watching it burn and slapping each other on the back?" He laughed aloud, but the laugh choked off into something else far less nostalgic. "Damn me, that didn't take long," he mumbled.

"I wouldn't have brought you into this if there'd been another way."

Jachad moaned and opened his eyes. Lahlil knelt down next to him in the bottom of the boat and checked his forehead. It was cold as wax.

"Go back to sleep," she told him, adjusting his cloak so that it covered him better. "We still have a long way to go."

"I had a dream we were in the desert and King Tobias was still alive," he said. His eyes were already fluttering. "He was chasing us, and I looked over and you were gone. I was alone."

"It was just a dream." She kept her hand on his back until his breathing slowed. Then she went back and sat down across from Dredge.

Her old comrade sucked his teeth. "He's not drunk, is he?"

"No."

"Is it something catching?"

"He's been poisoned."

"Oh. Tough break," said Dredge, not without sympathy. "Who is he, anyway?"

She watched the black water flow past. "He's my Jaspar."

The river narrowed a short time later, then they passed through a section where the trees grew out sideways from the banks to spread their canopies over the water, and the lantern light picked out the trembling leaves as they passed underneath. Lahlil smelled the stink of rotting vegetation and saw bright green pools of algae floating in the standing water around the trunks.

"You really want to leave the life?" Dredge asked.

"I already have."

"I'll admit," said Dredge, with his eyes locked on the lantern and the patch of water in front of the boat, "the quiet life gets to me sometimes. I miss the action. Still, I'll be sorry to see it end."

"Why do you think it's going to end?"

He raised his eyebrows, as if surprised he would have to tell her. "The empire can't hold. They're spread too thin. Mercenaries like us are fine for a siege or filling out your ranks in a battle, but afterward . . . The only reason the empire is still holding together is that no one wants to be the first to give 'em the chuck. One of these days, some nobody in some little shit kingdom somewhere is going to throw a rock at a Norlander's head, and then the whole thing is going to come toppling down and it'll be war for everyone, then: proper war, not that sneaky stuff we were doing toward the end."

She hardly heard his last few words over the sound of her pulse pounding. She could feel the slippery grass of the battlefield under her boots, and smell the oil and smoke. She could hear the sound of swords clanging, and that noise a blade makes when it notches into a bone, like an axe into a tree-limb.

"If I was you, General, I'd think again about leaving the life. It's hard enough for me to live with the things I've done. I can't guess the shit that would catch up with you if you stood still long enough to let it."

Lahlil woke up after her sunrise attack beneath the bench where Jachad slept on, still feeling the pain twitch along with her racing pulse. She knew she had only been unconscious for a few moments, but it was a few too many; anything could have happened. She craned her head back and saw Dredge still at the tiller where he'd been all night. Jachad's hand hung over the bench; his pulse was fast and dangerously faint, but that was still better than none at all. Looking under the bench, Lahlil could see Isa's legs stretched out and guessed that she was asleep as well.

"Almost there," Dredge called over to her, his voice softening in the haze of the encroaching dawn.

Not long after, Lahlil spotted the silhouettes of Prol Irat up ahead like a swarm of fat-bellied spiders on spindly stilt legs. The wind changed direction and greeted her with the swampy, inescapable odor of one of the richest cities in the world. She had a momentary impulse to let the boat go past into the bay, to find the nearest tavern and drink herself blind. Dredge wasn't the only one with old habits.

"Tide will be coming in soon, General," he warned her.

"Take us in at the edge of the Outer Ring, over by the Boards."

"Slumming it, eh, General? Whatever you say."

Jachad sat up. He looked a little better for having rested, but she could tell he was in pain, and he had no more medicine. She felt only a little easier when she remembered what Mairi had said to her before they left: as long as he was in pain, he had time. When the pain stopped, he wouldn't have much longer.

Dredge moored the boat near a rickety staircase leading up to what passed for streets in this section of Prol Irat. Crude coracles, rafts and less easily named craft wallowed in the mud in advance of the next floodtide. Dim lights flickered up above through the unglazed windows of the wattle-and-daub shacks of the dock-workers, rag-pickers, petty thugs and the lowest of the tradespeople who made their home in this district, a maze of ramshackle houses on stilt legs that didn't look like they could withstand a strong breeze, much less the pounding of the winter tides. It was a different world from the Inner Ring circling the bay, with its glittering houses, theaters, temples, workshops, moneylenders and brothels.

Dredge helped them struggle out onto the muddy sludge that passed for a bank.

"Well, good luck," he said, bowing in a mock salute. As he pushed the boat back out into the water, she heard him add, "And I hope by Pengar's short hairs I never lay eyes on you again."

"How far is it?" Jachad asked as she put her arm around him to help him up the stairs. Isa had already climbed halfway up and waited for them with her fingers tapping the railing.

"Not far."

Lahlil let Isa take the lead, calling out directions as they made their way through the crazy intersections of platforms and bridges jutting out in whatever direction people had nailed them together, trying to avoid the blind alleys ending in fifteen-foot drop-offs down into the swamp, or the single-plank shortcuts wherever anyone felt like setting them down. The hour of their arrival proved to be the only disguise they needed: they blended in perfectly with the drunks staggering home after closing-time.

"Disgraceful," muttered a sharp-faced old woman, who took a moment from sweeping her doorstep to frown at them limping past.

They passed single-file through a narrow alley where the porch of one building jutted up against its neighbor, and then found themselves facing a cramped staircase of about a dozen steps. Jachad struggled so much with each step that he needed to rest by the time they reached the top. Lahlil looked down the stretch of badly matched planks to the nondescript, two-story house at the end. A light glimmered in one of the upstairs windows, and smoke streamed out from a vent in the back wall in lieu of a proper chimney.

"I'm sorry," Jachad told her, clutching her arm as he fought to breathe. His face shone with perspiration, even in the cool dawn air. "I know I said I'd go on, but I can't do it any more. Please, let's stop. I know people here. We can find a bed—"

Isa stopped up ahead on the sloping planks and turned back, her silver-gray eyes shining too brightly.

"We're already here," said Lahlil, helping him lean back against a splintery railing to rest, and snagging her cloak on a loose nail in the process. "That's the house there. Just wait here."

<What should I do?> asked Isa.

<Wait with him.>

Lahlil walked down the sloping deck toward the house. The house had no windows on the first floor, but she could hear people moving around inside through the thin walls even before she banged on the door.

"Fellix!" several childish voices sang out. "Someone's at the door!"

The sounds of movement increased, and the door swung open. She had a glimpse of children of various sizes crowded into a fire-lit room before Fellix darted out and slammed the door behind him.

He was emaciated: a collection of bones rattling inside the thick, bark-like skin of the Abroans. She could actually see his heart beating through his shirt in his sunken chest, and he stretched open his faded yellow eyes enough to expose the veins twitching in the corners. His turban had slipped down onto his shoulder, revealing a bumpy scalp covered with fine gray hair and throbbing like a newborn rodent.

"Knew someone would come for me," he said in a trembling voice, speaking broken Iratian. "Heard she had disappeared. Ehya. Like a snake in the house, but where? Prayed to the gods you were dead. Prayed every day." He held up his shaking hands, palms out, so she could see the faint scars, none of them recent. "Don't do *that* any more. Make baskets, me and the children. Came back to kill me anyway. Knew they would. Been waiting."

The swamp smell rolled over them with another shift in the wind and she had a momentary vision of Fellix rotting away before her eyes and sinking through the cracks into the mud below. She had expected hatred and rage from him—like Dredge, only more so—but this morbid acceptance was somehow much worse.

"I'm not here to kill you," she told him. "I need you to take me some place. I need you to stride."

"No!" he wailed, hunching down in the doorframe. "Can't! She'll come back if I do. Kill us all. Told me, after last time: stride again, she'll kill us."

"*Who* told you?" Lahlil demanded.

"The Mongrel," Fellix sobbed, crossing his arms over his face. "Killed them all. Said I could live if I didn't stride." He clapped his hands over his mouth with a little cry of terror. "No, don't even say it. Hear you if you say it."

Lahlil didn't realize she'd been backing up until she felt Isa's chill behind her.

<He's mad, isn't he?> her sister said, grabbing her arm. <I can tell. I don't even have to know what he's saying. This is how we're supposed to get to Norland? What are we going to do now?>

Jachad needed to hold on to the railing for support, but he had his other hand pressed over his eyes so he wouldn't have to see the state to which Fellix had been reduced. Jachad's shame—shame on her behalf—burned like a hot iron.

"Ehya!" a voice called out to them from the end of the boardwalk. Lahlil looked over and saw a barefoot Abroan boy standing with bundles of rushes in both arms. "Ehya," he said again, slowly this time, leaving a trail of muddy footprints on the boards as he trotted toward them, "what are you doing to Fellix?"

Old habits. Time was running out for Jachad too quickly for her to make new ones.

Lahlil grabbed the back of the boy's shirt and yanked him down to his knees. His stiff turban fell off and rolled away across the boards on its side—his hair was the same mouse-gray as Fellix's, only thicker—and the rushes tumbled out of his hands. He tried to pull away, but a moment later she had the edge of her sword to his chest.

"Fellix," she said, "Fellix, look at me."

Whimpering, the man's eyes rose up over his arm and saw her captive. "Savion?"

"What do you want?" cried the boy. He was small and wiry, but older than she'd thought at first; sixteen or seventeen; Isa's age. She didn't remember him—she didn't remember anything about the faces from that day. She hadn't noticed unimportant details, like people, back then.

"Fellix, listen to me," she said. "There's somewhere I need to go, and you're going to take me. That's all I want from you. You'll never see me again after that. I'll never come back." She coughed back the acid burning in her throat. "But if you don't pull yourself together and do what I need, I'll kill this boy."

Fellix shrieked and curled into a ball. "Never. Said never. Tell them, Savion. Made you understand. Never, never."

<It's not working,> said Isa. <He's gone, Lahlil. That's it. This is over. You've dragged us here for nothing.>

A raindrop landed on the boardwalk in front of her, then another, and a gust of wind whipped through her cloak.

Isa was right: it was over.

Lahlil let go of the boy's shirt and stepped back, sheathing her sword. He scrambled away over the boards in what she thought was a frantic attempt to get away from her, but then she saw him pounce on his turban before the wind could sweep it from the boardwalk. Fellix just hugged himself a little tighter, still whimpering. He hadn't noticed the approaching storm. He didn't even try to go back in the house.

"He's all right most of the time. Sometimes he's like this," said Savion. He stood by the railing, watching her with yellow eyes, like Fellix's, but much brighter. "Be like this, days maybe, follow? He won't help you. He won't let us talk about it."

Lahlil squinted at him through the half-light. "What do you know about it?"

"This," he said, holding up his hands. Swollen, barely healed cuts bisected both of his palms. Then he turned around and pulled up his shirt. "And this."

The red welts of an emphatic caning crisscrossed his back just above his waist. Some of the cuts were still flaked with scabs. He turned back around, and now she saw the eagerness gnawing at his smile. She was beginning to understand why he hadn't run when she'd released him.

"I can take you," he said, "wherever you want. You *do* want to stride, ehya?"

"Don't, Lahlil," said Jachad. His hand slipped from the railing and she caught him as he fell. "Leave them alone," he said, pushing her hands away. The anemic light brushed his pale cheeks and half-shut eyes. "You've used these people enough already. I won't let you."

"I won't let you give up now," she told him.

"You were right, about your life." The collar of her cloak pulled down on her shoulders and neck as he seized the front of it, trying to haul himself up. His blue eyes were glassy and bloodshot, but all too lucid. "I didn't know. I didn't understand."

Then his eyes fluttered and he fainted into her arms as a peal of thunder shook the boards.

She looked up at Savion. "We have to go now."

"How much?" asked the youth.

"What?"

"How much? I say you pay me one hundred eagles," said Savion, folding his arms across his thin chest.

Lahlil actually gasped. "I've killed princes for less."

"Each," Savion added and then grinned, showing a line of small white teeth.

"All right," Lahlil told him, arms straining to hold Jachad up, "you'll get it—but when we get back, not now. There's no time."

Savion narrowed his yellow eyes. "How do I know you pay?"

"How do I know you won't dump us in the ocean?" said Lahlil. "Are we going, or not?"

"Ehya," Savion said. "The blood, follow? Need the blood of the person to meet."

Lahlil pulled the oiled-cloth envelope from her pocket and brought out the page from Trey's *Book*. A fat raindrop landed on the paper and the old stain bled blue around the edges. "Is this enough? Will it work?"

"Give me your knife," said Savion, holding out his hand as a flash of lightning forked the sky behind him. "Need to be touching, follow?"

<Hold on to me,> Lahlil told Isa as Savion slashed his palm with her knife. She saw him gasp, but the way his lips parted and his chest contracted did not look like pain. He let a few drops of his own blood fall to the boards—so he could find his way home again—and then pressed the stain with Trey's blood against the open wound.

"Where we going, anyway?" he asked Lahlil, giving her back the knife. He grinned again as he pinched a fold of her cloak. "Ehya, don't tell me. I like surprises."

His yellow eyes rolled back like he was having some kind of fit; then he took a step forward on the cracked boards, and they were gone.

Chapter 22

Kira crowded in among the others of her station on the porch of Eotan Castle to watch the workers smash apart the stone gods carved into the lee of the headland. The porch was too far away from Eowara's tomb for Gannon, though, who stalked right in among the low-clan workers trying to cart away the debris, terrifying them with his mighty presence. The number of triffons pressed into service had doubled to twenty in the last hour, and they could hear the dry clink of falling stone every time another boulder-filled net swung against the rock. The ancient barrier wouldn't hold much longer, and then Onfar and Onraka help them all.

Kira found herself wishing it would snow. The clouds were low and heavy, but they were holding their breath so far, along with everyone else.

She kept scanning the crowd for Rho—as if she would ever be able to spot him with five thousand soldiers shivering out on the Front. She regretted advising him to take the boy from the witch's tower while everyone else was distracted by the tomb-opening. He was bound to flub it and make matters worse: he was *Rho,* after all.

Every guard and soldier in Norland had been mobilized for Gannon's war except for the few contingents left behind to guard Ravindal's clan houses and other strategic points. Vrinna had selected two hundred Eotan guards to lead the strike force into the tomb alongside the more distinguished high clansmen. The soldiers recalled from the provinces would remain on the Front, waiting for their nightmares to swarm them.

Kira tried to work out if she was the only one who believed the tomb held nothing more than Eowara's old bones and the moldy scent of superstition. Obviously not Lady Jaen Arregador, with her hand apparently fused to the hilt of her dagger; and probably not Lord Gothar Peltran, who stood with his helmet under one arm, patting out a slow rhythm against his leg as he watched the progress of the demolition, and certainly not the eager Vartans, standing together with the fitful light of the torches playing off their polished helmets.

Another impact rattled the hinges on the castle gates behind her.

Until Kira knew for sure, the Mongrel and the cursed *could* be waiting for them down in that tomb, using Eowara's sword as bait. Three years was a long time. Trey, Cyrrin, the woman with the blotches on her face—even little Berril—might be down there with them, corrupted by Lord Valrig into something beyond recognition.

Another boom rolled across the Front. *Do not go down,* it said.

<I'm surprised to see you here, Lady Kira,> said Bekka Eotan, startling her by popping up just behind her. <You're not going down into the tomb? I thought the emperor wanted only those who'd distinguished themselves in battle to accompany him.>

<My, but you're well-equipped, Bekka,> Kira remarked. The helmet under her arm had a gold figurehead with jewels for its eyes and teeth and a swirling pattern of such complexity etched into the sides that it made Kira's eyes ache. There wasn't a scratch on it. Apparently sitting in a well-appointed tent and paying mercenaries out of coffers brimming with tax money counted as distinguishing oneself in battle these days.

<The emperor says this will be Norland's greatest triumph since Eowara's time,> Bekka said, practically glistening with anticipation. <Of course I want to be a part of that. Poems will be written about this day. Our names will be remembered forever.>

<Oh, I'm sure. Just think how you'll have proved yourself by going down there—against the laws written in the *Book* itself—with all those guards crowding you, and all of that rock above

you, and who knows what horrors waiting to swarm up from below.>

<Oh. Yes,> said Lady Bekka, after the slightest of pauses, <it will be glorious.>

A silent roar started outside at the headland and rolled back to them, swelling until Kira could feel it behind her eyes and in her chest. They had broken through. The privileged warriors representing the Eotans, Arregadors, Vartans, Rilndors and the rest of the twelve clans rushed forward as the castle guards barred the doors behind them against whatever was going to come swarming out.

Kira knew too well what it would be like, waiting behind here while the others went down to the tomb. She had spent the last three years waiting. She could not stand to wait any longer.

She snatched Bekka's helmet and jammed it over her head as she ran forward with the others, enjoying Bekka's wail of outrage behind her. She could see nothing except the people just in front of her and soon found herself caught up in a bottleneck behind the strike force.

<Kira Arregador,> Lord Betran Eotan droned when he noticed her, <you shouldn't be here. No, no, you can't—you've never fought in battle. This is no place for you.>

<I know,> Kira said petulantly, <I told the emperor that, but he insisted. He gets these ideas sometimes, and there really is no putting him off. I thought he was joking at first, of course. Who wouldn't? But no, he was serious. Frankly, I hope he changes his mind once we get in there. Eowara is *his* ancestor, of course, not mine, but I still don't feel right about it.>

<I don't follow you at all.>

She leaned back until her head brushed his hood, affording her enough privacy to explain.

<No,> Betran bleated in a rage when she had finished, <he wouldn't do that. That's desecration.>

<Not the way he sees it,> Kira tossed off, <and who am I to argue with the emperor?>

The fur-clad figures around her surged forward, sweeping her up along with them, and she had no time to reconsider her impulsive act before the ragged hole in the rock loomed up and swallowed her along with the others. An icy chill shot through her blood when she found the bumpy rock walls closing in on both sides and over her head, but the dozens of people in front and behind her made any escape from the narrow tunnel impossible now. The rock walls trembled with the sound of all their stamping boots. If the Mongrel was down there, she would have ample time to prepare for their arrival. A few of the guards carried lanterns and Kira tried to stay focused on the dim light bobbing somewhere up ahead. Surreptitiously, she reached out and clung to the fur coat of the man in front of her, looking for some small bit of comfort. She could just make out two silver triffons winding around the hilt of his sword: she was clinging on to Eofar Eotan.

The tunnel sloped down gradually at first, but then abruptly dropped away down a crude set of steps that twisted around on itself at no regular intervals. Kira had to brace her hands along the walls to keep from tripping as they climbed down into the dark, then down, and down some more. She tried to swallow but her mouth had gone dry, and the painful tingling that she had only just noticed in her fingers had begun to spread up into her arms. At least she wasn't alone: she could almost see the visceral revulsion of those around her smearing the walls.

Soon the steps grew less steep and the air steadily warmer. The space between her and Eofar widened unexpectedly and only a few steps further the floor levelled out in a small cavern, not much larger than her apartment in Arregador House. Guards filled the space up ahead of her and more pressed in behind; she had no room to draw her sword. They had blundered right into a snare, like a bunch of stupid rabbits—but no, the cavern opened up on the other side and the strike force had only paused to draw their swords before charging through. Kira fumbled Virtue's Grace out of the scabbard and went after them. As she passed through the crooked archway, she heard Gannon and then Vrinna give the order to keep going.

Kira charged into the cavern with the other high clansmen all around her, and just like them, she ran five paces and then stopped in awe before the people coming in behind her forced her forward again.

The cavern glowed with light, thanks to some silvery substance coating everything she could see with an iridescent, subtly colored sheen. Kira had often looked down into the cracks around Ravindal at the gently glowing mists, but nothing had prepared her for this. She felt like she was inside a snowflake, or an infinitely faceted jewel. Slender white cones hung down from the ceiling and rose up from the floor, but the vaulted spaces in between them were left in darkness. Streams and miniature waterfalls bubbled up and down out of the rocks and collected in pools; the steaming water filled the caves with a creeping, faintly aromatic mist. The weird glow and the vastness of the space played havoc with her eyes and they started twitching as she tried to focus. She tightened her grip on her sword, intimidated by a beauty that was as indifferent to her approval as it was to her existence.

The soft light illuminated a series of caverns on either side, while across the ethereal landscape the cavern floor rose in tiers, winding around the rock pillars toward the top of the cavern. Chasms fell away on either side, and from them came a faint but deep-noted roar that Kira thought might be the underground river gushing through the cliff and out into the sea. Death lined the way forward: bones lay everywhere, both singly and in heaps, yellowed, but blotched with the same silvery stuff as everything else. Some lay within nests of shriveled, hairless pelts, while others sprawled out across the floor. Skulls, some of them distressingly small, were scattered like pine cones under a tree, and abandoned among the bones sat the kinds of things people didn't normally leave behind: swords with leather-wrapped hilts still in their scabbards; chains of simple gold links; time-eaten spearheads without their shafts.

A white bat with red eyes dropped from an invisible niche up above her head and streaked off into the mist. So far, she had seen and felt no one else.

Gannon ordered the strike force into a tight phalanx behind him as he made his way across the cavern floor; the rest he left behind to safeguard the way out. The cave rang with the strike of metal-tipped boots and the jingling of buckles as the emperor's expedition led the rest of them through into a low-ceilinged tunnel. Kira found herself still just behind Eofar and his fussy sword, and she counted the gold claws on his silver triffons to keep from thinking of suffocation. Just when fear had squeezed nearly all the breath out of her they emerged into another cavern, this one running on longer and lower than the last. She strained to listen into the darkness beyond the reach of the steady silver glow and kept her eyes down to avoid stepping on the bones, but all she could hear was the pounding of her own heart and the constant drip and burble of the water.

There's nothing here, Kira told herself: not the Mongrel, nor Trey, nor the cursed, nor anyone at all but the bats and whatever they fed on. The stories in the *Book* were all lies. She was ashamed of herself for having given them even a moment of credence.

Several dark tunnels led out of the second cave, but after a quick conference between Gannon and Vrinna, their party moved toward the largest. For a moment Kira wavered, wondering if she should stay behind with the guards at the tunnel entrance, but she steeled her resolve and carried on. She had come down here to set her mind at rest. She would see this through to the end.

She regretted her decision when she came out into the next cavern, not more than one long leap from a wide crevasse where luminous mist rose into the stifling air. Cairns of rough stone mottled with the same silver slime crowded the wide ledges on either side, leaving hardly any room to walk between them, with precious possessions and offerings, rotting furs, tarnished jewelry, even daggers, swords and battle-axes, piled on top of each tomb. And there, standing alone at the back of the cavern, was the largest cairn of all, and Valor's Storm must surely be the sword laid across the top, bathed in the shaft of soft daylight shining down through the crack just above it. For the first time Kira thought about Ravindal, far over their heads, and awe lanced through her fear.

As Gannon continued forward the guards and remaining clansmen followed him, threading their way in single file through the tombs. Sweat dripped down Kira's back; she wasn't the only one to have removed her helmet and hood. The taste of chalk filled her throat, and the warm spray came at her like a triffon huffing in her face. The heat, the claustrophobic surroundings, the sound of running water were all combining to send her into a kind of stupor, and she imagined her body turning as insubstantial as the mist and sinking down into the rock beneath her feet, where she would see the army of the cursed crawling over itself like an insect swarm, ready to burst out in a storm of disease and destruction.

She stepped back, wanting to put more distance between her and the crevasse, and the heel of her right boot crunched down on something behind her. Gingerly, she moved to one side, dreading the sight of a crushed skull, but found only the shards of what might have been a clay vessel or a cup, still with traces of gold decoration. She bent down to touch one of the pieces and found it wet and just a little sticky. A little of the silver stuff rubbed off on her hand, but she could see the glow only very faintly. The feel of it between her fingers reminded her of the yellow scum that collected in the cracks around the hot spring pools.

A silent cry sent her straightening up again with her sword at the ready, but the guards were only responding to Gannon, who, wreathed in mist—like Onfar himself looking down from the Celestial Hall—was lifting the sword ceremoniously from Eowara's tomb. The scabbard must have been perfectly fitted, because not only was the sword intact after seven centuries but it had not a single spot of tarnish or blemish on it. The bronze blade tapered to a longer point than their modern swords, and a two-pronged guard separated the blade from a cylindrical grip ringed with time-darkened golden bands.

They all waited for something to happen, but nothing did. The water pounded ceaselessly somewhere down below, and though every eye watched the crevasse for some sign of movement, there was nothing: no Mongrel, no Lord Valrig, no cursed.

Kira managed her first real breath since she had entered the tombs—and then Gannon's wrath blew through the room like a gale.

<*No one!*> the emperor cried, turning back around and brandishing his sword at the silvered air. <The Mongrel isn't here—there's no one here. The rest of you aren't worthy, that's why. You've put them off.> He turned around and stalked back past the cairns, showing no fear of the chasm just a hand's width from his boots. <My father and his empire—he made Norland soft. He made you

all soft, buying your loyalty with taxes from places he'd never been. That's what being a Norlander is now: it's all feasts and jewels and dressing up like a bunch of dumb mummers: people who've never set foot on Norland soil before, thinking a high-clan name is all they need to be a Norlander, breathing out the stink of their foreign air—makes me sick.>

<Is that truly why the cursed haven't come out to fight?> asked Eofar, ignoring Gannon's pointed remarks. A loud noise at her feet made Kira jump back: a helmet had fallen off a tomb and was rattling along the black stone floor. Eofar reached down to pick it up, but came away instead with a jawless skull. He chucked it irreverently into the crevasse; they all heard the crack of it hitting the side, and then another as it struck a ledge or outcrop further down before the roaring waters deep in the chasm finally swallowed it up. <Maybe they're just asleep. Let's wake them up.>

<Don't do that,> Kira cried out in terror, grabbing him with her free hand and pulling him back before he could bend down and pick up another bone. He stumbled into her and now she smelled the drink on him.

<Don't? Why not?> he asked, looking down at her. His calm, handsome Eotan features belied his swirling emotions, all black and gray smoke twisting together, drawn up from the red-hot coals burning at the core of him.

<What's going on?> Vrinna demanded as she slid forward, and Kira cursed herself for being stupid enough to call attention to herself. <What are you doing here? You've never fought in a battle. You've never even left Norland. The emperor doesn't want your kind here.>

<Are you sure?> asked Kira. <But I was told to come—Lady Bekka delivered the message herself. She said the emperor insisted I come down with him into the tomb. Look, she even lent me her helmet. I very nearly didn't get the message in time, and then I had to run . . . Oh, it was a prank, wasn't it? Bekka is always playing tricks on me.>

<You're lying,> Vrinna growled, raising the point of her sword just a little. <You have some reason for being here. I can feel it.>

<Onraka's elbows!> Kira swore primly, flicking her fingers against the flat of Vrinna's blade. The dull ping died in the

stifling air. <Am I in trouble, Captain? I'm not the one who just flung my own ancestor's bones around, am I?—sorry, Lord Eofar, but you know you did.>

<Back off, Captain,> Gannon commanded, grabbing Vrinna's shoulder and pulling her away from Kira. Kira moved away from the crevasse, steadying herself and trying to catch her breath.

<But why did she come?> Vrinna broke in, so angry that the silver veins on the side of her neck bulged out. <She wouldn't answer me—>

<Cool down, or I'll put you some place—> Gannon broke off as a thought occurred to him. <Go and relieve the patrol at Onfar's Circle. If Valrig's army isn't coming through here, that's the other place they'd be. Take your squad out there. Look hard.>

Onfar's Circle—nearly within sight of where Trey and the others were hiding. Kira's throat closed up on her all of a sudden like someone was squeezing it, and a sharp pain flared in her chest. She didn't fall, but the cave went a little darker.

<I don't think Lady Kira wants me to go,> said Vrinna, her gray eyes flashing behind the mist.

<What? Oh, no, of course I don't want her to go,> Kira babbled, biting down hard on her tongue to keep herself from panicking. She was painfully aware that Cyrrin's enclave had gone undiscovered not because their ruined castle was particularly isolated, but because no one had ever thought to look for them. Dozens of guards searching for any sign of the cursed would find them with no difficulty at all. She had just brought about the very thing she had spent the last three years trying to prevent. <What if the cursed come here while she's gone? What will we do? All of these soldiers will be running every which way with no one to tell them what to do.>

<Are you feeling all right, Lady Kira,> said Vrinna, very nearly purring. <You don't look well.>

<I don't? No, and I don't feel well, either,> she said, clutching her forehead. <It's the air down here. It doesn't agree with me. I have to get out. I can't breathe. I have to get out, right now.>

She started backing up, but then Eofar took her by the arm and pulled her aside. <You don't think the cursed are down here, do

you?> he asked, speaking only to her. <You already know that everything you've ever been taught is a lie. Don't you?>

<No,> she said, sinking her shaking fingers deeper into the fur of his coat-sleeve, <I don't know any such thing . . . Please—there's nothing here. Let's get out.>

<Yes, let's do that,> said Eofar, guiding her out of the cave without waiting for anyone to comment.

She could hear Gannon behind her, issuing orders to keep guards posted in the caves at all times, and to send squads to search the tunnels they had not yet explored.

Even though her bad turn was genuine, she couldn't have found a better excuse for getting out of the caves ahead of Vrinna. Eofar kept hold of her as they made their way back through the caverns and to the dark stairs, but he never said a word, and she noticed he was keeping his emotions tightly locked down. In the darkness she could see the silvery stuff blotching her clothes and hands and even patching her companion's face. The color reminded her of lamplight shining on the snow through a green-glass window. She could still taste the mist; she wondered if her lungs were now glimmering on the inside like a glow-globe.

Eofar helped her over the last few stones and out into the Front. She turned her face up to the sky in relief as she slid through the slush, loath to tear her eyes away from the iron-gray clouds even as the points of five thousand weapons nervously rose up to greet them. The generals Gannon had left in charge came forward to find out what was going on, and as Eofar began to explain, she continued walking back across the Front toward the city, barging through the ranks of the soldiers, colliding with shields and pushing through the groves of spear-shafts without making any effort to hide her distress. Let them think what they liked.

<My Lady!> cried Aline, separating from the crowd and following her away from the Front, past the barricades and into Branch Street. Kira pulled her into the empty porch of a book-binder's shop as soon as they were far enough away not to be spied upon. <I've been looking everywhere for you—where have you been? Some people said you went down into the tomb!>

<I did,> said Kira, but then hesitated. She had never lied to Aline

before, but she balked at explaining how she had just drawn a target on her little sister's back by antagonizing Vrinna. <I want you to go back home and wait for me. There's something I need to do. I'll explain later: for now, don't talk to anyone, and don't do anything.>

She left Aline, but had only taken a few steps when she realized her hand-servant had not moved. She sighed, and came back.

<Are you going . . . *there*?> Aline asked.

<Yes,> she admitted finally, <I have to. The emperor is sending Vrinna and a whole squad of triffons there to look for the cursed. I have to warn them.>

<I'll get your riding clothes—>

<There's no time,> said Kira. <Please don't worry. I'm not going to let anything happen to your sister, I promise. And don't ask to come with me: you've been on a triffon exactly twice in your life, and besides, you'd freeze in that wool cloak.>

<Yes, my Lady,> said Aline, so afraid for her sister that she could hardly move. <Please take care of yourself.>

Kira started off again, but then turned back once more. <You might look for Lord Rho. He's probably gone by now, but if you can find him—>

<He's not gone. He came out of the Front just before you did. I wanted to ask him if he knew where you'd gone, but then I lost him.>

<Did he have a little boy with him? Or an old woman?>

<No,> said Aline. <He was alone.>

Kira swallowed. So he had flubbed it after all. <All right then. Go up to his room and tell him to meet me at the stables immediately.>

As Kira walked down Ward Street she tried to calculate how long it would take Aline to give Rho her message, but it wasn't until she turned the corner that she realized her mistake. She thumped her fist against her thigh in frustration: she shouldn't have told Aline to look for Rho in his room—she should have told her to look in the first place he'd be able to get a drink.

Chapter 23

As Kira hurried through the streets toward the stables, she couldn't stop picturing Vrinna and her guards following right on her heels. The caves had left her disoriented, and the echoes of her own footsteps chased her across Berry Street, along the covered walkway and into the alley behind tiny Alvarig House, where the snow covered everything with silence.

The stable complex sprawled at the opposite end of a deserted street—the usually bustling shops were all closed because of the opening of Eowara's tomb—and now Kira broke into a run. She had to get her triffon saddled and away before Vrinna and her squad reached the stables. She kept thinking the nervous energy charging through her should have made her run faster, but instead her boots stuck to the ground as if they'd been covered in sap. Her mind kept swerving back and forth: first she saw Trey running to her and pulling her into his arms, and then he was looking right through her and recoiling in disgust as she reached out for him. She tried to concentrate on just getting to the stable, but she could not stop thinking about how the last three years might have changed him.

She was halfway down the long street when a hand shot out of the darkness of a porch and grabbed her coat, pulling her sideways with enough force to drag her off her feet and send her flying into a dirty yard. Her sword banged hard against something that turned out to be an anvil standing outside a shuttered smithy and the impact knocked the wind out of her. A shape emerged from the porch as she looked up; it was obvious from the scarlet hostility burning in the air that Vrinna had beaten her here.

<I knew you would try to get to Onfar's Circle before me.> The captain drew her black-bladed sword and held the point to Kira's chest.

<Captain Vrinna,> she said, sitting up and feigning relief even though she wanted to scream. She didn't reach back to draw Virtue's Grace. They both knew Vrinna was ten times the fighter she'd ever be. <Blessed Onraka, I thought the cursed were here after all. Did you think I was one? You just don't know what's going to happen next any more, do you? It's all so exciting.>

<You're hiding something.> Vrinna stayed perfectly still while a conflagration of anger swirled around her. <I've always known it; I don't care what anyone else says.>

<Oh, come now, Captain,> said Kira. She stood up and dusted herself off, pretending not to notice the way the point of Vrinna's sword never moved away from her heart. There was no one nearby to help her, nor was there way out of the street except past Vrinna. <I wish I did have something to hide—a little mystery can be so alluring—but I never could keep a secret. Everything I think just comes straight out.>

<Why don't you want me to go to Onfar's Circle?> asked Vrinna, salivating with the prospect of finally catching her in a lie. <What's there? What're you afraid I'll find?>

<Nothing, that's not why I don't want you to go,> said Kira. She had known of this chink in the captain's armor for a long time; she'd kept it secret in case she ever found her back to a wall—or in this case, an anvil. <I think you should be by the emperor's side at a time like this, not running all the way out there to stare at trees—don't you feel the same way? I thought you of all people would. You know why—you don't need me to say it.>

Vrinna didn't lower her guard. <To say what?>

<Now don't be so cruel, Captain,> Kira said meekly. <You know what's really going on with me and you and the emperor—don't make me embarrass us both by spelling it out.>

<What are you talking about?> But Vrinna was lying this time; she knew exactly what Kira meant and she wanted to believe it so badly that Kira could nearly taste her neediness.

<Oh, very well, if I have to. You know the emperor settled for me—just like he's settled for all his lovers before me—because he can never have the one he truly loves; someone who is his equal in spirit and strength. You know he respects you too much to ask you to be his mistress—and he knows your pride would never permit you to accept such an offer. Of course we all know he had no choice whatsoever in his choice of wife. It's tragic, really. It would make a good poem, although I don't really like tragic poems. I prefer the comic ones. Did you hear the one about the—>

<You're lying,> said Vrinna, but her wrist drooped a little and the point of her sword wavered.

One more push was all she needed.

<I wish I was. I can admit it to you now, Captain: I'm jealous of you. I always have been. I knew from the beginning he'd never care for anyone but you. Don't you know that's why he's so sharp with you sometimes? He's trying to control his passion. You should really go back to him. I'm sure he's waiting for you. Go back to him now. He needs you.>

Kira waited for Vrinna to sheath her sword and fly back to her beloved, but instead, the captain stood perfectly still. She hoped Vrinna just needed a moment for the idea to find its way past the severed limbs and burning villages that took up most of the space in her head, but the pause went on and Kira's concern began to build. She took advantage of Vrinna's preoccupation to slip around to the other side of the massive anvil.

<This is a trick,> Vrinna said at last, snapping her sword back up. Kira was very glad she had moved out of easy reach. <You think I'm stupid. I'm just a joke to you.>

<Of course not,> said Kira, but she could feel the brittleness in her own words. <I was only—>

<Admit you were lying about the emperor,> Vrinna demanded.

<All right, maybe I was teasing you, just a little, but—>

<Lying,> Vrinna roared, <you're *always* lying! I won't have it—you're not going to lie to me any more.>

<Stay calm, now, Captain. You don't want to do something you'll regret.>

<Arregador—Aelbar—whatever you are,>—Vrinna's disdain was a noxious smell lingering in the air, like the reek of ashes from

the barrel against the wall—<you can't even fight. You're nothing but a coward. You're a disgrace to your clan.>

<You can't kill me and you know it,> Kira said, finally dropping the bubble-headed courtesan act. <I haven't even drawn my sword. Kill me now and you'll be shunned forever—not to mention what will happen to you when you get to the After-realm. And don't think you can just secretly dump my body somewhere, either. Everyone saw the way you spoke to me in the cave. They'll know who's to blame if I disappear. The *emperor* will know who's to blame.>

<I knew you were hiding something,> said Vrinna. Kira could hear her breathing through her nose. <The emperor didn't believe me, but I knew it.>

<Yes, you were the only one who saw through me—Onfar's balls, how can anyone be so canny and so stupid at the same time?> Kira asked, genuinely bemused, for all she was keeping Vrinna talking because it was the only way she could think of to avoid being stabbed. She wondered if Aline had managed to track Rho down yet. <You think the emperor feels any loyalty toward you, Captain? Gannon killed his *own father* to serve his ambitions. He doesn't care about anyone but himself; you're just someone who does his dirty work for him. Trust me, your fawning infatuation turns his stomach.>

<You think you're so clever,> Vrinna snarled, and at last the sword pointed toward Kira's breast started to wobble a little; the captain was on the verge of losing control. <You like talking down to me. Well, I know something you don't.>

<Oh, do you? This should be interesting. Please, enlighten me.>

<I don't want to *kill* you.> Vrinna sprang up onto the anvil as lightly as a cat and threw herself at Kira, who finally drew her sword and backed up—until she felt the stone wall behind her: she had nowhere to go. She crashed past the ash barrel and ran for the back of the yard until her knee struck the corner of a trough and sent her sprawling into the snow. Vrinna's imperial sword whisked through the air, guided by her battle-honed thoughts; she could have killed Kira effortlessly, had that been her aim.

Instead, she used her sword to batter Virtue's Grace to one side, then she took Kira by surprise by actually grabbing the blade at the unsharpened base near the hilt. Kira tried to pull it away from her, using her mind as well as her out-of-practice muscles to twist the sword from Vrinna's grasp, but she was concentrating so hard on regaining control that she never even noticed the pommel of Vrinna's sword before it crashed into the side of her head.

She fell with Virtue's Grace still in her hand, but she could do nothing with it. The gray sky above her went darker and the ground swung beneath her like a triffon going into a dive.

<Now you're going to tell me why you want me to stay away from Onfar's Circle,> said Vrinna viciously, <and I'm going to hurt you until you do.>

Kira saw a flash of light as the blow landed, and then her head snapped to one side with so much force that she was sure her neck must be broken. Hot pain like the touch of a brand zipped across her face a moment later.

<I will beat it out of you,> said Vrinna. <Believe me: I know just how much I can hit you before you pass out.>

Kira tried to lift Virtue's Grace, but Vrinna's fist smashed into her stomach and expelled the remaining breath from her body. She heard the clang of her sword hitting the ground. She instinctively reached for it once more, but Vrinna's fist streaked through the snow again and Kira had a moment to anticipate where the punch was going to land before the pain crashed through her. She tasted blood, and her swollen left eye didn't blink with the right one.

<What are you hiding?> Vrinna repeated.

<Nothing.> Kira's groping hand found an overlooked iron rod under the snow and she had a moment of pure pleasure as she imagined the pulpy sound Vrinna's head would make when the metal smashed into it. <It's all in your imagination. You've made this whole thing up out of your jealousy.>

<I'm *not* making it up.> Vrinna grabbed Kira's coat at the neck and hauled her up to her knees, then cuffed her on the back of her head and dropped her down again. Kira managed to turn her face to one side in time to keep her nose from shattering on the stone paving slabs, but the side of her head hit the ground and white light blazed in front of her eyes again. She had lost the iron rod and she was beginning to wonder if she would survive this encounter despite Vrinna's assurances.

<What are you hiding at Onfar's Circle?>

<Onfar's Circle? Where's that again?>

The enraged captain leaned in and kicked her in the stomach, and now Kira didn't know whether she should be trying to protect her face or her stomach; maybe it was too late, because her mouth had filled with blood. She spat it out and, coughing, tried to crawl away, but Vrinna picked her up by the back of her coat and shook her like a helpless kitten, repeating the same words over and over again until they no longer made any sense.

Finally the shaking stopped and Kira was thrown back onto the ground. For a moment she just lay there, shuddering violently; then she told herself she had to escape this madwoman and tried to crawl back to the anvil so she could use it to get to her feet.

But pain lanced through her like a spear-thrust; it burst under her right breast and knocked her back again and she ended up back on the ground with her forehead pressed against the freezing iron, fighting for breath.

A dark shape swelled in front of her, and out of it came Vrinna's fist once again . . .

Chapter 24

Rho left Kira's apartment with the map in his pocket. He watched dawn lighten the sky above Arregador House's famous green-glass atrium as he made his way back to his room, where he threw himself down on the bed—but sleep remained elusive, creeping up to him with promises of oblivion, but then disappearing the moment he closed his eyes. After committing Kira's little map to memory, he had nothing to do but wait until midday and the opening of Eowara's tomb. Eventually the walls of his cramped room pushed in closer and closer until they pushed him out to roam the cold corridors for what he fervently hoped would be the last time.

He and Trey had played war with their toy soldiers right there; that corner was where Trey had found him passed out and put him to bed the night he'd got sick on that Thrakyan wine; down there was the spot where Trey had broken Weld Arregador's jaw for starting a rumor that their mother had been set out for pockmarks. All of his clearest memories were of Trey, as if he didn't even have a past life of his own. He was his own ghost.

And here, next to this column, was where he'd been standing when Trey had told him he had been invited to join Gannon's regiment. Rho remembered his answer so clearly: that he couldn't see the point of putting so much effort into an empire that would eventually collapse, just like every other one had. He had been a little proud of his philosophical cynicism back then, but he had a sneaking suspicion that if he stuck his finger into it now, it would crumble away like the empty shell it had always been.

Someone called his name and he turned to find Trey's old friend Remi stomping down the staircase behind him in helmet and breastplate, carrying a very expensive shield with the Arregador pine-wreath cast in brass on the front.

<Rho! What are you doing here?> Remi asked him.

<I came back yesterday.>

<No, no, I mean, what are you doing *here*? Everyone else is down at the Front—I had to come back for my father's shield, even though I told him to bring it with him in the first place. He didn't think the others would be bringing theirs, but of course they did. I swear to Onfar, if I miss anything because of him, the cursed will be the least of his problems.>

Rho looked up at the green-glass roof. <You shouldn't worry—it's early. They won't have the tomb open for hours yet.>

<You're joking, right?>

Rho's stomach flipped over.

<They started opening the tomb an hour ago—the emperor and his friends are all there and every soldier in Ravindal—well, except the house-guards—is waiting out on the Front for the cursed to attack. Must be nearly five thousand, I'd say. General Yural is leading the Arregadors, except for the archers—they're with Lord Taryn. Didn't you wonder why the house was so empty?> He slapped Rho on the shoulder.

<But still, getting the tomb open will take a long time—>

<In case you haven't noticed, our new emperor is not a patient man.>

Rho tossed Remi a hasty word of thanks, then ran back to his room for his coat and was back downstairs again in a flash. The door-warden opened up for him and he rushed out into streets so deserted it might have been the middle of the night. When he reached Branch Street he found a crowd of onlookers, but his clan name got him past the line of guards sealing off the Front.

His view of the rest of the Front was blocked by a Garrador company leaning on their spears, but he could feel the discomfort of all five thousand soldiers. The Garradors didn't pay him any mind as he went past, but he noticed the rusty dents in their armor and guessed they were only just back from the provinces. He caught many of them checking out the innumerable cracks in the rock and bet that stabbing a few farmers in someone's bean field wasn't much preparation for facing down your childhood terrors come to life.

The crowd milling about in front of Eotan Castle was large enough that Rho was able to work his way through them, up the steps and through the castle doors without being questioned, or even noticed by anyone. In fact, the ease of his passage worried him a bit; it made him even more certain that a gut-punch was waiting for him around some unexpected corner.

<Rho?>

Eofar was standing in the corner next to a sputtering torch that cast jumpy little shadows on the stones around his feet. He wore a fur coat like everyone else but had tossed his gloves and hood into the silver helmet under his arm, and Rho guessed that the sweat sheeting his skin had something to do with why he wasn't wearing them.

<Eofar, you're not really going down there?> Rho asked. He moved into the corner with him, though the sweet scent of the thaw-vine torch oil almost choked him. <Why?>

<I have to make sure Gannon gets Valor's Storm.>

<Why do you care if Gannon gets to be a hero?> asked Rho. He'd have been tempted to shake some sense into him, except for the very real possibility of getting vomited over. <What are you doing about the Shadar?>

<I'm making sure Gannon gets Valor's Storm,> Eofar said again. <You know what Valor's Storm is made of?>

<No,> said Rho. <Steel? Bronze?>

<I don't know either. I only know it's not made from imperial ore,> Eofar replied, *<like mine.>*

<If you think you're going to challenge him for the throne, Eofar, don't do it. Please, don't do it. He's a killer—you'll never beat him, not even with Strife's Bane. I don't blame you for hating the Eotans for what they did to your family, but you didn't come here to be emperor. You came here to help the Shadari.>

<This is how I'm helping them.>

<Is it?> asked Rho, thumping him on the chest to wake him out of the daze he had fallen into. <I don't think so. I think this is about you and your family. I think you want revenge.>

Eofar straightened up and pushed him back. <I'm still your

commander. This is the plan. I don't need you for it, so there's no reason for you to be here. Why *are* you here?>

<I'm going to get Dramash,> said Rho. <I can get him out now, while everyone's busy with this. Kira told me where to find him. I'm going to take him back to the *Argent.*>

<So you were going against me anyway,> said Eofar. <And if they catch you? What then? You can't fight anyone off with that sword you're carrying. You know who will have to save you then? Dramash will: he'll have to use his powers to hurt and kill people because you couldn't wait to run away.>

Rho stood there for a moment, gritting his teeth. At last he said, <Well, good luck,> and backed out of the corner. <Someday I'll find your son and tell him how you died.> He kept walking until the smaller side door opened and he slipped into the steady stream of functionaries going and coming from the castle. Once inside, he made his way through the entrance hall and found the tapestry with the servants' door behind it. No one was paying any attention to him, so he ducked into the dark corridor, feeling like he was about to run straight off the edge of the world, until he reached the end and found a door.

The few people he encountered in the servants' passages were only too happy to pretend not to notice him and he followed the map in his head through the dimly lit warren, moving upward through the stories, chasing a spectral image of Kira's silver furs and wondering which of the doors he was passing led to the emperor's bed. He was afraid if he looked inside any of those rooms he would find Frea waiting for him with her leather jacket unfastened and her black-bladed knife strapped to her thigh.

Finally he climbed the last dark, zigzagging staircase and came out through another unbarred door onto the top of the tower. He kept his hand on the hilt of his sword as he stepped out onto the roof, sweating under his furs and trying to get his breath back, but he didn't see the guard Kira had mentioned—in fact, he saw no one at all. He looked around, then made an easy guess: he'd find them all in the square structure built around the tower's chimney and surrounded by stacks of firewood. The building had only one door that he could see—he must have flown past it a hundred times without ever noticing it before now.

He spared a moment to crane his neck over the spiked wall: the army had arranged itself over the Front like a general's map: regiments from all the clans were lined up facing Eowara's tomb, except for the penurious Aelbars and the Peltrans, who probably didn't have enough soldiers to form even one company. Gannon had had the spearmen set up on either side, with the remaining troops organized in wedges in between them. Armored triffons lined the headland, and archers were marshalled on the walls, their longbows and steaming cauldrons at the ready. Rho might have found it amusing to see all of this fuss over that one narrow little tunnel in the headland, had it not been for the dread that washed over him when he looked into that breach.

Do not go down into the deep places.

He crept to the little stone building and tried the door, which moved so easily that he'd swung it halfway open before he had the presence of mind to grab it and stop it. A gust of heat rolled over him like the breath of some fiery monster, but the room beyond was about what he'd expected for a prison cell: a single cot, a chair, a table and not much else—except that looking at the clothes and a pair of boots next to the table, this room was clearly used by the guard, not the asha.

Sweat was already dripping down his forehead. There was a wooden bar across a door on the other side of the room, but he stopped to take down his cowl and remove his hood before he lifted it up. He pulled the inner door open, slowly this time, and felt heat pouring out through the crack as if a creature of pure flame was about to burst through and scorch his flesh into blackened, oozing sores—but when nothing did, he stepped inside and pulled the door almost shut behind him.

Fire lit the room in streaks and shadows, and in the first confusing moment he thought no one was there. A fireplace took up the whole of the near wall, and some irregularly chiseled holes provided the only ventilation; the place was an oven. A long table took up most of the remaining space and was crammed with the kind of junk he had used to build his model on the *Argent*: chipped jars and bottles, biscuit- and nut-boxes, thaw-vine cones, all kinds of completely ordinary rocks, and a colony of live brass-beetles buzzing under a blown-glass dome that had probably cost more than a year of Rho's wages at the Shadari garrison. A small bed piled with furs stood in the corner.

Finally he picked out the hunched little figure sitting at a table by the wall, holding a pen in a tiny hand. Her Shadari face had the unnatural pallor of dyed cloth washed and washed again until the pigment had nearly drained away, and the brown deerskin scarf around her neck gave Rho the macabre impression that she needed it to keep her bird-like head from falling off. Her eyes, though . . . for some reason, they reminded him of the hollow eyes of the stone gods on the headland.

<Where's Dramash? What have they done with him?> he asked in a panic, before remembering that he needed to speak Shadari. "Where's Dramash?" he repeated out loud, then, "Isn't he here?"

Something moved beside the bed and what had looked to be a cushion on the floor turned out to be the boy, huddling under a deerskin.

"Dramash," Rho burst out in relief, "oh, thank Onfar. Come on, come out of there. We're going back to the *Argent* now. Hurry up; we need to leave right now."

"You're Rho," said the old woman, wiping her pen. She set it down with a deliberateness that felt oddly like a reprimand. "You can call me Ani."

"Both of you," he amended, looking down at her, and making a snap decision to ignore Kira's advice to leave her behind. If Ani was a threat to Trey, then Ani had to go. The tremendous heat was making him dizzy. He went to the bed and began rummaging through the scraps, searching for Dramash's coat. "I can take both of you, only we have to go now, before the guard comes back."

Dramash didn't move or make a sound.

"Dramash?" He took a step forward and a great rush of acid filled his throat as the boy shrank back against the wall. "I'm not going to hurt you, Dramash, I swear. I had to knock you out in the throne room. That was—" Words piled up in his mind, but none of them fitted properly. "I shouldn't have brought you to see the emperor. I swear I'll never ask you to use your powers again. I won't make you do anything you don't want to do."

The deerskin came down to reveal a mat of curly hair, a furrowed brow and then a pair of wary eyes.

"Dramash?" Rho called out again. One of the logs in the fire fell, sending sparks everywhere.

"I don't want to go."

"Why? If it's because of Ani, she can come with us."

"I don't want to go with *you*."

And there it was: the gut-punch. Everything around Rho went very, very still. Even the fire couldn't breathe.

"You saw my temple fall, in the Shadar," said Ani. Her voice was as frail as her body, but it had a resonance that made everything in the room vibrate in sympathy. There was a hint of sibilance there too, somehow both lulling and thrilling at the same time. "You were there?"

"Yes, I was there," said Rho.

"And my people," Ani went on, "did they weep when it fell?"

"Yes." Rho knew that the grating sound he was hearing was his own breathing, but it didn't feel like it belonged to him at all. "They wept."

Ani nodded to herself. He thought for a moment that he saw her smile, then he realized it was only her wrinkles and a trick of the firelight.

"You must go," she said. "This is not the time for me to leave. Dramash is not going to come with you now."

Rho picked up one of Dramash's gloves. "Isn't he?"

"You swore you wouldn't make him do anything he didn't want to do," said Ani. "Why would he go with you, after what you've done?"

"I know what I've done. Trust me, I know. But I can't just leave him here. I *won't*. Anyway, who are you to judge me?" Rho stopped and swallowed back his anger, remembering that Dramash could hear every word. "Emperor Eoban found out about the ore thanks to you. You're the reason he invaded the Shadar in the first place. You're as much to blame for what happened there as I am."

"I've done my penance," said Ani, sitting back down on her stool and folding her wrinkled hands in her lap. "Can you say the same? Do you have anything to offer the child except more pain?"

Rho remembered his panic in the throne room, how hurting Dramash had been the only idea to come to him. Even now he couldn't think of anything else he could have done. That night when Frea had told him to keep Dramash's mother quiet, the night she had taken him; there had to have been dozens of ways he could have stopped Saria from screaming. Instead, he had slit her throat.

Ani's dark eyes moved over his face and he felt as if every one of his sins were written there.

"What am I supposed to do?" he asked helplessly.

"Dramash will stay with me," said Ani. "He and I are the same. I am the one he needs now. You've brought him to me so that I can protect him. Now you need to let him go."

"Dramash?" Rho knelt down next to the bundle of fur on the floor. He could still feel Saria's hot blood spattering down onto his hands and neck and soaking through his tunic. Whatever penance he had done so far was not enough. He wasn't a better person now than he had been then. "Dramash?"

"Go away."

There was a sudden rush of cold air through the vents high up on the wall and the door opened a little further. The guard had not yet returned, but he would, and most likely soon. Rho stood up, feeling the heat of the fire passing right through him. He walked out through the open door and shut it behind him, then remembered to put the wooden bar back the way he had found it.

The sweat on his forehead chilled into an iron band as he walked back out onto the top of the tower. Halfway to the door he had left open and creaking in the wind, the breathless awe of five thousand people moved straight through him, tingling through every nerve. The emperor had found Valor's Storm. *Good for him.*

For a moment he mused on the fact that Gannon had gone down into a tomb sealed up for a thousand years and retrieved the fabled sword of an ancient monarch, while he had been unable to free one little boy and old woman from an unguarded room.

He started back down the steps, but stopped after a moment to compose himself. For Rho, this meant slamming his arm against the wall, then kicking the stone hard enough to feel the shock all the way up through his leg. He would have bashed his thick skull against it too, except he wasn't sure the wall could take it.

Chapter 25

The "stride" was the second-worst thing Isa had ever experienced—and the first was having her arm burned to a cinder.

Everything blurred by so fast that she felt like her eyes would burst, the speed blending it all into a tunnel of hectic colors. Panic kept her fingers clenched around the fold of her sister's cloak, but she couldn't feel Lahlil's presence at all. Her bones felt like they had slipped free from her joints and gone careening off into the nothingness. The pressure in her ears grew and tightened into a sharp stabbing pain. She was terrified they would crash into something and shatter like mirrored glass into a million pieces that would never fit back together again.

And still it went on, and on, and on, and with every squashed heartbeat Isa could feel herself moving further away from Daryan until she feared she would never get back. She realized that she would have to let go of that fear, just as she had had to let go of Aeda by the farmhouse. There simply wasn't enough of her to stretch all the way to Norland.

The world returned at first as a dull point of light that spread out in front of her until Savion took shape as a blurred silhouette; but then she had to shut her eyes as the speed at which they were traveling became apparent. She reopened them just in time to see the darkness at the edges of her vision burn away in a blinding white glare, and then they were through.

She lost hold of Lahlil and pitched forward, slithering down a rocky slope covered with something white: real snow, so much colder and wetter than she had ever imagined. Her pack caught on a bush and tore away from her shoulder. By the time she recognized the nature of the mist-covered oval she was sliding toward there was nothing to do but snatch a breath of freezing air and hold it in her lungs. She heard the splash as she broke the surface of the water, but then sank underneath where there was no sound at all. She wasn't sure if the others were in the water with her, or if they had even come out of the stride alive.

She kept sinking down until she hit the rocky bottom, then tried to kick up to the surface, but the weight of her sword and her wool cape made it impossible. Her lungs had already begun to burn, and she was too confused to know in which direction to find the bank. Then someone hooked their arms around her and an interminable moment later she crested out of the water and flopped out onto the rocks, coughing and gagging with her throat on fire.

The landscape around her gradually came into focus. The pool steamed like bath-water, and a greenish substance, crystalline like salt, ridged the rocks along the edges while a vivid yellow slime washed up and down in the cracks between them. Berry bushes of some sort ringed the pool, together with low trees furred with scarlet lichen, and further out was a dense forest—pine trees, she thought. Moisture hung in the air and carried a strong aroma that reminded her of the poultices made by her father's physics.

<Are you all right?> asked her rescuer, still standing waist-deep in the water.

<Rho?> she gasped.

A long scar zigzagged down his neck and terminated in a fist-sized, puckered mass along his shoulder. Another scar cut across his temple, notching his hairline. Neither interfered with his chiseled profile or the quintessentially Norlander symmetry of his features. She would have known him anywhere—but she felt no recognition from him at all. For a moment, she feared he had lost his memory somehow—but then she realized that it wasn't Rho at all.

<"Rho?" You know my brother?> asked the man.

<Your *brother*?>

<You just said his name,> he said while Isa checked his features

one by one. She could see Rho in everyone one of them. <Where did you come from? You just appeared out of nowhere.>

<The Shadar, to begin with,> said Isa. <Then we—>

<Where's Cyrrin?> interrupted Lahlil from somewhere behind Isa. Her legs were stretched out in the water, but she was cradling Jachad in her arms and had somehow managed to keep him dry. The flush of color from the stride or the cold made the Nomas king look a little better than he had at Prol Irat, but Isa could see he wasn't conscious. Savion knelt nearby, drained but ecstatic. He had no cloak or blanket and his feet and legs were bare, but the careless way he scooped up a handful of snow made Isa think that the cold had no power to penetrate his knobbly skin.

<Lahlil. You're here.> Rho's brother waded smoothly through the dark water toward her sister. As he walked up the rocky bank she realized he was naked. She stared stupidly at his softly glowing body, flushed blue from the heat of the water as he said, <I told Cyrrin you weren't dead. I told her the rumors weren't true.>

<Where is Cyrrin, Trey?> Lahlil said again. <Up at the house? I need her, right now.>

But the conversation went no further as half a dozen men and women in patched old furs ran out of the trees with blankets, cloaks and all kinds of things in which to wrap them up, along with a stretcher for Jachad. Savion waved them off and continued kicking up the snow with his bare feet, grinning wildly. The newcomers took off Isa's cloak and swaddled her like an infant, pulling her toward the trees before she even had time to ask who they were or where they'd come from.

She stumbled and slid through the snow as her new friends brought her through a subtle gap in the trees and onto a narrow trail. Lahlil came behind her, holding on to the side of Jachad's stretcher with one hand as if determined not to let him go. Patches of creeping shrubs stuck barbs into Isa's clothes, and broken pine branches left sticky trails of sap on her hands and face when she pushed them aside. Creatures she barely glimpsed darted through the undergrowth, calling to each other with savage little barks. A single blue bird streaked out of the sky and circled around them before alighting on a branch. It watched them for a moment with black eyes and then took flight again, knocking snow from the branches as it darted through the trees.

This was Norland. This was the place Isa had dreamed of for as long as she could remember.

And she hated it. She hated the way the gray sky pressed down on the tops of the trees, and she hated the glare of the snow under the colorless light. She hated the sound of the snow crunching under her feet and the way the cold reached its hands through her wet shirt and under her skin. She hated it just as much as its gods hated her.

The trees thinned out and gave way to open space; she was glad to be out of the overbearing woods until the wind slapped her in the face. Rows of pillars broken off at various heights marked out what might once have been a hall, and just behind them sprawled a vine-covered heap no taller now than the trees around it except for a bit of tower poking up on one side. One of the walls on the right side had collapsed, leaving rooms and staircases exposed. The left side of the building and the tower had fared a bit better, but the main section was nothing more than a wide set of stairs and a broken gallery with tree branches poking in through the doorways. Judging by the encroachment of the forest, this house dated back at least to the Second Clan Wars, maybe even the First.

She huddled inside the furs they'd given her and hurried across the slippery stone paving, caring about nothing except getting out of the perishing cold. Lahlil took the lead as they passed through a wide door made of split logs and into a corridor. People came out of the rooms as they went by, and suddenly Isa began to take note of the scars, the burns, the crutches, the missing limbs. She looked through some of the doorways as they passed and saw crude beds with deerskin curtains, lamps fueled by some sweet-scented oil sitting in niches in the walls, and little else. She counted people—around forty so far—but she sensed others less eager to be seen hanging back in the shadows. Not one of them said a word.

Lahlil finally brought them into a room furnished with fur-covered pallets and work-tables spaced out along three of the four walls; the fourth housed a big fireplace with a poorly drawing fire that did little more than take the edge off the unbearable chill. A woman was waiting there for them, leaning on the shoulder of a girl of about ten years old. The woman had no obvious scars or missing parts, but her torso was encased in a wood-and-bone contraption buckled on with leather straps and a strange piece of furniture sat behind her, a bit like a cross between an upended plank and a chair. Isa guessed it must have been made for her to lean against, since she couldn't see how anyone could possibly sit down while wearing that brace.

<Cyrrin,> said Lahlil. She said it as if she was calling out the identity of a dangerous animal coming at them through the trees.

Cyrrin said nothing in reply, but her emotions flickered and jumped like the fire behind her. She instructed the stretcher-bearers to move Jachad to the pallet closest to the fire, and then rattled off a string of orders that sent them hurrying off to fetch or do various things. Her tone of brisk efficiency never wavered, but underneath was a physical pain so deep and constant that it reminded Isa of the sound of the surf at home. <And find this girl some dry clothes, for Onfar's sake,> Cyrrin concluded. <I've got quite enough to do without nursing a fever.>

Savion said something Isa didn't understand and flopped down on an empty pallet in the far corner of the room. He curled up his thin body on the fur blanket and appeared to fall instantly asleep. Cyrrin's surgery only had one other patient at the moment. He kept his face turned to the wall and looked to be asleep as well, but the smoky air around him stank with his despair. Isa noticed the bandaged stump of his right wrist poking out from under the blanket as she moved close to the fire.

Jachad didn't stir as Lahlil knelt beside him and undid the clasps of his cloak, but he moaned softly when she opened his shirt. The black mark over his heart looked like the spatter from a broken ink-bottle. Vines crawled under his skin and reached out in every direction, twitching in time with his heart's labored beating. The buckles on Cyrrin's brace jingled as she hobbled over and stared down at him. The way her eyes moved up and down his body made Isa uncomfortable; she wouldn't want to be looked at like that, reduced to little more than blood and bones.

<He's not sick. He's been poisoned,> said Cyrrin.

<I know. I brought it.> Lahlil reached into her pack and pulled

out the wineskin with the yellow smudge. <They put it in the wine. Do you know it?>

<No,> said Cyrrin, <I've never seen anything like it before.>

<It only hurts magic users,> Lahlil added quickly. Isa could feel her sister's hopes teetering, like a drunkard on the edge of a cliff, but she wasn't giving up. <We figured out that much on our own. I drank it, and some of the Nomas did too, and nothing happened to us.>

<Take that from her, Berril,> Cyrrin said to the little girl, who took the skin and carried it back to one of the tables. <Poisons don't have minds of their own; they can't pick and choose whom they kill. Where did it come from?>

<The desert, near the Shadar,> said Lahlil.

<Is he Shadari?>

<No. He's Nomas.>

<Nomas,> Cyrrin said pensively, but then Isa felt a crack open in her clipped, impersonal demeanor and something more genuine reached through. <Shit, Lahlil—for Onraka's sake, please tell me this isn't King Jachad.>

Lahlil didn't need to answer. <Now you know why I had to bring him to you.>

Isa felt the tension straining between them and didn't want to be in that room any more, but the thought of taking even one step away from the fire made her hug her arm closer to her body. She looked at the little girl instead, watching her very carefully pour out a little of the poisoned wine into a shallow, red-rimmed dish. The girl was missing her first and second finger on her right hand, but she had no trouble at all taking the stopper off the skin, pouring out the wine or putting the top back on again. Isa watched her smooth movements with envy.

<The Mongrel's here,> moaned the man on the other bed suddenly, rolling over but throwing his arm across his face. <She's here—it's all true.>

<No, it isn't,> Cyrrin told him, with surprising force. <This has nothing to do with you. Stay quiet, or go back to your room with the others.>

Isa's hand dropped to her side as recognition stole over her, slowly, creeping like a shadow and draining the blood from her hand and face. She couldn't believe it, but she couldn't deny it, either. She should have recognized Ingeld at once—except how could she, when this was the last place she would ever have expected to find him?

<Isa?> Lahlil called out to her as she went to the pallet and pulled the man's blanket to the floor. He was skinny and filthy and had one less hand than before, but it was undoubtedly Ingeld. The bloodstained bandage over the stump of his wrist made her want to crow with joy—it was an ugly, brutal impulse, but in that moment she didn't care.

<What are you doing?> Cyrrin cried out.

<Get up, Ingeld,> Isa commanded, ripping off her borrowed fur. The cold hit her wet skin like a fist, but the pain only fed her rage as she swept Blood's Pride from its scabbard. <Do you remember this sword? You were going to follow it, and Frea, into battle against the emperor. Now you can die by it. I said, *get up*!>

<Who are you? Leave him alone!> said Cyrrin. She tried to put herself between Isa and Ingeld, but the best she could manage was to lurch into the skinny arms of the little girl who darted forward to catch her. <Lahlil, you brought her here. Control her!>

<This man tried to kill my brother and me and Rho,> Isa told them all. <He's a traitor and a murderer. You should have let him die.>

<That's not what we do,> Cyrrin answered icily.

<No, don't stop her,> said Ingeld, sitting up. Dry fir needles dropped from the bed and scattered the floor around him. <I want her to kill me. If I'm already damned, at least I can die by the sword. Go ahead, Lady Isa. Kill me.>

She readied Blood's Pride to oblige him.

<Lahlil, make her stop,> Cyrrin commanded, her anger burning like a red-hot poker.

Isa struggled as Lahlil grabbed her sword-arm, holding her with a strength she couldn't match while everyone else in the room stared at her, their emotions colliding and careening all over the place.

<Berril, give Ingeld some more of that elber root to calm him down,> said Cyrrin.

The girl snatched up a clay bottle from the table and hurried over. He was too exhausted to resist and she managed to get a few drops down his throat. He fell back onto the bed a moment later and shut his eyes.

<What did he mean, “it’s all true?”> Lahlil asked Cyrrin. Isa pulled away as soon as her sister loosened her grip. <What didn’t you want him to tell me?>

<The Shadari witch foretold your return,> said Trey, stepping though the doorway behind them. He was dressed in the same ragged clothes as everyone else, but on him they looked like a poor attempt at a disguise. <She said you would come to Norland and lead an army of the cursed, making way for Lord Valrig’s return. Emperor Gannon has been preparing for war.> He walked past Isa to Ingeld’s pallet and lifted the drugged man’s wrist. <He cut off Ingeld’s hand so he could deliver a message to you. He wants you to know that he’s waiting for you.>

<You said there’s a Shadari witch?> Isa asked him, ignoring everything else Trey had said. <You mean Ani? The one who brought the secret of the Shadari ore to Norland—?>

<That’s not why I’m here,> said Lahlil, cutting Isa off. <I’m here so Cyrrin can cure Jachad.>

<That’s why you came,> said Trey. Isa didn’t know how she could ever have mistaken him for Rho. He had a spark inside him, a bright, cold light that was the exact opposite of Rho’s careless dispassion. <It’s not why you’re here.>

<Everyone, just shut up,> said Cyrrin. <Lahlil, don’t listen to him. It’s all some stupid fantasy.>

<It’s true,> Trey insisted, dropping Ingeld’s arm. <She swore she’d never come back here, but here she is, just as the witch foretold.>

<What did Ani really say?> asked Lahlil, glaring at them all. <She saw me in Norland, and here I am. She saw me with an army of the cursed. Look around, Trey. Who do you see? This is exactly what the elixir does. I know—I spent the last year chasing down a bunch of useless visions.>

<This is different—> Trey began.

<No, it isn’t. I saw the visions myself, and every time one came true, it wasn’t what I expected it to be. Seeing the future isn’t the

same as understanding it. You can't know what it really means until it happens.>

Isa could feel Trey trying to hold back his anger. <I do know what it means. You just refuse to accept it.>

<I told you, I don't want to hear any more about it,> Cyrrin lashed out. <It's just a story from some crazy old woman who needs to give them a reason to keep her alive. You'd believe anything if it meant you could fight again, Trey, even though we both know you wouldn't last an hour with that shoulder the way it is, no matter how often you soak it. You'll never fight again. Everyone else around here has found a way to accept what they've lost—everyone except you. That doesn't make you special. It makes you an idiot.>

Isa felt as if a pail of freezing water had been thrown in her face. The image of Trey rising up naked out of the pool appeared unbidden, but it was the scars down his right shoulder that she remembered most clearly. She held her breath, waiting for him to say something fine and noble; something about courage and perseverance and strength of spirit, the kind of speech she made to herself sometimes when she was trying to thread a buckle or sharpen a pen.

But Trey just walked out of the room.

Disappointment curdled in Isa's stomach. As she moved closer to the fire Cyrrin lurched over to the table, shutting them all out.

Lahlil bent down and picked up the fur Isa had dropped. <Put this back on, before you freeze,> her sister said, holding it out to her.

<Ani is still alive,> said Isa. <She's still there.>

<It looks that way. We'll deal with it later.>

<But you heard what Trey said. There might be a war—don't you think we should get her now, before something happens?>

<No,> said Lahlil. <I told you, we'll deal with it later.>

<No, we won't deal with it later,> said Isa. She was shivering, but she still didn't take the coat her sister was holding out to her. <We'll deal with it now. I know you said you wouldn't leave Jachad—you don't have to. Just tell me where to find Ani and I'll go myself.>

<You're not going to Ravindal,> said Lahlil. <I brought you here so you would be safe, and for now, that means staying here.>

<I knew it!> said Isa. <You've been planning to dump me here all along. That's the only reason you wanted me to come with you.>

<It's about time you told yourself the truth, Isa,> said Lahlil. <You can't go back to the Shadar, with or without Ani. You must have figured that out by now.>

<Daryan—>

<Daryan is never going to make the Shadar into what he wants, and what's worse, he's too much of a dreamer to realize it. I've seen his kind before, and I've seen what the world does to them. They'll break him, Isa, and if you go back, you'll just be watching it happen.>

Isa hadn't realized how badly she was shivering until her teeth ground together and the buckles on her swordbelt rattled. <Did you think I would want to stay here,> Isa asked her sister, her words stuttering as if the cold had crept into her mind, <or were you planning on stranding me?>

<This is the right place for you,> said Lahlil. <You belong here. There isn't any other place for people like us.>

<Then why didn't *you* stay?>

<We're not talking about me. I . . . > Lahlil tailed off, and it felt like whatever she had been about to say had tumbled down into a dark pit. <I'm just trying to help you.>

<I know,> Isa shot back, <but you're *really* bad at it! Ordering people around and making decisions for them isn't the same as helping.>

Lahlil's anger licked out into the space between them and she dropped Isa's coat. <I'm *not* giving orders. This isn't a battlefield.>

<Isn't it?> asked Isa. <You never asked me what I wanted, or Jachad either. We're not real people to you; we're just pieces to be pushed around a map so you can make whatever moves you need to win this war of yours—against the gods or against yourself, if there's even a difference. You should have seen for yourself that Jachad never wanted to make this trip.>

Lahlil's mind went as blank as a sheet of paper, and Isa would have sworn her sister had disappeared if she hadn't been looking right at her.

<That's not true,> Lahlil said at last.

<He told me in the forest.> She was sick of being pushed around, and Lahlil needed to understand. She shoved any regret about betraying Jachad's confidence aside and drove her point home. <He wanted to be with you when he died and he knew you wouldn't have stayed with him—you'd have gone off looking for a cure without him and left him to die alone. He was weeping when he told me.>

Lahlil collapsed in on herself—Isa was reminded of a spyglass folding up, and all trace of her emotions just vanished, until Isa again became aware of the rest of the room: the snap of the fire; the small sounds of Berril grinding something with a pestle and mortar; the creak of Cyrrin's strange brace as she reached for something across the table.

She couldn't stand it any more. She picked up the coat and went out into the hallway and ran straight into an old woman with a small stack of clothes folded neatly over her arm. A complicated pattern of purple blotches roiled over the whole left side of her face.

<Boiling soup,> said the old woman before Isa could say a word, and handed her the clothes. <My name's Dara. I was a cook for the Olsdans. You can put these on in that room over there.> She pointed. <You'll have to dry your boots by the fire. I'll find some food for you when you've changed.>

<Thank you,> said Isa, noticing as she balanced the bundle on the crook of her arm that Dara hadn't shown any exaggerated care when she handed them over, or offered any unsolicited assistance. <What do you people call this place?>

The woman gave a wry smile. <We call it Valrigdal—you know, like Valrig's city in the Under-realm—well, Cyrrin doesn't, but it's just a joke.>

<Oh,> said Isa, wondering how exactly it was a joke. <Do you know where Lord Trey went?>

<Here,> said Trey, leaning out of a dark doorway a little further down the hall. His emotions were drifting around near his feet like a cloud of heavy smoke. <What do you want?>

<I thought you'd want to hear about your brother.>

Chapter 26

Lahlil turned back to Jachad, squeezing her fists until they ached as she watched him twitch and moan in his sleep, remembering the forest and how he had made her promise she would stay by him. If Cyrrin couldn't help him, then Lahlil had made his last few days a misery just to please herself. *Everything always has to be about you,* Callia had told her.

Jachad gasped in pain and called out her name.

"I'm right here," she said, kneeling down by the pallet and taking hold of his wrists as he tried to claw at his chest. Confusion clouded his eyes and Lahlil wasn't even sure he recognized her. Her wet gloves began to steam as black flames twisted around his hands, but she held on, whispering, "Jachi, it's me. Stop fighting me."

<Give him the rest of this,> Cyrrin said to Berril, handing her a little jar. <It'll help with the pain.> Lahlil could feel her anger roiling underneath her words: a swift current under a calm sea.

<No, Cyrrin,> the girl protested, <you—>

<Just give it to him, Berril.>

Lahlil took off her gloves and carefully took the jar from the girl's maimed hand without acknowledging her hostility. Everyone's anger would have to wait. She circled her arm behind Jachad's shoulders and lifted him up so he could swallow the last few drops of the syrupy liquid inside the jar, then held him until the moaning and writhing stopped. When he was no longer gasping for air, she pulled her arm away and took his wrist to check his pulse, but he took her hand instead.

"So, that's striding," he said. He was too weak and too pale for his smile to be reassuring, and his voice had a thin, reedy quality that made him sound like a little boy. "You won't hear me complaining about triffons after this."

"Good."

"You won't leave, now that we're here," he reminded her. "We're staying together. You promised."

Lahlil gathered up the edge of the blanket in her hand. The wool was stiff and smelled of damp and woodsmoke. "I haven't forgotten."

He let his head fall so he could see the fire. "That Abroan man in Prol Irat, the way he looked at you . . ." He tailed off, then said, "You were right. I didn't understand."

"Don't talk any more now."

"Do you think my mother is in Ravindal now?" he asked. Lahlil kept her eyes on the stitches unravelling along the blanket's hem so she wouldn't have to see the tears darkening the freckles on his cheeks. "I think she's close. Just a feeling."

"We'll find her as soon as Cyrrin figures this out."

He didn't say anything; she knew he no longer had the energy to pretend to believe in a cure, even for her sake. The hundreds of tiny nicks opened by Isa's accusations began to bleed.

Cyrrin and Berril came over carrying a small cloth spread with a thick red paste.

<What's that for?> asked Lahlil.

<Time,> said Cyrrin.

"Don't," Jachad pleaded in Nomas as Berril exposed his chest again, but he couldn't lift his arms to push her away. Cyrrin laid the poultice over his heart.

"It's cold—" he began, before his hands curled into fists and his whole body convulsed in pain. Lahlil clutched his arm as a tortured sound twisted its way through his clenched teeth.

<What is that? What are you doing to him?> she demanded of Cyrrin.

<What I said: giving him more time. His heart was shutting down, Lahlil; I've given it a push. The pain won't last long and he should sleep a little after that.> She picked up a staff leaning against the wall. <Berril, take the poultice off when the convulsions stop

and then cover him up again. He can't take the cold the way we can. See if you can get that fire a little hotter, then come over here and grind up some more of that blue-root. We might need it.> Using the staff, she made her way back to the table on her own.

Lahlil kept hold of Jachad's hand until he settled down again, then she moved out of the way so Berril could take care of the poultice.

<Did you give him anything before you got him here?> asked Cyrrin.

<The Nomas healer gave him something—I don't know what was in it, but it helped with the pain for a while. I bled him on the way here.>

<You shouldn't have done that,> Cyrrin said brutally; she never had been one to soften a blow. <Backward nonsense. You only made him weaker.>

<He told me that, but I kept doing it anyway,> Lahlil admitted. She expected a tart reply, but Cyrrin's silence was worse. When Berril went to tend to the fire, Lahlil walked over to get an extra blanket from one of the empty pallets. The musky smell of the fur brought back the memory of waking up in this room for the first time. She remembered thinking she would never leave, and then she remembered thinking she would never come back.

<A normal poison spreads through the body,> Cyrrin explained. <I've seen it a hundred times. The poison moves through the blood and invades the various organs, and they die.>

<And this is different?> said Lahlil, laying the blanket over Jachad.

<The poison's in his blood, but it's not spreading through his body,> said Cyrrin. <Only his heart is under attack.>

Berril was kneeling in front of the fire and piling on more logs.

<How much time does he have?> asked Lahlil, glaring into the fire until her vision blurred and the modest blaze swelled with rings of light.

<Not long,> said Cyrrin. <A few hours; a day at most.>

<But you'll save him.>

<I don't know,> said Cyrrin, dropping a pinch of white powder into the saucer of poisoned wine. <Maybe. Maybe not.>

<*Maybe?*> One of the logs slipped and sent embers hissing onto

the cold stone hearth. Lahlil grabbed the poker from Berril's hand, startling the girl. <That's not good enough. I didn't bring him all the way here just to have him die now. You *are* going to save him.>

<Or what, Lahlil?> asked Cyrrin.

The rough iron of the poker scratched at her hand and white ash from the end of it dusted her boots. There wasn't any point in saying she had taken it from Berril without thinking. That was exactly the problem.

<Berril, go and find Petra and get something to eat,> said Cyrrin.

<I'm not hungry,> said the girl, busying herself with brushing the ash and embers from the hearth.

<Well, I am. Get some cheese, and some of those pannis berries—but make sure they're ripe. You know I don't like them too sour.>

Berril put down her brush with exaggerated care and took her coat from the hook by the door. She left to follow Cyrrin's instructions, but not before making sure Lahlil felt her wrath like a shove from her small shoulder.

Cyrrin waited until Lahlil had put the poker back, then said, <You're not welcome here.>

<Because of Trey?> she asked. <Sending me away didn't make him any better. He hasn't "settled in"—he's more deluded now than when I left. When are you going to give up on him?>

<Never.> The physic looked at Jachad's waxen face. <If you can't understand that now, I guess you never will.>

Lahlil walked toward the back of the room, where what remained of an old mural was flaking off the stone: the last shreds of something beautiful. Sometimes she could almost make out the image.

Cyrrin said, <You promised you wouldn't come back. You *promised.*>

<I didn't know anyone else who could help him. Heal him, and I'll go. I swear it.>

<So how did this happen?> asked Cyrrin as she began grinding some roots in the mortar, the sound setting Lahlil's teeth on edge. Berril should have been doing that; the effort would make the pain in Cyrrin's back even worse. <He's the only person from your old life you ever spoke about. What kind of horror did you drag him into?>

<It had nothing to do with me,> Lahlil told her, turning away from the mural.

Cyrrin's derision licked out like a whip. <*Everything* has something to do with you.> She lost her balance and grabbed on to the table to steady herself, in the process knocking a clay flask to the floor. It broke with a popping sound and filled the room with the clean scent of pine sap. Lahlil looked around for a rag to wipe up the oil leaking out over the floor.

<Just leave it,> said Cyrrin, smashing the shards of pottery under her heel for good measure. <I can't believe, after all that happened, you would just—> She broke off as a burst of pain shot through her spine; Lahlil felt her silent cry and lunged forward to steady her before she fell.

<I'll get Berril,> she volunteered as she helped Cyrrin over to her chair.

<No, don't,> said Cyrrin. She was still trying to get her breath back, but she was already retightening the straps on her brace. <I don't want her to know. She's starting to get protective. It's irritating.>

<Where's that medicine you take? I'll get it for you.>

Cyrrin went on fiddling with her buckles.

<You gave the last of it to Jachad,> said Lahlil, working it out. <That's why Berril was so angry.>

<She burned the last batch,> Cyrrin admitted at last. <It wasn't her fault. I forget sometimes that she's still a child. It's not fair for her to have so much responsibility, but she's the only one here with the physic's gift—she has to be ready to take over when I'm gone.>

Lahlil didn't insult her by offering platitudes and reassurances. Cyrrin knew the reality of her condition better than anyone. Her spine had been deteriorating for years, and eventually it would come to the point where no brace, however firm, would help her.

<I meant what I said about the elixir,> said Lahlil. <Those visions are never what they seem. I'm done with all that for good. Besides, I swore to Jachad I wouldn't leave him.>

<Speaking of which, I need to finish that mixture before he wakes up. It may get the swelling down enough so I can get a better look.> Cyrrin pushed herself away from the chair and back to

the table, staggering a little, like someone crossing the deck of a listing boat. <What have *you* been doing for medicine? You must have run out of what I gave you a long time ago.>

<I made it last,> said Lahlil.

<Couldn't you find someone else to make it for you?>

<No one outside of Norland had the right ingredients.>

<I'll have to send Berril out to hunt down some lash-weed before I can make up a new batch. The marmonts got into the beds last month and trampled down all the shoots.> Cyrrin moved the jars on the table around like she was trying to find one in particular, but Lahlil could see she wasn't looking at what she was doing. Finally she admitted, <I've missed you. It was nice having someone around who didn't need me to be strong for them.>

Lahlil went back to Jachad and straightened his blankets. She had no idea how she was supposed to respond to that.

<That bird of yours is still here,> Cyrrin added.

The return of her impersonal briskness came as a relief. <I know. I saw it outside.>

<Rana's been feeding it, but it doesn't follow her around the way it did you.>

<It didn't follow me when I left.>

<Probably because it knew you'd be back,> said Cyrrin, sighing like a falling leaf. <Just like we all did.>

Chapter 27

The smell of the strong Norlander wine made Rho feel a little sick, but he drank anyway. He wanted to forget the way Dramash had pulled away from him in Ani's tower, but the wine only made the whole scene spin around in his head like a wheel, forcing him to watch his failure over and over again.

The huge refectory was exactly the same as Rho remembered it. He had taken a spot on one of the benches where the mid-clan household staff and the Arregadors who didn't have the money for personal servants took their meals; sometimes there'd be a few furloughed soldiers, or better-heeled Arregadors looking for something to settle their stomachs after a night of debauchery, but now he shared it with only three off-duty guards. Great joints of meat turned on spits in fireplaces the size of small rooms, and the old steward—whose primary duty, Rho had always thought, had been the stingy rationing of cakes—still kept a sharp eye on the cooks, scullions and innumerable other functionaries responsible for feeding the Arregador household. No one had paid any attention to Rho since a sharp-boned boy in an apron had first brought his wine, which had no doubt been added to the bill the house-warden had begun drawing up the moment he set foot in the door. He knew he should eat something, but his stomach was so jumpy he didn't think he could manage it.

He used one finger to push around a stray metal token left over from a dice game, engrossed by the sound it made sliding over the cracks between the wooden planks of the table. His primary reason for coming back to Norland had been to make sure that Dramash could have a safe future—and so far he himself had been the only one to hurt the boy. He felt like the victim of the world's least funny practical joke.

The token fell through one of the bigger cracks and rolled away under the table.

Ani bothered him. Something in that room had felt wrong, but he could not explain why. He recalled every word she had said, but there had been nothing there to warrant any particular alarm. Dramash obviously trusted her and wanted to stay with her, and Ani had made it sound like the elixir showed them getting safely away, so obviously interfering now would only make things worse. If his gut felt like it was full of rocks, it was probably because no one was telling him what to do next. He just needed to stay out of it and Dramash would be fine.

He took another swig, hoping it would help him believe all those self-serving reassurances, but it didn't.

This was all Eofar's fault. He was the governor of the Shadar, the one in charge; he should have followed their original plan—or come up with a better one—instead of just feasting and scheming with the Eotans like he was no better than the rest of them.

Rho stared into the cup, now as empty of wine as it was of answers. He set it back on the table, then knocked it down with an angry flick of his fingers and watched it fall over on its side. It lay there gently rocking, which made him think of that morning in the Shadar when he had sat on a rock and watched the Gemanese ship sitting way out in the bay. Dramash had just destroyed the temple and killed all of his friends, but he remembered how peaceful he had felt watching the vessel bob up and down. He could have sat on that rock forever, looking out at the rippling swells and the drifting flotsam. Then Isa had come along and ruined it. *Do something,* she'd said. *Fix it.*

Rho reached out and stilled the rolling cup.

From the moment this trip had begun he had stood aside while decisions had been made around him. Instead of taking matters into his own hands, he had sat back and waited for others to fail. He had backed off when Dramash refused to learn how to control his powers, even though he knew better than anyone how much damage the boy could do; he had let Eofar take the lead with Gannon, even though he knew how angry he was; he had let Kira keep him away from Trey—and now he had let Ani take Dramash away from him without even putting up a fight. These had all been his responsibility, and yet here he was, drinking alone in the kitchen, waiting for someone to come along and fix everything for him.

He crossed his arms on the table and put his head down, feeling more alone than ever before and with not the slightest clue what to do about it. For a while, he listened to the roar of the fires and the slow squeal of the turning spits. Then he heard someone swing open the kitchen door behind him and Aline appeared in the doorway with her cloak over her arm, flushed and out of breath. He sat up, blinking.

<What's the matter?> Rho asked her. The room swayed a little; he really shouldn't have been drinking on an empty stomach. <You look like you've been running.>

<I've been looking for you,> said the hand-servant. She came over to him, her distress almost tangible. <Lady Kira wanted you to meet her at the stables, but it's too late. She must be gone by now.>

<Gone where?> He sank back down onto the bench. <She went *there,* didn't she? She changed her mind.>

<Not just that,> said Aline. She reached out as if she meant to grab him, but then she remembered herself and instead curled her fingers into her palms. <The emperor sent Captain Vrinna to Onfar's Circle to look for the cursed, and Lady Kira was trying to get there first, to warn them. I was supposed to send you to her at the stables, but that was almost an hour ago. I couldn't find you. I looked everywhere.>

A sledgehammer shattered every other thought in his head, leaving only that one.

<She went to the stables?> He stood up and tightened the buckle on his swordbelt. <What's she going to fly? She can't afford to keep a triffon in Ravindal.>

<The emperor keeps one for her so she can hunt with him. What are you going to do?> she asked as he grabbed his coat from the bench beside him and started for the door.

<Something,> he said, and pushed through the door and out in the hall.

The restless crowd of Arregadors gathered to talk over Gannon's next move paid no heed to him as he slid through them. The door-warden gave him a second look before opening up, but no one questioned him. He strode through the ranks of the Arregador house-guards, ignoring the lieutenant's request to stop; Rho was a member of the Shadari garrison and still under Governor Eofar's command.

As he headed out into the streets, he saw triffons patrolling in tight patterns overhead—and not just checking the Front or even just Ravindal; he could see them circling the lower town and the forests to the north and west too.

He had a hard time keeping track of where he was going—three years out of the country had somewhat blurred his memory of the city's streets—and he sagged a little with relief when he caught sight of the cooper's yard with its skeletal half-finished barrels, and turned into the modest little street leading to the stables. The stalls had all been abandoned in the face of the coming—or more likely, *imagined*—crisis, and the fires had all been doused. Rho saw nothing moving except a snow-covered heap of fur in the blacksmith's yard; it looked like a big white dog.

Five paces away he realized with a shock that the heap was Kira's coat, and that Kira was still inside it. He stumbled to a halt for a moment, not convinced that anyone in that crumpled position could still be alive, then he shook himself and ran into the yard. He didn't see any blood in the snow around her, and as he knelt beside her and lifted her up he discovered to his intense relief that she was still breathing.

<Kira?> he called, gently prodding her mind, but he felt nothing but the velvety oblivion he recognized from years of frequenting low-class drinking dens. He carried her to a corner between the wall and an ash barrel, examining the bruises covering the left side of her face and her swollen eye. She had a big lump on the back of her head—that probably explained why she was unconscious. The way she had curled herself up in the snow made him think she had taken blows to her body as well. There were strange

silvery blotches on her coat, face and hair, but he didn't know if they had any bearing on what had happened. She had lost her hood somewhere, so he tucked the cowl around her face to keep her warm.

<Kira,> he said again, shaking her a little. He scooped up a little snow and sprinkled it on her face. <Kira, wake up, come on. You have to wake up now.>

She twitched awake suddenly and opened one eye. <Where's Vrinna?> she asked, already straining to get up.

<I don't know—I didn't see her. No one's here at all.> He held on to her as she tried to pull away, warning her, <You might not want to try that yet. I've taken enough beatings to know how this works.>

<I have to get to the stables,> said Kira, pushing against him, then bristling with pain as if her clothes were made of hot needles. She steadied herself against him and said, <Vrinna knows there's something at Onfar's Circle and she's on her way there right now.>

<I know—Aline told me. Vrinna gave you this beating, didn't she?>

<And she enjoyed every minute of it. She knew I was hiding something—she tried to make me tell her the truth.> She paused, looking at him, then said, <Thank you for not asking if I did.>

<You wouldn't look that bad if you had.>

Kira reached up to touch her left eye and winced. <We can still get there before her—she doesn't even know what she's looking for.>

<We'll never get there in time,> said Rho, standing up behind her.

<We have to try.>

<No, listen—> He didn't know how to break it to her gently. <Listen, you've been unconscious a long time—Aline said she'd been looking for me for an hour, and that was before I got here. Vrinna has to be almost there already.>

He felt the last of Kira's optimism plummet, as if he had tied a stone around her ankles and thrown her from a cliff.

<Then what do we do?> she asked in despair.

<I don't know,> said Rho. He kicked the ash barrel and then winced.

Using his arm, she pulled herself to her feet; by the time he realized she was reaching for Virtue's Grace, she was guiding the sword back into its sheath.

<Where are you going?> he asked as she lurched past him, swaying badly.

<Where do you think?>

<You can't fly all the way to Onfar's Circle like that.> He dashed after her. <All that bouncing around in the saddle will kill you.>

Kira turned back to him; he watched as snowflakes settled on her hair and white eyelashes and was shocked anew at the damage to her beautiful face.

<Do you have a better idea?> she asked.

Another triffon passed by low overhead, and very much to his surprise, Rho realized he *did* have a better idea. He turned his face up into the falling snow and whistled as loudly as he could. The triffon turned around and flew back toward him, then the rider obeyed Rho's command to land.

<Rho?> Kira watched warily as the guard carefully maneuvered the triffon into the narrow street.

<Don't say a word—*not one word,*> Rho warned her as her questions burst open in his mind like scarlet blossoms. <I need you to take us to the castle,> he demanded of the guard, walking forward as the triffon drew in its wings and tossed its head, showering him with snow. She was wearing an Eotan tabard; Rho did not recognize her.

<Why?> asked the woman.

<Why, *my Lord,*> he said to her, mimicking the high-clan entitlement he had always so despised. <And it's none of your concern; you will do as you're ordered.>

Kira stepped up behind him, buzzing with anxiety. <Just tell me—>

<No.> He took her arm and led her over to the triffon. He saw the soldier shy away with repugnance when she saw Kira's battered face. Kira tried to pull her cowl down to hide the damage, but he gently pushed her hand away. <No, don't do that. Leave it.>

<Rho, I can't go,> Kira said, suddenly digging in her heels. <I can't show up at the castle looking like this.>

<Yes, you can, and we don't have time to walk there.> He pulled

her along, hating that he was causing her more pain, but he had no choice. The soldier kept the triffon in place, staring resolutely at the top of its head while Rho helped Kira up into the saddle as gently as he possibly could, then climbed up behind her.

<Rho—>

<We're going to demand that Gannon arrest Vrinna immediately, for unlawful attack,> he told her. <You're just going to have to trust me. This is going to work.>

Rho was astonished to find that he actually believed it.

Chapter 28

The force of the triffon swooping down over the Front forced Kira back against Rho as the Eotan soldier looked around for a place to set down safely among the fidgeting troops. Kira saw the soldiers stamping their feet against the cold and casting glances at the empty entrance to Eowara's tomb; she winced as waves of their edginess pounded against her throbbing eye and cracked ribs. Triffons still lined the headland and archers still gathered around the braziers, using the warmth to keep their bows supple, even though Gannon had always considered archery little more honorable than throwing rocks from a blind. She should have known that Gannon would not be put off by the failure of his villains to appear on cue; he was going to have his day of glory even if it meant making his soldiers wait out on the Front until icicles dripped from the corners of their eyes. No one was going anywhere until something *happened*.

<Rho—> she began, but he cut her off with a wordless warning.

The soldier flew low beside the terrace and Kira braced herself for the jolt of landing. Rho put his arm around her waist to support her, but she still felt as if she had just fallen from a window when the triffon's claws scraped across the black rock. She managed to undo the harness herself, but Rho had to help her down from the saddle. She was beginning to feel like a parcel that had passed through too many hands on the way to its destination. They moved up onto the first few steps to the porch so the triffon could take off again.

<Now can I say something?> Kira asked as the soldier flew away. She was holding on to Rho's coat, not just to keep him close, but to keep herself upright too. She looked over her shoulder to make sure no one was listening, and did her best to hold back a gasp as the twisting motion sent a stab of pain across her abdomen. <Listen, we can't go in there–it'd be as good as telling Gannon we're hiding something. We don't even know for certain if Trey is in any danger. After all, Cyrrin must have some way of hiding those people if she's kept them safe without anyone's help up until now.>

<We can't take that chance,> said Rho. <I'm sorry, but this isn't the time to lose your nerve.>

Kira bit back a curse. <That's not– Rho, this is madness. Gannon is not going to arrest Vrinna because of me; not now, not when he's waiting for the cursed to turn up.>

<He will.>

<Oh, of course,> Kira snapped, <because you know him so much better than I do.>

<Vrinna's gone against him by attacking you,> Rho reminded her. <He won't tolerate that: it's like an itch. He'll have to scratch it. Now just wait here and I'll be right back.>

<Rho–>

But he was gone, and she hurt too much to run after him. She had lost her hood and the cold that had been soothing to her bruised skin at first now struck her like a lash. At least no one was paying any attention to her: not with the tomb's dark doorway whispering to them of the Under-realm. Even Kira found herself drawn to the power behind that black arch.

Rho soon returned with two guards to escort them to Gannon. As they were led up the stairs and across through the smaller side door, Kira pinched the edges of her cowl together to keep it closed. If Rho was going to force her to act out this mummers' play, she could at least keep the audience to a minimum.

Maintaining her modesty became even more difficult when they got inside. High-clansmen in full battle-dress clogged the hall and the stairs, all checking and rechecking their blades and the rivets in their shields, while messengers pushed their way through the crowds and frightened servants tried to stay out of everyone's way. Kira dragged her feet as they moved up the steps to the second-floor gallery, her jaw clenched, hemmed in by the guards in back and Rho in front.

When they reached the throne room and the guards inside opened the doors, a rush of air as cold as outside pushed against her. Gannon had turned the room into his command post. His favorite generals—Denar, Olin and Gerstan—stood around a large table staring down at a huge map of Norland; the weighty battle-gear they wore explained why no one had lit the fire. Scribes sat around a second table, sharpening their pens or flexing their fingers to keep them limber in the freezing room. Youths not yet old enough for battle hugged themselves on the benches lining the eastern wall, waiting to carry messages that had yet to be transcribed.

<Will you pick up the pace, please?> Kira urged her guards, feeling the stares as they walked down the length of the room to the terrace doors at the opposite end. <We're not out for a stroll, you know. I'd like to see the emperor *before* the cursed attack and kill us all, thank you very much. How long do you think we'll give the Mongrel on that, by the way? Can we stop waiting for her when it gets to be dinner-time? I mean, we can't fight the greatest war since Eowara's time on empty stomachs, can we?>

Servants pulled the terrace doors open at their approach and more cold air swirled into the room, rustling through the maps and the scribes' paper and blowing in a cloud of snowflakes that didn't melt when they fell to the black stone floor. Rho let go of Kira's arm and stepped away from her as they crossed the threshold. She felt surprisingly adrift without his presence next to her.

Gannon stood motionless in the center of the terrace, looking up toward the beacon fire twisting in the wind on the headland while his dogs ranged around him, lifting their heads to sniff at everything and nothing. He had already traded his imperial sword for the restored Valor's Storm, and the newly burnished gold on its hilt and its bronze scabbard gleamed in the early evening light. Kira waited with Rho while the guards who had brought them went to explain.

Gannon did not move or even turn to look at them as they were ushered across the snowy terrace to stand before him.

<Your Majesty,> said Rho, <Captain Vrinna should be arrested immediately.>

<So they told me. What's she supposed to have done?> asked Gannon.

<Supposed to have done? *Supposed?*> Kira wailed, stepping forward and lowering her cowl with all the theatricality she could muster. <As if everyone can't see what she's done to me!>

Gannon finally turned around and reeled back in disgust at the sight of her battered face. <Vrinna did that to you?>

<Jealousy, that's what it is,> said Kira, putting up her cowl again with numb hands. He didn't believe them; they were going to fail. <She's always been jealous, and now she's finally snapped. She came at me like some kind of rabid beast. Honestly, I don't believe she's responsible for her actions; that's why I couldn't bring myself to kill her, because of course you know I could have if I'd wanted to. She's gone to Onfar's Circle, then, has she? Well, someone should go after her at once. I don't care if we're going to war, she can't do this to a fellow high clansman and get away with it. We'd lose the respect of the gods if we let something like that happen—and we would deserve it, too.>

Gannon regarded her with a kind of steely inquisitiveness, studying her like a map of enemy territory. He said nothing for a long time, letting the moment stretch until she didn't think she could stand the agitation buzzing in her bones another moment.

<Send a squad after Captain Vrinna,> Gannon said to the guards, <and see that she's brought straight to me.>

Rho's triumphant relief rolled toward her like a crystal-blue wave and she straightened her spine to keep from sagging down onto the snow-covered flags. She felt him in her mind, looking to share the victory with her. His plan had worked. For the first time she thought she might be able to forgive him for running away and leaving her alone with the shame of having betrayed Trey.

Gannon suddenly said something to the guards behind Rho's shoulder and they kicked Rho's legs out from under him. He dropped, cracking his knees on the stone flags, while a pair of heavy hands landed on his shoulders and held him down. Another guard grabbed Kira's arms and pinned them behind her back, making her whole body scream with pain.

<What's wrong?> Kira yelped. <Your Majesty? What's happening? Don't you believe me?>

<I believe you,> said Gannon. <Vrinna's broken my laws, and she'll pay for it. There's something about Vrinna, though . . . she doesn't do anything without a reason. You must have done something. >

<Lady Kira hasn't done anything,> cried Rho. <You have to believe me!>

<No, I don't *have* to believe you, Rho Arregador,> said Gannon, focusing on him as if he was a spider scuttling up the wall beside him. <I felt sorry for Trey. He deserved a better older brother than you; that's why I let him stay by my side. He hated how weak you were. He hoped you'd die in the Shadar—I bet you didn't know that.>

Kira stared down at the black stone marked with the guards' slushy footprints, feeling like her heart was about to burst.

<That cousin of mine over there, Eofar, he told me how you killed that Shadari bitch. Cut her throat, right?> Gannon circled around behind him.

Kira remembered the night Gannon had cut off Ingeld's hand and tried not to faint.

<Didn't you?>

<I did,> said Rho.

<Bet there was a lot of blood. Just pours out from a cut like that, eh?>

<Yes, it does. It did.>

At a gesture from Gannon, the guards grabbed Rho's arms and pulled him back up to his feet. Snow matted the bottom of his coat where he'd been kneeling on it, and Kira could see the wet stains on his trousers. Gannon bent down and squinted at Rho's abdomen.

<Eofar told me the whole story: the boy's father cut you, right around here, wasn't it?> Gannon looked around, and that's when Kira saw Eofar standing in the shadows by the terrace doors. She felt nothing from him; he was as blank as a snowdrift.

Gannon reared back and struck Rho in his side; Kira felt his pain like glass shattering, but had to listen again to the blunt sound of fist against muscle even as she looked away. She heard another punch, felt another scream, and then saw Rho fall over in the dirty snow before the guards pulled him up so Gannon could hit him again.

Rho coughed and spat out blood as the dogs loped over and circled around him hungrily.

Gannon turned to her, shaking out his fist. <How come you haven't asked me to stop?>

<Oh, was I supposed to?> asked Kira, scraping up all of her will to keep herself under control. <You never said. If we're going to play a game, it's only fair to explain the rules before we start.>

<There's only one rule,> said Gannon, and he hit Rho again while she looked on helplessly. <I'm the one who says when the game is over. I thought you knew that.>

Gannon finally stopped and issued a few orders to the guards, but Kira couldn't focus on what he said over the need to keep back the nauseating swell of her hatred. She would flay her own skin before she let Gannon touch her again, and if she had been able to reach her sword, she would have gone for him then and there, even though he would have ended her life in less than a heartbeat.

<Eofar!> Rho called out as the guards dragged him back into the throne room by his arms, straining them so badly she was afraid they would snap out of the sockets. She was marched along behind. Eofar still said nothing as they passed by him.

They were brought back through the room to the small door to the left of the dais, the one which led into the little room Emperor Eoban had used for private meetings when he was holding court. Kira's foot caught on the raised threshold and she stumbled as they shoved her inside. Stone surfaces slammed into her from various angles as she rolled across the floor. By the time the door banged shut, she couldn't move. She lay curled up against the pain, wheezing into the darkness.

<Rho?> she called out at last. She could feel his presence nearby like a bleeding wound, but he didn't respond. The only light came from the transom over their heads and their own luminous skin. When she was finally able to sit up, Kira looked down at the silver blotches left on her coat from her trip down into the caves; they looked bigger to her than before.

<Well, except for getting the shit beat out of me,> said Rho, as he

sat up against the wall and pulled off his hood, <my plan worked brilliantly.>

<That's one way to look at it.>

The door swung open again, sliding dim light across one-half of the room and showing the hazy outlines of a pair of chairs and a table. Eofar Eotan came through the door and shut it behind him.

<Why didn't you help him?> Kira demanded, fury giving her enough strength to clamber to her feet and face him. <You could have stopped Gannon—you watched Rho being beaten half to death and you did nothing!>

<I warned him to stay out of this,> said Eofar. <I never wanted him to get hurt.>

<That would be easier to believe if you hadn't told Gannon exactly where to hit him,> she shot back.

<You don't understand.> The reek of wine saturating his clothes made her eyes water; she had a pretty good idea of what he'd been doing since they'd left Eowara's tomb. <I've made up my mind: Gannon is the real monster here and he has to be stopped. No one in the Shadar—or anywhere else—will be able to live in peace until he's gone.>

<Stopped, how?>

<He means he's going to challenge Gannon for the throne,> said Rho, pulling himself up on the wall. <And that's suicide. I'm not going to let you do it, Eofar. I'm so angry with you I would choke you myself if I could reach you, but I still don't want to see Gannon cut you in half.>

<That's not going to happen,> said Eofar. <Gannon gave up his imperial sword for Valor's Storm, just like I planned. Strife's Bane gives me the advantage now. I will defeat him.>

<Eofar, I know you think this is the best way to free the Shadar—>

<Not just that,> he said, cutting Rho off. His silver-blue eyes shone brighter than anything else in the room. <Freeing the Shadar isn't enough; not any more. The rot of this place goes too deep for that. I'm going to free the world from the Norlander scourge. I'm going to end the empire itself.>

<You're a fool if you think you'll end the empire by taking the throne from Gannon,> said Kira, not bothering to temper her

scorn. <The Eotans will get rid of you soon enough and the empire will go on just like it did before.>

<You *still* don't understand.> Eofar's emotions rocked between heady expectation and plummeting dread in a way Kira recognized all too well. It came from trying to deceive yourself about the wrongness of something you were about to do. She'd felt the same the night she'd slept with Rho. <If the elixir predicted the cursed would come, then they'll come. I'm going to wait for them, and then I'm going to kill Gannon, and after I do, I'm going to let the cursed have their way with Norland. I'm going to walk away and leave it bleeding behind me.>

<Nations don't bleed, Eofar,> said Rho, stumbling forward and grabbing Eofar's coat. <*People* bleed.>

<What does it matter?> Kira asked, trying to pull Rho away, but she didn't need to; he fell against her, breathless with pain. <Let him kill Gannon if he wants. There is *no* army of the cursed. We both know that.>

But Rho ignored her, even as he clutched her shoulder for support. <So, that's your plan, Eofar? Save the world from the empire by letting the cursed kill everyone in Norland? Say you succeed: what then? What if Lord Valrig decides that Norland isn't enough for him, what happens to the world then?>

<Stop talking about this,> Kira demanded. <Just stop it, Rho.>

<You were there in Eowara's tomb,> Eofar said to her. The force of his resolve pushed into her mind, powerful enough to back her up a step. <I know you felt it, too. Something's coming. *They're* coming. You can talk yourself out of believing it all you want, but you won't stop them.>

<No!> said Kira stubbornly. <No, I will not allow this discussion to continue. You don't know what you're talking about, Eofar. You know nothing about the cursed. They're not beasts. They're not what you think they are at all.>

<He knows what they are.> Rho sighed, loosening his grip on her shoulder. His words ached with something Kira had never felt from him before and it confused her. <That girl I told you about? The one who lost her arm? That's Eofar's sister. He cut her arm off after she'd been burned. He saved her life.>

Kira's mind just stopped, like she'd turned a page in a book and found the next one blank.

<This isn't what Harotha wanted, Eofar,> Rho pleaded. <Don't wait until after you've done something you can't undo to find that out. Trust me, I know. I should have stopped you before things went this far. Please don't give me something else to regret.>

<I'll see that you both get out of Ravindal when the time comes. Dramash, too,> said Eofar, striding to the door.

<Wait!> Rho reached out to grab Eofar's coat as he walked by, but he missed and reeled into the wall clutching his side. Eofar opened the door and went out again, leaving Kira and Rho alone in the near-darkness.

<I don't care what he says,> said Kira, as a strange shudder wound through her, starting from the half-healed cut under her left eye. <Nothing is going to happen. It's going to be all right.>

<No,> Rho moaned from the shadows, <no, it's really not.>

Chapter 29

Isa found an empty room in Valrigdal where she could put on the clothes Dara had given her. As soon as she was alone a pang of homesickness shivered through her. The fire in Cyrrin's surgery waited just down the hall, but so did Lahlil, with all her stifling, self-serving interference. She needed to be away from the twist and pull of others' emotions so she could think of some way to get to Ravindal, because she was certain now that Lahlil had no intention of helping her.

From Trey, she had learned that a fast triffon could reach Ravindal in less than two hours, and that someone who knew the route and how to survive the terrain could reach it on foot in a few days. None of that helped. She didn't have a triffon, or any way to get one, and her odds of survival out there on her own would be about the same if she stripped naked and covered herself in jam first.

She went up onto the gallery and then kept climbing, stretching over gaps where the stones had fallen away. She'd tucked a piece of hard biscuit and some dried meat into her pocket—she knew she should eat something to keep up her strength—but the gamey smell of the meat only worsened the sour cramp in her stomach.

She emerged onto a stretch of battlement where holes for long-gone iron spikes lined the walls. The short walkway terminated in what had once been the tower, but was now just a few walls with the remains of a fireplace and a doorway to a four-story drop straight down into the woods below. Thaw-vine crept over all of it, and the constant dripping of the snow melting through it tapped against her raw nerves with tiny insistent fingers.

She went across to the wall and looked out over the landscape, out to where Ravindal taunted her somewhere beyond the horizon. Heavy snowflakes blended into a white haze over an empty plain; beyond that, the forest sloped up before giving way to a range of rocky hills. By screwing up her eyes, she thought she could make out a smoky shape far, far off in the distance to the southeast where flag-topped spires and spiked parapets rose up from the clouds of her imagination just as they had in the days when her mother had spun tales of far-off Norland.

A flock of dark birds swept across the sky right above her in a wave, then veered off the opposite way. A flash of color caught her eye just as the little birds scattered in all directions—the blue bird from the forest was streaking after them. The flock regrouped and headed down into the trees with the blue bird following, and she lost sight of them as they disappeared below the wall.

Panic sat just below the surface of her thoughts; she had no idea what her next move should be. Every idea she tried to form just spun away. *Had she come this far, only to get no further?* She squeezed her eyes shut and tried to let the heavy silence calm her mind, leaning back into the warmth of a thick spray of thaw-vine and soon falling into a fitful half-sleep, where she dreamed of walking in endless circles.

The whir of the blue bird's wings startled her awake again as it alighted on the top of the wall just opposite.

"Go away," she said to it in Shadari.

The bird walked a few steps one way and then walked back again, watching her all the while. Isa tore off a little strip of the dried meat and tossed it toward the bird, who flew up after it and snapped the morsel right out of the air. Then it returned to the top of the wall to gulp it down before cocking its head at her again, clearly waiting for more. She put the meat between her teeth to tear off another piece—but a familiar sound intruded on the silence: triffons, sweeping across the sky, then turning and going back the other way. They were close. She counted two full wings and each of the twelve beasts was carrying a pair of riders. *If only she could get hold of one for herself.* She could almost feel those muscles straining underneath her, those wings beating the sky as she urged it on toward Ravindal.

Then she saw that they were not just close but getting closer, and that the precise and methodical pattern of their flight could only be a search pattern: those triffons were looking for something—or someone.

Isa dropped down behind the wall, tugging her cowl down to cover her face while she wondered how to let the people below her know about the danger. Then a scratching sound came from the top of the wall above her and she twisted around just enough to see the bird strutting back and forth again, puffing out its blue-feathered breast. Its bright plumage shone like a beacon.

"Go away," she whispered, but the bird stood up taller and flapped its wings, scattering the snow around it.

The light dimmed as one of the triffons passed just above her; she bowed her head and counted the gray shadows, waiting for them to go by—then a greedy cry from the bird pulled Isa's nerves as taut as a bowstring. At the sound, one of the triffons broke formation and swung back around just as the bird hopped down off the wall and right in front of her. She tried not to move, even though it was pecking at her cloak. She could see the triffon's massive head coming toward her, changing the snow to mist with its warm breath.

Isa stood up and drew Blood's Pride. She didn't know how she was going to fight them, and she didn't care; she only knew that she would not cower before them. She screamed out loud, the effort ripping her throat to shreds, but she was sure her sister and everyone else below had heard her. The closest rider called out her presence to the others and the formation shifted, but no one came to engage her. She sheathed Blood's Pride and picked up the largest rock she could find, and then flung it at the nearest triffon, cracking it on the base of its tail. It bellowed in annoyance, but it was too well trained to buck. Isa ran across the battlement as the rest of the formation broke apart and three or four triffons wheeled back around toward her.

<Leave her,> commanded the only rider without a partner in the saddle. The guard's eyes glared out from beneath a bronze helmet. A blue crown had been stitched onto her tabard above the

Eotan wolf's head, and the authority in her words ran down Isa's back like an iron rod. <She's trying to distract us. That means there're others.>

They flew off, leaving Isa alone on the battlement. The moment they'd moved off she ran to the stairs and half-climbed, half-fell down to the floor below. She pounded along the half-floored gallery, but Cyrrin's people were already running frantically, shouldering bundles and helping those less able. She saw Dara the cook; she held a frightened child by the hand as she followed others Isa had met earlier—Weldsin, with a foot lost to cold-creep; Erlis with the twisted nose; blind, cloudy-eyed Petra, and Thora, whose scars she never saw . . .

But not Trey; she saw him standing back in a corner of the gallery, watching the people scurry about below him. It was impossible to tell where her hatred for the Norlanders ended and his began.

<You're not going to run,> she said.

<Neither are you.>

<No,> she replied. <No, the only place I want to go is Ravindal.>

The cold spark inside him twitched, bright and eager. <As do I. If Lahlil won't come, I'll go without her.>

Isa followed him down the opposite stairs to the ground level of the empty side of the building, leaping down over the last three missing steps. She could see the triffons overhead now, fanning out, and she and Trey waited in the shelter of a pile of rubble, watching to see where they would land.

<Isa?>

Lahlil stood just outside on the other side of the building, tensed like a cat ready to leap. She could do nothing to stop them from over there.

<I told you if I had a chance, I would take it,> Isa called to her as the triffons began landing all around Valrigdal in a wide circle. <Daryan can't wait, and neither can I. I want to go home and this is how I get there.>

<They'll kill you, Isa.>

<If they do,> she told her sister, <I want you to remember that bringing me to Norland was your idea. Sorry it didn't work out the way you planned.>

Trey broke for the woods, and Isa pelted after him as fast as she could, running with a wild freedom as if a rope holding her back had just been cut. She skated across the icy stones, darting through the pillars, then leaped through a gap in the jagged line of the old back wall and into the trees. As soon as the triffons started their descent she followed the path back to the spring, willing herself not to slip and fall.

She burst through into the clearing. Mists from the hot springs were drifting over the ground, and a triffon had landed on the open space between two of the steaming pools. The two riders were already dropping down from the saddle and Isa froze: both guards were carrying imperial swords and she had only Blood's Pride. Then branches snapped behind her and Trey charged straight for them. Isa clenched her teeth, remembering Cyrrin telling Trey he would never fight again, and she couldn't help but remember all that scarred and knotted flesh she'd seen as he rose up out of the pool.

But if he could do it . . .

With furious resolve, she drew Blood's Pride and charged out to meet the man coming for her.

His black-bladed sword flew toward her, already shining from the falling snow, and she came on guard and blocked his first two cuts, moving instinctively, though Blood's Pride felt as slow and stupid as a cudgel in her frozen fingers. Her heels skidded on the ground. The Norlander guard forced her back past the pool and into the clinging branches. She had already lost track of Trey's position, but she could hear the sounds of combat.

She had to focus: her position went from bad to worse among the trees where she risked lodging her blade in the black bark of some looming pine. She would never get anywhere like this, weaving backward over the unfamiliar terrain, fighting the grasping bushes and tangled patches of ivy as much as her enemy's sword. Several times she tried taking the offensive, but the guard had his block up the moment her arm changed direction; he was just too fast for her.

Then the inevitable disaster happened: she stumbled into a thicket where a host of thorny branches stuck fast in her borrowed cloak, pulling it open and pinning down her sword-arm.

Her opponent slashed his way in after her and she could feel his loathing like fetid breath in her face as he caught sight of her missing arm. Good. She didn't want his compassion. She wanted to be the monster he knew her to be; the contagion that was going to deliver Norland into the twitching, feverish fingers of the cursed.

She pulled herself away just in time, and his blow sliced through the spindly thorn branches instead of her shoulder. Her shirt ripped as she twisted around, but she had him now: too close to cut him, so instead she rammed the pommel of her sword into his shoulder as hard as she could manage, and he fell back, just as she had intended, leaving the way clear for her to thrust the point of Blood's Pride just under his chest-plate and into his stomach. His weight nearly pulled the blade out of her hands as he teetered there, then she yanked it back and watched him pitch face-down into the slush.

Wicked jabs of pain pulsed down her missing arm as she ran for the nearest gap in the trees, but she set her teeth against it. But just as she had almost reached Trey, she lost her footing on a bit of sloping rock and went slithering down. Black bark and bristling green branches flashed by; she was sliding completely out of control, and not toward a bush or a tree but straight at Trey. She tried snatching at a clump of gnarled roots, but she didn't dare let go of Blood's Pride and they just grazed her freezing fingers, rubbing them raw without even slowing her progress. Her boots collided with the backs of Trey's legs and knocked him on top of her, but not before he had grabbed hold of the guard's cloak and brought him down too.

The next few moments were a hideous confusion of boots, blades and cloaks and Isa tried to roll free, only to find herself throttled by her own cloak as it caught underneath Trey's leg.

He managed to roll over on his side to free her, and she and the guard sprang up at the same time.

The guard was still off-balance from the pile-up, but his instincts were fast and he whirled to face her anyway. She saw the silver eyes beneath his hood slide to her missing arm and she felt his disgust roll over her like the stench of rotten meat. The cold cracked through her shirt like a whip, but her muscles worked smoothly as she rushed him, playing on her opponent's horror.

Moving faster than she had ever moved before, she soon had him backed him up toward one of the massive trees. He stumbled on roots hidden by the snow, so Isa leaped at the chance to slash at his exposed side. The sharp blade slid through skin and muscle and she jumped back, but not before a gush of bright blood marked her trousers with a wide wet streak.

She turned away from the dying man, expecting to see Trey climbing into the saddle, but the triffon was still standing calmly with the warm mist swirling around its feet, sniffing at the bushes.

<Trey?> she called out, and ran over to where he was standing on the edge of the clearing, stock-still and staring at a spot in the trees. She didn't need to ask why; a tall, wiry woman was forcing her way through into the open: the woman in the bronze helmet, the solo triffon rider.

<Vrinna,> said Trey.

<I knew that bitch wife of yours was hiding something,> the woman said. Her words swung at Trey's head as if they could cave it in. <All this time, while she spent her nights rolling the wrinkles out of the emperor's bedclothes like a split-clan whore.>

Isa felt Trey's bright red rage unfurl behind him like a cape in a strong wind. <I don't have a wife, nor an emperor—not since you and your gods cast me out.>

<Where is the Mongrel?> asked Vrinna, her black blade twitching. <The emperor is waiting for her. And just for fun I'm going to throw your head in your bitch wife's lap.>

<Go,> Trey told Isa as Vrinna rushed him. <Go now, before the others come.>

Isa sheathed her sword and vaulted up onto the triffon, snatching at the pommel to keep from sliding right across the smooth leather saddle and over the other side. She slid Blood's Pride into the saddle's sheath as the startled triffon swung its head and sidestepped into the pool, splashing up the warm water and sending a cloud of mist into the air. Isa didn't have time to manage the buckles with her only hand, so she wrapped the straps around her arm as best she could, then took up the reins.

It felt strange to have any other triffon except Aeda beneath her. She brought them up as high as she dared until she had a better view of the situation. The guards had landed all around the castle and were closing in, obviously intent on driving anyone they found into the middle. Five of the guards charged into the pillared yard from different directions, but none of them had any prisoners in tow, nor were there any waiting to be taken. Cyrrin's escape plan must be working.

Trey and Vrinna had fought each other to the edge of the clearing; from her vantage point their blows were so quick that she could hardly see their black blades flicking through the air. The snowy trees ate up the clanging as if feeding on their animosity. Trey's fluid footwork and skill took her breath away, but she could see the tremendous determination he needed to move all of that stiff scar tissue. As difficult as it was for Isa to admit it, that fight was only going to end one way.

She turned the triffon and dived straight toward them.

They both saw her battle-trained triffon coming for them, but neither of them broke off the fight—finally she gave them no choice but to dive out of the way, each leaping in opposite directions. She drove Vrinna back to the trees, flying so low that the end of the triffon's tail skated through the snow. She didn't veer away until the last possible moment, forcing her mount to turn almost sideways to avoid the trees, remembering too late that she wasn't properly strapped in. She gulped down a panicked breath as she hooked her arm around the pommel and held on until they levelled off again. When she looked back, she saw Vrinna clutching her chest and thought she saw blood: only then did she realize that one of the triffon's needle-sharp back claws had caught the captain as they turned.

She flew back around and slid into a landing just behind Trey. <Get on,> she called down to him, and started struggling out of the harness so she could slide back into the seat behind.

<I didn't need you to rescue me,> Trey fumed, rage lighting him up like a beacon.

<I need you to come with me.> She tried to thread the buckles faster as she saw the bleeding woman stagger up and come at them at a run. <I don't know the way.>

He looked off in the direction of the ruined castle.

<Trey!> she cried out, as the woman closed the distance between them.

Finally he climbed up in front of her and strapped himself in with a few practiced tugs. He took up the reins while the triffon stretched its wings to take off, keeping the charging woman at bay. He turned east as soon as they were in the air.

<They'll come after us,> said Isa.

<They're focused on the ground,> said Trey. <I'll fly above them. All they'll see is our belly. That should give us a little time before Vrinna can send out new orders.>

The ruined castle shrank beneath them as they spiraled up, leaving behind the strider, Jachad, Lahlil and her last links to the Shadar. Isa could not go back the way she had come. The only way home now was to go forward.

Chapter 30

Isa squeezed her knees tighter and tried not to think about the deep dusky green forest beneath them. She had never flown so fast before; she didn't think Aeda was even capable of such speed. Her arm and shoulder ached with every bounce, and suddenly the terror she had felt that long-ago day as she watched her mother fall, right in front of her, held her once more in its claws. Trey was saying something to her, but she couldn't make it out over the memory of her mother's scream. She shut her eyes and tried to use the icy touch of the snow to keep her in the present. A tug came from around her waist: Frea, with a knife in her hand—but no, it was Trey, tightening the buckles for her now.

<Are you all right?> he asked her.

<Yes.> When he turned back around she could see how stiff his neck was by the way he held his head; she could sense the pain running like cracks through his military discipline. <How long will it take to get there?>

<Longer than it should. Vrinna will send her guards after us so I'm taking us out of the way to avoid them.>

They flew on through the empty sky, leaving the ruins far behind them, and Isa eventually stopped clutching the lip of the saddle every time they pitched up or down to take best advantage of the wind. Snow quickly piled up on her cowl and shoulders, even sliding through the eye-holes of her hood. The forest was endless, interrupted by white plains or snow-dusted hills before the trees crowded back in again. Trey was avoiding habitation and

Isa saw towns or manors only in the distance: great stone houses with spiked towers and parapets and concentric walls, with hot springs hidden under clouds of vapor; towns and villages of little houses made of stone or wood. The closest one they passed had a tall tower wedged into a chink between two rocky cliffs. Her family owned an estate somewhere, not that she ever would see it now.

<Not long now,> he reassured her as below them a stream cut through banks lined with flowers in startling shades of red, blue and purple.

<Where are we going to land when we get there?> Isa asked.

<Near the stables,> said Trey. <No one should notice us there.>

<What then?>

<I'll know when I get there.>

She strained her eyes, trying to see through the driving snow, and thought she could see towers in the distance. The gray sweep behind it must be the sea.

<Trey . . . > She looked again. <Trey!>

<I see them,> he said. Two triffons, flying just south of them. One of the triffons had armored plating covering its head; the other was missing the tip of its tail. It was too late to fly high enough to pass over them.

<They're turning—they've seen us. I think they know we don't belong here.>

<Hold on,> Trey warned her, and then banked sharply to the left, their triffon snorting with the effort.

<They're following,> she warned him.

She thought his handling of the reins nothing short of brilliant as he forced their pursuers to throw themselves around the sky, teasing out a little more distance with each maneuver. Isa gritted her teeth and did her best to endure it without distracting Trey, but even with his adjustments, her harness wasn't tight enough to keep her backside from sliding across the saddle and smashing her hip into the curved side with every sharp turn.

<We can't outrun them,> she said, leaning over to draw Blood's Pride. The screaming wind tried to pull it from her hand, but she held on determinedly. <Bring us in striking distance of the armored one.>

She waited for him to argue with her, but he said nothing, just brought their triffon round into position—his movement caught the soldiers by surprise and the man on the back had no time to readjust his harness for fighting. He tried to take the offensive anyway, slashing at her as the triffons passed, but he wasn't able to stand tall enough to extend his arms properly. She parried, and though her muscles were stiff from the long ride and the snow was blinding, still her thrust found its mark past the soldier's block and into his shoulder. She tightened her grip on Blood's Pride and used the momentum of the triffon's movement to pull the blade out again.

<Other side,> Trey called back to her as the triffon with the stubby tail came round into position; Trey hauled on the reins, trying to pull theirs back the other way, but the other rider, anticipating his move, altered course to force the confrontation. Isa swung around in the harness just in time to make the block, but her angle was wrong and the oncoming black blade skidded off Blood's Pride and bit into her thigh. Blood welled up over her knee like a warm blanket and she could feel the soldier's triumph.

<How bad?> Trey called back to her, trying to look at her as the first triffon came around again. The soldier in the back was slumping, but the man in front clearly intended to fight.

<Keep going. I'm all right.>

The lead rider on the armored triffon looped the reins over the pommel and drew his sword and as Trey sped past, Isa leaned over—perilously far over—and struck three quick blows. The first two missed, but the third sliced deep into the man's arm. She had wounded both riders now. He bellowed in pain, then whistled an order at his triffon, who broke away and headed down toward the rocky ground below.

Isa's head spun and she found herself dropping back down in the saddle, but before she could pull herself together, Trey had stood up in the stirrups and was taking the next attack from the remaining triffon, the one with the ugly tail. Her dizziness blurred his swordplay into a series of indistinguishable flashes, but a moment later he was sitting down again and wiping the blood from his sword with a rag he pulled out from under the saddle. The triffon was gone, just like the other.

<Here,> he said, handing the rag back to her, <tie up your leg, tight enough to slow the bleeding.>

For the first time she was glad of her enforced idleness in the Shadar, for she had spent a long time practicing things like one-handed knots. The depth of the cut surprised her, but likely the cold was dulling the pain and slowing the bleeding.

<Over there,> said Trey, and she saw towers up ahead, with yellow watch-fires flickering like candle-flames behind the snow.

<Ravindal?>

<Almost there. They won't stop us now.>

Isa squinted through the snow as the city grew closer and closer and wondered how Trey could possibly be looking at the same sky if he still believed they would get through alive. There was a great plateau down there at the foot of what could only be Eotan Castle, and triffons covered the whole area above it like a net. They had shaken off their pursuers, but that would hardly matter once they were spotted by these others.

Trey brought them along the northern edge of the walled city, the side furthest from the sea, racing along just below the wall as mounted soldiers hailed them. Trey ignored the first hail, and the second, and the third.

Low buildings and narrow alleys streaked past, then big houses like the ones in Isa's picture books, with spiked towers poking up in the air and clan pennants flapping in the breeze. In between the buildings, spires, vine-covered walls and gigantic green-glass figures lay stretches of snow-covered rock and black fissures stretching open like eager mouths.

Trey brought them up again, rocking her back in the saddle: three triffons had swung into position behind them and were in hot pursuit. Isa gripped the saddle so hard that she was afraid her fingers would permanently lock in that position. Trey dropped them down suddenly between two high walls; only a battle-trained triffon could have been forced into such a narrow space without bucking, but even so, it roared out a deep-throated bellow of annoyance as its wings scraped along the stone walls. They shot out from between the buildings a moment later, straight into a thick plume of woodsmoke that stung her eyes and clogged her already-straining lungs.

They overflew several huge houses, then she got her first real look at the lusterless oval of the harbor down below them, bristling with masts and reminding her of a beetle flipped on its back. Then she looked down at the plateau—it must be the Front, she now realized—and her heart leaped into her mouth. Soldiers covered it, as thick on the ground as a flock of gulls on a rubbish heap.

Two more triffons ahead of them broke away and headed toward them.

<Trey!> she called out, twisting around and craning her neck to see if they had any chance of escape. Their original pursuers had disappeared and she wanted to believe they'd lost them, but the burn in her chest told her otherwise—and she was right. Her warning came out as a wordless scream as the first triffon came barrelling out from the widest of the cross-streets, cutting right across their path. From the corner of her eye she saw the other triffon coming from the opposite direction.

<They're trying to force us down,> said Trey. <Hang on!>

He pulled their triffon up into a climb so steep that Isa worried her spine would snap like a dry twig. She wrapped the harness even more firmly around her arm, then gripped the saddle again and squeezed her thighs as tightly as she could to keep from being flung right off as the other two triffons converged on them. The angle at which they were flying was precipitously sharp. A knot of pain exploded at the back of her head and her stomach flopped as the horizon swung by faster than her eyes could track. Trey was hauling on the reins, but they were boxed in now: more and more triffons forming a circle around them. The charged emotions of the Norlanders watching from the ground reached up to her like the warm, grasping tendrils of the thaw-vine, trying to pull her down to them.

<I have to land,> Trey told her.

<I know.> Isa clenched her teeth together as the triffon stretched its wings out to slow its descent, but they still hit the ground much too hard and the impact threw her forward against the saddle, then jerked her back as they slid across the snow-covered rock, soldiers dodging out of their way and then rushing to surround them, their weapons out and ready.

*

Isa fought them when they came to drag her down from the saddle, and she refused to stand or walk, forcing them to half-carry her and revelling in it, because she could feel how much it sickened them to touch her. She kicked at them when they wrestled Blood's Pride away from her and when one of them lost his grip on her arm, she punched and clawed at him until he was able to haul her back up out of the snow. She would have sunk her teeth into any of them if they'd showed her any skin. They thought she fought them because she wanted to escape, but she fought them because every scratch and bruise she inflicted made her existence a palpable fact; because they would deny her the right—the right of anyone like her—to exist. She fought them just because she could.

They wrenched her arm behind her back and pushed her down on her knees, twisting with her to keep her from writhing out of their grasp. This was her real homecoming: on her knees before these beautiful people, *her* people, who could barely stand to look at her.

She was still trying to get her breath back when she heard Trey's name sweep through the minds of everyone there: first in confusion, then in horror and revulsion. Another whisper went through the ranks and the people in the crowd closest to her backed away. She couldn't see any further than the first few rows of soldiers encircling them, then a channel opened up before her and she found herself staring up at a terrace made of green-glass that looked a confectioner's fever-dream, all curlicues and furbelows. A man in a rippling silver-blue fur wearing a breastplate and a silver helmet stood at the balustrade, backed by yet another squad of Eotan soldiers. He looked so much like one of the legendary heroes from Isa's storybooks that she caught herself looking over his shoulder for the painted background. Then her stomach turned as she recognized the wolf's-head device snarling down at her from the peak of his helmet. It was identical to the helmet her sister Frea had worn every day, the one which was still on her corpse, lying at the bottom of the sea.

The ranks parted in another direction, this time to let through a man in the tabard of an Eotan lieutenant. He went straight to

Trey and waited with his arms folded across his chest while the soldiers pulled him to his feet.

<Take off his hood.>

They yanked it off Trey's head, revealing his scars, and the people around him reacted as if they were watching a man being flayed alive. The soldiers dropped his arms and backed away, and it was Trey himself who threw off his cloak, displaying the scars on his neck, much to the onlookers' disgust. But he wasn't finished. With his gaze locked on to the man on the terrace, he ripped his shirt open from the collar to the shoulder, sending wooden buttons tumbling to the ground and making sure everyone could see the shiny, puckered scars that marred his flesh.

<It's him, your Majesty, without a doubt,> the lieutenant called up to the man on the terrace, who curled his gloved hands over the balustrade and leaned forward for a closer look.

The emperor said nothing at first, but everyone could feel the tension between him and Trey humming like a bowstring.

<What's this supposed to be?> Gannon called down at last, as brusque as if he was asking a fishmonger what he had in his basket.

Trey stepped forward, his skin streaked with cold-rash. <I'm here to challenge you, Gannon Eotan,> he said. <I'm the champion Lord Valrig has sent to defeat you.>

The emperor never moved, but Isa could feel his attention tightening around them like a garrote. <Where's the Mongrel? Where's the army of the cursed? Is this some kind of joke?>

Trey kept silent, but the emperor's derision had broken open something inside him.

<Why are you still alive?> Gannon asked him. <You wanted us to leave you there to die.>

<I wanted to die,> Trey answered, twisting his wrists against the cords binding them together, <but Lord Valrig wanted me to live.>

<Lord Valrig.> Gannon pushed back from the balustrade and paced along the edge. <So, after everything I did for you, you went ahead and betrayed me.>

<No,> Trey protested, moving forward toward the balcony

before he saw the soldiers readying to restrain him. <I did what you always told me to do: *fight,* you said. Live and die for glory above everything.>

Gannon brought his fist down on the balustrade. <I never told you to be a traitor!>

<Valrig offered me the chance to die in battle, the way I deserved,> Trey shot back. <What would Onfar and Onraka have done for me? They would have set me alongside schemers who never drew their swords and old cowards who died in their beds. For all time! I deserved better!>

<You're right, you should have died in battle. But you didn't,> said Gannon, dismissing Trey as carelessly as he would have the fishmonger. <Cut his throat,> he added, and turned his back.

The soldiers grabbed Trey, averting their eyes as much as they could while they forced him to his knees. The lieutenant in the Eotan tabard drew his sword.

Isa struggled to get up, but they kept her down as Trey raged, <You can't kill me like this! I am Valrig's champion—you have to fight me!>

<The Mongrel is Valrig's champion,> Gannon said.

Trey's shrill amusement cut like a flail. <You think Lord Valrig needs to hire mercenaries? You think he couldn't find a Norlander worthy enough to go up against you?>

<This *is* a joke,> said Gannon, turning back around. A pair of triffons streaked by over his head, darkening the green-glass terrace like the clouds of an oncoming storm. <Valrig's playing a trick on me. He thought since I bothered with you once I'd dishonor myself by fighting you out of pity. As if I would sully Eowara's sword on a banged-up wreck like you.>

Isa's blood burned like pure venom through her veins.

<I've changed my mind,> Gannon told the lieutenant. <Slit him open and spill his guts on the ground. Lord Valrig sent him here to be sacrificed and I feel like obliging him.>

<No!> Isa screamed out, unable to bear the thought of doing nothing while they sliced Trey open like a goat.

<That one,> said Gannon. <I don't know her. Show me her face.>

The soldier behind Isa snatched off her hood, then grabbed her braid and pulled it hard enough to force her face upward for the emperor to see. Fat snowflakes dropped down on her cheeks and slid between her lips, making her realize she was incredibly thirsty.

<An Eotan,> said the emperor, cataloguing her features but never looking into her eyes. <She must mean something to him. Kill her first; I want him to watch.>

Isa flailed against the people holding her, making herself a dead weight as they tried to haul her up. They didn't bother to unfasten her cloak but just pulled it off her, and the collar choked her almost to death before the clasps finally popped open. They grabbed her under the arms and jammed the hilt of a knife into the small of her back while she was still gasping for breath.

She tilted back her head; she wanted to feel every drop of hate and loathing raining down on her; she *needed* it. She had to find a way to live through this, for Daryan's sake . . . But Daryan wasn't here, and there were so many of them; too many, and she was alone.

But the timbre of emotion changed as someone new came out onto the terrace, forcing a path through the line of soldiers behind the emperor. Isa could see nothing but a fur coat and the flash of a silver hilt as the newcomer walked straight up to the emperor, well within striking distance.

<What do you want?> said Gannon, turning around to face his uninvited guest. His bodyguards surrounded him, but he waved them back. The crowd in front of Isa shifted and suddenly she could see what was playing out on the terrace: it was Eofar standing there, with his triffon-handled sword in his hand, looking so beautiful in his helmet and Norlander clothes that she could have cried. She had never pictured her brother in furs before, but now she couldn't remember him any other way. In the gray light, Strife's Bane looked magnificent, not gaudy and out of place as it had in the Shadar.

<I want you to let her go,> said Eofar.

<Her? Why? Look at her—you can see what she is.>

<I *do* see what she is,> said Eofar. Fury roiled inside him, not only for Gannon, but for her, for being a world away from where she was supposed to be. This was a grudging rescue at best. <She's my youngest sister. Her name is Isa. Isa Eotan.>

<This was some kind of plan?> Gannon demanded incredulously.

<You're with them, is that it? You all thought you could trick me into dishonoring myself?>

<You're not going to kill her.>

<I am,> said Gannon comfortably, <and then I'm going to have you killed, as a traitor.>

<Do it now, then. Draw!> Eofar insisted, circling around him.

<Draw on you?> asked the emperor, his words slippery with disdain. <I wouldn't fight you any more than those two abominations down there.>

<I had intended to wait for the cursed to rise, but my sister's forced my hand.> Eofar pulled off his helmet and then his hood and tossed them both down beside him. The helmet rolled over the green-glass surface, appearing then disappearing behind the fussy posts of the balustrade. <You *will* fight me. You don't have a choice.>

Gannon's emotions sharpened to a single needle-sharp point. <I'm the emperor: all the choices are mine.>

<And everyone knows how you got to be emperor,> said Eofar, pitching his tone so that as many people as possible would catch his words. <You challenged your father for the throne, and by law, he couldn't refuse you.>

Gannon's anger started as a trembling that Isa felt in her bones, and then it flashed over her all at once, like bone-dry kindling thrown on the fire. She didn't understand what was happening, only that her brother had somehow trapped the emperor into something. Gannon pulled off his helmet and hood and threw them into the hands of one of his guards.

<Bring those two inside and put them with the others,> Gannon commanded his lieutenant, and then he drew what looked like a bronze-bladed sword, although she couldn't be sure from this distance. She only knew that it touched something ancient and proud inside her, something still whole among all the broken pieces.

Eofar came on guard and Isa suddenly understood what he meant to do. She had not been alone after all. The swell of pride and fear and grief for a family lost and betrayed echoed back to her, transformed into the raw thrill of five thousand Norlander soldiers.

<I, Eofar, of the ancient and noble clan Eotan, the personage most dear to our progenitor here within the walls of Ravindal, do challenge you, Gannon, supreme champion of our bloodline, the right to reign over all Norland according to the custom of our people; to sit on Eowara's throne; to serve the Norland Empire with my blade; to protect it from its enemies, and to preserve it in glory until the end of the world.>

Chapter 31

Lahlil stood at the end of the hall, watching Isa thread her way around the broken pillars behind Trey until both of them disappeared into the trees. Cyrrin's fears had all come true: Trey had gone to ruin, thanks to her, and Isa had followed, caught up in the net of chaos Lahlil dragged with her everywhere she went.

The frenetic pace of the people fleeing finally shook her free from her stupor and she raced back down the corridor to Cyrrin's surgery, nearly colliding with two heavily laden people who came running out of the doorway. They pounded off down the corridor in the opposite direction, heading for the escape route Lahlil herself had laid out when she'd last been there.

<There you are,> Cyrrin said as she entered. Lahlil didn't know how to tell her that Trey had gone to Ravindal; she glared into the fire, looking for the words. The physic was measuring something into a jar while Berril packed solutions and instruments into a box filled with pine needles. <No, Berril, leave that one—the stopper's loose. We don't want it spilling and ruining everything else. Don't forget the herbs on the drying rack. We'll need those. Lahlil! Stop that daydreaming. I have something for Jachad—I think I know how to help him.>

<You do? Are you sure?> Lahlil asked, thunderstruck. Jachad hadn't stirred in over an hour; not since the pain had got so bad that Cyrrin had given him a dose of the brew she usually reserved for those she was about to cut open. <What is it? Have you given it to him?>

<No, I can't do it here. It's complicated—I'll explain when we're on our way. Funny how it just came to me, when I started packing up these things. But I can't be sure—Berril, where's the lid for this jar? Did you pack it already?>

Lahlil thought of the log houses they'd built for just such an emergency, and of the three leagues of lagramor-infested woods between here and there. Jachad would never make it that far, even carried on a stretcher. And as for Cyrrin—

"Ehya, so much running." Savion came up behind her, new grooves etched in his knobbly forehead by his scowl. He had been asleep so long that Lahlil had all but forgotten about him—but now a desperate plan began to take shape in her head. "You don't leave without me, not owing me money."

She seized his shoulder and he flinched, knocking his turban askew. "Can you stride again?"

"Now?" asked Savion. They both stepped aside as two women tried to get through the door carrying Ingeld between them. Savion blinked the last of the sleep from his eyes as he watched them go. Then he tilted his head and said warily, "Someone is coming, I think."

"Norlanders: the ones who want your people dead."

The Abroan hissed. "When?"

"They're already here."

Savion swore and backed away toward the fire. He took a deep breath and flexed his arms and legs, as if testing them out. "Ehya, I can stride, but not so far. Where can we go? No place to hide, here."

"I have a place. Just wait."

He straightened his turban, then sat on the nearest pallet with his thin elbows digging into his knees and his yellow eyes fixed on the doorway.

<I need to talk to you,> Lahlil told Cyrrin.

<Go and find Trey, like I told you to do, then we can talk. Berril, get that stuff at the end of the table, too.> Her attention was completely focused on packing. <You know how to use all of them; there's nothing complicated there. Just remember to go easy on the lash-weed until we figure how to keep the marmonts out of the bushes. That's enough now, tie it up. Go on. I want you to get out with the others.>

<I want to wait for you,> Berril protested, and Lahlil felt the girl's distress like the floor disappearing from under her feet.

<I need you to go,> Cyrrin said firmly. <You're the only real physic here besides me. You know how slow I am and some of the others are going to need help before I get there. Now stop arguing and get out. I don't need you giving me something else to worry about right now.>

The girl clutched the box in both arms. She looked as if she was waiting for Cyrrin to say something else, but after another moment of being ignored she finally left.

When she was gone, Cyrrin stopped trying to find the lid for the jar and clapped her hands over her eyes. She allowed herself that one moment of anguish, then she went back to what she was doing.

Lahlil took Cyrrin's coat from the hook beside the door and brought it to her. <Put this on. We have to go.>

<Just wait,> said Cyrrin, waving her away, then she suddenly turned to her. <You're hiding something.>

Lahlil heard a sound out in the hall; she tossed the coat over Cyrrin's chair and dashed to the doorway. Dust was still swirling in the open-ended corridor where dozens of people had just passed through, but in all other respects it looked like the deserted ruin it was supposed to be. <They're coming. We have to go.>

<So you keep saying, but we can't leave without Trey and your sister.> Cyrrin finally found the right lid for the jar and looked up. <Where are they? Didn't you find them?>

<I did,> said Lahlil. She heard the sound of metal-tipped boots coming toward them: the heavy, confident steps of soldiers. Savion sprang up from the pallet, then froze like a statue.

<Just stay back,> Lahlil told them.

She drew her sword as quietly as she could, then took a quick look into the hallway. Three of them were coming, stopping to check each of the empty rooms as they passed. The man in front had powerful shoulders and a helmet stuffed full of a great blocky head. The man in the middle was the only one carrying a shield, and the very young woman in the back clutched her sword with such eagerness that her arm was visibly shaking. They all had imperial blades.

Lahlil leaped out into the hallway and ran straight for them. She hadn't been in a real fight in a long time, but her muscles eased a little more with each step and she was as loose and supple as an eel by the time she reached them.

The blockheaded soldier ran straight back at her, but he needed a moment to adjust his swing for the narrow hallway; before he'd figured it out, her blade had sliced into his neck. The other man stayed back and steadied himself, as she'd expected, while the female soldier was practically breathing down his neck trying to get past him. Lahlil knocked back the man's first three blows with ease, then kicked him, taking him by surprise—effective, if not heroic—and flung him back against the wall. His shield went spinning down the hallway like a wheel.

As soon as her comrade was out of her way, the woman leaped forward with all the fire of a great warrior and none of the skill to back it up. A moment later she took Lahlil's blade in the left side of her chest. She hadn't landed a single blow. Lahlil pulled her sword out and turned back to the other soldier. His helmet had slipped a bit, just enough for her to chop into his neck, sending arterial blood spurting into the air. He managed to stagger a few paces by hanging on to the wall, then collapsed into a heap.

The young woman was still alive, but barely. She was trying to use her power over her black blade to slide it along the floor and into her hand, though she hadn't the strength to lift it. Lahlil could see now that she was not even as old as Isa: sixteen at most. She started toward her—why, she wasn't sure—but then stopped as the girl's black sword gave one more shuddering lurch and then stopped. The rounded hilt rolled gently over the stone floor.

"You killed them all," whispered Savion, who had been watching from the surgery doorway. He looked up at her with wide eyes. "You did it so fast. They're all dead . . ."

"The blood you need to stride—does it have to be from the same person?" she asked. She raised her sword to wipe off the blood and realized her hand was shaking. She had seen other people shake after a fight, but it had never happened to her before.

"Don't understand," said Savion.

"Does it have to be from the person you're striding to? Could it be a blood relative, instead? Someone close, like a mother?"

"Mother?" Savion swallowed. "A mother, yes—yes, I think so. Never done it, though."

Lahlil told him her plan.

"Ehya." Savion sucked his teeth, but she saw that same hectic gleam in his eye that he'd had at Prol Irat. "Yes. Yes, all right. I hope you can swim—just in case, follow?"

Lahlil handed him her knife. "It's the only way out now. We'll have to risk it."

Cyrrin had finally put on her coat and was trying to cross the room, but she hadn't made it any further than her chair. Lahlil guessed she wasn't strong enough to walk the length of the hallway, much less to the camp. Knowing that didn't make her feel any better about what she was about to do.

<Lahlil?> The physic stared down death every day of her life—particularly her own—and yet Lahlil had never felt her so close to real terror before. <We're trapped, aren't we?>

<No,> Lahlil reassured her. She crossed over to Jachad's pallet and knelt down beside it. When she dug his fingers out from under the blankets they had no warmth in them. <Do you have the cure for him?>

<Right here. But I won't leave without Trey,> Cyrrin declared. <Don't even try to make me. You have to go and find him.>

<I did find him,> Lahlil told her, keeping her eyes on Jachad's pale face. <He went to Ravindal with my sister.>

Cyrrin's emotions hit her like a brick. <Go and stop them.>

<I can't. They're gone.>

<Stop them!>

<They're already gone, Cyrrin. I tried to stop them, but there was nothing I could do.>

"We go now, yes?" said Savion, coming to stand by Jachad. He had Lahlil's knife in his right hand and his left hand already balled into a tight fist. A single drop of blood trickled down his arm.

<What is he doing?> Cyrrin asked frantically. Lahlil checked to make sure the physic was still holding the jar with Jachad's medicine, then gripped his lifeless wrist a little higher up. She could hear someone else out in the hall now, coming toward them.

She reached over and grabbed a fold of Cyrrin's coat. "Do it," she told Savion.

Just as Savion pricked Jachad's palm with the point of the knife, a woman with a bloody gash across her chest stepped into the doorway. Lahlil recognized her from the battlefield: Vrinna, by her uniform now a captain in the Eotan Guard. Her sword was drawn, but her shoulders were hunched and she looked feverish. Her silver eyes ignored everyone else in the room except Lahlil. She had found what she wanted.

<Tell the emperor he can't win,> Lahlil told Vrinna as Savion's eyes began to roll back. She watched the triumphant halo around the captain fade, replaced by dismay as Vrinna sensed what was about to happen. Just before everything disappeared, Lahlil said, <Tell him the Mongrel's not playing the game any more. Tell him I quit.>

Chapter 32

Lahlil felt the boards beneath her almost before she had time to brace herself for the stride. Snow was falling in tiny, stinging flakes, and they were in a cove just beyond Ravindal Harbor: there was no mistaking the vine-covered towers looming over the promontory in the distance, or the frozen waterfall arching from the cliffs, or the triffons wheeling in the sky above—too many triffons.

"Did it," said Savion, flashing a grin before he swayed and dropped to the deck.

<What just happened?> Cyrrin asked, staggering. <This is a ship—why are we on a ship? Where are we?>

<This is the *Argent*. Just stay calm.>

<What have you done?> Cyrrin grabbed the front of Lahlil's coat and pulled it hard, spinning both of them around. <*What have you done?*>

<We couldn't have stayed there,> Lahlil told her, <and you know Jachad would never have survived in the open.> She very carefully took the jar of medicine from Cyrrin's hand. <We're in Ravindal Harbor. We didn't go far.>

<But Berril, and the others—they need me. They're waiting for me—>

<I'm sorry,> said Lahlil, <but I did what I had to do.>

Cyrrin let go of her and staggered to the mast, grabbing on for support. <Gods, I hate you. *I hate you!*>

Lahlil knelt down next to Jachad just as Nisha's cabin door burst open and Grentha charged down the ladder. Doors crashed open and five other women came close behind her. Recognition crossed the old sailor's face as her eyes met Lahlil's—before the sight of Jachad sprawled across the deck changed it to something else entirely. Grentha instantly whirled to block Nisha's path.

"Meiran!" the queen was already calling out to her; she had almost forgotten her old Nomas nickname. "Sweet Amai, girl, did you drop out of the sky? What—? Get out of my way, Grentha. What are you doing?"

"Easy, now," the first mate cautioned as she stepped aside. The sound Nisha made when she saw her son lying on the deck almost split Lahlil in half. She made way as the queen threw herself down on her knees next to her prostrate son, pulling him into her arms and calling his name in a throaty sob. Jachad managed to grasp his mother's hand and say some words of reassurance to her, but Lahlil couldn't make them out.

Sailors bundled into anonymity against the cold started bursting onto the deck. Grentha ordered four of them to carry Jachad into the captain's cabin and they lifted him from Nisha's arms with the wordless efficiency of people accustomed to working together in a crisis. Other women helped Savion up and urged him into the galley to warm up by the stove. By the time Lahlil had gathered her wits about her again, he had already gone inside.

It wasn't until Nisha found herself kneeling alone on the deck that she seemed to remember Lahlil.

"What have you *done*?" asked the Nomas queen, rising and striding over the deck, her presence the force of a tidal wave as she swept past Grentha's staying hand. "What have you done to my son?"

"He was poisoned—I brought him here to help him." She gestured toward Cyrrin, who was still sagging against the mast. "Cyrrin has a cure."

"*Who* poisoned him?" The prickling snow reddened Nisha's cheeks and made the fury in her sea-blue eyes flash even brighter. Some of the sailors had clustered together by the rails and were eyeing them with distress.

"We don't know—someone from the Shadar, we think."

"From the Shadar—where *you* brought him," said Nisha, but something occurred to her before she went on with her recriminations.

"You're supposed to be with the caravan, with Oshi." Even now, the thought of Oshi softened her into the woman Lahlil remembered; the one who had pulled her down onto her lap and brushed the tangles from her hair with silver combs; who had murmured lilting songs about selkwhales and mermen. "Where is Oshi? What have you done with him?"

"Oshi is fine. He's with Callia."

"On the *Dawn Gazer*?"

"No, she's with the caravan," said Lahlil. She had no choice; she must spit out the rest like the bitter pill it was. "Callia was poisoned, too. She survived, but her baby died."

Lahlil saw Nisha's last breath stop in her throat, suspended there in a moment of perfect dismay.

Then the Nomas queen's rage cracked wide and she lashed out, pounding on Lahlil's chest like someone banging on a locked door. Lahlil remained motionless as the blows rained down on her, but she couldn't stop her head from recoiling when Nisha's flailing fist caught her chin and knocked her eye-patch loose, or when her ring tore a gash over her eye. By then Grentha was pulling her captain away.

"It's not her fault," said Grentha. "Nisha, she didn't poison them. Think. She brought Jachi to you."

Lahlil replaced the eye-patch and dabbed at the blood running down into the corner of her eye. Grentha could say what she liked: it was her fault, somehow. Everything was her fault.

"Then I'm sorry, Meiran," said the queen, regaining her composure as quickly as she'd lost it, but not her warmth. "You said you had a cure?"

Lahlil nodded.

She stayed behind as Grentha shepherded Nisha to her cabin. A pool of warm lamplight spilled out from the door when it opened to admit them, and then disappeared when it clicked shut behind them.

<Take me back,> Cyrrin demanded, still clinging to the mast. <Take me back to the others.>

<We don't have any way to get there,> said Lahlil. She could feel Jachad's precious time draining away. <I'll take you up to Nisha's cabin so you can give Jachad the medicine.>

The physic looked at her. <No.> The single, chilling word came from the black point at the center of her spinning emotions.

<You wouldn't let him die just to get back at me.> Lahlil tightened her fingers around the jar. <I know you wouldn't. You're better than that.>

<You don't know *what* I am,> said Cyrrin. A gust of wind thumped against the furled sails over their heads. <You keep telling me you've changed—well, maybe I've changed too. Nothing says we all have to change for the better.>

<I have the medicine,> Lahlil reminded her, already skirting around a locker to get to the ladder leading to the deck above. <I'll give it to him myself.>

<You'll kill him,> Cyrrin warned, stopping her in her tracks. <Give him too much and you'll kill him; too little, and he'll still die. And don't ask me to tell you how much he needs, because I don't know. I have to give it to him gradually, and watch him until I can tell when to stop.>

<What more do you want from me, Cyrrin?> Lahlil cried. <Right from the beginning I told Trey I wasn't going to help him fight Gannon, or anyone else. He made his own choice.>

<Your sister was right about you,> said Cyrrin. <You came here for your own selfish reasons—you never asked or cared what Jachad or anyone else wanted.>

<I was trying to change,> said Lahlil, throwing back her cowl, ignoring the swirling snow. <I don't know what else I can do.>

<Go to Ravindal,> Cyrrin commanded, pushing herself away from the mast. <Get Trey out of there before they kill him. *That's* what you can do.>

Lahlil's jaw ached as if it had frozen in place, and the snow coming down made it hard to see the door to Nisha's cabin. She knew the ship wasn't rocking, but she could have sworn she heard the swaying mast creaking and groaning over her head.

<Don't ask me to do that,> she pleaded with Cyrrin.

<I already have.>

<The prophecy—> Lahlil clenched her fist behind her back to keep from hitting something. <*This* is how I get to Ravindal. *You make me go.* You're making it happen, now.>

Cyrrin looked away. <Don't blame some prophecy, Lahlil. You made your own choices, just like the rest of us.>

<I told Jachad I wouldn't leave him. I made him a promise.>

<If he knows you like I do, then he knows exactly what your promises are worth,> Cyrrin sniped. She let go of the mast and started to shuffle slowly across the deck. <I won't help him unless you agree, so you'd better make your mind up fast. He doesn't have much time.>

Lahlil felt the Mongrel surge up inside her: a ball of flame ready to burst. <I could *make* you do it.>

<Oh yes, you've changed, haven't you: until you don't get what you want,> said Cyrrin, bracing herself against one of the lockers. <I've never been afraid of dying. Why would I be afraid of it now, when you've taken me away from everyone I care about and everything I've spent the last ten years building?>

<And what if I do bring Trey back?> asked Lahlil. <Are you going to drug him to keep him with you, like you did to me?>

Cyrrin's anger hardened into a diamond. <All right, then. Tell me why you don't want Jachad to die.>

<What does that have to do with anything?>

<I want to know.> Cyrrin's words had the same blunt force she used when, knife already in hand, she explained to her patients what she was about to do to them. <Go ahead, tell me: why do you want him to live?>

The wind blew; the snow fell. Ice floes bobbed in the dark sea far beyond the rails and the silent spout of a selkwhale plumed up. Silence invaded her, pushing back the words she needed to say. <You want me to say I love him.>

<It hurts, doesn't it?> Cyrrin's bitter satisfaction glowed cold and white.

<All right,> said Lahlil. The sore spot above her eye where Nisha had cut her throbbed in time to her pulse, sending a dull pain thudding through her head. <If that's what it takes, I'll go to Ravindal. I'll find Trey and I'll bring him back.>

<Help me up, then.>

Lahlil went to Cyrrin and offered her shoulder and together they navigated the obstacles at an infuriatingly slow pace until they reached the ladder to the upper deck. Lahlil lifted her up, one step at a time.

<What are you going to tell Jachad?> asked Cyrrin, and Lahlil recognized that tinny bite in her words: she was trying to distract herself from the pain.

<I'll think of something.>

<Why don't you tell him the truth? That I'm making you go?>

<Because I know Jachad,> said Lahlil. <He wouldn't take your bargain. He'd rather die.>

They didn't speak again as they made their way to Nisha's cabin. The door opened at Lahlil's knock and Mala, the *Argent*'s healer, rushed over and led Cyrrin to the table where she'd hastily laid out some supplies. Lahlil handed her the jar. Nisha had pulled up a stool beside her bunk so she could hold Jachad's hand and stroke his hair. A tall woman Lahlil didn't recognize stood behind Nisha with her hands on the captain's shoulders and Grentha stood in the shadows by the door.

Lahlil stepped back outside and closed the door, shutting herself out. She shut her eyes, letting the falling snow sting the cuts made by Nisha's assault while she listened to them talking inside.

<This isn't a poison at all,> Cyrrin was telling them, <at least, not the way we usually think of poisons. It's not attacking him the way poisons do.>

<Then what is it doing?> asked Nisha.

Cyrrin said, <It's splitting the bond between his mortal self and his god self, if that's what you want to call it: the part of his nature that gives him power over fire. The two aspects of his nature are normally in balance, but now they've turned on each other and they're tearing him apart.>

There was a pause, then Mala said, <Which would explain why Callia's baby died, but not Callia.>

<We need to stop that struggle,> said Cyrrin. <If I had more time—a lot more time—I might be able to come up with another way, but now . . . the only thing that will save him is if one side wins, so we need to make that happen, and very quickly.>

<I don't understand,> said Nisha. <How do we do that?>

<With anoline, mostly.>

Lahlil heard the floorboards creak as Mala jumped up. <Anoline is a poison—it will kill him.>

<If you set two armies of the same strength against each other, they'll fight until they're both destroyed,> Cyrrin explained. <Pit a much larger army against a much smaller one, and the smaller one surrenders.>

"Sweet Amai," Mala breathed in Nomas. "She's talking about killing him *on purpose*."

<How could he survive that?> asked Nisha. <Even if it destroys the poison, how can he survive without part of himself?>

<I'm not sure he can, but I don't have another solution. If we don't act now, his heart will tear itself apart and he'll certainly die. We can wait for that to happen, or we can take a chance.>

Nisha was silent for a long time. Then she said, "Either way, I'll lose my son."

The door cracked open beside her and Lahlil jumped as Grentha's lined face poked out.

"He's asking for you."

She went inside and knelt down beside Jachad's bunk. Nisha said nothing, lost somewhere no one else could follow. No one made a sound except for a spoon clinking against the jar of medicine as Cyrrin measured out the dosage. The quiet was unnatural; it was the absence of all the anguished words Nisha and her women were choking back for Jachad's sake.

Jachad's mouth moved and he said her name.

"Jachi." She moved closer to him, but she couldn't take his hand. Nisha had claimed it and she wasn't letting go. Lahlil swallowed. "Jachi, I have to go to Ravindal."

Jachad stared up at the carved ceiling over the bunk for such a long time that she fixed her eye on the subtle rise and fall of his chest to make sure he was still breathing. His eyes closed, but she saw his free hand curl into a fist and clutch at the blanket.

"Why?"

"Isa went there on her own. I need to go after her."

"You swore," he said. "You swore we'd stay together. That's the only reason I came. I came for you."

She felt something wet slide down her cheek. "Jachi—"

"There's blood on your face."

She wiped away what she had thought was a tear, then looked at the dark smear on her gloves. Blood was the one thing she always brought with her, wherever she went; it was her gift. Beside her, Nisha made a soft noise that contained an impossible amount of pain.

"I have to go." She couldn't say it any louder than a whisper.

"Just go, then," said Jachad.

She stood up and walked across the cabin, all of her senses as numbed as if she'd spent a night sleeping in the snow. She could feel the Nomas waiting for her to leave. When she opened the door and stepped across the threshold, she heard everyone inside take a breath, as if she had fouled the air just by being in the room.

By coming to Norland, Lahlil had pushed a snowball up to the top of a hill and now it was about to roll down the other side. She didn't know how big it would get, or where it would end up; the only thing she knew for certain was that she would be rolling down with it. At dusk, her gods-ridden attack would come again, and if she hadn't found Trey by then, she was as good as dead. She needed Savion for one last stride.

Something wet trailed down her cheek again and she took a moment to wipe away another droplet from the cut over her eye. Still no tears; only more blood.

Chapter 33

Rho shifted in the corner of the little room where he and Kira had been imprisoned. He'd been hoping to discover what was happening in the throne room on the other side of the door but all he could hear was the clicking sound of Kira nervously tapping her fingernails together. He tried to focus on what they were going to do next and not on whether or not Vrinna had found Trey. No one had come to ask them any questions or take them away—maybe they were going to be left here to die of hunger and thirst. Rho could think of worse deaths; he had seen plenty of them with his own eyes.

<I can't stand this. How long do you think it's been?> asked Kira. She still had that silvery stuff all over her, and in the half-light she looked as if she'd been dusted with ground glass.

<I don't know.> He examined the wedge of light on the floor, but it didn't help. Telling time had been easy in the Shadar, where light was bright and shadows were dark. Here, everything was always the same shade of gray. <An hour, maybe.>

<There has to be something we can do besides sit here.>

<I'm working on it,> he promised her. <This was my plan. I'll find a way out.>

He expected a sardonic remark in return, but she didn't say anything.

<Are you all right?> Rho asked her. <Are you still in a lot of pain?>

<Not so much, but I feel a bit odd. I'm probably getting the ague

from lying out in the snow. Wouldn't it be just too whimsical, if that ends up being what—?> Kira broke off and lifted her head. <Did you hear that?>

Rho could also hear the sounds of people running in the throne room, and he sensed a sudden spike in the emotions of the people on the other side of the door.

<Wait, I'll look.> He pulled the door open, very slowly until he could see the guard standing in front of it. Someone had left Fortune's Blight and Kira's sword, Virtue's Grace, lying on the corner of the dais, almost within reach. The scribes had pushed back their stools and run to join the crowd already jostling by the doors to the green-glass terrace. As more guards rushed into the throne room from the hallway outside, Rho shut the door as carefully as he'd opened it.

<Something's happening out on the terrace.> He leaned back into the corner again, grateful for the support of the wall. <But I couldn't see anything.>

<Is it Vrinna?>

<I don't think so—I think I would have felt her if they'd brought her in.> Rho decided not to tell Kira about their swords, abandoned so close to them. They might be able to push past the single guard in front of the door, but neither of them were in any shape to fight their way out of the room, much less out of the castle itself.

<I want to see,> said Kira. <Do you think that inebriate friend of yours is going through with his plan?>

<Eofar wasn't always a drunkard,> said Rho, surprised to find himself defending him after everything that had happened. <Well, maybe he was—but he had his reasons. He didn't deserve any of this.>

<I'll take your word for it.> She reached up for his arm and he supported her while she rose. He could feel her arm twitching very faintly, and she did seem a little feverish.

Then the door swung open and Rho looked up with his heart pounding, expecting to see guards coming to haul them to their execution, but instead they ushered in a muscular man with his hands tied behind his back and impotent rage hanging like a noose around his neck.

The jolt of recognition pushed Rho back into the wall, and he reached behind him to keep himself from falling. The guards turned and shut the door behind them. They had not said a word.

Kira breathed out a name.

<Trey!> Rho echoed, throwing himself forward and pulling his brother into an embrace. Trey allowed himself to be held, but he gave Rho nothing in return; he stood as still as a green-glass statue, his skin just as cold, and something pernicious chewing away at his insides. Rho held him all the tighter for it. <I would have come home—I would have done anything for you—I still would.>

Trey pulled away and waited while Rho fumbled with the knots tying his hands together until the rope fell to the floor. He could feel the effort it was taking for Trey not to try to hide his scars, even in the near-darkness, and choked on his helpless anger. This was his perfect little brother, torn up by a tree and left to die: the hero of Redland, or at least what was left of him.

<You told him?> Trey asked Kira, freezing Rho out as if he wasn't even in the room. <You swore you wouldn't do that—you swore to me.>

<It's not her fault. She didn't want to tell me,> said Rho, shaking off the shock. <I came back to Norland because of something else. I just blundered into all of this—it just happened.>

<It just *happened*?> Trey's bloodshot eyes darted back and forth between them.

Rho didn't realize his unfortunate choice of words until he felt Kira's mortification freeze her to the ground. He swallowed, struggling to keep his footing as an avalanche of feelings swept toward him. <What happened before—what we did . . . We never wanted to hurt you. Just the opposite, really. The only thing Kira and I had in common was that neither of us ever felt like we were good enough for you.>

<It doesn't matter any more,> said Trey, turning away from them both and going over to the table. <That's all over now. *This* is what I was meant to do: bring the cursed to defeat Gannon. I've never doubted it. That's why I came to Ravindal.>

<You *wanted* to come?> asked Kira. <After everything I've been through trying to make sure no one found out about you? Trey, how could you do that?>

<I never wanted your help,> Trey told her. <I told you to forget about me.>

<No one's coming, Trey. *No one.* I've been down into Eowara's tomb. There's nothing there but bones,> Kira insisted. She crossed the room toward him, reaching out to him. <I should never have let you send me away before, but we're here now, together. We can escape together. We've got another chance, if you'll just stop this ridiculous quest—>

<Don't touch me!>

The table legs squealed over the stone floor as Trey backed away, pushing it into the wall.

Rho pressed his fingers into his temples. The pain in his side was nothing now compared to the throbbing in his head. He was mildly surprised to find that he was sweating, even though the room was freezing cold. No one spoke, and as Kira retreated into miserable bewilderment Rho began to fear he was on the verge of going mad. He didn't know what he was supposed to say; he didn't know how to argue with Trey. In his world, Trey was always right and he was always wrong.

<Gannon refused to fight me,> Trey told them at last, finally breaking the unbearable tension. <He was going to slit open my gut like a beast for the slaughter, on my knees, in front of everyone.>

<Gannon is a delusional piece of shit,> Rho said. <He always has been.>

<Delusional,> Trey repeated acidly, and Rho could feel the dam his brother had put up against the two of them cracking down the middle; he feared he would be swept away by the flood. <You were right, Kira: there's no Lord Valrig, and no army. I saw the Mongrel, and she's not coming. I wasn't chosen for anything. I was just another broken body for Cyrrin to put back together. That's what you've been waiting for me to say, isn't it?>

Kira had shut her eyes while he was talking as if she couldn't bear to look at him. <No, Trey,> she said. <That's not what I've been waiting for you to say. Not even close.>

<Kira—> Trey turned to her and she rushed to him, throwing herself into his arms.

Rho's body was so stiff that he had a hard time moving, but he struggled into the far corner to give them at least the illusion of privacy.

After a long while, Trey called out to him, <You know what I just remembered?> His tone had warmed a little, but his words still had the same brittle edges.

<What?>

<That time when we were boys, when old Kurt caught me stealing Exemplar Orina's ring on a dare. You stepped in and took the blame.>

<I remember,> said Rho. <I'm sorry.>

Kira's confusion floated toward them. <Sorry for what? What were you supposed to do, let them punish your little brother?>

<No,> said Rho, <I was supposed to stop him from stealing it in the first place.> He took a breath. <It's time to get out of here, I think.>

He went back to the door and nudged it open like before, only this time a cold wind ruffled his hair and he could see the maps and papers skidding off the edges of the tables. Everyone he could see had left their posts except for a pair of frustrated guards at the throne room doors, but they were still in the room; they were all at the end straining to see over each others' heads out onto the terrace. Rho caught the briefest possible glimpse of a figure on the green-glass outside, but one glimpse was enough.

<What's happening out there?> asked Kira, turning around in Trey's arms.

<I don't know,> Rho told them, burying the truth away so deep that Lord Valrig himself would never find it, <but the guard's gone and we're getting out of here.>

Chapter 34

The soldiers pushed Isa toward the castle as her brother and the emperor began to fight. As they brought her under the shining green-glass terrace she raised her head and tried to see what was happening, but the glass was too thick and she could make out nothing more than the dark streaks of their coats as they circled and darted at each other. She could still hear the clanging of their swords, though, and feel the swelling emotions of the spectators as she was marched ever closer to the black stone castle that might once have been her home.

Trey had been taken in ahead of her while they tried to figure out how to bind her with only one arm. They had eventually given up and now one man walked beside her holding her single arm twisted behind her back, while the other carried Blood's Pride. She could feel the man holding her grimacing in distaste at being forced to touch her.

The great castle doors were shut, but the guards brought them around instead to a small, unadorned door that Isa guessed was used mainly by the servants. When she looked up, she saw the castle's towers looming above her, so tall from this angle that they appeared to poke up into the After-realm. Isa stumbled over the threshold on her wounded leg and fell, breaking the guard's hold on her arm. He swore at her and prodded her with his boot, but she curled up into a ball when they came to get her, forcing the man carrying her sword to put it under one arm so he could help his comrade drag her along the hallway.

But instead, she swept her leg back and knocked the guard behind her off his feet, then leaped up and slammed the one carrying Blood's Pride into the wall. She made a grab for his knife and they grappled for a moment, but all his training was no match for the horror of finding the stump of her arm so close to his face. She wrenched the knife from him and stabbed at his neck, missing the first time but driving the blade deep with her second blow.

Isa had Blood's Pride in her hand and the swordbelt over her head before the first soldier had got back up to his knees. He reached behind him to draw his own sword, but she drove her heel into his back and knocked him down again. She snapped her sword up between his shoulder blades and pricked him to make sure he knew it was there.

<Where do they keep the Shadari witch?> she demanded.

<I don't know,> said the man, shrinking away from her. He was scrawny for a Norlander, particularly a soldier.

<Yes, you do,> said Isa. <I grew up around soldiers and I know they can't keep secrets.>

<You won't make me tell you,> the man answered, stupidly confirming that he knew exactly where to find Ani. <I'm not afraid to die.>

<Oh, I have other plans for you,> she said, crouching down beside him and repositioning her blade on the back of his neck just under his helmet. She poked the stump of her arm through her torn sleeve and thrust it into his face. Cold had made the blue veins throb under the skin. The soldier squeezed his eyes shut and tried to bury his head under his shoulder. <I'm going to make you into one of us.>

<No, please don't,> he pleaded, but she just pressed the sword a little harder against his neck until a shiny line of blood sprang up on his quivering flesh. <She's in the tower.>

<Which tower?>

<Southwest,> he gabbled, <right above us.>

Isa turned her wrist, preparing to bash him in the head and knock him out, but she hesitated. Someone was bound to stumble across him sooner or later, and he could tell them exactly where she was going. She had made it here to Ravindal and she would not be stopped by a couple of common soldiers. She changed her grip. She knew what Lahlil would do. She knew what Frea would have done.

Then the guard flailed about and punched her in the chest, knocking her to the ground. She lost her breath for a moment but never loosened her grip on Blood's Pride. The soldier got to his knee and reached for his sword, but Isa rammed her sword straight through his armor and into his heart before he could draw. He gave one great wheezing gasp as she yanked out her blade and she swayed backward to avoid the blood as his face smashed into the stone.

Southwest tower.

She sheathed her sword and made her way along the dim servants' hallway, running her hand along the wall the way she remembered Daryan doing in the Shadar. The rough stone under her fingers made her feel close to him, and she could picture him running in front of her, turning back to urge her on when the numbness in her leg made her stumble, or dizziness sent her crashing into the wall.

Around the next corner was a staircase and she began to climb, passing through a landing with corridors opening out in three different directions, and then another with a door she had no intention of opening. The next landing had an iron grate at one end with nothing but blackness on the other side.

Either the stairs were getting steeper and Blood's Pride was getting heavier, or her strength was failing. At the next landing, she sat down with her back against the corner to rest for a moment. A slit in the wall next to her let in thin gray light, and she could see her breath misting. She just needed a chance to recover, and then she would keep going.

A door in the opposite wall swung open and a man in a brown shirt with a pail dangling from his hand stopped on the threshold. Isa couldn't move. With her shirt torn and her cloak gone, the naked stump of her arm hung from her shoulder like something obscene. The man dropped the pail, splashing the water down the stairs as the bucket spun around right to the edge of the top step. The servant backed out through the doorway from which he'd come and very quietly shut the door.

As soon as she heard the latch click into place, Isa pushed

herself up and staggered up the steps. She passed no more landings, and the glimpses she had through the slits showed Ravindal dropping further and further beneath her. She had to grab hold of her trousers to pull her wounded leg up that last flight, but she soldiered on in the faith that the wooden door rattling in the wind above her would be the gateway to her salvation.

The wind pushed the door toward her the moment she lifted the bar and it banged against the opposite wall, echoing down, floor after floor. She had to put her head down to fight against the gale, and once outside the snow whipped against her exposed skin and the cold brought tears to her eyes. Triffons soared in the sky around, above and below her, but their focus remained on what was happening on the green-glass terrace down below. She wanted desperately to know if her brother was all right, but she couldn't allow anything to divert her attention from the steady stream of black smoke, bent sideways by the wind, coming from the chimney of the small structure ahead of her.

The snow crunched under her boots as she made her way across to the building, leaving a crooked trail of blue blood behind her. She leaned her shoulder against the wall when she reached it: she could feel the shadowy presence of a Norlander on the other side: *Ani's guard?* Then alarm tightened her throat as she realized she had no way through the door: there was no keyhole, which meant it had to be barred on the inside. Kicking it down was not an option, not with her leg barely able to support her weight, and hacking it open would take too long. She could have used a log from the woodpile to ram it, if only she'd had two hands to hold it.

She put her back against the wall to hide from the specter of defeat now circling toward her like a triffon's haggard ghost. There had to be a way in. *What would Lahlil do?* she asked herself bitterly. Lahlil wouldn't do anything. The door would just open because she wanted it that way.

And then the door swung open all by itself.

A thrill went up Isa's spine.

The door wobbled when it encountered a little resistance from the snow and stopped when the gap was about a hand-span wide, but she could see someone sitting on a bed at the far side of the room with his back up against the wall. After a second, longer look, she pushed the door open and went in.

The Norlander was dressed like a guard, and completely indifferent to the world around him. His silver-blue eyes were cloudy and dull, and his presence had an unsettling indistinctness, as if he were wrapped in layers of something thick and soft, like the Shadari moths in their dust-colored cocoons. When Isa probed a little deeper, she found a hole dropping straight down into nothingness. She backed away from his mind before she slipped over the edge.

There was a second door in the opposite wall, but the cleats where the bar should have been stood empty. She limped across with Blood's Pride still in her hand and pushed it open. Heat poured out like a furnace, and everything inside jumped and shifted in the light of a blazing fire. She listed against the doorframe, the smoke stinging her eyes.

"Ani?" she called out in her throaty rasp.

"Here." A bundle of fur in the corner moved and a pair of bright, dark eyes looked out at her from an impossibly lined face. Then the old woman smiled, and even more wrinkles sprang up at the corners of her eyes. "Interesting. Though just as I expected."

Isa tried to step into the room, but her right leg folded and she dived onto the floor face-first, crushing her chest and scraping her chin along the ground when she failed to catch herself. The warmed stone beneath her whirled and dipped until she thought it would fling her off into space, like those games of snap-the-reins she had always lost to Eofar and Frea when they were children.

"You knew I was coming?" she asked, pushing herself up until she was no longer sprawling on the floor. Ani rose from her stool and came toward her, but Isa still couldn't see much of the old Shadari except for the wrinkled face and long white hair. She didn't understand how anyone could wear so much fur in a room this hot.

"The elixir," said Ani, standing over her. She spoke slowly, and her low voice had a strangely sibilant quality, like the sound of the desert sands shifting in the wind. "You know about that, yes?"

"That's why I came—that, but mostly to bring you back to the Shadar." A movement from the bed in the opposite corner of the room caught Isa's eye, but she saw nothing there except more fur blankets. "Are you ready? Can you come? I think they're following me—"

The moment Isa tried to stand, all of her hopes toppled back down again like a tower of blocks. She managed to stifle her scream, but she couldn't stop herself from falling to the floor. Pain gripped her leg like a fiery ring, answered by a throbbing spasm from her missing arm.

"I have to close this cut," she told Ani, pulling herself over to the fire on her knuckles so she could bring Blood's Pride with her. The old woman watched her without comment or any indication of anxiety; Isa thought perhaps she didn't understand how much danger they were in.

She heated the blade, and the smell of hot metal helped clear the mist from her head. She forced herself to wait until the blade changed color, and when the metal began to glow white-hot, she drew it out and pressed it down hard against the bloody cut. The moment the blade touched her flesh, the memory of her brother Eofar slicing through her arm that horrible day in the temple grabbed her in its steel talons and squeezed the breath out of her. She dropped Blood's Pride onto the hearth and rolled onto her side to get one of her pills out of her pouch.

"Is this what you want?" asked Ani, kneeling beside her with the deliberate care of the elderly and untying the pouch for her with small, nimble hands. Isa reached out as Ani pulled out one of the few remaining green balls, but instead of handing it over to her, she brought the pill close to her own face and inhaled its scent. "Interesting," she said, again drawing out the sibilance. "It's bitter, yes? It makes your tongue and the inside of your mouth a little numb? Where did you get it?"

"From the Nomas. Can I—?"

Just as she stretched out her hand to take it, Ani crushed the pill between her thumb and forefinger and caught the crumbs in the palm of her opposite hand.

"No!" cried Isa, sliding forward. "Don't, please! I don't have many left."

"Calm yourself." Ani poked at the bits in her hand, smearing a few against her papery palm. "They've tricked you. This is mostly marly grass. Worthless."

"No. That can't be," said Isa, shaking uncontrollably now. "I've been taking them for months. They help with the pain."

"Only because you think they do."

"They wouldn't trick me." Isa wrapped her arm around her chest and held on to her stump. "Mairi wouldn't do something like that. She must have made a mistake."

"You have a lot to learn about the Nomas. I'll correct that." Ani scattered the crumbs on the floor, then stood up with a lurch and a soft groan. She picked up a little stoppered glass bottle from the table and set it down on the floor next to Isa. "This will be of much more help."

"What is it?" Isa looked at the bottle, noticing how similar it was to the one that had contained Lahlil's elixir.

"Something you'll need, if you're going to be useful to me," said Ani. When Isa still hesitated, she added, "You said they're coming for you, yes? Then take a sip."

Isa picked up the bottle and took out the stopper with her teeth. The stuff inside smelled sweet and a little too pungent, like spoiled fruit. She was just about to drink the liquid when she saw movement from the bed again, and this time she was quick enough to see a head and a pair of small hands whisk back under the blankets.

"Dramash? Is that you?"

He poked his head out again and she expected one of his chirrupy greetings, but he said nothing. Even the firelight couldn't disguise his pallor, and the way he looked out at her from under his hooded brow worried her. If Dramash was imprisoned here and her brother was fighting the emperor, then where was Rho?

"Isa," said Ani, drawing her name out like the wind through a field of dry grass.

She turned her attention back to the bottle in her hand. The taste of the few drops she poured on her tongue reminded her of the sticky candied fruits her brother had sometimes bought for her when she was small. She bowed her head and waited for something to happen.

"That's my girl," Ani said, as everything within Isa's sight grew smaller and faded to black before she slumped peacefully to the floor. "Everything's going to be all right."

Chapter 35

This time Lahlil could see when the stride was about to end. Just as the light began to return, the world gave a shuddering heave and tilted like a boat about to go over a waterfall. She pitched onto her knees onto a few inches of kicked-up snow and looked up into at the same sky she had been watching from the deck of the *Argent* just a moment ago. Eotan Castle thrust up through the snow on her left; on her right, the headland with its flaming beacon wrapped around the cliff until it met the city walls. Closer to the ground, a press of heavily armed soldiers blocked her view, but no one had noticed her abrupt arrival except for one saddled and very nervous triffon, who reared and ripped its bridle out of the hand of the soldier who'd been holding it, attracting the attention of the others.

Savion's bare feet were no match for the snow-covered rock and he slipped and fell on his back, hard. Then he looked up and saw himself surrounded by Norlander soldiers. Lahlil didn't need any elixir to tell her what was going to happen next.

"No," said Savion, sounding just like Fellix as he scrambled away from them before he realized they were surrounded. "No, don't let them take me!"

Lahlil jumped to her feet and headed toward him, but he stood up and spun in a circle under the astounded stares of all those helmeted heads. She couldn't stop him now; he'd only take her with him if she grabbed him, and she couldn't go back, not without Trey. Savion's eyes rolled back in his head and he disappeared.

Now she would have to find another way back after she found Trey, and dusk was already on its way. The fear that she might fail dug one sharp talon into the back of her neck.

Recognition started with someone's finger pointing at her, then someone else's hand reached to grasp the arm of the person next to him, and soon it was spreading through the crowd like a wave, moving from the front to the back and then spilling back toward her: a wave of hatred and desire all churning together. She only had a moment before their shock gave way to action.

<Where is Trey Arregador?> she demanded.

No one would answer her, but she had expected that: she was watching for the involuntary movements of their eyes. Even with their helmets and hoods on, she saw enough of them look at the piles of fur and wool lying on the ground nearby to tell her what she wanted to know. One belonged to Trey, and the other to her sister. The size of the patch of blood in the snow did not indicate a life-threatening wound, and it marked out a clear trail toward the castle.

Then three soldiers came for her, all at once: two from in front of her and one from behind, not coordinated, just the ones who were quickest. But the Mongrel was ready for them, just as she had been outside Cyrrin's surgery, and the sweet relief of handing control over to her was so great that Lahlil had to clutch the sun medallion under her shirt to remind her of Jachad and why she was here before raising her sword to face off against them.

She drew her knife with her left hand and faked a move forward, then threw her weight backward into the soldier coming at her from behind her, crashing into his shield before spinning to her left and thrusting an elbow into the side of her adversary's head. While the man shook his head, momentarily off-balance, her left hand darted out and she stabbed deep into his shoulder; as his arm spasmed involuntarily, she wrenched his shield from him and slipped it over her own wrist, turning in time to deflect the blows of the two soldiers coming at her.

While she kept the soldier on her left at bay with her shield, she engaged the other one, but he was so frantic with battle-lust that his imperial sword twitched awkwardly and it took only one pass to get under his guard long enough to cut through his boot and into his calf: not her most decisive victory, but it brought him down.

As he fell, clutching at his companion's tabard, Lahlil grabbed the triffon's reins. More soldiers had shaken off their shock and broke after her, but she used sword and shield to keep them off as she leaped up onto the triffon's back and grabbed the pommel. The fastest of the guards tried to hack at her ankle; he only managed to nick the triffon in its thick hide and the creature roared in pain and launched itself into the air, giving her no time to strap herself in. She looped her arm through the vacant harness and grabbed the pommel again, then let the shield drop from her arm onto the heads of the mob reaching out for her from below.

But there were dozens of triffons already in the air; they'd be after her before she'd even turned toward the castle. At least she had their sheer numbers to her advantage: they'd be in danger of hurting each other if they all rushed her at once, and they could not shoot at her without fear of hitting their comrades. She had nothing but the stirrups and her one-armed hold on the harness to keep her from being flung out of the saddle, but she didn't have time to worry about that. She needed to get inside the castle, but rows of iron spikes protected the tops of the towers, and all the roofs were steeply peaked to stop the snow from settling.

Her gaze fell on the wide green-glass terrace stuck on to the castle to the west of the main gates: it would have made a perfect landing spot if not for the gigantic statues blocking her access. She banked as gradually as she could to avoid a triffon coming at her and went down for a closer look. Two swordsmen were circling each other in what looked like a duel, and a line of Eotan guards were keeping back an eddying crowd of spectators. As she got closer she recognized Gannon; she'd seen him on the battlefield and over a besieged castle wall. And she realized she knew the face of his opponent even better, but the sight of her brother came as such a shock that she had to blink several times before she could believe what she was seeing. She had to admit that Eofar was fighting better than she would have thought. He was keeping his attacks sharp and fast, making the best use of his imperial sword and not foolishly trading speed for the power of a killing thrust. But Gannon would still finish him soon if she didn't intervene.

As her triffon banked lower, she could feel her name repeated on all sides like a chant, and the commotion sparked by her arrival spread to the crowd gathered on the terrace. She felt Gannon's attention latch on to her like the fangs of a snake, his elation dripping into her blood like venom.

Eofar had enough sense not to waste the distraction and went straight for Gannon at a run. He managed to catch the emperor a little off-balance, not enough to land the thrust but at least to cut Gannon's forearm in the exchange that followed, earning a surprised exclamation from the onlookers.

Then, Eofar's back foot slipped on something—the green-glass itself, maybe, or a rock hidden beneath the snow—and as he lurched backward Gannon's heavy thrust caught him in the left shoulder. Only the fact that he was already falling backward kept the blade from passing straight through. Eofar staggered, his hand pressed to the wound and blood leaking out between his fingers.

Lahlil loosened her arm in the harness to make sure she could pull it out smoothly and headed straight for the terrace. The triffon stretched its wings out to slow its descent, but even so its tail smashed into the nearer statue of Eotan and sent the green-glass wolf's head bowling into the crowd. When the beast flew over the space between Eofar and Gannon she swung over the right side and jumped clear, falling at least ten feet onto the terrace. She knew how to stay loose and let her body absorb the shock of the fall; even so, it hurt.

The triffon flew on, pushing Gannon and the spectators back toward the opposite end of the terrace and giving her a moment with Eofar, who was leaning against the balustrade still clutching his bleeding shoulder. Lahlil oriented herself: she was facing east with the broken statue on her right. Gannon was about thirty paces away and a crowd of at least a hundred had gathered in front of the balcony doors and on the other side of the terrace, mostly soldiers, plus two generals decked out for war, ink-stained scribes and even a few children, with at least forty Eotan guards keeping them all back—but there was no sign of Trey or Isa.

Eofar stared at her, aghast. <They said you weren't coming.>

<Find a torch and close that wound,> Lahlil told him. He looked

ill: flushed and feverish, like Vrinna had looked in Cyrrin's surgery, and he also had those strange silvery blotches all over his clothes.

<Where's Oshi? Where's my son?> Eofar demanded, pitching wildly toward her. <Is he all right?>

<He's fine. He's with the Nomas.>

<No, stop,> said Eofar, grabbing her sleeve as she started toward Gannon. His eyes were too bright and his silver-blue irises had swallowed the pupils entirely. <This is my fight. Do you understand me? I'm going to do it myself this time. *I'm* going to save the Shadar.>

<All right. We'll take turns,> Lahlil promised, <but oldest goes first.> She moved away from him toward the center of the terrace and whisked her unnamed sword out of its sheath. The guards and soldiers all tensed, preparing to rush her, but then Gannon did exactly what the highest-ranking Norlander within reach of her always did.

<Stay back!> roared the emperor. <This is *mine*!>

Gannon walked slowly toward her with her brother's blood dripping into the snow from the tip of his sword, shimmering with smug assurance. The cut on his right forearm looked sour; if she had not seen Eofar give it to him just a few moments ago, she would have guessed it had been festering for a while.

<Where is Trey Arregador?> she asked, standing her ground but declining to raise her guard.

Gannon looked her up and down like an ursa he'd just wrestled from a tree. For a moment he took his silver eyes off her to look down over the Front. <Where's the army of the cursed?>

<No army.> A rush of air from another swooping triffon blew back the hair straggling out from her neglected braid and she could almost hear Callia's wearied sigh. <No Valrig. Just me.>

<If there's no army, you wouldn't be here,> said Gannon. <The witch told me the cursed are coming. They're mine to defeat. I'm the mightiest Norlander since Eowara.>

<Give me Trey Arregador and then you can do whatever you want.>

<No!> Eofar cried out, and she turned her head a fraction and watched him trying to pull himself up on the balustrade. Now she

was certain something was ailing him beyond the wound in his shoulder. She could feel him trying to struggle his way out of it, and wondered if he was losing his reason. <Gannon can't be allowed to live. The world has to change.>

<Stay down!> Lahlil commanded. <Think about your son.>

<I *am* thinking about him,> her brother seethed. <I'm thinking about everyone back home who's suffered because of Norland. It has to stop!>

Then for no visible reason Eofar screamed like something was shredding him from the inside. He dropped to his knees as some kind of convulsions hit him, bending his limbs, then straightening them again, leaving crazy patterns in the snow around him. Before Lahlil could do anything to help him, he leaped up and ran straight at the emperor. A few in the crowd tried to rush forward, but the guards still had orders to keep everyone back. Gannon met the attack with surprise, but not without ease as Eofar hammered at him with Strife's Bane as if the tactics of his earlier efforts had never even occurred to him.

Lahlil dashed forward and grabbed the back of her brother's coat the moment she saw an opportunity and he went spinning off and collapsed against the broken statue. She half-expected him to bound up again and rush at Gannon, but he just lay there, surrounded by shards of green-glass, as if he had spent all of the energy he possessed in that one attack. That wasn't all: his eyes had the hollow look of a corpse and his mouth hung open. This was some illness she had never seen before, and the wash of fear she felt for him caught her by surprise.

<Go home, Eofar,> Lahlil pleaded. <Find Oshi and take him somewhere safe. Forget any of this ever happened. Tell yourself it was just a dream.>

Gannon raised his sword. It was a beautiful thing, bronze, and ancient without being old: Valor's Storm. Lahlil couldn't have counted how many wooden replicas there had been among the toys in the secret room where she had lived as a child. Her mother had told her the stories of the first ruler of Norland, great Eowara, over and over again, even after she knew Lahlil's scarred arm meant she no longer had any claim to that birthright, or any other.

<Trey Arregador,> she repeated, very slowly. <Give him to me.>

<Or what? D'you think I'll bargain with garbage like you?>

Lahlil had not seen her father since she was three months old. She didn't remember him. She had tried to imagine what he looked like many times, picturing him like an older Eofar, only that image had never really come clear. Now she knew that her father had looked exactly like Emperor Gannon looked right at this moment, standing in judgment over her.

<If you don't, I'll tell everyone here the truth,> she threatened.

<You don't know any truth,> said Gannon. <You serve the god of lies. I'm smarter than he thinks. He can't trick me.>

<He's already tricked you,> Lahlil told him, <or somebody else has. I don't have an army. You're not going to win any great victory today—but you can wait out here in the cold if you want. You'll wait for nothing.>

Lahlil turned her back on him. She felt his fury, but he wouldn't hit her from behind. He needed his defeat of her to be legendary; nothing less than a fight to the brink of destruction would satisfy. She walked to the front of the balcony until the entire army below her came into view. Their tabards shone like the colored tokens on a campaign map. The watch-fires looked a little brighter that they had just a few moment ago and she knew she didn't have much time left before her attack. She leaned over the balustrade so that everyone could see her as the role of Destroyer—of life, of hope, of sanity—slid over her like a hangman's hood, familiar and suffocating.

<Listen to me,> she said, pitching her voice out wide, even though she already had their rapt attention. Even the beats of the triffons' wings melted away. <The people you set out for being "cursed" aren't any different from you. They don't change once they're scarred.>

She could feel their surprise and knew in a moment it would give way to angry denial.

<Some of the cursed survived being set out—they've been living not far from here, living right next to you, without you even knowing about it. They're ordinary people, just like you. They feel pain. They get lonely. They wonder how you could have abandoned them.> The leviathan skull on the headland eyed her with its

empty sockets. <Trey Arregador is one of them. So am I. My father, Eonar Eotan, set me out to burn to death in the desert when I was eleven years old. But here I stand.>

<I told you. Lies,> Gannon said behind her, but his certainty was beginning to drain out of him.

<You're wrong about the *Book,*> Lahlil told them all. <Dead wrong. You've set all those people out for nothing. You're responsible for the murder of every man, woman and child you ever left to die out there: people you loved—people who needed your *help.*>

<Don't listen to her. Valrig is trying to confuse you,> Gannon broke in again. <He wants you to think he's not coming so he can take you by surprise.>

<I'm not finished. You wanted me to bring an army for you to fight. Instead, when you close your eyes, I want you to see the faces of the people you abandoned to die, the ones you left out there, freezing and alone. You want an army of the cursed? Shut your eyes—go on! Picture their faces, those people you claimed to love, those people you betrayed.> She gripped the green-glass so hard she could almost feel it melting beneath her fingers. <There. There's your army. Fight it, if you can.>

A breath went through her body; longer and deeper than any other breath before it. It found the spaces she had locked away, drifted through cracks and keyholes, blowing away the ashes of the fires that had finally burned themselves out.

Gannon brought Valor's Storm around to face her. <Your speeches mean nothing to me,> he announced. <You're going to fight me.>

<I'll fight you for Trey,> Lahlil told him. The guards and the rest of the spectators had spread out along the back of the terrace and she could almost see their anticipation, like sparks of static crackling between them. <If I defeat you, you give me Trey Arregador. That's all.>

<No. That's not all,> said Eofar from behind her.

She glanced back as she circled Gannon. Her brother had lifted himself up using a chunk of green-glass until he was kneeling in the snow. Lahlil had seen enough people die to know that her brother was dying. She forced her attention back to Gannon, sensing his impatience; waiting for her to strike. So many swordsmen gave everything away in that first strike.

<You're fighting for the empire now. For Eowara's throne,> Eofar announced, speaking as forcefully as he could in his weakened state. Out of the corner of her eye, Lahlil saw him point to her. <I'm not the highest-ranking Eotan in Ravindal any more. *She* is.>

Chapter 36

As soon as Rho was sure no one was waiting to pounce on them from the dais, he led the way out of the little room. Their swords were still there, lying forgotten in the corner. He reached for Fortune's Blight, but somehow managed to knock both Virtue's Grace and Honor's Proof to the floor in the process and had to listen to the hilts bang against each step as they rolled down. He cringed, fully expecting their guard to come charging back, but he didn't, and neither did anyone else. Not only had none of the people already crowding around the terrace doors noticed their escape, but the guards at the throne room doors had their hands full trying to keep more people from barging in to get to the terrace.

Rho bent down to pick up Virtue's Grace, but the wound in his side had other ideas.

<What's wrong?> Trey asked him, handing Kira her sword and then retrieving his own. <Are you hurt?>

<Here, put this on,> said Rho, sheathing his sword and then taking off his coat. <You're shivering in that torn shirt.>

Trey lifted the coat over the hilt of his sword and put his arms through the sleeves. <Something's wrong with your side,> he persisted.

<It's nothing to worry about,> Rho said. <I'm indestructible.>

<We can go this way,> said Kira, pointing to a curtain in the corner. <The servants' corridors are through there. I know how to get us out of the castle, at least. Don't ask me how we're going to get out of the Front, or where we can go after that.>

Rho turned to her and was suddenly taken aback. She was obviously ill: her eyes were glassy and far too bright, her shoulders were hunched, and he could feel the hectic undercurrent of fever in her words.

<We'll go to the *Argent,*> said Rho, while his brother watched three more Eotan guards rush in through the doors to join the crowd on the terrace. <Only . . . >

<Dramash,> Kira finished for him.

<I have to get him. I was wrong to leave him with Ani. Something's not right there.>

<Go, then,> said Kira. <Meet us on the ship.>

Rho turned to Trey and found his brother drifting back toward the terrace. Cold fear rushed through him: he knew his brother would never leave if he found out Lahlil had come to Ravindal after all. They had to get him out quickly, before the perverse hopes Trey had spent the last three years of his life cherishing strangled him again.

<Wait for us in the hallway,> he told Kira. <I'll get Trey.>

She hesitated for a moment, but then she clicked open the latch and slipped out of the room.

<Trey, get back here,> Rho called softly to his brother. <Come on. Kira's waiting.>

<I hear swords,> said Trey. Rho heard them, too. <Someone challenged Gannon for the throne, right before I was arrested. I never saw him before.>

<That was Eofar Eotan,> said Rho, trying to hide his anxiety. <The son of the Shadari governor. Come on, it has nothing to do with us.>

But Trey continued edging toward the terrace.

<Trey, think about Kira and me,> he said urgently. <You might be able to fight your way out of here, but we can't. We need to go.>

<No, it's the Mongrel. I can tell,> Trey assured him, and Rho felt his hectic joy. He thought he was going to be sick as Trey said, <I was right. I knew she would come.>

<So what if she did?> said Rho, dashing around the deserted clerks' table and stretching his arms out to either side in a ridiculous attempt to prevent his brother from getting past him. <That's

all over for you now. The elixir brought us back together again. Isn't that enough?>

The sound of swords continued outside, along with the swell of emotion typical of the spectators at a tournament. Trey reached up with his left hand and kneaded his scarred shoulder.

<I can't leave—>

A commotion cut him off, this time from the hallway outside the throne room, and a company of guards brought in Captain Vrinna. She wasn't bound, but they had taken her sword, belt and all. She had obviously found *something* at Onfar's Circle, going by her bloodstained shirt and the jagged tear across her chest. The wound looked more like the result of a mauling than a swordfight, but it didn't explain her feverish shuddering or her burning eyes. *Just like Kira,* Rho thought, getting more and more worried, *only worse.*

Vrinna's guards tried to pull her toward the terrace, but she stopped short when she caught sight of Rho and Trey.

<What did you do to me?> she demanded of Trey. Her voice felt like spiders crawling into Rho's brain and down his throat. He had never felt a Norlander presence like that before. At the second glance, he saw the way her muscled shoulders hunched up toward her neck, and how she thrust her jaw all the way out on one side. Even the rage swirling around her felt odd: an unfocused maelstrom of blood and bile. <*You* did this. That bitch wife of yours tricked me into looking for you so you could mark me. I can feel it: you're turning me into one of you.>

They were interrupted by the physical upheaval of the crowd on the terrace as the people in the front tried to back away, while the people who had been trying to see over their heads continued pushing forward. The tense excitement of a few moments ago melted away to reveal a bubbling, viscous dread, and suddenly people were running through the throne room in a frenzy. Rho darted forward and took hold of the first guard he could reach. It was someone he knew.

<Dell! What is it? What's happening out there?> Rho asked the man, hanging on to his uniform as he tried to pull away.

<Rho? Let go of me!> said Dell. <It's the cursed—they're here!>

Rho pulled him closer so Trey wouldn't be able to hear what he was saying. <The cursed? *What* cursed? There is no army of the cursed.>

<We have to stop them,> roared the man, and looked over Rho's shoulder to where Trey was standing. <There's one of them, over there!>

<That's Trey Arregador, for Onfar's sake,> said Rho. <The hero of Redland.>

<Rho . . . > said Dell, fixing him in a blank-eyed stare as he drew his sword. The imperial blade was black as the bottom of a well, shiny as a pool of oil. <They've got to you too. You're on their side. You're one of them now.>

Panicked people were still running through the throne room, and the ringing clash of swordplay was still echoing from the terrace. Rho took the chance to kick the stools out from under the table, tripping Dell and buying himself a moment's respite. As pen-holders and ink-pots rolled to the floor he repeated, <There is no army of the cursed.>

<I know what I saw,> Dell insisted, coming for him.

Rho ducked over to the wall where the map stands stood in a neat row. He thought about pushing one at Dell until he saw they were chained to the floor, so he slid in between two of them instead, then darted around and came out on the other side with Dell following close behind. He kicked at an iron fire-dog and sent one of the smaller logs on the top of the pile rolling down and bowling Dell over like a child's wooden block. The soldier fell down, landing awkwardly and turning blue as the impact knocked the wind out of him.

<Tell me what's out there,> Rho demanded, holding the point of Fortune's Blight over Dell's chest.

<I told you,> said Dell, <it's the cursed—they're all around us!>

<Where did they come from? Eowara's tomb? Up through the cracks? From outside the city?>

<You really don't know?> asked Dell as his certainty about the situation swirled into confusion, like the snow billowing in through the open terrace doors. <They didn't come from anywhere. They're *us*—they're marking people; changing them as they go.>

<Rho!> Trey called out, coming toward him through the confusion. <They're saying it's the cursed. What do they mean?>

<It's some kind of mistake,> Rho assured him.

<It's no mistake,> Dell cried. <For Onfar's sake, Rho, there's one of them right behind you!>

Rho looked over his shoulder. <Where?>

But then his eyes landed on the captain. Her guards were nowhere to be seen—either she had broken free or they had fled—and her sword lay cradled in her arms. The fetid wound in her chest dripped with slime, and the same silvery fluid leaked out from both corners of her mouth and dripped from her eyes like shining tears. The hunch of her back and the painfully unnatural angles at which her limbs were twisted struck Rho like a bolt of lightning as an image from his father's huge copy of *The Book of the Hall* rose before his eyes.

<Rho! Trey!> Kira called out to them, weaving toward them from the other end of the hall. They had kept her waiting too long, and she'd come back to find them. <Why are you still here? What is going on?>

Vrinna's head swiveled around like a hawk's until her eyes fell on Kira. Then she thrust her sword aloft and gave a silent Norlander scream that turned Rho's blood to ash.

Chapter 37

The hate-filled battle-cry stopped Kira in her tracks just in front of the dais.

<I'll kill you this time!> Vrinna shrieked as she came charging down the length of the throne room. It felt like she was throwing off shards of madness as she ran and her voice squirmed inside Kira's mind like the manifestation of her most terrifying nightmare, made even worse by her oozing, crooked body. Kira drew Virtue's Grace in a blind panic, but Vrinna lunged straight for her and beat back her blade with one savage swipe. She tried to block the captain's follow-up lunge, but her wrist turned at a strange angle and she only just managed to divert it. Vrinna lunged again, and this time Kira just stood there like a sparring dummy until she heard Trey screaming out her name and jerked away.

Kira looked down at the spot where Vrinna's blade had gone, but she didn't see anything except a rip in her beautiful lagramor coat. It had been so lovely just this morning, and now it was covered in filth and sticky with the still-glittering slime from Eowara's tomb. Aline would scold her when she got home.

Then Kira cried out as a strange, twisting pain pounced on her like a crag-cat, grabbing hold of her limbs and contorting them in ways they were never meant to go, curling her spine into a tight hunch. Something took hold of her: a fistful of rage like nothing she had ever felt before, as if Vrinna's madness had burrowed inside her, seizing her body for itself, wrapping around her heart and twining down into her limbs. Its strength coursed through her, whether she wanted it or not, and the weight of Virtue's Grace dropped to a feather's lightness in her hand.

Vrinna's black blade flew at her again, and this time Kira swept up Virtue's Grace to block. The shock as the blades met shimmered through her body and the thing inside her writhed with pleasure as they fought. She might be holding Virtue's Grace, but it was like having a lagramor by the tail as the sword darted here and sliced there with sinuous menace, entirely of its own volition. Vrinna's blows came down like sledgehammers but Kira's arms had turned to steel: she could go on like this for days—in fact, she never wanted to stop. Once she killed Vrinna she would have to find someone else to fight, and someone else after that.

Trey danced around on the edge of her vision, calling out to her, but she had no time for him now.

She made a break for the steps of the dais. Vrinna swiped at her legs as she leaped up to the second step, but she blocked the blow and went for a quick follow-through, aiming to hit Vrinna's side under her right arm—the captain couldn't get into position to block in time and instead jumped back. Kira had her now: she aimed her blade, ready to charge down the steps and finish Vrinna once and for all.

Then the thing twisting in Kira's limbs suddenly snapped back, like someone yanking a fishing line out of the water, and the power and strength she had thought would last forever gushed out of her all at once. The wave of euphoria she had been riding crashed back down again, taking her with it. She clutched at her head as Vrinna's bloodlust howled inside her, trying to squeeze the madness out again, and staggered back in terror until she latched on to the smooth bones of the throne behind her for support.

<Leave her!> said Trey, charging at the thing that used to be Vrinna, hurdling fallen stools and shards of broken ink-pots and pen-holders.

<Trey, don't,> she called to him, and tried to take a step forward, but instead she dropped her sword and sank to the ground. She told herself the weakness was just the effect of Vrinna's beating, but a wiser voice inside her wouldn't quite let her believe it.

She could hear them fighting in front of the dais, but she had something in her eyes that was making it hard to see what was happening. Most of the other people in the room had fled, but through the now-unguarded throne room doors she could hear a frightening uproar coming from the main part of the castle. She cast around and found Virtue's Grace on the floor next to her and used it to try to get up. She had just managed it when Trey pushed Vrinna back to the foot of the dais.

Something had changed: Vrinna's blows weren't coming as hard now, or as fast. Her boots were stumbling over the ink-stained stones and she only just turned aside Trey's next thrust, staggering sideways, with her sword arm drooping. Kira would have found that more heartening if she had not been able to see the stiffness in Trey's shoulder making every movement a misery.

Kira pulled off one of her gloves and wiped the thick fluid from her swollen eye, then pulled back her fingers to look at them. They were coated with silver.

<Kira!> Rho limped up to her, his arm jammed against his side. Kira turned her face away from him and curled her fingers in her palm so he wouldn't see the silvery pus.

<Get Trey away from Vrinna,> she begged her brother-in-law. <There's something wrong with her. You both have to stay away from her.>

<But—>

<*Please,* Rho.>

He staggered back down the steps but then hesitated, as if he was trying to decide whether to grab Trey and haul him away, or jump in between him and Vrinna and take over the fight. Then Vrinna lost her balance and fell back against the wall. Trey rushed toward her, but as he raised his arm for the thrust his shoulder finally seized up completely and he stopped short with his arm shaking, desperately trying to transfer the sword into the other hand.

Kira's eyes clouded over again and she ground the heel of her hand into the swollen sockets, trying to clear them. The room came back into view again, but everything was swimming behind a veil of smoke. Trey appeared to her in front of the throne, in the same place she had seen him for the very first time, when she could not have conjured a more wonderful specimen of Norlander perfection. The gray smoke drifting around him now hid his scars and he looked just the same as she remembered. She could finally forget the bitterness of that day in the forest, with the snow and the blood . . . so much blood.

So much blood now, too, because Vrinna had just pulled her sword out of Trey's chest before melting away into the nonexistent smoke.

Kira couldn't move or say anything, even though her body screamed to go to him. It was Rho who rushed forward and caught him as he fell. Somehow she got down the steps to them, but by then Trey's eyes were closed and she could feel his mind a long way off.

<We have to seal that wound . . . > said Rho.

He tailed off as his despair swept him under, and her with him. She sank to her knees beside her husband.

Trey suddenly drew in a gasping breath and his eyelids fluttered. She leaned in closer; he couldn't open his eyes completely, but he could see her. She saw him trying to reach his hand out to her, but he couldn't lift it high enough. She took his warm, limp fingers in her own.

<We're here,> said Rho. He was holding on to Trey stiffly, as if the slightest movement would shatter him. <I'm going to take care of you. Everything's going to be all right.>

<Rho,> said Trey. His words came from an odd angle, as if they had to find their way around a blockade too heavy and too well entrenched to be shifted. <Is it true? Is the army of the cursed here? Was I right?>

<Yes, it's true,> said Rho, and Kira believed him; he was committing to the lie with the whole of his heart. <The Mongrel is here, and she brought the cursed with her. You were right. Lord Valrig chose you. It was all true.>

<Are you sure?>

<I'll prove it,> said Rho, lifting him up. He was already covered with his brother's blood. <Come over here, Kira. We've got to take him outside.>

Kira stood up, forcing her weakened legs to move, and smeared her eyes clear again—and saw Vrinna leaning against the wall with her head cradled in the crook of her arm. The captain staggered forward, coughing in wheezy hacks and with her bulging, dripping eyes sparkling like a fish's scales, until she finally fell over ten paces shy of the throne room doors. Kira picked up Virtue's Grace and went to her, watching her twitch like a bird with an arrow through its wing.

<Kill me,> Vrinna begged when she saw her coming. Her words felt thick and sticky in Kira's head, like no amount of scrubbing would ever get them out again. <I won't be one of them. It's not too late—I can still die by the sword, like a real Norlander. That's what Trey wanted, too. I gave it to him. You give it to me.>

Kira took Virtue's Grace in both hands and raised it up over Vrinna's helpless body.

Then she found something left of herself, tucked up in a little corner that the other thing hadn't yet found and rooted out. She should have guessed that the last thing left of her wouldn't be her love or her intellect or her compassion: it would be her sense of irony.

She sheathed her sword and turned her back, instead joining Rho as he carried Trey through the room toward the terrace. Snow was blowing in, along with the last of the daylight. Outside, Gannon and the Mongrel were still fighting in the corner next to the now-headless statue of Eotan. At least a hundred people remained on the terrace, and a good half of them were displaying some variation of Vrinna's symptoms—*her own symptoms*—and the rest were trying to battle them back. Kira wanted to tell the healthy people to get away while they could; the sick would be no threat, not once their mad strength ended, and that lasted only a little while. They should just be left to die.

A single flake of snow pricked her cheek like an icy finger as Rho knelt down on the threshold with Trey dying in his arms. Kira could hardly feel the stone beneath her numb limbs and her coat weighed down on her shoulders like a lead collar. She managed to open it, though her fingers felt dead already, and let it fall on to the ground.

Do not go down into the deep places.

<Can you see her?> Rho asked Trey, lifting him up a little higher. <She's right over there; and the army of the cursed is all around us. You brought them.>

Trey couldn't speak now, but Kira could feel a light at the very center of him, glowing brighter and brighter until it burned some of her darkness away. It held her, that light, and made her a part of it; a part of *him*.

<Lord Valrig is going to be there in the After-realm, waiting for you,> said Rho. <You're going to get a hero's welcome, just like you deserve.>

Kira lurched over and fell beside Trey, pulling him into her unfeeling arms and resting her cheek against his head.

They both felt the moment when he left them. Rho's grief burst open, and she would have taken some of it for him—she would hardly notice it, mingled with her own—but it was his, and he didn't want to give any of it up. Kira felt like they stayed that way for hours, but when Rho stirred, she realized no time had passed at all.

<I'm going to get Dramash,> he said, hauling himself to his feet, <then I'm coming back for you. We're leaving here together.>

<No. Don't come back,> said Kira. She knew there was no way to stop what was happening to her, and she didn't really mind, not now. <You have to get away from here as fast as you can.>

<Kira.> He looked more like Trey now than ever.

<Rho. Please go.>

She felt the touch of his hand on her head for a brief moment, then he disappeared back into the darkness of the throne room. She held Trey in her arms and watched her world crumble to bits through the wavering green-glass, like a dry leaf crushed in a gloved hand.

Chapter 38

The floor bobbed up and down and Isa could see her sister Frea in the water, trying to pull off her dented helmet.

"Isa."

"It's the cape, Frea. It's pulling you down."

"Isa. Wake up."

With her eyes still closed, she felt the tightness in her throat and realized she had spoken aloud, in Shadari. She kept her eyes closed, trying to remember where she was. The stables: that was it. She had tried to ride a triffon again and she had fainted. Eofar would come and carry her back to her room and put her to bed. No, that wasn't right. The stables were gone, along with the temple, along with Frea–along with the pain.

The pain was gone.

That creature that had been gnawing at Isa's insides since the day she'd lost her arm had unfurled a pair of great black wings and swept up out of some lair deep inside her. She gasped aloud as it passed through her, shocked that something so big had been crouching down inside her all of this time, and so lightened by its passing that she felt like she was floating up into the air. The pain was gone: *all* of the pain.

"It's working, yes?" asked Ani, when Isa finally opened her eyes. "I knew it would."

The old woman was placing a few selected items inside a leather satchel, deliberately, as if she had no need to hurry. Her voice sounded different–quicker, and somehow further away–but Isa wasn't worried. She wasn't worried about anything now, because she trusted in what Ani had promised.

Everything was going to be all right.

Isa rose with ease now, carrying her full weight on her injured leg without feeling a thing. She rubbed the stump of her left arm and felt nothing. Even the heat of the fire didn't make her uncomfortable. She went closer, thinking how it was odd that she'd never really looked closely at a fire before. Beautiful colors danced in the flames, so varied and alive.

Still one problem nagged at her.

"I don't know if it's safe for you in the Shadar," she admitted to Ani. "Things are very bad there. Someone's been killing all the ashas."

"Yes, I know," said Ani. Her voice never rose any louder than the soft desert wind, but something roared underneath, like an inferno somewhere just out of sight, on the other side of the dune. "I'm in no danger."

"How do you know that? Because of the elixir? Is that how you knew I was coming? Did you see who's killing the ashas?"

"Ashas," said Ani, with a little sound like the one Daryan made when he spoke of Binit and his band of pot-stirrers. "They dared call themselves that, though they were nothing but puppets, always doing the same dance. There have not been any real ashas in the Shadar for three hundred years."

Dramash crawled back out from under the covers. "Are we going?" he asked dully.

"We're going home," Ani told him. "We're going back on the Nomas ship."

"Do we have to?"

"Put on your coat," Ani told him, still without raising her voice, but with the fire beneath it burning a little hotter. She had paused in her packing and was holding a small scroll in her hand. Isa stared at the Shadari woman, a little perplexed. Something was wrong with the picture before her, but when she tried to concentrate on it, the bad feeling slipped away. "I have been waiting a very long time for this—for you, Isa. So has the Shadar. A dark age is ending, and you're going to help me begin a new one. My people have completed their penance at last."

"Penance?"

"Yes. They had to be punished."

"For what?"

"Their fear." Ani was sorting through a box of ordinary-looking stones and carefully choosing one for her sack that looked exactly like all the others. "Their hubris, for thinking they had the right to set limits on me." Her mellow voice dug into Isa's head like a hot knife, carving deep grooves into her consciousness. "For starting a war they knew they couldn't win and destroying everything I had built for them. They needed to understand just how helpless they are without me."

"But they didn't start the war." Isa stepped away from the fire; the heat had started to creep up on her again. "My people started it after you told them about the ore, and how to make swords from it."

"Not the war with the Norlanders," said Ani. She stared at the wall for a moment as if she could see all the way back to the Shadar. Her voice dropped so low that Isa could hardly hear her. "No, the war the ashas started against *me*."

The scroll. Now Isa knew why it had bothered her: the Shadari never wrote anything down. It was forbidden by their religion, ever since . . .

"You know who I am now, yes?" Ani asked her, coming toward her. No more than three paces separated them, yet Isa felt hours pass as the old woman crept closer. The red firelight was glowing at the ends of her wiry white hair. "I know Harotha told you all about me; I could see everything she saw when she took the elixir. She even sensed I was there, the clever thing; I'm a little sorry she's dead, but she served her purpose. She told you how the ashas betrayed me, and how I jumped from my temple. She saw, but she didn't understand."

"That couldn't have been you." Isa shut her eyes for a moment. She felt a little dizzy, but no pain; the pain was completely gone. "That was hundreds of years ago."

"That's why you see me like this, old and weak," said Ani. "I've needed to use my powers to keep myself alive. I've had to do my penance as well, but that's all finished now. The way has been prepared for me. I'm coming home, thanks to you, Isa."

Ani went back to her table, opened a wooden box and drew out a bottle.

"Is that the elixir?" asked Isa. Something in her mind tapped out a little rhythm; something it wanted her to do; something wanted her to know that everything was *not* all right. "Can I take some?"

She needed to know if she and Daryan would ever really be together again. She needed to know if there had been a point to all of this. No, more than that: she needed to know if bringing Ani back to the Shadar was the right thing to do.

"You could," said Ani, "but it would kill you. I've poisoned it so no one can take it but me now."

Ani held out her hand to Dramash. He came over to her obediently enough, but his head was bowed and he pulled his hand away for a moment before he put it into hers. Isa looked over the room again. She felt like she had put something down and was about to leave without it, but she saw nothing but some old furs and bits of wood and stones, and some beetles buzzing under a glass dome. The humming sound found the little prickings of doubt in her mind and smoothed them over, soothing her back into certainty. She opened the door.

Dramash spoke at last. "What about Rho?" he asked, stopping just before the threshold. "He probably wants to come with us."

"You chose," Ani told him. "You sent him away. He isn't coming back."

The three of them went into the next room. Ani's guard was still slumped against the wall. Isa did not try to touch his mind this time; she knew he was dead now. The door to the outside creaked on its iron hinges as Isa opened it wider, and they went out onto the roof. The flakes were falling in heavy sheets now, but the snow beneath the worn soles of her boots felt as soft as sand and she didn't feel the cold any more than she had the heat of the fire. Far down below, inside the castle and out on the Front, and spreading like a pool of blood into the city beyond, she sensed the deep boom of a terror beyond anything she had ever imagined. But that didn't worry her.

Everything was going to be all right.

Chapter 39

Lahlil held her ground as Gannon charged, tracking Valor's Storm as he swept it down with enough force to cut her in half. At the last moment she whirled out of the way and heard Eowara's sword whisk past just over her head.

Gannon was already using the momentum of the missed strike to swing back around, but Lahlil had changed to a two-handed grip as she spun and now she hammered down with all of her might, trying to smash Valor's Storm to the ground. Maybe it was Gannon's strength, or perhaps some unseen property of the bronze blade, but her strike glanced off and left her off-balance, and she only just managed to turn aside his next thrust by locking their blades. Both of them pushed as hard as they could while Eotan's headless statue loomed over them, aloof and impartial.

They both timed their move out of the impasse so perfectly that Lahlil herself didn't know who had moved first, but she didn't waste time wondering; she went all-out for Gannon, blade and muscles shifting in perfect harmony.

She tried to push him back to the balustrade, cutting at him first from the left and then the right, employing the agility that had vanquished a hundred imperial blades; keeping him always on his back foot. She had hoped all those years of wielding an imperial blade would have made Gannon slower and clumsier when he couldn't control the blade with his mind, but he matched her speed and bettered her strength, leaving her unable to take advantage of any opening even when she managed to find one.

She could not even find a way to use the weeping wound on his arm to her advantage.

She failed to capitalize on a brief moment where he left himself open on his left side, then had to scramble as she misread a feint and found a thrust coming straight at her heart. The bronze blade slid past as she shifted out of the way, coming close enough to rend her coat.

She came back into position again and started working through all the little tricks and maneuvers the Mongrel had perfected just for the sake of it, but nothing worked. She felt scattered; disjointed. She needed to focus entirely on Gannon, but instead her attention skittered around like a little bird, wanting her to notice the fighting that had broken out among the crowd on the other side of the terrace and the tumult of the troops below her on the Front; wanting to know what had happened to her brother, and where Trey Arregador had been taken. Mostly she wanted to know if Jachad was still alive, and if he hated her for leaving, and what he would say if she ever found her way back to him.

Finally she forced herself to let everything disappear but her opponent: she was just a blade, a vessel of destruction with no conscience, no sympathy and no objective other than the kill. She waited for the relief that came with giving over to the Mongrel once more.

But this time it wouldn't come, and instead was the image of Jachad, pale and dying, turning his face to the wall so he wouldn't have to look at her.

Then Gannon let out an agonized cry and fell back against the statue, contorting into one unnatural pose after another, as if someone had got hold of the muscles from the inside and was yanking them this way and that. She should have hit him then, but she was thinking of the convulsions she had watched Eofar endure right before he flew at Gannon in a mad rage.

And he came for her again, battering her with hatred and fury in every stroke of his sword. She had fought princes and generals maddened by the carnage on the battlefield around them, but this was beyond anything she had known. She fought him until her arms ached, but she could do nothing to stop him.

Succumbing finally to frustration, Lahlil squared her blade and charged, trying to push him back with nothing more than brute force. The strategy worked—something so stupid had probably caught him off-guard—but then she saw a slackness in his jaw and the way his right shoulder sagged a little with the weight of the sword and realized he was finally vulnerable. Dozens of possible attacks flipped through her mind like the pages of a smeary training manual. She wanted one that was quick and ugly, and she wanted it to hurt.

But before she could choose, an armored triffon streaked out of the sky and smashed right into the front of the green-glass balcony. A cloud of pulverized ice flew up, hiding bigger and sharper pieces within, and a crack zigzagged back as far as the castle wall. The impact knocked Lahlil off her feet, but she caught a look at the contorted soldier in the saddle before both he and the triffon fell two stories through the breach. The sickness that was killing her brother had claimed another victim.

The floor shuddered beneath her and she crawled back away from the rupture while the terrified triffon shoved through the columns below, trying to find its way back out into the open. Each impact from its iron-plated forehead shook the whole terrace until finally one pillar cracked and went down, and then another. The terrace split in two along the fault line, each side swaying on its remaining supports.

She and Gannon were cut off from the castle, as was Eofar, if he was still alive. The crowd on the other side of the terrace bolted for the throne room, but there were too many of them to get through the doors all at once.

Lahlil sprang back up to her feet. <Where is Trey Arregador?> she demanded.

Gannon backed away from her, holding Valor's Storm in front of him like a talisman. The fur on his blue ursa coat shook with his trembling, and she could tell by the way he dragged his feet that his legs had gone numb. A silvery pus had started to ooze from the innocuous cut Eofar had scored during their duel and the emperor's eyes were wide with primal terror.

For by these marks on their flesh—

<"For by these marks on their flesh,"> she recited for the man to

whom all of Norland owed allegiance, <"their twisted limbs, the corruption in their blood, our brother Valrig has claimed them.">

She had witnessed every type of terror, but this . . . The tiny black dot of Gannon's realization condensed all the fear of an entire lifetime into that one moment. She wanted to savor it, to roll it around her mouth and suck the marrow out of it, let its warm juices run down her throat. Instead her teeth clamped down and her lips sealed tight, shutting it out. Somewhere along the way, she had lost the taste for other people's horror.

<What have you done to me?> the emperor screamed at her, dropping Valor's Storm and clutching at his head with both hands. <You put it inside me!>

Lahlil looked down over the Front and instead of colored tabards in strict formation, she saw a riot of dots and streaks of color like the work of some demented artist. Armored triffons flew erratically through the towers or out over the city, while others tried to force them down or engage with them. Jittery archers fired down from the walls and up at the sky at anything that might be a target. Frantic servants and commoners, armed with whatever they could find, flooded from the castle gates and tried to find a way past the soldiers, desperately trying to escape. Wherever Lahlil saw empty space, she found someone indiscriminately attacking those nearest them, spitting silver foam from their mouths or writhing and screaming in pain. All this horror, because something was turning people into the one thing every Norlander had been taught to fear from their first sip of milk.

Let all so afflicted be numbered among the damned.

A heavy, sucking energy behind her made her turn back around to see Captain Vrinna come out onto the abandoned terrace, leaking silvered blood down over her Eotan tabard. The passion of her purpose kept her upright as she flung herself over the teetering ice toward the breach separating her from her emperor. She fixed her dripping eyes on Gannon as if he were a god demanding her sacrifice, then ran straight to the edge of the gap between the two sections of the terrace and jumped.

She didn't make it.

The gap was only a few feet across, but Vrinna's legs collapsed under her just as she leaped. She managed to grab the jagged edge of the green-glass with one hand, and now pulled the other one up beside it. Her legs swung below the thick ice, but she had nothing to brace herself on to pull herself up the rest of the way.

Lahlil watched her trying to hold on and felt like she was watching herself clinging there by her fingertips, as she had been ever since that morning out in the desert when she had watched her mother fall from her triffon. Every day of her life she had felt that ice slipping away from her, knowing the darkness at the bottom of that drop would be the end. Only one person had been there to give her the strength to hang on: Jachad. He had kept her from falling all these years, even when she had resisted; even when she didn't deserve it. He had never stopped trying to pull her back up, even when he was dying himself.

Lahlil ran to the broken edge of the terrace and rammed the point of her sword down into the green-glass to give herself a little bit of leverage on the tilting ice. She held on to the hilt with one hand and seized Vrinna's wrist with the other. The captain let go of the ledge and grabbed Lahlil's arm and with one good heave, scrambled over the edge and slid across the listing ice.

As Lahlil pulled out her sword, she noticed that the crack had grown wider and the two ends of the terrace were leaning further from each other. The brittleness of the green-glass columns below them would not hold out against the stress forever. She looked across the gap toward the doors, trying to guess how long she could wait before she had to get back across, when she noticed a woman sitting just across the threshold, cradling the body of a man in her arms.

Lahlil's mind splintered into jagged black shards as she recognized the dead man. She felt as if the gods had stuffed the whole night sky in there and then shattered it with hammers of lightning. The explosion hollowed her out, making room for the dread to sink deep down into her. *Trey was dead.* She had forfeited the bargain she had made for Jachad's life. She had broken her promise, and left him alone for nothing. She had ripped Cyrrin away from her people, and then failed to save the one person the healer had ever allowed herself to love, even if he had never loved her in return.

<Lahlil!> Eofar warned her—still alive—and she turned to see Vrinna with her sword in hand, but not coming for her. The captain was dragging herself along the ice toward the emperor.

<What are you doing?> Gannon cried out to her, still caught in his terror as he backed away from her into the broken statue.

<It's not too late,> Vrinna told him. Love bled from her, twisted and possessive, as sticky and foul as the silvery stuff killing them both, and everyone around them. <I can't let you become one of them. You have to die by the sword.>

<Vrinna, no!> Gannon screamed, but she sank the blade straight through the hands he had thrown up in front of his chest to protect himself. The emperor's head fell back to face the falling snow and his mouth dropped open with a gurgling cough. His loyal captain clasped her arms around him and threw herself over the balustrade, taking him with her. If they made a sound when they hit the ground, Lahlil could not hear it over the wall of noise rising up from the still-raging battle below. She followed the trail of Vrinna's silvery poisoned blood and looked down to see both of their bodies lying broken over one of the fallen pillars.

The familiar words came back, repeating themselves over and over again, trying to tell her something.

Let all so afflicted be numbered among the damned. Let them not remain among you, for they will be your destruction; let them be stripped of their garments and set out in the wilderness, for by these marks on their flesh, their twisted limbs, the corruption issuing from them, our brother Valrig has claimed them and will have dominion over them. He will bring them to his hall of Valrigdal in the deep forbidden places, and they shall be his Army of the Cursed. Then be ready against the day they will rise up and strike at the Righteous. On that day let a Hero be prepared with the sword we have given you, to subdue them, lest they corrupt all that is pure in this land. Yet as Lord Onfar is merciful, and as Lady Onraka is just, if the afflicted be found worthy, so their wounds shall be healed and their steps guided back to the fires of their clan. For by this sign, they are to be embraced without prejudice.

Lahlil looked down at Eowara's sword lying on the ground. *Do not go down into the deep places.* She threw her worthless unnamed sword into the gap and picked up Valor's Storm.

<Eofar?> she called, crossing to the back of the swaying terrace

where her brother slumped against the wall. The increased pitch of the other side of the terrace did not escape her notice, nor did the snapping noise that sounded like ice breaking up in a spring thaw.

A pair of shining silver tears rolled down Eofar's cheeks, but Norlanders didn't cry. More fluid gathered behind his parted lips. He jerked his head away when Lahlil reached out to touch him.

<The deep places,> said Eofar. <We're the ones who did it. We went down into Eowara's tomb and we brought this plague back with us.>

Lahlil took a closer look at his wound. The edges had already started to knit together, even without sealing it, but that ubiquitous silver pus bubbled out from the cut. She could feel his strength draining away, like snow melting through her fingers.

Her next breath snagged in her throat. She had been looking at a picture her whole life without being able to make any sense of it, and now someone had come along and turned it the right way up.

Let them be stripped of their garments and set out in the wilderness.

<It's too late for me. It's in my blood,> Eofar told her. <Go, before it gets you too. You have to take care of my son. Please, Lahlil—please, go.>

<We need to get your coat off.> Lahlil started on it before she had even finished saying it and he couldn't fight her; he was too weak even to wipe the snow from his face. She pulled him out of the fur coat like she was extracting a snail from its shell, and then used her knife to widen the rip in his shirt and tear it off him until he was lying half-naked on the frozen green-glass. She weighed her knife in her hand, only pretending to herself that she was making up her mind.

<This is going to hurt,> she warned him, and before he knew what was about to happen, she pinned him down and slashed the wound in his shoulder open again. His scream contributed nothing to her task, so she ignored it while she gathered up handfuls of snow and packed it into the wound. Cold shuddered through him until his teeth rattled, but she kept him down.

<Wh— wh— what are you doing?> he asked, as she rubbed more snow into his wound, and then onto his chest and neck.

<The cold will kill the infection,> said Lahlil. <You have to stay

out here. I don't know how long. I'd say right up until you freeze to death.>

<There's a cure?> her brother asked. His presence in her mind already felt stronger. <Are you sure?>

<That's why they set people out: so they wouldn't hurt anyone else when they turned violent. They figured out that was how the sickness spread, through wounds and into the blood. If the cold cured them, they could come back.>

<How did you figure all that out?>

<I didn't,> she told her brother, looking down at her dirty, callused hands as she brushed the snow from her fingers. <It's all in the *Book*. It's been right there all along.>

<Lahlil.> Eofar curled his fingers into her coat for a moment and held on.

<Get your strength back,> she commanded after she swallowed past the lump in her throat. <If this spreads as fast as I think it does, I'm going to need you to cure me soon enough.> The scabbard for Valor's Storm was still on Gannon's broken back, so she rested the naked blade against her shoulder as she stood up.

<Where are you going?>

Lahlil said, <Down there. I need to show them what to do.>

<Just don't let them kill you,> said Eofar, dropping his head back and letting the snow fall on his naked skin. <I don't think I want to be emperor any more.>

Chapter 40

Rho had thought losing Trey for the first time was the worst grief he could ever feel, but he knew now that guilt and self-pity were not the same as grief. He could still feel Trey's weight in his arms; it was a burden he would never put down. Nor would he hand it over to someone else. He clutched it to his heart, as he now embraced his mission to take Dramash away from that woman. He would allow nothing to stop him this time, not even Dramash.

The stink of chaos hit Rho when he came out of the throne room and onto the gallery looking down over the entrance hall. The castle gates had been breached somehow—probably from the inside, by people trying to get out—and now as many people were running inside looking for sanctuary as were frantically trying to escape. A few of the boldest ones hurried through with armfuls of looted treasure, dropping jeweled cups and gold dishes behind them like a trail of shiny crumbs. A soldier with dripping silver eyes took a sword to the neck at the top of the stairs just as Rho leaned over the railing; she went barrelling down, knocking over anyone who didn't get out of the way fast enough. If the sickness spread from blood to blood, then every knife and sword was now a wand of pestilence and every cut a conscription into Valrig's army.

Rho pushed his way through to the tower stairs with his whole right side vacillating between fiery-hot and icy-cold. He was sure now that Gannon had pulled apart something inside him that wasn't going to go back together on its own, but he didn't care as long as he got back to the *Argent* with Dramash. He gathered as much momentum as he could by running down the last hallway and using it to propel him up the steps, though he was forced to slow as the climb grew steeper. Then a gust of wind moaned past him and he realized that the door up above had been opened. He moved back on the next landing and brought his right hand up to his shoulder, ready to draw, but when he looked up the steps, he saw Dramash's small face peeking out from layers of fur. He was holding Ani's hand, and a third person was coming down the tower steps behind them.

<Isa!> he called out in shock.

<Rho?> She reacted slowly to his hail, although she was looking right at him. He could tell immediately that something was off about her. She was out of focus, like she was standing just to the side of where she appeared to be.

A door opened on the next landing down and Rho heard people running behind him. His reunion with Isa would have to wait. He backed up and turned around just as an Eotan guard with an imperial sword charged up the stairs. He was leading five others that he could see, and probably more behind that.

<Isa, get them back up to the tower!> Rho shouted out to her as he drew Fortune's Blight. He didn't care how ridiculous he looked, coming on guard against so many when he was so battered that he couldn't even stand up straight. But Isa chose not to listen to him, which was at least comforting in its familiarity. She slipped past Ani and Dramash and ducked right under his arm to stand in front of him. Every one of the guards could see the stump of her severed arm as she drew Blood's Pride.

<One of 'em's up here,> said the man in the lead. <Kill them! Kill them all!>

"Run!" Rho called back, checking over his shoulder to make sure Ani and Dramash could get away as the guards rushed them.

He saw Ani take a long pin from somewhere under her coat and prick her palm—without flinching—until she drew up a drop of red blood. Then before he could understand what he was seeing, much less stop it, she lifted up Dramash's hand, pulled off his mitten and did the same to him. He squeaked when the needle pierced his skin and his eyes stretched wide in surprised pain.

A terrible sense of foreboding made Rho look behind him.

The imperial sword of the second guard shot forward, and she stabbed the man in front of her straight through the back. Blue blood bubbled out of the victim's mouth and he collapsed in a heap at Isa's feet. The guard who'd killed him dropped her black-bladed sword in horror and backed into the man behind her, who screamed out a warning even as he swung his blade into her neck, nearly taking her head off. The same man then sliced into the shoulder of the man behind him like he was splitting a tree stump. After that, the scene turned bloodier than Rho's worst nightmares. Frantic screams and cries of pain blended into one soundless roar as the swords turned against their owners' wills, and still more soldiers kept charging forward up the stairs behind them, trying to get to the enemy they knew must be up ahead.

Rho turned back around.

Ani was still holding Dramash's hand. Tension shivered through his limbs and his eyes stared at nothing, but that particular look—that one that plagued Rho's dreams—wasn't there. Dramash was not the one doing this. *Then how—? Oh, sweet Onraka,* he said to himself as his gaze slid to the old woman at the boy's side. The look on Ani's face wasn't one he had ever seen on a living, breathing person. It was the haughty, serenely curved lip and the unblinking eyes of a carved deity: somber, powerful, and utterly pitiless. *She* was the source of this carnage, and she was wielding Dramash like an axe.

"What are you doing to him?" he cried out to her. "What *are* you?"

She considered the question for a moment. "Patience," she said. "That's what all gods are, in the end."

He would have lunged toward her then but Isa flowed in front of him with her liquid grace.

<Stop,> she said, blocking his path.

Rho couldn't understand how everything had gone so wrong so quickly. It was like the world was a table and someone had come along and heaved up one side, sending everything rolling down onto the floor into one tangled mess.

The slaughter had ended, and now instead of boots pounding up the steps and jingling sword belts, he heard the sound of bodies sliding slowly down, a few steps at a time.

Rho lifted Fortune's Blight and pointed it at Ani. "*You* are not a god."

"Don't, Rho," Isa said as she slid her shoulder in front of his to move him back. A hectic wash of pink and burning orange flowed out from her, a torrent of emotion. He had never felt anything remotely like it from her, or anyone else before. "I'm taking them back to the Shadar. That's why I'm here, to help Daryan. Everything's going to be all right now."

"Isa—" More alarmed than ever for her now, he reached out to her with the easy intimacy of their friendship, but all that color just swept him back again. His heart gave a heavy thump. "Isa, you can't take her to the Shadar. Didn't you see what she just did?"

"I was protecting us. Isa knows that," said Ani. "She knows it's time for me to go back to the Shadar. It will be different this time, with Dramash to help me." The boy's eyes were beginning to focus again, and his limbs had lost that horrible rigor.

"He's just a child," Rho cried out. "He's been through enough. Can't you just leave him alone?"

"Oh, he doesn't want that," said Ani, "not now he's seen what he can be."

The boy tilted his head up to the old woman and Rho saw something kindling in Dramash's eyes that he feared was a dark kind of triumph.

"No," said Rho, through clenched teeth, "you can't do this to him."

"What would *you* do with him?" asked Ani. Her voice spiraled down the walls toward him, hissing like a sandstorm. "Hide him away? Make him ashamed of what he is? You want him to be something you can control, but you never will. The other ashas burned up because they weren't strong enough to channel my power, but not Dramash. I'm taking him home with me. We have work to do."

<Isa, I know you can't be all right with this,> said Rho, reaching out to her for help, but it was like trying to look into clouds glowing with sunrise color: indistinct, but incredibly bright. He could not even tell if she understood what was happening. <We have to stop her—she's not what she's pretending to be. Help me get Dramash away from her first and then we'll figure out what to do.>

He saw the pommel of Blood's Pride coming at his head, but his body in its present state was too slow and stupid to do anything about it. It smashed into his skull over his right ear, and Fortune's Blight fell from his hand as he stumbled back against the wall and crashed to the floor. The dead guard with the severed neck lay beside him with her fingers still curled in the shape of the hilt of the sword Ani and Dramash had ripped from her hand.

Rho heard the shuffling of their boots across the landing and then down the stairs. He couldn't move, but he was still conscious. Isa could have killed him easily, so he found a little hope in the fact that she had only knocked him down.

He crawled over to Fortune's Blight as soon as he could and fought his way to his feet. Going down: down was like falling and he could do that. He hugged the walls to get past the bodies of the murdered guards, trying not to count them or categorize their wounds, and then made it back down past the other landings, moving as quietly as he could. Thankfully, he encountered no one else.

Even before he emerged back out into the entrance hall, he knew something had changed. A huge silver urn rocked on its side in front of the doors and the hall held nothing but rubbish and dead bodies dumped into corners, lying on the ground or across the stairs. The looters were gone but so were the guards, the high clansmen, even Gannon's dogs, and Rho thought he smelled smoke.

Isa, Dramash and Ani had already disappeared. He made his way across the hall, trying to ignore the pounding in his head, using anything he could for support. He could hear the tinny rattle of swords clashing in the distance so the situation outside had not improved, but the loud cracking and groaning sounds nearby worried him more.

He made his way out onto the darkening Front where the freezing air instantly chilled his lungs. He stopped at the top of the steps, intending to throw himself after Dramash as soon as he spotted him in the crowd, but now he understood why the looters had fled the castle: the afflicted were everywhere, and they were terrifying. The colored tabards had ceased to have any meaning; the only distinction that mattered was between "cursed" and "not cursed," and even that designation was looking horrifyingly fluid. He could see hundreds of lurching, convulsing creatures screaming and slashing at anything that came near them, and just as many others on the ground, writhing in agony and begging for death.

He slid to a dead stop and then inched back through the slush as another high-pitched groan rose above the general clamor. A sliding shadow turned the snow in front of him to a pale green and just as he realized that some catastrophe had smashed the terrace in two, the eastern half listed over on its green-glass columns and the whole thing up-ended.

The statue of Eotan smacked down right in front of him, splitting into sections where the separate castings had been joined. The wolf's head bounced on the black stone, kicking up a cloud of crushed ice, and then landed upright on its severed neck with nothing but indifference in its green-glass eyes. The platform slid down on one edge and cracked apart into flat chunks that went spinning away across the Front. Three soldiers in Garrador tabards were plowed down right in front of him, while everyone else scrambled out of the way.

"Dramash!" he called out, searching for them in the heaving crowd, but no one responded. He careened down the steps until Eotan's severed green-glass torso blocked his way, then lumbered around it before nearly walking straight into the point of Isa's sword.

Ani and Dramash were standing behind her, next to a saddled and armored triffon. Amidst all the chaos, the beast had its head down between its paws so that Dramash could reach across to scratch the bristly fur at the top of its snout, just where the armor skullplate ended. Rho remembered Dramash doing something similar the first time they met, the night of the mine collapse. He had tried to bribe him with a sweet to leave before Frea got there, but the boy had refused to go.

"You shouldn't have followed us," said Isa, speaking in Shadari so the others could understand—or maybe because she didn't want him in her mind. Whatever was the matter with her was breaking Rho's heart, but he didn't know how to help her. "Dramash doesn't want to go with you."

"It's funny you put it that way," Rho said as he took a step back and raised Fortune's Blight, "because I don't care what Dramash wants. He's a little boy and I'm his guardian. I'll decide what's best for him, and that's absolutely *not* going with her."

Dramash stopped petting the triffon—only for a moment, but Rho saw it.

"I won't let you stop us," said Isa. The point of Blood's Pride never wavered.

"Yes, you will," Rho said, with the cold burning his throat. "I don't know what this woman's doing to you, but you're stronger than that. Look at what you've done—just look where you *are*."

"Step away from him, Isa," said Ani, and took Dramash's hand again. The needle in her hand already had a drop of red blood swelling at the end of it and Rho thought of those bodies on the stairs and the amount of blood spilled by just eight imperial swords. Not twenty paces from him, five guards surrounded one of the cursed; between them, they had six imperial swords. To their right, General Olin sat on the ground, pressing a cut on his thigh. His imperial sword lay next to him in the snow: that made seven. He could keep counting; to ten, to twenty, to fifty, without even trying. He could count to a thousand, and still not have counted every black blade on the Front right at that moment. And Ani could control them all through Dramash.

He pushed Isa aside and ran toward the boy just as every single one of those black-bladed swords ripped out of the hands of those who held them and shot up into the air. They hovered there, turning gently, suspended by an energy that tightened Rho's jaw and felt like a fist clenching his heart. Those swords would come back down like a flight of arrows when they dropped, and no place on the Front would be safe from them.

One sword swung like the needle in a compass until it pointed straight at him. Ani's eyes flashed and her body tensed; Rho held his breath. The black blade sliced through the snow toward him, but then jerked to a stop as if someone had grabbed the hilt.

"Dramash," said Rho sternly, "I've had enough of this."

A shadow moved through the boy's eyes. Then he smiled, except it wasn't really a smile, not at all. Rho stepped back as Ani's face twisted into the exaggerated snarl of a mummer's mask. She tried to pull her hand away, but Dramash didn't let go. She gasped, and her frail body stiffened.

Isa ran toward Ani and Dramash with a silent howl, throwing away Blood's Pride so she could chop her arm down to break the connection between them. Ani dropped to the ground and a blast of unseen force shoved Rho back into the fallen statue. His shoulders cracked against the ice; he dropped Fortune's Blight and clutched at the statue to try to keep himself upright, but the green-glass just slid out from underneath his gloves and he slipped down, plowing up the snow in front of him.

He lifted his face to the snow-filled sky in time to see the black blades burst into dust.

Each sword—a thousand and more—puffed into its own little black cloud and remained suspended there by the wind, even as the empty hilts came tumbling back down. Rho threw his arms up over his head as all of those bits of metal fell, banging on shields and bouncing over the rocks. The black dust began falling on him and everything around him, turning it all the same dirty gray. All movement on the Front ceased except the writhing of the people who had fallen ill.

Dramash tottered dizzily for a moment, and then fell face-down before Rho could heave himself off the ground to catch him. The boy was so bundled up that Rho couldn't tell if he was breathing, much less conscious.

"Dramash?" he called out, scrabbling through the black-crusted snow to get to him.

The boy rolled over, displaying a bright red nose and cheeks and a jutting bottom lip.

Rho wiped the grit from his own eyes. "Are you all right?"

"Yes," said the muffled voice.

"Can you get up?" Rho asked, tugging on his sleeves to help him. "Where's your other mitten?"

It was getting dark; at least Rho thought it was getting dark, but the way it was darker around the edges than in the middle made him a little suspicious. His side felt numb now, but not numb enough that he didn't still have the sensation that something inside him was leaking like a punctured wineskin.

"I don't want to go with Ani," said Dramash. Tears spilled from his eyes and soaked into his fur hood.

"I know. You're not going to. She's gone, anyway." Rho had seen the shadow of the triffon as it flew away and knew without even looking that Isa had taken Ani away. He was certain he was going to regret letting that happen someday, but for now he was just happy to find Dramash's mitten caught in his scarf. He handed it to the boy and went back to get Fortune's Blight. On the way, he found a bloody rag stuck to one of the chunks of the statue. The fabric looked familiar—Rho realized he'd seen it tied around Isa's leg earlier. For no sane reason, he took it and stuffed it into his pocket.

Then he bent down to pick up the sword, and the light snuffed out like a candle.

Chapter 41

Lahlil jumped across to the other side of the terrace, looking to see if anyone had escaped the carnage. Blood had turned the green-glass into a slippery mess, and the swaying of the unstable structure only made it worse. No one there was still alive.

She made her way to the other statue of Eotan, the one that still had a head. Putting her back up against it, she threw one leg over the balustrade and waited. On the next swing, the supports finally gave way and she rode the balustrade as the terrace tilted down toward the ground, sliding off before it smashed and running as fast as she could to clear the shards of green-glass flying in all directions.

She shoved her way through a dizzying spectrum of tabards as people smashed into her, darted around her or rolled at her feet. Blue blood leaked out from under hoods and tabards and rolled down necks and arms, mixing into the silver-tainted snow. Triffons circled overhead and an arrow clattered down nearby, but no one was looking for glory now: this fight was far uglier and dirtier than that. There was no objective, no castle to take or river to cross; these were just people trying to escape the curse that had just transformed their friends and family—their brother, sister or lover—into a horrifying monster. And they were doing it all wrong.

They came for her in a constant stream, the sick and the well from every clan and every strata of Norlander society, and she fought them off with Valor's Storm bending and gliding in her hands like no weapon she had ever wielded before. She pushed them back unharmed where she could, wounded when she could not, all the while searching the ground around her for the signs—twitching or convulsing, weak movements, a faint cry for help or plea for a quick death. She knew no one would listen to her; showing them was the only way.

The first person she found was someone she recognized from campaigning against the Norlanders: old General Denar Eotan was lying next to his sword with a shallow gash across his throat. The familiar silvery pus leaked from the wound and from his eyes and mouth, and tremors pulsed through his twisted limbs. He had already passed the violent stage and was now succumbing to weakness, just like her brother and Gannon and Vrinna. Lahlil shied clear of his mind, knowing he would beg for death.

She had started to pull Lord Denar out of his cloak when a man in a Garrador tabard came at her. His imperial sword was writhing in his grasp and he was drooling and twitching with madness. She kicked him in the stomach before he could land a blow and turned back to her patient, setting Valor's Storm down and stripping the general of as much of his clothing as she could. Then just as she had done for Eofar, she grabbed handfuls of snow and pressed them into the wound.

As soon as she finished, she took up Valor's Storm and looked for her next patient and saw three without even turning her head. She raced to the nearest one, only to have an Eotan guard jump out to block her.

<I need you to listen to me,> Lahlil commanded.

<We did listen to you.> The man's anguish filled him so that he could hardly speak. <You lied. You said there were no cursed—so what do you call this?>

Lahlil gripped Valor's Storm a little harder. No one would stop trying to kill her long enough for her to explain the cure and at this rate the infection would spread completely out of control. She needed some kind of distraction: something dramatic that would stop everything, just for a few moments.

The next instant, every imperial sword on the Front flew up into the air. She watched them hang there, spinning, and then burst into dust. Even before the empty hilts came crashing back down she had rushed to the nearest sick person and started packing the seeping wounds with the cleanest snow she could find.

<You see?> she said, jumping up and grabbing the dumbfounded soldier nearest to her, a woman in an Arregador tabard. <You can cure them—just like it says in the *Book—Let them be stripped of their garments and set out in the wilderness.*>

The uninfected people around her began coming out of their daze. Lahlil found the next person who needed her help, only this time she grabbed an Eotan soldier and at sword-point made him do it instead. She repeated that over and over until her back ached, but finally the information was spreading across the Front, and everywhere she looked she saw people stripping others and snow being applied to silvery wounds. She even saw people trying to prevent those in the violent stage from hurting anyone until the mania wore off instead of killing them.

She was trying to get the tabard off a man determined to fight her even though he could barely sit upright when a woman in a lagramor coat knelt down next to her. Lahlil knew she had seen that bruised face somewhere, but she couldn't place it.

<Eofar said I have you to thank for my life,> said the woman. She looked like someone who had been on the brink of death and only just come back. <Lahlil—is that your real name?>

<Yes. Lahlil Eotan.>

<Kira Arregador.>

<You were with Trey,> said Lahlil, finally remembering: she had been lying there on the terrace with Trey in her arms. <You're his wife.>

<Yes, I am.> A pause. <I was.>

<I'm sorry,> said Lahlil, turning her attention back to her patient, who no longer had the strength to fight her. <I failed. I came here to save him.>

<You did, in a way, and I wanted to thank you for that,> said Kira. She stood up as if she meant to leave, but she didn't go anywhere. <Lahlil?>

<Yes?>

<I think I may be dead after all. Do you see that too?>

Lahlil followed her gaze out to the western horizon, and then lifted to her feet without any conscious volition, wonder swirling around her like a cyclone. Someone had rolled up the bottom of the gray Norland sky like a blanket and color was pouring in from the other side like a waterfall of red lava and melted gold. The clouds took on broad swathes of orange, pink and purple behind the snow, and the gentle curve of the sun itself—the sun that had never shone in Norland, since time immemorial—stretched from one end of her vision to the other. She felt its warmth on her face. Everything shimmered.

Sunset had come without her knowing, because she had felt no pain.

She laid her hand against her shirt where the medallion hung over her heart and pressed down until she felt the points of the golden sun mark her flesh. Then she pulled the eye-patch down around her neck. The world spread out before her, clear and whole.

<You're not dead,> she told Kira. <I see it too.>

Chapter 42

Isa pulled the reins again, turning the triffon back toward the harbor, even as he tried to fly back to land. The colors down below blurred together as they wheeled around. She checked behind her to make sure that Ani's harness had not come loose. The old woman's head bobbed along with the beating of the triffon's wings as if she was asleep. Isa screwed her eyes up as she tried to remember how she had got her in the saddle and strapped in by herself, but she couldn't do it; all of her memories had a thick haze around them now.

People had hurt and betrayed her: she remembered that. She needed to remember who—not Jachad, who was dying, or Cyrrin, who had devoted her life to helping people like her. Isa didn't know what had happened to either of them. She knew Trey was dead: she had seen his body on the terrace when they were flying away. She had seen Eofar too, but he was alive. She remembered how angry he had been to find her in Norland. No, it was Lahlil who had betrayed her, and Dramash, and Rho. Rho had tried to kill Ani. She would never forgive him for that.

She looked over an expanse of dark green water dotted with bobbing ice floes, merging in the distance with a blurred horizon with just the faintest suggestion of blue. The harbor bristled with masts, but many of the ships were sailing away on the tide. A steady breeze kept the flags waving and she soon found the silver moon flag of the *Argent* far out past the point where the green line of the shallower water shifted to black. A few of the women were up in the rigging, unfurling the sails; they waved to her as she circled the mast.

A chill ran across her shoulders and down through her missing arm, followed by a hot flush: not pain, but the memory of pain.

Women crowded back against the rails as she brought the triffon down on deck. A few familiar faces smiled into hers, but she couldn't remember any names. They spoke to her in Shadari, but their voices sounded strange and she knew she was answering their simple questions too slowly. She explained about Ani as best she could while they helped the frail old woman down from the saddle and whisked her off to some place warm, but afterward Isa wasn't sure exactly what she'd said.

A door opened on the upper deck and Captain Nisha ran to the railing. Cyrrin came behind her, dragging herself along, her steps small, painful.

<Isa, are you here, too?> Nisha asked. <Where is Lahlil? What happened to Rho and the others?>

<They're not coming,> said Isa, a little surprised at how easily the lie flowed out without her even thinking about it: if it even was a lie. She knew only that she wanted this ship to sail away from here, right away. <They want you to leave without them. It's too dangerous to stay.>

<What about Trey?> asked Cyrrin.

<Trey's dead,> said Isa, remembering his body on the ground by the fallen terrace, covered in blood. Cyrrin's grief burst up, bright and quick as a conjurer's flash-paper, then she just folded up and disappeared from Isa's mind.

Another woman came out of the cabin and called them back in. "Come quick. Something's happening—I don't know— Please, *come*."

Nisha helped Cyrrin back into the cabin and Isa followed after them, drawn by something. She could feel Jachad through the walls the way she never had before, not even the way she could feel other Norlanders. She didn't know if he was reaching out to her, or she to him, but her connection was pure and clear while everything else receded.

A dozen people crowded into the little room, but they were all shadows next to Jachad.

His mind locked into hers and she felt like she was being shoved over a cliff. She could feel herself falling, and she could do nothing to save herself. Chunks of her broke off as she fell, and all she could do was watch those precious and irretrievable pieces disintegrate into smaller and smaller bits until they floated away and disappeared. Part of her understood that this was Jachad's experience, not her own.

She grew lighter as she went down, as if she had been trapped inside a clay shell, and the more that fell away, the lighter she became. Her descent from the cliff slowed and then stopped. She wasn't falling any more; she was floating, and whatever she had lost no longer felt important. She was glad to be rid of it, because it meant she could float this way—and she wasn't only floating, she was expanding. The brightness that had been pressed down into a tight little ball deep inside her churned up, pushing past boundaries that toppled like blocks and then reached out, further and further, finding nothing to stop it.

A scream brought Isa back to herself and she opened her eyes to find Jachad's blanket smoldering on the floor with one of the sailors stomping on it. Little tongues of flame zipped all over his body, twining around his limbs, darting over his chest, wrapping around his neck, covering his face like a mask until they finally died away.

"Jachi?" Nisha whispered, both hands covering her mouth and her eyes spilling tears. Everyone began talking at once and the noise drove Isa back out onto the deck. No one noticed her. Sailors bustled all over the ship, getting the *Argent* out to sea. Isa climbed up to the stern deck and looked up at Ravindal.

She had done everything she had set out to do. She had rescued Ani and found the elixir and she was bringing both home to Daryan. She wondered if she felt happy. She couldn't remember what "happy" felt like any more, or "sad," or "angry." All emotions were the same.

Down below her, Nisha and Jachad came out of the cabin together and walked to the closest rail. Nisha kept fussing with the blanket around her son's shoulders, but Isa didn't think he really needed it, judging by the way the snow melted under his feet as he walked across the wooden planks.

"It's not too late to turn back," Nisha informed him. "Do you want to go back for her?"

"Who?"

A strange expression twisted across Nisha's face. "Lahlil."

"Oh," said Jachad. He looked back up at Ravindal like he could see Isa's sister there—but then, perhaps he could. He could see everything: the curve of the horizon; the tiny dot the *Argent*'s sails made in the vast sea; a single loose thread in the sail billowing over their heads. "There's no reason to go back."

"Are you sure?"

Even as the snow continued to fall, the impenetrable Norland sky split open and ripples of light in every fiery hue streamed across the water, sparkling so that Isa had to raise her hand against the glare.

"Take me to the desert," Jachad said. "Take me home to the sun."

Epilogue

When Rho woke in his old room in Arregador House, the first thing he saw was a small form huddled up under a blanket in front of the fire, as if a boy was lying there, sound asleep. He closed his eyes, telling himself it was just his fur cloak on the floor.

"You're awake!" cried Dramash, jumping up and sprinting for the door.

Rho spent a moment prevaricating, and then slid his hand down to his side. A fresh bandage covered the spot where Gannon had punched him, where Dramash's father had cut him.

The boy came back with Eofar in tow, then hopped up on the chair and sat cross-legged, pulling his neck down into the collar of his fur coat like a turtle. He still had circles under his eyes, but his cheeks were pink with cold. Rho wondered if anyone had thought to give him a bath.

<How long have I been here?> Rho asked as Eofar pulled the other chair over beside the bed and sat down.

<Two days. The physics weren't expecting you to sleep so long. They were starting to worry.>

<What happened?> Rho sat up on his elbows. <The last thing I remember was the Front, and Dramash turning those swords to dust.>

<Including mine,> said Eofar, not without amusement. <He said you collapsed, and he dragged you inside all by himself. The physics cut you open, put you back together and sealed you up again.

They said the only reason Gannon didn't kill you with that beating was because the Nomas fixed you up so well the first time.>

<Well, if I can ever tear myself away from soldiering, I've got a future in the market square: "Rho Arregador, the Indestructible Man." If I have to get beaten up anyway, I might as well get paid for it.>

Eofar slumped back in the chair a little and tapped the carved wood with his knuckles. <I'm sorry about your brother. Vrinna's dead, too, if that helps at all. As is Gannon.>

Rho fell back onto the bed feeling like he'd taken another punch. The grief that had been waiting for him had found its moment and it siphoned into him like water through a funnel.

<Are you all right?> Eofar asked as Rho rolled over to face the wall.

He didn't have an answer, so he didn't give one. <Kira's dead, too, isn't she?>

<No, Kira's still here,> said Eofar. He explained what had happened while Rho had been rescuing Dramash, and then after he'd collapsed. <I've never heard of a sickness spreading so fast; it explains why our ancestors were so afraid of it. We've sealed up Eowara's tomb and closed the port and the city, but I don't know if it will be enough. Many people don't survive the cure, particularly . . . > He tailed off, and Rho didn't have a hard time guessing he'd been about to say "babies." <We've made it illegal to set people out alone now, but change isn't going to be that easy.>

Rho had another question, but he wasn't sure he could accept the answer yet. <What about Isa?>

<She's gone. She got Ani to the *Argent* before I even knew why she had come to Ravindal in the first place. By the time Dramash told me what had happened, we'd already closed the port and there was no way to reach them.>

Rho threw off the blankets and sat up, surprised to find himself in far less pain than he had anticipated. <We have to stop them. That old woman has done something to her and I have a sick feeling that whatever she has planned for the Shadar is far worse than anything our people ever did to them. We have to go after them.>

<Not me, Rho. You're going to have to do it yourself this time.>

<Why?>

<I was an ass. I'm sorry for that, too. I know you tried to stop me

and I should have listened to you.> Eofar's apology lacked the sloppy remorse that had been weighing him down since Harotha's death, bleeding out every time he'd spoken. Rho realized that for the first time in months he was neither drunk nor hung-over.

<I don't care about the past,> said Rho. <There's no reason to let it stop you from going back to the Shadar.>

<Oh, that's not why I can't go,> said Eofar. <Lahlil officially abdicated this morning. I'm the emperor now.>

Kira gave the signal to the two waiting stonemasons and they slid the lid back over Trey's tomb, then left her alone to her grieving. Her belief in the After-realm had died three years ago along with her belief in the cursed, but she desperately tried to make herself believe it now so she wouldn't have to accept the fact that she had just seen her husband's face for the last time.

<Kira?> Rho came limping toward her through the stone avenues. He wasn't wearing a hood, and the lamplight on his face left too much room for her imagination. She had to look away.

<I've missed it, haven't I?> he asked her.

<Yes,> said Kira. <His tomb isn't empty any more.>

He moved past her and looked down at the effigy. <I keep having these moments when I remember he's dead, but then I think, "No, he's not really dead. That was just a lie" and then I feel better. Until I remember holding him, and feeling him die in my arms.>

<Gods, Rho, don't, please . . . >

He pulled her into his embrace, clutching her to him, sagging down and burying his face in her hair, and then she held him just as tightly in return. They stood together that way for a long, long time. But they couldn't stay there forever.

<I'm leaving for the Shadar as soon as I can,> he told her when they finally ended their embrace. He still kept hold of her hand.

<I thought as much,> said Kira. <I got to know Dramash very well in the last two days. He refused to leave your room, you know. He insisted we bring all his meals in to him. Oh, and he likes the sweet pickles, but not the sour ones. Don't forget that: he was very stern with Aline the last time—he quite frightened her.>

Rho said, <You could come with us.>

<To the Shadar? Do you think I'd like it there?>

<Oh, no,> said Rho, <Onfar's balls, no. It's a terrible place.>

The weight on her heart lifted for a moment, giving her just a hint of hope that she wouldn't feel like this always. She leaned over and kissed his cheek.

<What are you going to do then?> Rho asked her. <Stay here in Ravindal?>

<Lahlil has promised to help us find Aline's sister, once people are allowed out of the city again. There's a little house in Aelbar I'll inherit from my mother someday—no size at all, really, hardly more than a shack—and no one lives there now but the caretaker and her family. There's nothing but goats for leagues around.>

<It sounds lonely.>

<Yes,> she said, already imagining the sound of goat-bells tinkling in the distance and unbroken snow as far as she could see. <I think lonely is just what I need right now.>

Lahlil climbed to the highest point of the headland, near the skull of the old sea monster, and looked out at the waves. They reminded her of the desert in the very early morning when the dunes rippled away in waves of gray and purple. Two days of sunrises and sunsets with no pain had finally convinced her that her attacks were really over. She wrapped her arms around her chest as a gust blew over the headland: the wind had changed direction, and she could taste the sea.

She felt her brother calling to her, but she didn't turn away from the waves until she heard his footsteps right behind her. <What?> she asked, as Eofar started.

<I'm sorry—it's strange seeing you without the eye-patch, that's all. Listen, I need to ask you something important, and I know you're leaving soon.>

<The city's closed. I can't leave.>

Eofar's pause served as a rebuke. They both knew perfectly well that nothing like a closed border was going to stop her from leaving whenever she chose. <I need to ask if you intend to take Valor's Storm with you when you go.>

<Why?>

<I think it should stay here,> said Eofar. <Two days ago we discovered that we've been murdering our innocent loved ones for

hundreds of years. Think about what that means. Think about how the father who set his daughter out a week ago is going to feel. Think about the next scarred person who won't be set out, and what their life is going to be like. Everything is going to change, and unless we're careful, Norland is going to pull itself apart. People need to understand that we've lost our way and that we need to go back and start again. I think Valor's Storm is the symbol we need. It can remind us that we should be looking at ourselves and our past and learning how to rule ourselves instead of trying to rule over the rest of the world.>

<You're going to disband the empire,> said Lahlil. <They won't let you, you know. They'll kill you.>

<They'll try. I'm not going to make it easy for them.>

Lahlil drew Valor's Storm and held the bronze blade up against the gray sky. She had made it a point never to carry a sword of her own, instead picking up whatever blade came to hand, and then discarding it just as easily for the next. Valor's Storm was different; it was the first sword that had ever felt like it belonged to her.

<You can have it,> she said, sheathing it again and then unbuckling the swordbelt to hand over to him.

<I thought you would say that,> said Eofar. He unslung the pack from his shoulder and brought out something of a highly irregular shape wrapped up in a cloth. <That's why I brought you this.>

She took the object from him and unwrapped the cloth: two silver triffons, wings unfurled, with gold claws and eyes of faceted red jewels: the hilt of Strife's Bane, bladeless now, like thousands of others.

<I thought you'd want to commission the blade yourself,> said Eofar. <Father gave me that sword on my Naming Day. Since you never had a Naming Day, I think you should rename it whatever you want.>

<Thank you,> Lahlil said to her brother, wrapping the hilt back up carefully, focusing hard on each twist of the cloth so she wouldn't have to look at him. <Strife's Bane is a good name. I think I'll keep it.>

Isa felt a touch on her shoulder. "She's in Sabina's cabin," said the girl behind her. "I'll show you the way."

She followed the little girl out onto the deck and down the ladder, then down the hatch to the dim lower deck. Shapes of things—square things, round things, hanging things—went past. The girl led her to a pair of doors and pointed to the one on the left. Isa opened it to find Ani sitting on a stool in the tiny cabin. Her attention was drawn first to a little harp resting in the corner, and then to various items Ani had unpacked on the table.

"What do you want, Isa?" asked Ani.

The question was simple enough, but she had no answer for it.

"How are you feeling?"

"Fine," she said. Then, "I don't know."

"Do you want more medicine?"

"Yes," said Isa with a burst of relief at having remembered why she'd come.

"I'll give you some. Soon," Ani amended, as Isa stepped forward to take the bottle from the table. "Sit down now."

The woolen blanket rubbed against her coat as she sat down on the bunk. The view from the porthole high up on the wall showed nothing but a gray circle, but the sun must have come out because the light in the cabin brightened all of a sudden, and the outlines of the furniture came more into focus.

"You knew I needed Dramash," said Ani, "and you left him behind."

"Rho wanted to kill you—I had to get you out."

Ani put her head to one side and folded her wrinkled hands on her lap. "I know I will have him in the Shadar, and soon, so you are forgiven. Just remember that I've had three hundred years to learn the price of indulgence."

Isa heard a strange rattling and looked down to find her own legs shaking so violently that the buckles on her boots were jangling. A flush of cold went through her whole body, disappearing in an instant, but not without leaving something behind in her mind.

"Do you know who's poisoning the ashas?" she asked.

"Of course," said Ani. "My acolytes, at my command—or their descendants, to be more accurate."

Isa's arms were shaking now as well. "Then they poisoned Jachad too."

"The Nomas king?" said Ani, as if they were talking about disposing of a rat. "Perhaps. The Nomas are not worth my attention."

"I have to tell them the truth." Isa tried to rise from the bunk, but her legs were wobbling so badly that they wouldn't hold her and she fell against the cabin wall. The cold came back, only it didn't leave so quickly this time.

"Do you? Interesting." Any remaining beneficence drained from Ani's face all at once, like water down a plughole, and behind it blazed the naked visage of an unhappy god. "You may want to wait until you're feeling better."

Icicles stabbed at Isa's forehead and the pain pushed her down to her knees. She banged her head on the side of the bunk, accidentally the first time, but then she did it again, trying to use that smaller pain to knock away the freezing pain that was nearly unbearable. Then the cold vanished and instead came a heat so intense that she felt she was being burned alive from the inside out. Sweat soaked her clothes in an instant and she tore off her coat in a panic.

Ani lifted the medicine bottle from the table. "Is this what you want?"

Some part of Isa worried that if she went down this road, she might never find her way back; but it was the other part, the part of her still in agony, that reached out a shaking hand for the bottle.

"Everything will be all right," said Ani, "as long as you do exactly as I say."

Then the drops hit Isa's tongue. Afterward, she found herself curled up on her bunk without remembering how she got there, or how day had suddenly turned to night. She would be fine as long as she could stay like this forever, without thinking, without questioning. She didn't need to eat or sleep. She didn't need anything except Daryan. Daryan, and the little glass bottle.

Omir came around the rocks and found Falit and Tamin already waiting for him, furrowing the wet sand with their pacing. The rocks shielded them from anyone walking along further up the beach but no concealment was necessary; there was nothing unusual about three friends talking on the beach. Falit had been smoking a pipe of some stinking herb, but he knocked it against the rock to clear it out after Omir gave him a look.

"Did you find her?" he asked.

"No," Falit answered, scowling at a patch of bird dung on the rock in front of him. A gull flew over and landed just above it, stretching its wings out to catch the late afternoon sun. "The little bitch went to ground, just like a rat."

"She went to the resurrectionists," said Omir. "I know it. They've been waiting for a chance to get their hands on an asha."

Tamin cinched his robe closer around his wiry frame and asked, "Then shouldn't we move against the resurrectionists right now? I mean, we can't wait, can we?"

"We can't go in there slashing," said Omir. "They need to be arrested. I need more time to convince Daryan. He's still upset about Isa and I can't get his mind to fix on anything else."

"You said we were well rid of that Dead One—you said you'd have proper control of the daimon with her gone," said Falit.

"We're not here to talk about that," said Omir, stepping back as the tide rushed up to his sandals. His footprints in the sand looked twice the size of Tamin's. "We have to decide what to do about Yash."

"I say we do nothing," said Tamin. "So he did something on his own? So what? I say it can't hurt to have that Nomas bastard out of the way."

"Can't hurt?" said Omir, wetting his lips and tasting the salt from the sea air. "If the Nomas figure out that wine was poisoned, they'll trace it right back here to the Shadar."

"So what?" Falit repeated. "Our families—our cabal—kept these plans secret for three hundred years, even through invasion and thirty years of occupation. Those sand-spitters won't ever find us."

Omir walked around the rocks, looking at their wind-worn crags and pits and knitting his big, clumsy fingers together. His shoulders were still sore from lifting stones to build their new prison, and tonight he had to represent Daryan at another pointless meeting about what they were going to do about the feral triffons.

"I don't like it. It's messy," he said, when he came back around the rocks to where he started. "Deal with him."

"Omir—" Falit began.

"It's my decision. If you can't do it, I'll do it myself."

"No, I'll do it," said Falit, swiping the back of his dirty hand over his bearded chin. "We dug in the mines together for ten years. It should be me."

"Good. You think I'm being harsh, but I'm the First Acolyte, just like my father and his father and back to the Fall. It's my job to make sure everything is perfect for her." Omir walked down toward the waves, letting the water run over his sandals, and looked out to sea as if he could already see her ship on the horizon. "And after three hundred years, Anakthalisa is finally coming home."

The story concludes in
the final part of
The Shattered Kingdoms

STRIFE'S BANE

Acknowledgments

Comparing the creation of a book to childbirth is both hackneyed and insulting to anyone who's had a human being come out of her body, but if a book is "birthed," then this book was twins in the back of an unlicensed cab on the southbound FDR Drive at rush hour on the Friday before Memorial Day weekend. It owes its life to the many people who came to its rescue: Stacy Hill, who gently but firmly steered me away from the cliff from which I was so determined to hurl myself; Miriam Weinberg, who swooped in with her enthusiasm, wit, and quick-fire brain; and Jo Fletcher—detector of quirks and eradicator of same—who taught me the word "furbelows" along with a million ways to be a better writer. Zoë DiMele helped me dig out of a deep, dark hole with patience, humor, and a love that I am only just learning to accept. I need to thank Julie Heron Harreld, my beta reader and tireless booster, whose suggestions were dead-on and who took time away from curing cancer (really!) without ever making it seem like a chore. I have to thank Ann Pinto McCarney because she knows where the empty wine cooler bottles are buried, and because she's a wonderful friend, certifiable lunatic, and just maybe the most caring person I've ever met; and Dean McCarney for making her so happy and for fathering their four precious children. Fellow authors Alison von Rosenvinge and Laura Snyder and my agent, Becca Stumpf, are to be thanked for their stalwart friendship, and for listening to me whinge about problems I'm lucky to have. Lisa Rogers has to be thanked for her (usually) thankless job of keeping me relatively sane and getting me out of the house, even when she had more than her own fair share of crap to manage. Finally, thanks to my mom, Joanne—sorry for all the times you received monosyllabic answers to your phone calls—my husband, Lou, who continues to get smarter and more handsome just to spite me, and to my daughter, Prudence, the love of my life.